SHORT SHARP SHOCKS
VOLUME TWO

STOMPING GROUNDS

An April Moon Books Publication
Published in arrangement with the authors
Edited by Neil Baker

First Edition 2014
Published in Canada.

www.AprilMoonBooks.com

ISBN: 978–0–9937180–2–1 (softcover)

Dedication

In memory of C.J. Henderson.

Thank you for the stories, Jack.

Neil

Contents

The Joy of Wrecks
by
Neil Baker

In my previous anthology (Short Sharp Shocks Vol. 1: AMOK!), I stated in the dedication to the writers that it is far better to create than it is to destroy. This is certainly true, from a certain point of view...

However, just one look at the face of Calvin as he stamps through a sandbox city while Hobbes looks on aghast, or the sheer, unadulterated joy of Stitch as he trashes a carefully constructed city in Lilo's bedroom, reveals the stark truth; it must be a hell of a lot of fun to reduce a city to rubble under your mighty, scaled feet. Sadly, very few of us are mountainous monstrosities hellbent on worldwide destruction, so we have to get our jollies from movies, old Sega games and books.

Being a child of a certain age, it is little wonder that colossal, rampaging monsters hold a special place in my heart. Having grown up watching Harryhausen flicks, all the Godzillas (good through bad), and the various iterations of Kong, I, like many of my ilk, will never tire of watching monsters torn from their environments and placed in a jungle of concrete and pesky bugs. Unlike more 'human' monsters with their questionable agendas and elaborate thirsts for death, giant monsters are forces of nature, cyclones tearing through suburbia and ruining your day. It really isn't our job to understand them, rather it is our job to survive them, and to watch other poor saps try to out run them.

When I first announced the theme for this second volume of amusingly shocking tales, I was keen to stress that I didn't want a slew of Godzilla clones. The lovable lizard certainly has his place at the top of the pile, but I was looking for stories that featured enormous beasts I hadn't seen before; monsters that would catch the reader off-guard. My authors did not disappoint. While some creatures make perfect monsters (hellgrammites, wasps and three-headed hounds), others have been dragged from their comfortable roles as good subjects for Beanie Babies, and transformed into gargantuan, blood-crazed fiends (giraffes, beavers, frogs,

1

humming birds, kangaroos and a platypus). Less Godzilla - more Night of the Lepus.

Then we encounter the afore-said forces of nature in the form of giant, God-like entities (sea creatures, the Karkadann, even planetary bodies) and finally round off the roster of rampagers with Lovecraftian entities (a Mayan deity, a monster conjured from a treph, a cosmic blob, an ancient machine that transforms your darkest urges into monsters and a hound of Tindalos).

At the end of the day, we are all good people, but even good people need to let off a little steam.

I suggest you let the monsters in this book let that steam off for you - all you have to do is grab a bowl of popcorn, sit back and enjoy the carnage.

Neil Baker - Dec. 2014

Juggernaut

by
C.J. Henderson

Juggernaut

by

CJ Henderson

IT'S A GRUESOME THING, from what I'm told. An unstoppable monster - all legs and claws and molten muscle that fangs down on a man like water cascading across pavement. Everywhere at once, always coming, always from every direction, relentlessly. As endless as the sea, as patient as the mountains. They say it can't be killed, can't be turned, can't be avoided. Inevitable as tomorrow, final as judgment. That's what they whisper, anyway.

Circles confuse them. Spheres, the very thought of bending frightens them like a shadow that isn't cast by anything in sight, and yet is still there crawling across the ground toward you. Curves are their unknown, and they fear them. But it's never been quite understood that curves cannot block them forever; nothing is so fearful of anything that it can be held in check forever. Creatures of sufficient intelligence can figure *anything* out sooner or later. And despite what most people believe, the Hounds of Tindalos *can* think. Trust me, I know.

My name's Teddy London. I used to be just a simple New York City private detective. Then I died. It wasn't long after that initial revelation, the first time I walked the dream plane - just removed my physical form from out of time and space for a moment to avoid dying, or more to the point, dying by being dragged off to some nether dimension by something or other that would torture me for my arrogance from now unto eternity - when I decided that perhaps it was time to change my line of work. Or at least, how I went about it. Since then I've spent a lot of time learning new tricks. A bit of on-the-job training, so to speak.

"So, boss, what'dya think these things look like anyway?" The question was from my partner, Paul Morcey. Balding, a bit overweight, but as loyal and sharp as you could want in the person watching your back. He's seen most everything I have, and he's still around, which says a lot. People don't tend to last long in this business.

"Well, some reports," I told him, indicating the papers on my desk, "say they're greenish, hairless dogs with blue tongues. Some describe them as black, formless shadows. Then there's a layer of the dream plane where they're seen as mercury-like creatures whose bases glide smoothly over anything at lightning speeds, but the surface, due to contact with the air, is a constant boil of unbreakable spines..."

"So, in other woids, they're tough to get a positive I.D. on before it's too late."

"No I.D.," I admitted, "but we've got their M.O.. Why don't you explain a little about them, Doc."

Professor Zachary Goward took center stage. The Doc's always been good for background on this or that beyond-the-edge nasty that I've run into. I've gotten help from all manner of people along the way. Just trying to stay alive, which is really all I've been doing since I got my first peek behind the curtain and learned there really are things out there going bump in the night. You see, the problem with stumbling into something like this is... well, basically, just what do you do once you know about these things?

Most of the world thinks beings like vampires and dimensional shamblers and the walking dead and all are just stories. Oh, a part of their mind believes, but ultimately they're too intelligent for all that, don't you know. And so, when they finally do stumble across something -something all teeth and tentacles - they freeze. It's the slightest of moments, that infinitesimal split second they need to adjust to what's being seen, to run through the files in their brains to find some kind of label for the horror for which they have no immediate designation. Of course, by the time they do find a name for it, they're usually dead.

"These things, the hounds of Tindalos," said the professor, "aren't really dogs of any kind, of course. They're creatures of immense power possessed of the ability to travel through time, itself. Millions of years ago, the reports say, they dwelled in a city of corkscrew towers somewhere here on Earth. Where this was, what has happened to the city, where the hounds are now, what's become of them, et cetera, all unknown. Not even any guesses worth mentioning, although I do have a theory."

"Spill them beans, Doc," said Paul. My partner has a way of cutting through the red tape that has to be admired. He's the only person I've ever come across who wears his enthusiasm for this work openly. Most of the rest of us could leave it behind, permanently, without a second thought. I know I could. Not Paul, though. Smiling, he added, "It's been a while since I've wrestled with something beyond me comprehension."

The problem with getting mixed up with this "from beyond" stuff is that there's just too much of it. The concepts are all big and overwhelming. Little is known for sure, and what is known is wrong half the time, or insufficient. For instance, there really are vampires, but they aren't afraid of religious icons. Or sunlight. And they don't drink blood, either. They simply pull the energy out of you. There's no sexual thirst, no entrancing kiss - that's romantic bullshit cobbled together by a century of hacks to trick money out of the gullible. Real vampires just break your legs or your back and then strip away your remaining years while you claw the ground in pain.

"If the hounds are anything we know of already," Goward told those assembled, "it would be the fallen angels of the Christian Bible, actually, the rebels who followed Lucifer when he attempted to overthrow the Heavens."

"Angels?" asked Cat, an electronics expert still willing to gamble her life now and again on one of my stunts.

"Sometime in prehistory," answered the professor, "there was a great upheaval between two powers. If you like 'God and his angels,' fine. If you want other labels, I'm not opposed. These Tind'losi appear to be the basis for the legend of the fallen angels. Whatever they and their masters were, are, what-have-you, they seem to have rebelled and then been sealed away in their city outside of normal time as a punishment. You see - the hounds cannot navigate curves. . ."

"Oh, excuse me, doctor," asked Pa'sha, a weapon's maker from the Caribbean whom I've known longer than anyone else in the room, "but if you could explain that concept even just a tiny bit more thoroughly."

Goward sighed. I didn't blame him. That's what this game is like - you're just constantly shattering people's notions of what is and isn't real or permanent or whatever. And worse yet, once someone who's just gotten a taste of the beyond finds out you've stopped something, some thing that's weird, supernatural, paranormal, ultradimensional, whatever, suddenly you're supposed to be able to do anything, stop *anything*. 'Hey, Marge, ain't that the guy who killed a rat with a shotgun? Let's give him a Bowie knife and point him at Godzilla.'

"As briefly as possible," Goward answered Pa'sha, "Tind'losi occupy the angles of time, while mankind, as well as every other living thing, I imagine, live within the curves of time. I know this is a difficult concept to grasp, I'm not really comfortable with it myself, but it does make a certain mathematical sense. You see, if the hounds were pulled outside of normal time as a punishment, they would have to be bound away from humanity by some sort of cosmic geometry. This notion of them being Lucifer's troops, why not? The hounds of Tindalos are the only creatures in all arcana which are described as existing under such conditions. Perhaps Tindalos *is* Hell. It would explain a great deal, why there is no trace of their city on Earth today, why they hate humanity so. . ."

"How's it explain that?" asked Paul.

"Tind'losi can only come after human beings whom they have seen. Which, because of their unique situation in the universe, means that humans have to make the first contact."

"But how could a person contact these things if they exist outside normal time and space?" asked Cat.

"There are ways," said the professor. "For instance, a man by the name of Harvey Walters once found a gemstone which, when meditated upon, allowed him to look into the far past. When he did so, he was seen by a Tind'losi which apparently, once it had made visual contact with him, was able to track him through the millennia, traveling through the angles of time until it..." Goward paused for a moment, then composed himself, finishing with, "Anyway, it's from Mr. Walters we have so many of the descriptions of Tindalos and the hounds, et cetera."

"Okay, okay," said Morcey. "So, dese things is tough to kill and they come after ya worse than the IRS. So what's all this got to do with us?"

A while back I'd thought that maybe we might've finally seen it all. I mean, as a group, we'd tangled with vampires and succubi, werewolves and winged lizardmen, cast the abomination known as Lilith back into the pit and thwarted the rapacious desires of more than one inter-dimensional traveller.

"Ah, you see..." answered Goward with hesitation, "The reason I know about Mr. Walters' gem is... it was sent to me for study. I didn't know what it was when I first began to examine it. But, after I looked into it under a microscope, and saw that terrible face leering back at me across the endless tracts of history..."

The professor paused to remove his glasses, wiping away imaginary grime as he said, "Anyway, according to the best information available, the hound should arrive here somewhere in between four and five days from now. At which time, I imagine, it will destroy my physical being and then return to Tindalos with my soul which it will keep, and torment, throughout eternity."

Seen it all, I told myself. We hadn't seen anything yet. But we were about to. And it wasn't going to be pretty.

We put the next few days to good use. Knowing that a sphere would keep the professor safe, our first priority was to come up with a safe house. Pa'sha solved that problem for us by taking us out to the Brooklyn docks. New York's shipping industry used to be one of the greatest in the world. Times change, though, and over the years more and more of the city's harbor area had been allowed to drift into disrepair.

What Pa'sha knew about was a foundry that at one time had worked in dye casting wrecking balls. The firm had sold all its molds to the Japanese just before World War II. When hostilities broke out, the massive casting blocks had been stored rather than shipped out to the enemy. Too bulky to move, they'd simply been warehoused, then forgotten. The dye stood some fifteen feet in height. When Cat noted that the sphere inside was rather cramped, Paul quipped that it was a lot more roomy than a coffin. Goward agreed. That closed that deal.

Our plan was simple. As the final moments arrived, Goward would enter the spherical interior of the mold through the pour hole in the top. After that, we would wait for the arrival of the hound. As soon as we got a fix on it, a second mold would be lowered on top of the other to eliminate the entrance and keep the Tind'losi at bay. The only things we stocked the sphere with were water and scuba gear. There wasn't any use in wasting space on food or a chemical toilet or most of the other things that got suggested. Oxygen tanks are fairly bulky for the amount of breathable atmosphere they can hold. The professor was going to run out of air long before he got very hungry.

After the defense was set, it was time to work on the offense. This was where Cat and Pa'sha came in. Cat, of course, worked on our sensors, setting up a relay system that would drop the second mold atop the first as soon as we had confirmation that the hound had arrived. She also worked out a few other tricks to help give us an edge.

We were stymied for a while on how to aim our weapons, but Goward himself gave us the answer to that one. Not knowing from which angle in the warehouse the creature would appear, he suggested we simply eliminate all but one of them and then concentrate our fire power there. We did. The entire warehouse was lined with chicken wire and then sprayed with plaster foam. As the foam set, we carved the corners into pockets. None of them were perfect, but that didn't matter. As long as we didn't leave any angles steeper than forty-five degrees, the Tind'losi would be denied entrance. Only one corner, the one furthest from the mold in which we would hide Goward, was left untouched. In that space we concentrated our bombs and nets and everything else we had to throw against the monster.

We didn't, however, expect any of this to stop it. We would happily accept a miracle, obviously, but if Goward's research was accurate we pretty much knew nothing we were doing there in the warehouse was actually going to stop the beast. Bullets, electricity - petty annoyances like these were only going to enrage the thing. Madden it beyond reason. Which, of course, was our plan.

The last night before the Tind'losi was supposed to arrive, I sat up with my fiancé, Lisa Hutchinson. I couldn't sleep and neither could she. Lisa is a partner in my agency. We met when I saved her from an experience that didn't do either of our mental states much good. I spent a long time in the hospital after it was over. Lisa was there every day at my bedside, refusing to let me just slide into the madness that beckoned so comfortingly from the edges of my mind. Since then she's done her best to keep me sane. I try not to let on what a crummy job I think she's doing.

"What're you thinking about?" she asked me. I told her.

"Tomorrow, mostly. How I'm going to... um, handle this whole mess."

"Translation... 'how you're going to live through it'... was that more what you meant to say?"

"Well, something on that order, I guess." I stared into Lisa's eyes, drinking in the shining blue of them, concentrating on their color, letting blinding nuisances like thought and reality fall aside into disrepair.

"You want to talk?" she asked, knowing I didn't, but that I had to. I'm the kind of person who thinks well on their feet, but I'm not much of a planner.

"Like to," I admitted, "but there isn't much to say. Sometime tomorrow this thing is going to show up. We'll seal Zach in the mold and then we'll try to get rid of whatever it is that wants to get him."

"And if you can't?" Her voice was tense. Not tearful or threatening, she covered herself well. But there was no getting around that she was worried. Then again, why shouldn't she be? I was worried, too. "What then?"

"Then," I told her, "I guess people are going to die."

Her fingers tightened around mine, her body falling in closer to me, pushing us deeper into the couch cushions. She didn't start crying, or asking foolish questions like why was I the one who had to face this thing. She knew why. For some reason when Lisa had been in trouble a few years back, fate had shoved her in my direction, made me her protector whether I wanted to be or not. A lot of people didn't live through the experience. I did, though - barely. I survived with the knowledge that these things are powerful and fearsome and evil. Some will try to tell you that these creatures are so cosmically almighty that they're beyond good and evil, but that's a crock.

Everybody acts with intent. Everything has motivation. Nothing is random, and that means the actions of gods, monsters and heroes are no exception. Surviving that first attack moved me up a square, made me more visible. After that, stuff just kept finding its way to my doorstep - faster and faster. For me to turn away from any of it would be to surrender. Not facing this Tind'losi, whatever it turned out to be, would be a death sentence for the professor. If I didn't try to stop it, I might as well just put a gun to Zach's head and pull the trigger myself. Certainly it would be more merciful than leaving him to it.

Lisa knew all that, though. She knew I had to play the hand I'd been dealt, like we all do. I could have turned my back on her when we'd met. If I had, of course, she would have died and shortly thereafter the entire world would have been nothing much more than a cosmic cinder. But I didn't. I faced what was after her and managed to stop it. I ended up with four broken ribs, a shattered leg, pneumonia and scores of gashes and burns. I also went somewhat insane. But I was rewarded with Lisa's love, a pure and guiding comfort that in the end seemed worth a thousand such conflicts. Feeling her next to me on the couch, the pattern of her breathing, the rhythm of her heartbeat, the anxiety that had been digging its ragged nails under my skin began to dissolve - dissipated by the care of a loving woman's heart.

I was counting down the minutes to when I would be forced to face a creature that was, for all intents and purposes, quite literally straight out of Hell. In a matter of hours I would pit my few score pounds of flesh and brain against a monster every source available to us considered unkillable, unstoppable by any means. Looking into Lisa's eyes once more, however, I simply couldn't find it within myself to worry any further. I had no illusions about my chances.

Most likely, a voice from the back of my brain told me, *there is no way we can survive.*

Nodding in unconscious agreement, I smiled at my beautiful Lisa and then bent toward her. Our lips touched and the next day was forgotten. Eventually one of us turned out the lights, but for the life of me I can't tell you who it was.

"So," called out Paul, grinning as he stood in the center of the foundry, hands on his hips, "are we all ready to kick a little monster ass?"

"Oh, ho," answered Pa'sha, "And tell me, my friend, what is it that leads you to believe this approaching monster has a small buttocks?"

"Dis guy," complained Paul, grinning as he did so, "he's so stupid he's makin' me look smart."

"Now, now, Morcey-mon," answered Pa'sha with feigned indifference, "you know full well there's none in all this wide world quite that stupid."

The two laughed, coming together for their ritual drink. Pa'sha's been known to toss down more than his share of alcohol, true enough, but Paul isn't that much of a drinker. The pair of them always get together before things get started, though, to knock back a couple of shots together. Pulling his usual silver and glass flask from inside his jacket, Pa'sha handed it to Paul, telling him warmly;

"A coconut rum from my father's own hometown. Fiery and dangerous, but a true flash of lightning, you shall see."

Paul unscrewed the cap and took a whiff.

"Whooo–" he exclaimed. "Some strong stuff here. Kind that puts hair on your chest."

As he hoisted the flask in a momentary salute, then moved it to his mouth to take a drink, Pa'sha answered him, saying, "This one does not put hair on the chest, Morcey-mon... it burns it off."

The two laughed and drank, Pa'sha waving various members of his crew over to join them. His "Murder Dogs," as he calls them, were happy to oblige. The heat in the foundry was punishing and after the grueling preparations we'd readied during the previous few days, there weren't any of us who weren't primed to take a break. All of Pa'sha's troops set aside their weapons, crowding forward to partake in their boss's bounty.

10

While they did, I turned away for a moment, needing to complete a ritual of my own. Opening my bag, I began the process of slipping into my shoulder holster. I already had my ankle sheath in place, my stiletto, Veronica, secure inside. With a shrug and a twist I had my holster on, my .38 Betty snug under my arm.

Don't ask me why I named my weapons after the girls from the Archie comics. For some reason, a very long time ago, I thought it was funny. Don't ask me what I thought either one of them was going to accomplish in a battle with a Tind'losi, either. I knew neither weapon would be of much use considering what I was going up against, but there're things we do that make us feel prepared, relaxed, more confident. It was a morning for such rituals. Those who didn't have any were advised to start making some up.

Professor Goward was smoking his pipe, maybe not a ritual, but certainly a relaxant. All things considered the Doc looked to be holding up pretty well. Sure, he was worried, being the one directly in the line of fire - who wouldn't be? But still, he was calm enough on the outside to help keep the tension level down, which is always a good thing. Wiping a handful of sweat from my brow, I crossed the room to check on him. I made sure all the rebreathers that'd been loaded into the die with him were full, then I reviewed how to use one properly with him. He reached out while I spoke, catching hold of my shoulder. Grasping it firmly, he said in a low voice.

"You know, I never really have thanked you for taking all this on."

"Don't thank me yet, Zach," I answered him honestly. "We've got a long way to go before we see who lives through this."

"True enough, Theodore," he told me. "But you know what they say about 'thoughts and deeds' and the such. I just didn't want to appear ungrateful, especially considering the fact that I might not get a chance to say it later on at all."

"Jeez," I answered, only half in jest, "and they call me a cynic."

The professor extended his hand toward me. Although the angle was difficult due to how high off the ground he was situated, I reached out to take his hand when suddenly a burning, acrid scent pushed its way into and throughout the room. It was an unbelievably pungent odor, one so nauseous that for a split-second everyone's attention was frozen. We sprang into action, however, as Cat's voice bellowed through the speakers we'd strung throughout the foundry.

"Incoming!"

I snapped my hand back as the top half of the spherical mold began to lower into place. The professor flipped his pipe outside the dye and then began fumbling into his breather. Above, the second mold followed the top half of the first weighing the first down and sealing it shut. Racing across the room, Paul threw himself upward forcibly, climbing the ladder two rungs at a time to the control room where Cat was waiting. Pa'sha and his men scattered as well, each man heading for his prearranged station. Gas masks and earplugs were hurriedly slipped into place. The muffled sounds of footfalls and weapons being cocked filled the large room, echoing off the cold concrete walls and floor and ceiling.

All eyes stared at the entry point. The one remaining corner in all the building gushed with a thick, purplish billow. Tendrils of it lurched awkwardly upward and outward, looking more like one liquid forcing its way into another than smoke filling the air. The impenetrable haze grew heavier, crimson sparks flashing randomly within its spreading body. Then, suddenly, something solid emerged from the depths of the cloud.

"It's here!"

An awkward, almost crab-like paw stepped down out of the putrid swirl of gases and scratched along the concrete floor. A bulbous snout followed, red and hard, masking a jaw possessed of multiple layers of needling teeth and fangs. What we could see so far indicated a being roughly the size of a large cow, or perhaps a rhinoceros. Bluish pus dripped from the creature's sides, splattering the floor, burning into the poured stone wherever it landed. Another paw followed the first, striding forward, pulling more of the loathsome body into view. It was long, like a hound, but the comparison was strained - like describing a hand grenade by saying it was oval-shaped, like an egg.

The thing's mouth opened, and a black and yellow mix of gases shrieked out into the room. As hands cocked weapons, I stepped back further away from the stacked molds, my eyes firm on the creature's advance. Then, once I was certain its entire mass had exited onto our plane, I dropped my hand. In the control room Cat flipped a massive connecting toggle, electrifying the steel mesh net we had spread across the floor.

The beast howled as current filled it. Hundreds of thousands of volts filled the thing's massive body. Its screams were ghastly, bright gray things, darts of sound that shattered glass throughout the building. At the same time, Paul threw a second toggle. This dropped a reinforced mesh net from the ceiling, one layered with thick, but sharp, metal hooks, each of them covered with scores of wicked barbs. The Tind'losi, bucking and straining against the current only succeeded in snarling itself totally in the two nets, a score of the hammer-sized hooks tearing into its body. In addition, the barbs were coated with every available poison - hemlock, arsenic, strychnine, everything we could find. The hounds of Tindalos might be power incarnate within their own realm, but to walk amongst men they had to take on flesh of one form or another, and in that one tiny weakness we'd put our hopes. For a moment, it seemed as if our hopes might not be vain ones.

The horror in the nets screeched and bellowed, sizzling pus and bile flying from its body as it writhed in electrical pain. In the control room, Cat targeted the creature with a ringed battery of white sound cannons, blasting the demon with high frequency noise. As she guided both attacks, she also watched over the power meters, making certain we stayed at maximum output without going into overload. While she did, Paul started setting things into motion for the second part of our plan. We'd selected the Tind'losi's entrance point carefully, making certain it brought the beast directly beneath the foundry's pour bucket. As the nets below began to smoke and spark, Paul prepared to drop the load of molten metal we had waiting.

"The power's topping out," shouted Cat. "We've got to slice it or we're going to burn down the neighborhood."

Paul nodded, his hands gliding through the routine he had practiced a thousand times over the last few days. As the power to the nets was cut, we all prayed the poison had had a chance to have some kind of effect as the pour bucket released its contents. Ironically, the Tind'losi looked up just as the molten metal dropped down onto it.

New razor-bellowed screams lashed through the building, the force of them etching scattered cracks in the walls and ceiling. The smell of burning bone and organs filled the room. Combining with the smell of the creature's arrival, the stench grew almost overpowering, easily reaching us through our gas masks. As the pour bucket emptied, the entire room hued over in reflected oranges and reds. A torrent of molten splash was flung everywhere, hot metal burning the floor, melting the nets, searing the alien flesh of the Tindalos hound. Not ready to leave anything to chance, however, I gave Pa'sha the high sign from my hiding place. He cued his men. Explosions filled the air.

The Murder Dogs targeted the glowing, thrashing figure in the center of the room, pumping hundreds of bullets a second into the monstrous thing. A two man team fired anti-tank missiles into the burning form, blowing out successively larger chunks of the creature with each fearsome strike. Shotguns and flamethrowers were added to the mix, our redundant efforts hoping to enrage and confuse as much as to weaken. It was amazing how little good any of it seemed to do.

With a hissing whisper the Tind'losi stood erect once more. Poison gas canisters were released by Pa'sha and his men, as well as chemical burners and flash bombs. More miniature missiles were launched. Grenades followed. Even though every man fought from behind a steel-reinforced lead shield of considerable thickness, three of the Murder Dogs were already out of the action, one felled by an unfortunate ricochette, two hit by molten slag thrown off by the screaming monster in the center of the foundry.

And then, suddenly it seemed like we were getting somewhere. For a moment it'd appeared the creature was rallying, but then the moment passed and the

Tind'losi sank to its knees, crippled beyond repair. Pa'sha and his Murder Dogs kept firing, throwing everything they had left into their attack. Thousands of rounds were launched, enough fire power slamming into the burning thing on the floor to pierce the side of a battleship. And still, somehow the terrible form threw itself up off the floor, it's forward legs pawing the air violently.

But then came another massive howl, an almost sonic blast of hate and fear, erupting from the creature. Lashing through the room, the horrid screech shook the entire building, piercing our ear plugs, rocking the floor, even moving the five ton mold we'd used to seal in Goward by several inches.

The thing fell to the ground completely then. Its burning head slammed into the concrete, cracking it open to the depth of eighteen inches. Its massive legs kicked brutally against the air, sending more molten slag and super-heated bits of netting flying through the air. But, as each second passed its thrashing grew less and less violent. And then, suddenly, the unstoppable beast simply ceased moving.

In the control room, Cat switched on the massive roof fans. We hadn't dared run any power equipment while trying to electrocute the beast, but the moment for caution seemed to have passed.

"We did it!" shouted Paul. Dancing a victory shuffle in the control room, he pulled Cat from her chair, laughing as he twirled her around the room. "We killed it! Ding, dong - the humpin' bastard is *dead!*"

A part of my brain was amazed at how easy it had all been. Another voice from within my mind snickered at my naïveté. We had gone through enough power to keep Time Square lit up for several months. We had fired some fifteen thousand projectiles into the thing - followed by several hundred compressed pounds of various gases and chemical poisons. All told, we had spent nearly a million and a half dollars of the company's money. The rest of my brain told the single dissenter to shut up, though. Yes, we had thrown everything we had against the creature. If it had lived another few minutes we'd have been reduced to hurling rocks at it. But it hadn't. We'd beaten it. The battle was over. The professor was safe.

Or... so we thought.

"Hey," called out one of the Murder Dogs, "what dey hell be dot, mon?"

From the initial entry point, once more there came a gushing, thick, purplish billow. Once more tendrils lurched awkwardly into our dimension, the same heavy, crimson sparks flashing through the mounting haze, the same vague solid stirring moving forward from deep within the depths of the cloud.

"Sweet bride of the night!" shouted Paul. "There's *two* of them!"

Again, a misshapen paw stepped down out of the newly forming swirls of smoke and gas stretching through the foundry. But, unlike the first attack, this time there was a substantial difference. This time, there was more than one of the creatures. As everyone around the room simply stared in amazement, a second bulbous snout moved out of the haze, followed by another, and then another. Behind them, receding down the corridors of time, stretching off through some unbelievable chain of right-angled space, waited an infinite number of the pus dripping creatures, all of them straining to pass through into this world.

My eyes darted throughout the room, time splitting into micro-seconds as I checked on everyone. Cat had fallen back into her chair, stunned into immobility. Even through her gas mask her eyes showed wide and unblinking. One of her hands was raised to her face, her forefinger upheld, the entire hand trembling.

Paul was still standing, his shoulders stiff and tight. He had already pulled his Auto-Mag from his shoulder holster and was headed for the control room door. The same held for Pa'sha and his men. None of them had more than a few rounds of ammunition available to them. Most had nothing left, but they were ready to fight nonetheless. If only one more of the creatures had arrived it might have been different. One more might have inspired terror within us, or a sense of futility. But, there were so many coming toward us that fear became useless.

So was throwing away lives, however. Knowing there was no sense in every-one dying, I stepped forward into the room, drawing as close to the volcanic heat of its still molten center as I dared. Hoping the fans had already completed their job, I tore off my gas mask and addressed the Tind'losi in the lead.

"And just what the fuck do you want?"

The creature was taken aback for a moment. It sniffed the air between us, its cautious movements halting its massed fellows. The thing stared at me with interest, like a child wondering exactly what kind of bug it was that stood on its hind legs and dared bark so. There was no fear in the thing - its curiosity was borne more of an awesome delight, the joy in finding an unexpected treat. Some of the Tind'losi behind it began to snarl and jabber, bucking to push their way forward into the foundry. The leader silenced them with a tearing hiss that blew bloody steam from its nostrils. Then, returning its attention to me, it spoke.

"To step into the world once more, and to find man so utterly unchanged." Its voice was a harsh, yet elegant sound - the clattering growl of a cultured cement mixer. "As if a hundred billion revolutions round the center were but a yawning brief pause."

The creature smiled, horrible rows of devilish teeth grinding against one another in its terrible jaw. Taking another step into the foundry, the thing reared upward, then sat down on the floor, its body towering over us all. Looking down at me, it announced;

"You may call me, Belial. It means. . ."

"It means," I cut the thing off, "'Without a master.'"

15

"Why, what a clever puny you are." Turning to its fellows, Belial snarled contemptuously, "You see, I told you. There will be more sport here than simply slaughtering them all."

"You're not going to slaughter anyone."

A great angry barking arose through the crowding horde. Their leader silenced them with another steaming shriek. It turned languidly, its torso twisting unnaturally, and then struck the two closest Tind'losi devastating blows with its forepaws. As it did, I bent my head slightly, trying to corral my runaway nerves. I knew what I had to do next.

You do, do you? A voice from the back of my consciousness, some ancestor from the early recesses of my racial memory, shouted at me, *This isn't what you expected–is it? No–things have gone far beyond anything you imagined, haven't they?*

We still have a plan.

You had a plan for dealing with one of these things–ONE! screamed another, albeit less stable, one of my forefathers. *This is more than ONE!*

SILENCE, I thought darkly, flooding the single word throughout my consciousness. Several other dissident voices were trying to speak up, but the creature had turned back toward me and I had to be ready for it. The struggle for power between us was about to commence and it wouldn't do if I was too busy comforting myself to play its game.

"So, my little puny, you are the one called 'the Destroyer', yes?"

"There are some who call me that," I admitted.

"Well then, tell us, Destroyer, how is it that we are not going to do that which we have come to do, that which we have dreamed of since a trillion centuries before you had form?"

"Because you're all going to turn around, right now, and go back to where you come from. And then you're going to stay there."

Clearing my mind, pushing panic and all her sisters away from me, crushing terror and fear, I sent my senses out beyond my body, feeling my way into the city beyond. On any given day there are at the very least well over five million people in New York City. Gently, from each one of them, from their pets and all the trees and plants of every shape and size, from every living thing in every direction I began the siphoning of tiny bits of power.

"And why would we do this, my puny?"

"Because I'll destroy you all if you don't."

Globs of mucused spittle spat from a thousand throats, yellow-brown fangs clattering in raucous glee. I got the feeling the Tind'losi didn't believe me. Not that I cared. The longer they allowed me to stall, the better my chances got. Unfortunately, they didn't give me all that long.

"Anduscias," snapped the creature. "Attend to my puny."

As the thing to Belial's left moved forward, I continued stealing what power I could - the energy to run up a flight of stairs, a week's life here and there, the power to mix a pan of batter, a toss of a bowling ball, five minutes walking, et cetera - storing it all in an ever-tightening clutch as I casually asked;

"This Anduscias, not a close friend, is he?"

The second Tind'losi stared at me, taking my measure for a split-second. The right side of its maw curling in a wicked sneer, it dug a claw into the foundry's floor, flicking brick-sized chunks of concrete this way and that.

"Why do you ask?"

Anduscias sprang, his motion a blur. My hand shot up of its own volition, releasing a huge blast of the energy I had stolen. The Tind'losi was torn in two, its organs splattering across the floor, a length of its spine splashing up through its back, shattering against the ceiling, various bits of it clattering back to the foundry floor. My nerves tingled throughout my body from the release, burning flashes tearing at my flesh, unraveling my tendons, grinding my bones one against the other. I kept my face calm, somehow, and answered Belial.

"I just hate to break up happy couples." I gave the words a second to penetrate, then tried my bluff again. "Be that as it may, that's all the time we have. I want to thank you for playing with us. Be sure to pick up a copy of our home game on your way out. You know where the exit is. Don't let the door smack you while you're leaving."

"I do not believe you understand the situation, my puny." Leaning forward, Belial bent its massive head downward until it was within a few feet of my own. "We were locked away from this world for not bowing. We chose to be the lords of Tindalos rather than to bend our knees to others, to be told we were not the equal of what was to come. Of you."

"My heart's bleeding, pal. Tell it to someone who cares. Now are you going calm, or do we have to have trouble?"

"Thrown from this world," snarled Belial, "we were refused entry to it, unless called by human voice. Only a handful of times have you punies reached out so far as to touch us. We have always come. But when puny blood has cooled our throats, back always have we been flung. Until now."

I followed the creature's eyes as it looked at its fallen comrades. Knowing where it was going next, I prepared myself for the inevitable.

"No anchor would we have in this world. One puny found allowed one of us to escape, but contact was always fatal, and fatality always sent us back. But, you, Destroyer, you have ended that. You have spilled Tind'losi blood. You have given us our anchor here. Now, this world is ours. We shall scatter across the face of it, and everything shall be consumed. Beginning with *you*."

I threw myself back just as Belial came forward, its wicked fangs snapping the air where my head had been. Instantly those others behind the monster pushed their way into the foundry. As they turned their attention this way and that, their master commanded,

"No! None other than the Destroyer! He dies, then we live!"

I threw a mental challenge out to all the Tind'losi, driving it straight into their brains, daring them to come after me. Then I turned tail and ran, heading for the outside. I didn't bother to waste time looking over my shoulder. The sound of walls being smashed, of the ground itself being ripped asunder as the monsters tore through everything in their path, let me know I had no worries about being followed. Diving into my waiting car, I punched the ignition and headed for the gate.

My rearview mirror was filled with the sight of scores of slavering monstrosities galloping down the road after me. Even over the roar of the car's engine I could hear the screams of those people who spotted the horde tearing through the streets. Did any of the monsters stop, changing targets, gobbling down those innocents who just happened by? They did. I couldn't see them, but I could feel each strike, each stopped heart and silenced brain, all of them cutting through me like thrusts from wide, dull knives.

I couldn't worry about that, though. We'd miscalculated, badly. Seeking only to save our friend we had unleashed a Hell throng upon the Earth, one that would wipe out every last living soul if they weren't turned or stopped. Luckily, we had a plan that might just do the trick. It had been our last ditch reserve, a dodge we'd cooked up in case our more conventional weapons failed. It had seemed a foolproof fail safe - for taking care of the single hound we'd expected. As for hundreds of thousands... that I didn't know. What I did know, however, was that the trap we'd come up with was the only chance we had, and that I'd better concentrate on springing it.

With a lurch I threw my car into a hard right, sending it flying down a broken side street. The Tind'losi piled up on each other, clawing and biting their own, giving me a chance to get a few blocks ahead of the pack. I gunned the motor, ignoring red lights, laying on the horn, chasing cars out of my way, using any lane I needed to, or even the sidewalk, to keep moving forward. Behind me the monsters charged headlong, crashing into buildings, tearing storefronts away with glancing blows of their bodies.

People staggered in the street, reeling with disbelief at what they were seeing. Fangs and claws tore them apart without compunction, practically without notice. A bus ground its brakes, screeching to a halt as the wave of Tind'losi filled the street behind me. I swerved around it, crashing against the mini-van behind. Careening off the damaged vehicle, I reached out with my mind toward the souls in the bus, even as I fought with the steering wheel to straighten out my car. As I found each pulse on the bus I extinguished it, seconds before the Tind'losi could tear the fragile steel and iron to shreds.

"After him!" came the great, growling shriek. "Kill the Destroyer - kill him! Only him!"

I'd led the attack that destroyed one of their own. I'd killed another right before their eyes. Now, whenever they tried to take the souls of the humans that crossed their paths, I reached out and stole those first, as well. I was hoping this tactic would outrage the monsters. From what I could see in my rearview mirror, it was working. Praying that it was working well enough, I floored the gas and threw my car onto the ramp exit leading down to the Battery Tunnel. Breaking through the toll barrier, I shot down into the descending opening. Behind me, Tind'losi tore great gashes in each other trying to be the first to enter the tunnel after me.

Reaching a point beyond the monster's line of sight, I slammed on the brakes and stopped the car. Leaping out as fast as I could, I concentrated deeply, working to open a doorway to the dream plane. I knew where I wanted to go, I knew when I wanted to arrive. I just had to make certain my timing was perfect. Sensing the approaching Tind'losi, I closed my eyes and stepped forward, disappearing into the dimensional rift I had opened. Behind me, I could hear the creatures running forward, screeching over what I'd done. They had seen me, had figured out what I was doing and were following me through the gateway.

Excellent, I thought. Now if I could just get them all there on time.

I used nearly half the energy I'd gathered from the dying to cut a swath across the dream plane. I needed to take the Tind'losi to another location on Earth. Opening the doorway there in the tunnel in Brooklyn, I opened another into a tunnel in Switzerland, in Geneva to be exact. The Cern Facility is built in a tunnel some three hundred feet underneath Geneva. It is a circular burrow some twenty-seven kilometers in length. I didn't open the gateway exit into that tunnel, however, but rather into the metal pipe suspended in the center of that tunnel. The Cern Facility is the world's largest particle accelerator, a massive, city-sized machine scientists use to split atoms and create new elements. It is a perfect cylinder, designed so to keep radioactive particles–which can only travel in straight lines, from escaping its confines.

"Good God," exclaimed one of the control technicians. "There's some massive build-up in the core pipe."

"Yeah," I snapped. Stepping into the control room, from out of thin air for all the scientists there knew, I ordered, "start it up, now."

"You're mad, there are hundreds of thousands of alien particles in the cyclotron chamber. They're simply appearing from nowhere. The vacuum isn't..."

"Don't even talk to him," interrupted an older man. Snapping his fingers at another, he ordered, "Call security. Get someone in here right away."

They were all speaking French, of course. I was talking to them by thought, putting words directly into their brains which they translated themselves. Not having time to argue, I started putting orders in instead of suggestions.

"You've got plutonium tests scheduled all day today. I know the rail gun is loaded and waiting. Fire it, *now!*"

The man's hands moved to obey my orders even as his conscious brain protested. It didn't matter. I had influenced the day's schedule when we'd first decided on this plan. By leading the Tind'losi into the tunnel, I'd hoped to trick them into not noticing they were being moved from one type of tunnel into a vastly different one. I wanted them to think I was trying to escape them so they would rush in after me. Once in the gateway, our relative size would become unmeasurable. There would be no way for them to notice they were being shrunk by the exit portal to sub-atomic size. Sidedooring on them, I had led them into the particle accelerator while I dropped into the control room.

The rail gun was primed to fire an atom of plutonium into the accelerator. We had assumed if this was done with the Tind'losi that was coming after the professor inside, that the thing would be atomized, split asunder in a nuclear reaction that would create a new element with a half life of a millisecond. That was one Tindalos hound, of course. What would happen with hundreds of thousands was anyone's guess. But, it was the only chance the world had. If the Tind'losi escaped, billions would die. Casting aside the seductive pleasure of doubt, I pushed my anger into the operator's brain and squeezed his soul until his hands did my bidding. The single atom of plutonium was fired into the accelerator tube. And then, their world ended.

As the technicians screamed, the entire control room began to vibrate. One by one the monitors covering the accelerator tunnel glowed then exploded. The curving atoms merging with the angles of the Tind'losi set off a chain reaction which shattered the central tube, incredible explosions ripping along the miles of subterranean passages. In seconds vast sections of Geneva began tumbling into the ground. Gas lines erupted, flames shooting hundreds of feet into the air. Buildings crashed against each other, falling into the vast, mile wide cracks opening everywhere throughout the city.

In my head, I could feel thousands dying all around me. Those in the control room had gone first. I'd plucked the energy of their wills to power my escape, feeling them curse me with their dying moments. Fine by me, I thought. They weren't the first.

20

Sliding into the dream plane, I gathered what force I could from the legions of the dying below. Staring down into the city from the safety of my ethereal vantage point, I steeled myself against the wail of sorrow I could feel drenching my soul. Thousands dead. Crushed, ripped apart by shrapnel, burned, asphyxiated, atomized in nuclear-force blasts. I was as staggered by the enormity of what I'd done as that of why I'd done it.

An accident had brought a friend under the sights of a thing from Hell which meant to wear his soul for lunch. Determined to save him, I had put together a group that stood up to the beyond thing and annihilated it. Which, it turned out, was exactly what the horrors had wanted us to do. Simply trying to save a friend's life had resulted in a staggering loss of life - blood spilled and souls consumed on both sides of the world - thousands sacrificed so that billions could live.

Was it worth it?

The question came from the back of my brain, not one of the sneering voices I so often have to argue with, but one of my calmer ancestors, one given to asking direct questions without any ulterior motives. I looked at the horrible welter of black clouds rising up out of the billowing rage of fire consuming Geneva, and I wondered - was it?

Should I have let the Tind'losi consume the Earth rather than risk having the tragedy below on my conscience? Should I have simply told Goward he'd sealed his own fate and allowed him to be taken away?

No, I thought, it had to be done. Whatever they were, whatever force had sealed them away in the dark origins of the Earth, the denizens of Tindalos had waited eons to attack mankind. If they hadn't been stopped now, they would have had to have been dealt with later. Coldly, I looked out at the horror spreading across the face of Geneva and decided that, monstrous a measure as it had been, it had been worth doing if it stopped the Tind'losi.

The only problem was, they hadn't been stopped.

As I watched in blank and numbing horror, scores of the nightmare beasts began to pull themselves up out of the burning wreckage of the city. Many of them were gone; most of them. But still, thousands had survived. Thousands of immortal Hell beasts. Thousands of supremely powerful agents of chaos. Thousands of...

"Destroyer!" Belial's voice growled clear and harsh across the dark madness of the blazing havoc. "There will be now a reckoning!"

I hadn't stopped them. Some of them, yes. Their forces were crippled, certainly. But, stopped? No. Were they still a force to be reckoned with? Could they still end all life on the planet? Had Armageddon finally arrived? Before I could decide on an answer, I turned and ran instead. I didn't return to Geneva, but stayed on the dream plane. Not that it mattered. I had led the Tind'losi to that separate dimension beyond man's normal consciousness and now given the monsters free reign within it. It wouldn't take them long to realize its many uses. Indeed, with access to the powers it gave its users over the dreamers of Earth, there was no telling what insanity they might visit on the planet. Running straight across the vast open plane before me, I taunted the Tind'losi madly, doing everything I could to keep them concentrating on me.

"There is no escape this time, Destroyer."

"You might be right," I agreed truthfully. Playing off the honesty Belial could sense in my voice, I added, "But then again, maybe I'm just toying with you."

"I have read you now, my puny," the thing answered, its galloping strides dragging it quickly across the dream plane. Red dust splashing up around its great legs, Belial growled, "That was your master plan. You have nothing left now. You are finished. And we are coming for you."

"You come right along, pal," I shouted back. Something was stirring within my memory, one last place I might be able to take the remaining Tind'losi. I'd learned to twist space on the dream plane, to make it do my bidding, to open doorways to here and there at the slightest whim. It took power, of course, life force stolen from the world about me, so it wasn't a skill I utilized often. Still, if I could mold space… why not its cousin?

What was that date, I whispered to myself, begging my brain for the answer. When? When do I want to be?

"We are coming for you, Destroyer!"

I reached the base of a staggering orange and purple mountain range. Throwing myself upward, I clawed at the brilliant rocks, my hands tearing on the glass-sharp facets. I ignored the pain, though, ignored the blood, ignored the baying of the creatures behind me and the mindless screams of the thousands of dead Swiss still howling in my brain. I ignored everything, demanding of my memory one simple thing. A date and a time.

April 26, 1986, came a whisper. *1:23*

A smile crossed my lips. I had them now. With the horrors clawing their way up the mountain after me, I knew they would now follow me anywhere. To anytime. So I took them where I wanted. To the Soviet Union, and the nuclear reactor at Chernobyl.

My memory had given me the exact time of the accident that had shocked the world. I would open a doorway into the reactor core at the top of the mountain. It would take the Tind'losi and myself directly to that moment and place when the world was presented with its first nuclear meltdown.

Giddy with anticipation, I threw myself up and over the top of the summit's edge. As I did so, I found myself in the doomed Soviet plant's main generator room. All around me people stood staring. People with clipboards. People who did not look as if they were in the middle of the most terrible man-made disaster of all time. Not knowing how many seconds I had before the Tind'losi crossed the threshold into the same reality, I grabbed the nearest person I could. Shaking him, I screamed a thought into his brain.

"What're you doing? Don't you know the reactor is melting down?!"

The technician looked at me as if I were a lunatic. Mostly, he was correct. I was dirty and bleeding, my clothing in tatters, my hair soaked with sweat and blood, my eyes wild and stained with tears. Others approached to free their friend, but I knocked them away with a sonic blast of energy. The man I had seized was stammering, confused by my presence, frightened by my urgency. I probed his brain with a thought, forcing him to answer me.

Suddenly coherent, he said, "There is no meltdown. We are only carrying out tests today. We need to prove that the coasting turbine can provide sufficient power to pump coolant through the reactor core while waiting for electricity from the diesel generators. The circulation of coolant, you see, will be sufficient to give the reactor an adequate safety margin while we wait for..."

Because I had ordered him to explain, he continued to speak even after I no longer needed him. Looking around myself, I began to laugh. Suddenly, everything had been made clear to me.

"Destroyer, now you will learn what it means to dare the wrath of Tindalos."

I turned and stared at Belial. The thing was burned and scarred, but hardly injured. Scores of Tind'losi were already in the massive generator room. Hundreds more were cramming in behind them. My laughter had now turned into a wild cackling. Belial and his fellows stopped their forward progress for a moment, staring in wonder at my antics.

All of the workers from the generator station had fled the area. Searching my mind, I remembered that the only thing the investigating authorities could agree upon about the Chernobyl disaster was that there had been an unexpected fall in power. Knowing what had to come next, I reached into my shoulder holster and pulled out Betty. Aiming her at the reactor's main control panel I fired, squeezing off round after round. A warning siren sounded as suddenly the control rods began sliding back into their slots. This set into operation additional pumps which began removing heat from the core causing the spontaneous generation of steam. Almost instantly, the reactor's power rose to more than one hundred times its design value. Inside, fuel pellets started shattering, fuel channels ruptured, and while monsters howled, the explosions began.

As always, I lived. How many died, I don't know. Think what you want, but at this point, I don't even care. Somehow I managed to slide back through the dream plane to New York, right back to the foundry. The others bundled me up and took me home. It was only a week before I was coherent again.

The professor, of course, is very grateful. He says it was something that had to be done. Knowing what we know now, it's certain the Tind'losi would have found a way to invade the Earth sooner or later. They'd been waiting a long time. They'd have found a way. Everyone else agrees. Hell, maybe they're right.

But then again, they didn't sink a score of square miles of Geneva under the mantle of the Earth. They didn't decide it was all right to set off mankind's only nuclear disaster and let a bunch nobody particularly liked take the rap for it. And they don't have to live with the screaming in their ears of the souls they harvested, using their life energy like a marathon runner does pasta - pounding them down without a second thought, all sacrificed for some overwhelming goal.

Of course, we don't even know if the Tind'losi are gone for good. Yes, as best I can tell they sank into the ground, trapped in the molten core of the Chernobyl reactor. But, what are we supposed to do, gaze into the professor's goddamned gem once more and pray we don't see anything? Not bloody likely.

And that's the other problem with investigating this stuff. You never really kill any of these things off. Maybe you disperse one, stall it for a while, shut a door in its face. But end one of these things for good? Not really.

The only things that ever die permanently are human beings. I should know, I've killed plenty of them. All in the name of protecting humanity.

Oh yeah, the hounds of Tindalos - gruesome things - unstoppable monsters - all legs and claws and molten muscle that fangs down on a man like water cascading across pavement. Everywhere at once, relentless, unkillable, unturnable, unavoidable. Inevitable as tomorrow, final as judgment. That's what they whisper, anyway, about the Tind'losi.

I wonder what it is they whisper about me?

Koom Koom: The Frog from Hell

by

Aaron Smith

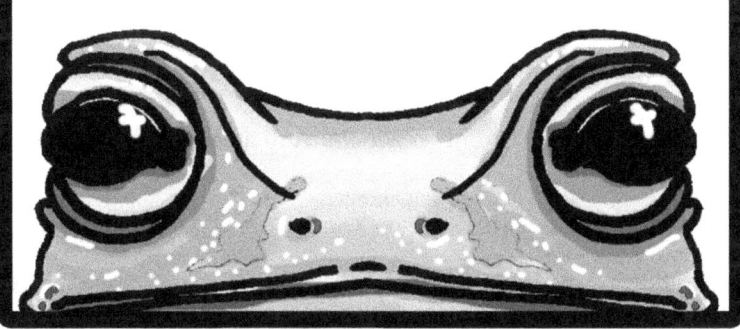

Koom Koom: The Frog from Hell
by
Aaron Smith

Today:

"THIS IS MY FAULT I did this," Magda said in a shocked whisper as she stared into the television screen. Though the volume was turned up high, the voice of the reporter only penetrated the edges of her awareness, as if the tragic news was coming from a separate reality a thousand universes away.

"You have our pledge," said the newsman, "that we will remain on the air to give you the latest information for as long as power is available in the city, though we have no way of knowing how long that will be. A great many citizens have died, but efforts to count and identify the dead must wait for the chaos to subside. Damage is estimated to be in the billions, and still the destruction continues with no way yet found to stop the terrible... thing... that has seemingly come out of nowhere to devastate Warsaw. Assistance is on the way from the British, French, Spanish, and Americans, but it will be too late for the thousands of dead, injured, and homeless victims of this horror. The Pope has issued a statement asking Catholics all over the world to pray for the people of Poland."

The lights went out, the voice from the TV stopped, and, with that barrier gone, Magda could hear the sirens, screams, and looting outside. She put her hands up to cover her ears, closed her eyes as tight as she could, but it was no use. Shutting down sensory intake only made the guilt attack her harder from within.

Yesterday:

They just wouldn't stop. The same stupid, sentimental, sickeningly sweet accolades, over and over again, louder and louder with each increasingly drunken repetition.

"Bless you, Patryk!" must have been shouted a thousand times that afternoon, Magda thought, and would be cried out a thousand more as the evening went on. She tried once to hide in her room and let her iPod drown out the noise from

26

the other room, but Aunt Renata barged in-not bothering to knock, of course, since the adults in the family still treated Magda like a child, even at sixteen - and accused her of being antisocial.

She sat through another hour of her aunts, uncles, cousins and neighbors getting louder with every drink. Her parents were getting tipsy too, but still trying their best to be good hosts, soaking up the attention, enjoying the perks Patryk's new profession would lend to their social status.

When she could stand it no longer, Magda crept through the kitchen and out the back door to the dark stairwell nobody used much, made her way down to the ground floor, and finally, mercifully, out into the open air. She rushed through the courtyard and made her way onto the street. She stopped running, but kept up a brisk walking pace, convinced the sharp eyes of her mother or aunt would detect her exodus and force her back to the celebration.

It wasn't until she'd put three blocks between her and the apartment that she slowed to a stroll. She wandered around the neighborhood as the sky grew darker, letting songs play in her head, trying to forget her annoyance at the day's events, but it just kept nagging at her. She was angry at Patryk, at her parents, at herself.

"Wow! Look at you!"

Magda stopped, turned to face the source of the voice, not in the mood for company.

It was Lukasz. Of course it was. It had to be the last person she wanted to see. He was strange, a moody loner one minute, with his leather jacket, heavy metal T-shirts, and straggly hair, then irritatingly opinionated the next, with his anarchist views, rants about horror movies, and comments designed to test people's tolerance for offensive remarks.

"You look different," Lukasz said, lighting a cigarette.

Magda wrinkled her nose as the tobacco fumes drifted toward her. Lukasz was the only kid in her grade who dared to smoke out in the open. The few others who tried cigarettes were careful to hide the act from adult eyes.

"You look good," he continued, poking for a reply.

Magda's usual attire, jeans and sneakers, had been replaced by the dress and heels her parents made her wear when company was coming. She was uncomfortable dressed up, which added to her irritation with the day as a whole and with Lukasz's sudden appearance.

"I'm not in the mood for your crap," Magda said.

"What's the matter?"

"Why would I tell *you*?"

"Because I'm here and you're here and I'm bored."

"It's none of your business!"

"You know what I do when I'm upset? I punch things. But I don't think you can do that without breaking your knuckles open. You haven't had practice like I have. So you can slap me - but I wouldn't recommend it because I hit back, whether you're a girl or not - or you can vent."

Magda stared at him for a moment. Lukasz was usually a jerk. Was he really trying to help? Was he so bored he was willing to act human for something to do, someone to talk to?

But, she realized, maybe he was right. It *would* feel good to unload, and she wouldn't even consider telling her family what was bothering her. As angry as she was, she'd never hear the end of it if she ruined their celebration.

"You really want to know?" Magda asked.

"Sure," Lukasz said. "It beats doing nothing."

"It's all this crap about my brother!" Magda began. "Patryk this and Patryk that and they're all drunk and happy and celebrating and none of them realize what a stupid thing he's really done!"

"Yeah," Lukasz said, "I figured it had to do with that, since you're out roaming the streets in that dress."

"Don't interrupt!" Magda shouted. "Do you want to hear this or not?"

"Go ahead, but what did you expect? Patryk just got ordained as a priest. He's a big deal now."

"This is not the kind of big deal he should be!"

"And that's up to you because... ?"

"It's not, but you have no idea what Patryk's thrown away by giving himself to the church!"

"Magda, what are you talking about?"

"Can we sit down? I'm not used to these shoes."

The local café was closed for the evening. Magda and Lukasz sat on the bench near the front door. Magda thought they'd look like an odd pair to anyone passing by, with her in a party dress and Lukasz with his leather, denim, and sloppiness.

"Look, Lukasz, Patryk's six years older than me. You know what my earliest memories of him are? He was always drawing. And it wasn't comics he was copying from the paper or kid stuff like that. He was making up machines when he was nine, sketching how they'd work, what the insides would look like, how wires would connect, and how the parts would move. And if he wasn't drawing new machines he was reading science books about how electricity works or why airplanes fly. I always knew he was smart, so smart it kind of scared our parents, I think. I grew up hearing about how Patryk was going to be an engineer or an inventor. His teachers were blown away by how far ahead of the other kids he was. His marks were perfect in school and he could have graduated early except that my parents wouldn't allow him to be skipped ahead because they didn't want people talking about them."

"So you're upset because you think your brother's a genius and now he's just a priest instead of the next Einstein," Lukasz said.

"And nobody else sees what a tragedy this is!" Magda shouted.

"What did you expect?" Lukasz asked. "To your parents and grandparents and my parents and all the older generations, the church is everything. To them, Lukasz is a hero, giving up everything else to serve God."

"But he dropped everything! All that potential! He woke up one morning and walked into the kitchen and said he'd heard a calling. What does that mean? Was it a dream, a hallucination, something caused by an upset stomach? What kind of god takes a smart kid, a kid who could solve the world's problems and invent new ways to do all kinds of things, and tells him to give all that up and spend the next four years reading the Bible and praying and kneeling on a church floor so he can be ordained and have his family sit around getting drunk and talking about how great he is while all the ideas he's had in the past and all the great ideas he might come up with in the future get flushed straight into the sewer?"

Magda stopped talking, let out a long sigh, stared up at the sky.

"Wow," Lukasz said. "Feel better?"

"No."

"So are you mad at your brother, your parents, or God?"

"All of them."

"Do you really believe in God?"

"I'm not sure what I believe in."

"Come with me, Magda."

"Where?"

"Someplace where you'll feel better. You need to lash out at God, and I know just how to do that."

"What are you talking about?"

"You'll see. It might seem absurd, but it might be fun too. Come on!"

Lukasz stood, started to walk away.

Magda hesitated for a moment, but followed. She had nothing better to do.

"I can't believe we just broke in here! If we get caught ..."

"We won't get caught," Lukasz said. "I've done this a dozen times. Once we're in the basement, we can turn the lights on. No windows down there, so nobody can see us."

Magda followed Lukasz down the stairs. The high school looked so different with shadows everywhere, Lukasz's keychain flashlight guiding them through the corridors, past classrooms that would be familiar during the day, and finally into the catacombs that students rarely saw. They went through one last door, which Lukasz closed behind them as he flicked on the light. A single bulb hung from the ceiling, chasing the dark away as it activated, illuminating a large square floor space surrounded by stacks of boxes with the names of various school subjects written on them in wide black marker.

"What is this place?" Magda asked.

"It was the bomb shelter," Lukasz said, "but now they just store books down here. Look how dirty the floor is. Nobody comes here much."

Magda looked down. Her shoes had disturbed the layer of dust, causing small clouds to rise a few centimeters into the air. In the middle of the room, she could see the light remains of a circle that had been drawn in chalk and then wiped mostly away.

"So what are we doing down here?"

"You'll see. Just close your eyes for a minute, Magda. This won't take long."

She did as he said. An uncomfortable feeling crept up her spine as she heard Lukasz moving about.

"Okay," Lukasz said, "It's ready."

Magda opened her eyes and gasped.

The floor was covered with strange symbols. The circle had been redrawn in white chalk, with a red triangle inside. Weird curved sigils had been placed at regular intervals within the circle's perimeter. Lukasz stood in the circle, just outside the triangle, with a mischievous smile on his face.

"What is it?" Magda asked.

"This," Lukasz said, "is Satan's telephone. If you're so mad at God, maybe it's time to talk to his opposite."

Magda burst out laughing. "You can't be serious! This is stupid!"

"Is it? Don't make up your mind before you try it."

"Satan doesn't even exist!"

"But you said you're not sure what exists."

"Yeah, I did say that, but ... "

"Are you scared?"

"No."

"Then step inside the circle."

"I'm going home."

"Don't be such a wimp, Magda. If nothing else, you can let some of that anger out. Just think of it as a game."

"Have you done this before?"

"Yes."

"And what happened?"

"Try it and find out."

"Lukasz!"

"I dare you."

"That won't work on me."

"Come on, Magda. Think of your brother and all that wasted intelligence. Think of how your parents worship him and ignore you. Think of God and how he stole Patryk's potential. Makes you want to slap him in the face, doesn't it?"

"This is stupid," Magda muttered again, but she kept staring at the symbols on the floor. She started to feel strange, like something, somewhere was calling to her, inviting her. She wondered, for an instant, if this was how Patryk had felt when he'd received *his* calling.

All fear, all hesitation, and all feeling that this was just Lukasz being silly vanished. Magda was overcome by curiosity, driven forward by the mixture of emotions she'd been feeling all day: anger at her parents and at God and, most of all, at Patryk; confusion as to how such a promising future could be thrown away on a set of beliefs without evidence, and desperation to find something, anything to help her release her frustrations. She kicked off the uncomfortable shoes, no longer caring how dirty the concrete floor was, and walked barefoot over the chalk border, into the circle.

Lukasz smiled, gestured for Magda to step into the triangle.

She entered the three-sided shape. She shivered.

"The floor is colder here. This is weird."

"See? It's working!"

"What ... what do I do now?"

"Speak to him, speak to Satan. He's not like the other one. He might answer!"

Magda fell to her knees. She felt the cold wrap around her like the arms of an invisible reptile. She let go of her self control, began to speak, first in a whisper, then louder.

"I hate this! I hate them all! My stupid brother for throwing away his life on the church and my stupid parents for encouraging him! Don't they see what they've done? And God and his call! Why? Why would you take away Patryk's future? I hate this stupid world and this stupid city and everybody in it! Curse them! Curse them all!"

The light bulb on the ceiling shattered. The room went dark. Magda screamed.

"Whoa!" Lukasz shouted. He took his keys from his pocket, pressed the button on the flashlight, followed the narrow path of brightness out of the circle, and turned back to check on Magda. She was still kneeling, staring blankly ahead.

"Magda, we have to get out of here!" Magda snapped out of her trance, saw Lukasz waving the flashlight. She stood, stepped out of the triangle. She stumbled as she felt broken glass bite into her bare foot. She steadied herself, limped out of the circle, grabbed hold of Lukasz's hand. They ran from the room, the door slamming behind them. They rushed up the stairs, down the hall, through the exit door and onto the front steps, where they sat, out of breath.

"What just happened?" Magda asked after a few minutes had passed.

"Nothing," Lukasz said, wiping sweat from his brow. "The bulb was old. It broke. That's all."

"No ... it was something else. It was so cold and ... Crap! I left my shoes in there!"

Lukasz looked down at Magda's feet where they sat perched on the next step down. "Are you bleeding?"

"Yeah," Magda said, lifting her foot into the stream of light coming from the nearest street lamp. "I stepped on a shard of the bulb, but it's just a scratch."

"Magda, did you get blood in the triangle?"

"I may have. Why?"

"Shit!" Lukasz shouted. "We have to get out of here!" He stood.

"Calm down," Magda said. "What's the big deal?"

"Blood acts like a door. It makes it all real! Don't you understand? You cursed people in that circle, and you shed blood! Shit! Shit! Shit!"

Lukasz started to run. Magda watched him disappear around the corner. She knew where he was going. He would cut through the soccer field to the street behind the school grounds. His house was in that direction.

She started to laugh. She didn't really think anything supernatural had occurred in the basement. Yes, she was shaken by the sudden darkness and the injury to her foot and the eeriness of the whole experience, but it was easy enough to explain in hindsight. She'd felt sudden chills because of her bare feet on cold cement. The sigils on the floor had a dramatic essence that made them both get carried away by imagination. She'd been lost in the role of angst-ridden teenager, let Lukasz's weirdness get under her skin. She didn't believe in Satan or curses or any of that. But if Lukasz did, she wasn't about to pass up a chance to pick on him as much as possible before it got too late. She got up and ran after him, forgetting about her abandoned shoes.

As she ran the way Lukasz had run, turned the same corner, followed the alley between the school's two buildings, and headed toward the field, she heard it.

The noise was loud as thunder, a powerful, almost deafening croak that made her skid to a halt.

"KOOM-KOOM!"

Then, "My God! My God!"

Magda recognized Lukasz's voice, was about to call out to him, but was cut off by the other noise's second assault on her ears.

"KOOM-KOOM!"

She willed herself forward, made it to the end of the alley, then stopped again, horrified by what stood bathed in the glow of the soccer field's lights.

It was enormous, as wide as five cars parked side to side, as tall as five cars stacked atop one another. Its eyes were vivid yellow. Its skin was a putrid green. The smell made Magda choke. Slime dripped from its body. It was a frog, a huge disgusting frog.

Lukasz stood a few meters from the creature. He looked paralyzed with fear.

"Lukasz, run!" Magda screamed.

Her cry was too late. She watched the frog's mouth open. A long tongue jutted out like a red carpet unrolled at a film premiere. The tongue scooped up Lukasz and reeled him in. The giant lips closed. The frog swallowed. The mouth opened again and a loud, satisfied croak issued forth.

"KOOM-KOOM!"

Magda turned and ran.

Magda arrived home to find her parents and Patryk in front of the TV. She stood behind them, watched the screen over their shoulders. The reporter was uncertain whether the reports of a giant frog rampaging through Warsaw were part of a hoax. Patryk was laughing. Magda didn't know what to say. She was glad no one turned around and saw her tears.

Moments later, the sound of sirens came from all directions. Crashes could be heard outside.

"I'm going to check it out!" Patryk said as he rose from the chair. He was still wearing his new priestly garments.

"No!" Magda's mother screamed. "We must stay together. Lead us in prayer, Patryk!"

Patryk sat back down. Magda watched and listened as her family begged God to save them from the unexpected horror that had appeared so close to their home. She did not join them.

The creature, the news reports indicated as the night wore on, seemed to be moving about the city in a random way. It forged a path of chaos through the center of Warsaw, leaping from place to place, crushing cars and pedestrians under its enormous weight. Those who weren't pinned beneath its bulk were consumed, pulled into the terrible mouth by the rapidly grabbing tongue.

The police surrounded it, fired at it, but its hide was too thick for bullets to dent. Power was lost on block after block as electrical wires became collateral damage to the frog's bounding journey.

They sat staring at the TV through the night. Patryk commented now and then, still sounding like a young man, not the priest he was now supposed to be. Magda's mother let out a squeal of terror from time to time. Magda's father stared, stone-faced, at the images of wreckage on the screen. Magda did not speak, just sat and watched, looking from the TV to her family and back again.

Today:

As dawn broke, sirens still wailed in the distance. The neighbors' cars began to roar out of the apartment complex's lot, one after another.

"We should leave too," Magda's mother said.

"Yes," her father agreed.

"I'm not going anywhere," Magda said.

"You'll do as you're told," her mother warned.

"But," Magda struggled for a reason to stay, something they'd believe, "I took first aid classes. I can help the wounded."

"She's right, Mama," Patryk said. "Those poor people need all the help they can get. And I can't go either. I have to do God's work now, and that work is here. You two go, find a safe place. I'll watch over my little sister."

Magda and Patryk watched the news for another hour after their parents had gone, promising to call when they'd found a hotel safely out of the city.

Patryk's cell phone rang. He answered, but Magda could tell it wasn't her parents. Her brother was using his serious clergy voice.

"Yes, I'm on my way," Patryk said before closing the phone and stuffing it into his pocket.

"Where are you going?" Magda asked.

"To help set up a field hospital. The regular hospitals are all overflowing."

"Let me go with you."

"Not yet. I want to see how it looks out there before I put you at risk. I'll come back and get you when I can. I promise. Stay safe."

Thirty minutes after Patryk left, the power went out. The sudden silence in the apartment let in the distant sounds of panic, chaos, and destruction. Magda put her guilt on hold and dressed quickly, discarding her dress in favor of jeans, sneakers, and a T-shirt covered by a thin jacket. She left her home, running along the Warsaw streets.

She barely recognized her city as she ran. Broken glass was everywhere. Cars were crushed. Pools of blood sat slowly drying in the morning sunlight. A police car sped by, sirens wailing and lights flashing.

She heard crashes and screams from not far away, a little to the south, she thought. The last news reports had the frog heading away from her neighborhood. Was it coming back, she wondered? Looking up, she saw helicopters circling. She ran toward them.

The sounds grew louder as she neared their source. The whirring of the helicopters' blades, the shouting of orders from officers to soldiers, and the horrifying croaking of the thing Magda's anger had brought to this world: "KOOM-KOOM!"

She stopped and stared at the battle. Bullets ricocheted off the skin of the giant demonic amphibian. Its tongue lashed out, sweeping the soldiers aside, slamming them into walls. A grenade was dropped from a helicopter, rolled under the fat belly of the frog, its explosion muffled by the dense hide, only a few scraps of hot metal shooting out to the sides to shatter windows.

Through the thunder of war, Magda heard a voice, desperate and repeating. She thought it was calling her name. She felt a body slam into her, felt the ground vanish from beneath her feet as she was lifted. She turned her head just enough to see the face of her carrier.

"Patryk?" was all she could say before another grenade blast cut through the air and she fainted from fear.

"Where am I?" Magda asked as she woke. She felt hard floor under her body, only a blanket between her back and the boards.

"On the uppermost floor of the church," Patryk said as he handed her a bottle of water. "We're with some of the other priests. It's pandemonium down on the street, but, for some reason nobody's been able to explain, that creature hasn't attacked the church yet. There's rubble all around, but this building's remained undamaged."

"Maybe he can't smash the church," Magda said as she sat up, "because he's from Hell."

Patryk looked at his sister for a moment. "You sound very certain of that statement."

"I am."

"How?"

"Patryk … I made the frog come here. All this … all those people dead … it's my fault."

"What are you talking about?"

She broke down. She cried, and, through the tears that made the world one big wet blur, she choked out the whole story, told Patryk about her leaving the party, roaming the streets, and encountering Lukasz. She told him about the circle on the school's basement floor and how she'd stepped on broken glass and bled in the triangle after cursing Warsaw and everyone in it and crying out against God.

"You can't blame yourself, little sister," Patryk said when he'd heard it all. "You were being controlled by forces few can resist."

"But all those people," Magda said, "are dead!"

"We can't do much about that now," Patryk told her, "but we *can* figure out how to stop this before it gets any worse."

"KOOM-KOOM!" thundered through the air again, as if in defiance of the priest's words.

Patryk ignored it, closed his eyes, swayed back and forth where he sat.

"What are you doing?" Magda asked.

"Praying and thinking," Patryk said. "I don't know what else to do."

Magda watched her brother sit there for what felt like hours, his lips moving, but no words audible. She waited and hoped.

Three other priests, all older than Patryk, looked out the window five meters from Magda. She watched as one of them drew something from his pocket. She couldn't see what it was.

"Foul abomination!" the priest yelled as he threw the object out the window.

"My Lord!" the second priest shouted.

"Did you see that?" the third said.

"It smoked, for only a second, but it seemed to have burned it!" cried out the one who'd made the throw.

Patryk, hearing his fellow clergymen's excitement, stood and joined them at the window.

"What just happened?"

"Father Filip threw a vial of holy water at the beast. When the glass shattered, it appeared to burn for an instant!"

"Are you sure?" Patryk asked.

"I know what I saw," Father Filip said.

Patryk fell to his knees.

Magda rushed to her brother. "Patryk, what's happening to you?"

"I'm thinking, Magda! I'm thinking like I used to think and thinking like a priest too, as if both parts of my life have come together in this moment of need!"

"Even if the holy water did burn the monster," Father Filip said, "the small amount we have here cannot do much harm to such an enormous creature."

Patryk stood. He was smiling.

"Does anyone have a cell phone that's still working?"

The third priest handed Patryk a phone. Patryk dialed, barked into the phone.

"I need the chief of the fire department! Yes, I'm sure he's busy, but I must speak with him immediately! Get him now or more people will die!"

Twenty minutes later, Magda looked down from atop the church. Though most of the roof was arched, there was a section flat enough for her to not slide off. She stared down at the street below. Wreckage was strewn everywhere. Most civilians had fled the area.

The enormous frog still rampaged, its tongue lashing out at any soldier or police officer who got close enough, its unearthly voice still croaking forth, "KOOM-KOOM!" at regular intervals.

Patryk had told her to remain inside the church, but she couldn't. She had to see what would happen next. Once Patryk and the three other priests had left, she climbed out the window, carefully scaled the exterior wall, and made her way to the roof, from where she had a clear view of the blocks surrounding the house of worship.

She was horrified to see Patryk suddenly dart out into the street and throw a small vial of holy water at the creature. The glass shattered against the frog's hide, a small cloud of smoke rose as the blessed liquid did its work.

"KOOM-KOOM!"

The frog squatted lower, then pushed down with its wide legs, made a vertical leap into the air, flew forward a dozen meters and came down again.

Patryk, young and fast, had moved by the time the frog landed. He stood in front of its new position, arms raised, yelling, taunting.

The frog waddled forward. The mouth began to open.

Magda, from the roof, screamed, though she doubted her brother could hear her, "Patryk, the tongue! Look out for the tongue!"

Patryk ducked as the enormous red tongue slashed across the air, skimming just above his head. He felt the slime drip down onto his hair as he rolled out of the way.

He stood again, stared up at the huge frog, screamed out, "A little further, you unholy thing!"

Magda could hear her brother's words now; he taunted the frog so loudly.

Patryk backed up, the frog advanced.

Magda saw the frog creep closer to her brother. If it jumped again, Patryk would be crushed. They were in the middle of the street, buildings on both sides. Patryk took a few more backward steps, with the frog waddling toward him, matching him meter by meter. As he stepped over a manhole cover, then further back until the cover was centered halfway between his position and that of the frog, he called out again.

"Now, my brothers!"

Magda watched the manhole cover fly up and out. From the hole in the street, a tall firefighter emerged, holding the end of a hose attached to an underground water hookup. Father Filip crawled out of the hole after him. The water started to spray the frog. On either side of the street, another firefighter appeared, each with a hose attached to a nearby hydrant, each accompanied by a priest.

As the water began to stream toward the frog from three directions, the priests, Patryk included, began to speak in a loud, steady rhythm, their voices rising in volume with a musical quality behind their words.

"Oh water, I bless you in the name of God, the father, and in the name of Jesus Christ, his son, and in the power of the Holy Spirit. I bless you so that you may put to flight the enemy and root out and supplant that enemy through the power of our Lord Jesus Christ who will come to judge the living and the dead. Amen."

Magda listened to the priests chant the words over and over as the water shot forth from the hoses, drenching the enormous beast that had brought such havoc to Warsaw.

The frog stood there, its eyes open, its cheeks bulging as if it wanted to open its mouth and lash out with its tongue but could not.

The great roar of "KOOM-KOOM," thundered no more.

Magda watched as the pool around the frog grew and more of the blessed water struck its target. She blinked, doubting her vision for a moment, as the frog seemed to shrink.

The bulk of the beast, which had been the height of five cars and the width of the same, now decreased, slowly but steadily under the torrent of holy water. It was the size of a bus, then that of a single car, then no wider than three men standing side by side. The horrible mouth opened one last time, struggling to release its furious sound, but it was more a squeaking cry of desperation than the booming croak it had been before. The thing that had come from Hell was now the size of a large dog, then of a cat, and soon could be seen no more from Magda's place atop the church.

The hoses stopped spewing water. The priests stopped chanting.

Magda climbed back through the window, into the church. She ran down the stairs to the ground floor, rushed out the front door and into the street.

The priests and firefighters stood in a circle in the middle of the street, their feet in a large puddle. Magda ran up to them, pushed her way into the circle, stood next to Patryk and looked down at the tiny frog that sat in the water.

Had anyone not known of the chaos that had nearly consumed Warsaw that past night and day, they'd have thought it was just a normal frog that had wandered from some forested area into the city.

"What do we do with it now?" one of the firefighters asked.

"We send it back to its master!" Magda shouted as she stepped forward and crushed it beneath her sneaker.

Green sludge shot out from under her foot. She stepped back and watched the slime disperse into the water and disappear. She took a deep breath, the smells of destruction hitting her with full force: the smoke of burning buildings, leaked gasoline, the coppery scent of blood, and the stench of fear. She heard sirens still crying in the background and the moans of those trapped under rubble. Tears began to stream down her cheeks. Her stomach knotted up as guilt hit her like a sledgehammer. She fell to her knees, looked up at Patryk, and forced out the only words that would come to her.

"Bless me Father, for I have sinned..."

The Bulb

by

Patrick Loveland

The Bulb
by

Patrick Loveland

A CITY-SIZED bumpy sphere of pale-green luminescent flesh dangled hundreds of tendrils the length of highways as it glided northward over the Hudson River near Hoboken, New Jersey.

Rachelle "Hyna" Sandoval and her team watched it float high above from inside their powered armor suits on the deck of a small, cloaked ship on the river. If the noontime sun hadn't been obscured by dark, pouring clouds, the huge thing would have blotted it out from almost any point underneath.

The tendrils were covered by thousands of clouded eyes, or sensors, the size of halved basketballs, and they gracefully picked over any remaining energy sources in a three-mile radius, as if they were under individual or guided automatic control. They slithered and caressed buildings, machinery, long-abandoned vehicles, and any other possible source of whatever energy it sought.

Electricity had been the obvious early assumption, but it also absorbed heat and radiation, as was discovered when the Bulb hovered above Chernobyl and Fukushima for days just caressing the meltdown sites. It had also fondled the ground above the Lucens underground test facility partial meltdown, which had been sealed for decades, and examined Three Mile Island, before moving on and meandering from one functioning plant to the next. After that it had refocused on major population and infrastructure centers, and at present, it was picking back over the ones it had started with after appearing initially.

Sandoval looked back and forth in her shell-suit's head case, a sideways egg of thick, opaque armor on the suit exterior. It was nestled atop the suit's twelve-foot-seven-inches of roughly human-shaped (but boxy here, too smooth there) bleeding-edge military tech. Its real-time exterior feeds allowed her to see the decimated remains of the industrial areas and the West Village lining this stretch of the Hudson as if there weren't five inches of plasteel armor physically obscuring the natural view. The only things breaking the illusion were an AR heads-up display showing translucent readouts of tactical information and her suit integrity and weapon statuses, and those of her team members' suits. Also, the pouring rain slapping and running down the armor exterior was vaguely visible as a kind of curved surface several inches from her face, which was comforting in an ineffable way.

She contemplated for maybe the fiftieth time what the creature might need the endlessly sought energy for. Most of the planet lay quiet and dark, sucked dry by the monster, and with absolutely no answers as to why. Actually, many had put forth the possibility that it wasn't a huge monster at all, it could be a ship, and maybe needed to recharge. Sandoval guessed it was a mix of both, but in a way humans couldn't relate to. Some even thought it was some form of God.

"The Bulb" was what most everyone called it due to the colossal ball on top, the tendrils clinging to its lower hemisphere before draping almost straight down and fanning out, plus its eerie glow. Billions dead and the remains of humanity a scared, desperate mob... Sandoval didn't care what she should call it, today, the monster would be brought down for good. It had been traversing the northeastern United States for days now, but this was the first time it had been over a body of water viable for their purposes. She looked around again, this time at two other shell-suits on her left, Reilly, Quaker, and two more on her right, Beech, Laidlaw. Her team. They were ready, as ready as they could be, considering their very possible impending death. Most of them had children they knew they wouldn't see again, actually, Sandoval remembered, Reilly's wife was pregnant now so, in a way, they all did.

Sandoval's only solace was that after today, their grieving spouses and partners could raise their children in a world without this monster... and hopefully one united by a cosmic truth it almost certainly represented. As the acting prime minister of the North American Coalition had said in her most recent speech, "We are not alone... and all of our manufactured problems and stubborn selfishness have kept us from becoming one global humanity for a greater good."

The five power-armored warriors were secured leaning back at an angle atop special apparatuses installed onto the deck of a Coast Guard Fast Response Cutter they had repurposed for this mission. A relatively small, fast water vessel had been settled on because all attempts to approach the creature by air directly had failed.

Manned helicopters and a succession of drones had been obliterated by its whipping tentacles in impressive and terrifying shows of defensive awareness. After this violence and continued lack of any communication, they had also failed to harm it with orbital particle beam platforms. The Bulb had drooped a bit in the air after the beam successfully penetrated its entire vertical girth, only to float up into orbit and destroy the offending platform, then go on about its business.

This would probably fail too, thought Sandoval, but she tucked it away in her mind.

43

Beech had an extra cylinder of metal on her suit's back, a six-foot bomb they hoped would be enough to end this, which had necessitated a different apparatus design for her suit. Sandoval had wanted them each to have a bomb to increase their chances, but with the world in the state it was in, there had only been enough resources globally for the one. She just hoped it worked when it came time.

At least as far as the instruments and sensors were concerned, everything was in fact functioning as designed and intended, so the decision came down to her discretion.

Sandoval said, "Okay... suits, 'pults, and bomb look ready... but are you guys?"

-Ready,- Quaker said, always eager.

-Ready,- Laidlaw said.

-Sure,- Reilly said, casual as possible.

Silence from the bomb carrier.

"Beech?"

Sandoval heard a long intake of breath, controlled exhalation, and some form of murmured prayer from Beech over the squad comms feed.

She watched the Bulb sliding through the air high above the river and noticed it changing direction somewhat to now pass over the river at a slight northward angle. Soon, it would be back inland over New Jersey then probably Upstate New York, and the operation would be a wash.

"We can wait another minute maybe... "

Beech said, -I'm ready.-

"Okay, good. 'Cause I can't think of anything *I'd* rather be doing," Sandoval lied.

Beech started to chuckle, but it caught in her throat.

Sandoval said, "Alright, no speeches. Once this starts, it's gonna happen fast. You know I love you guys... *and* you know why this needs to happen."

-Word,- from Reilly.

-Awww, shucks, girl. Love you too,- Laidlaw said.

Quaker took his time for once and just hummed a tune. It had become a running joke for them since the bar brawl during his bachelor party that they hadn't asked for but *had* won.

Beech sniffed, obviously holding back tears, and said,

-Dammit, Quaker...-

"Amen..." Sandoval said, then keyed over to global comms and said, "This is Sever-One, Sever Team. Commencing Operation Lights Out on my mark. Warm up all actors."

She made a thumbs-up in her suit, and its big multi-tool and weapon-flanked bionic hand did the same. The ship operators turned over the engines, and everything powered up from stealth trickle level to full.

She raised her synched suit arm and held it as she said, "Five... four... three... two... one..."

Sandoval swung her suit arm down and said, "Blitz."

As the modified cutter ship heaved forward and picked up speed toward the slowing (confused?) Bulb, the sky was set ablaze. Artillery batteries and mobile platforms fired from all over a five-mile area. Drones filled the sky as they ascended toward the massive creature, firing Vulcan cannons and rockets with no hope of doing real damage, but that wasn't the point. This was without a doubt the largest, most potentially destructive, and most expensive distraction in human history. Especially when its utter harmlessness to the focus of its assault was taken into consideration. But that was exactly what Sandoval and her superiors were hoping for when they devised the plan; a distracted, annoyed Bulb might not focus on a small ship on the river.

So far, that seemed to be the case. The artillery battered the Bulb's lower half and even reached higher sporadically. Quad-rotor and VTOL drones buzzed and flew around it like hummingbirds and hawks, peppering the Bulb with their own weapons. If this attack had been focused on anything else in this human world it would have been utterly obliterated. Anything. The Bulb was, at best, irritated.

Unimpressed as it seemed to be, the monster still took action, whipping and slicing some of its tentacles from on high. They cut through buildings and streets and all other infrastructure with no great effort, throwing up clouds of dust and sending rubble and debris flying as far as the eye could see. High-rises, skyscrapers, office buildings, etc. collapsed and tumbled down, some diagonally cut sections of large buildings were thrown with the rubble, taking out any flying drones in their paths.

In a small part of her mind not focused on the planned task at hand, Sandoval was glad that she had demanded the artillery be manned by remote-controlled bipedal Hüm drones. The Hüms were a bit twitchy in "rehearsals," but they were performing just fine, and she knew only plastic, rubber, and metal were being shredded and disintegrated in the Bulb's attacks.

The task at hand dangled and slithered ahead, below the looming sphere, the tentacles that weren't attacking. Sandoval broke motion-synch and keyed a code into a pad within her suit's shell arm. The apparatus bases extended and bowed, forming into the arms of what amounted to five high-tech catapults with a shell-suited human in each harness.

Sandoval used a contact pad to focus a glowing box in her AR overlay on her choice for ascension. Once she confirmed it, it locked on. The ship pilot crew received her selection, locked on the shifting coordinates, and steered the cutter upriver toward it. She re-engaged synch between her shell and real arms and readied herself.

In the periphery of her eyes, Sandoval registered the shores of the river blurring by through the streaking rain on the head-case exterior. The heart rates of her team members were high, but that was to be expected, what they were about to do was worlds away from what they had spent their lives training for before the Bulb arrived.

The AR box began flashing in their overlays.

Sandoval said, "Fail-safes... released."

The cutter captain said, -Now within optimal range...-

"Copy," Sandoval confirmed, then to her team said, "Prepare for launch." Four small green lights winked on then off to answer affirmative on her team-suit readouts. That along with all the technical systems in the green sealed it.

Sandoval ordered, *"Launch."*

Hydraulic clamps holding Sandoval and her team members in place on their catapults released, and each shell-suit was flung in an arc toward the huge tentacle, sailing over the river and outpacing the cutter through momentum mixed with sheer kinetic release. Just before the shell-suits reached the apex of their ascent, jump thrusters on each of their rear upper exteriors fired and sent them flying straight for the writhing sensor-covered appendage.

"Go to manual thrust control!" Sandoval barked, surprised at their speed of approach. They didn't actually want to make contact with the tentacle if they could help it, their suits had every kind of shielding humanity's scientists could layer in below the shells themselves, but they still didn't know if it would save their suits from being sucked dry. They each steered just to the left side of the vertical length, all but Quaker succeeding.

"Fire tethers!"

Each suit raised its arms, and tungsten carbide harpoons on unbreakable lines fired out with puffs of compressed gas, then their own small thrusters engaged, closing the gap between the suits and the tentacle and sinking into its surface.

Sandoval, Reilly, Beech, and Laidlaw flew just wide of the tentacle's left side and let the harpoons reel them in until they were within about fifteen feet of the surface. Upon reaching this distance, nonconductive spears of rubberized plastic telescoped out of the suit's rough shoulder and hip areas. The spears plunged in, and then smaller spears shot out of their main shafts like barbs under the surface. This all held the four shell-suits in place away from the energy absorbent surface and its cloudy-eyed half-basketballs.

Quaker's spears didn't shoot out, because he came up on the tentacles surface too fast and was still trying to veer away when he fired his harpoons. As he was trying to trigger the spears, he hit the surface. "Quaker, jump off and engage spears!"

Quaker fought the harpoon-line tension as he tried to follow Sandoval's instructions. He got his suit's feet onto the surface, squatted toward the surface to jump, and disengaged the harpoons, Quaker's suit power and vital levels went flat in Sandoval's AR overlay.

"Quaker!"

The shell-suit fell to the river.

Sandoval blinked a few times and just stared at the spot where Quaker's suit splashed down before she remembered the situation, they needed to keep on task or they would all die for sure. She fought herself hard to sound cold and professional...

But instead she belted out, *"Exam!"* in a sorrowful moan.

The "Exam" was something they had observed on only a few occasions when the Bulb caught a tentacle on something or vice versa. It would raise the offending tentacle to a nondescript grouping of the sphere's bumps nearest the tentacle's tether point.

The lower tentacle area they were speared to started to curl and rise toward the sphere midsection.

Sandoval succeeded in mastering her tone this time as she said, "Prep for *Flick...*"

After they were dangled in front of the huge hemispheres of the bumps along the sphere's equator, the tentacle was flicked up and away from the bumps. At the moment before it finished its upward climb, the shell-suits retracted their spears and flew upwards. If she hadn't been so close to possible death at any moment, Sandoval might have been able to appreciate the spectacular aerial view of what was once the thriving New York / New Jersey area as they spun up and away from the Bulb.

"Parachutes."

Several large parachutes popped from the upper sections on the shell-suits and flapped open.

"Reorient."

Small thrusters all over the suits fired, using the tension of the suits against their parachutes to place them back on a Bulb-ward course.

"Cloak."

They each engaged a visual cloaking system developed during the last global conflict, it was imperfect and at best odd-looking in overcast daylight, but close enough to invisibility for their immediate purposes. Sandoval just hoped visual sensory input was what the Bulb relied on most.

Sandoval and her three remaining team members forced themselves to remain as calm as possible as they descended toward the upper half of the Bulb at the end of huge, fluttering, invisible parachutes. In her mind, she kept seeing the moment

Quaker's signs blanked but knew his wouldn't be the last to do so and tried to force the images out with thoughts of her son growing up without fear.

Most of the artillery was destroyed below, but the flying drones were still distracting the Bulb well, and Sandoval was thankful for that.

Sandoval, Reilly, Laidlaw, and Beech touched down on the mottled, meaty surface near the Bulb's apex. The Bulb's exterior bumps surrounded them like half domes in a curved, rain-battered desert of flesh. With the help of nanotech in their weaves, the parachutes became like fine nets and retracted into their storage compartments.

"Okay, guys, focus..."

Three tiny green lights winked on for a moment in her overlay.

"Lasers."

Four sets of three beam-throwers extruded from rings around the shell-suit midsections and pointed down at the surface. They warmed up, shot down, and rotated, cutting circles just wider than each suit's bulk in the surface. Sandoval couldn't decide if the surface reacted like organic or manufactured material, but maintained that maybe they just didn't have a frame of reference.

Either way, the suits plunged through meat, frame, and fluid as their lasers cut farther and farther into the Bulb. As their suit re-breathers kicked on, Sandoval was also grateful she had demanded true pressure and air seals on the suits. As their lasers cut downward, they dived deeper into the bowels of the Bulb...

They stopped abruptly, connecting hard with a thick ball of something the lasers couldn't penetrate. Sandoval gathered herself and examined her readouts, they were deep but not at ideal projected bomb depth.

She couldn't see a thing.

"Thermal..." the internal makeup of the Bulb made that a mistake, blowing out their internal views with bright nonsense.

"High-contrast sonar!"

Their suits started pulsing with a layered audio ping system, showing on their head-case interiors as rough visual information. Sandoval studied the visual abstractions: they were on some form of skeletal internal protection sphere. Organs and/or machines pulsed and pumped all around, some seeming to malfunction due to their violent penetration.

"Okay, let's move, we need to find a way down... "

-Shit!- Laidlaw yelled, then screamed...

A pod of several bumpy spheres, six to ten feet in diameter, descended on his suit and pierced it somehow. All Sandoval could see was his suit pressure being lost, followed by bio flatlines.

Reilly shambled through the fluid toward Laidlaw and the spheres and started firing concussion shotguns in his suit's forearms, the closest sphere took it point blank, collapsing inward almost halfway. He fired at the other spheres as they attacked his suit, peppering and denting them, but they worked in unison to pop and open his suit. Sandoval could only guess as to what had actually killed Reilly when his readings went flat.

"Beech. . . " Sandoval started, unable to voice what she was thinking.

-I know, I know, we have to. . . -

"Do it, Beech!"

Sandoval primed her concussion guns and fired on all the approaching spheres while Beech detached and armed the bomb. Sandoval danced and rolled through whatever the Bulb's interior fluids were, pulping and disintegrating all comers.

Beech started, -Okay, it's set! Let's. . . -

Sandoval looked back at Beech, whose body was exposed in the fluid and being taken apart by the spheres.

"No!" Sandoval fired on the spheres until her guns ran out.

More bumpy spheres swam to meet her, replacing their fellow shipmates or antibodies. Sandoval knew they wouldn't be able to stop the bomb now that she could see its countdown in her overlay. She considered just letting them take her. . .

Then thought better of it and hit her suit thrusters. They clogged quickly but gave her the push to sail away from the skeletal sphere surrounding whatever the Bulb's core was.

When Sandoval was clear of the internal sphere's outer edge, she re-engaged the laser system and set all mini-thrusters to push her down toward the direction of the circular cut.

Sandoval cut all the way out of the Bulb's lower, south-facing curve and dropped into the sky above New Jersey, followed by a river of the internal fluids. After falling away some, she hit her parachutes and felt their welcome pull against her descent. She reset her visuals to normal view and rotated to look up so she could watch the explosion when it came. Instead, she saw the outer surface of Bulb pulsing and swirling in a psychedelic fashion.

She looked down in time to watch New Jersey disappear. . .

The sphere of psychedelic distortion had swallowed the Bulb and enough area around its exterior to swallow Sandoval's suit with it. The weird swirling sphere collapsed toward the Bulb's surface, and Sandoval saw that she was somewhere else entirely. She was in deep space, her view a daunting maw of black, glowing planets, and a field of bright pinpricks stars.

The suit's parachutes collapsed in front of her and shriveled in vacuum due to the air filling them abruptly not existing, and they obscured her view. She keyed in their detachment, and as they floated away from her egg-shaped head case, she was met with a sight she had trouble comprehending. . .

"The" Bulb glided through space toward what could only be described as a family of Bulbs, of which it would have to be considered the runt. If it was huge, these dwarfed it, the largest few easily the size of Earth's moon. The larger Bulbs' tentacles caressed and prodded the smallest Bulb, maybe diagnosing its recent injuries.

Even with her basic knowledge of the stars, she knew she was screwed. This wasn't even her solar system from what she could tell...

As Sandoval watched the bomb count down and pictured it in the Bulb's gut, she mustered all of her remaining energy and will to curse the Bulbs from her airtight suit interior:

"Watch your child die and *understand*... Come to Earth again, and *my* son will kill every fucking one of you..."

As the bomb counter ticked down to zero, Sandoval raised the shell-suit's right hand with its middle finger extended and closed her eyes, picturing her baby boy.

The Humming

by

Christine Morgan

The Humming
by
Christine Morgan

W INGS WHIRR wings blur zip zip zip and sip. Dart head. Beak and tongue. Sip sip. Pulse race flutter flutter. Up down forward back sample sip sip sip. Liquid sweet. Dart and zip. This one. That one. Wings whirr whirr whirr.

Craving hunger craving need. More more. Sweet. Sip and drink. Beak poke. Tongue flick.

Need need.

More-more-hurry-faster.

Zip. Whirr. Up-down. Thiswaythatway.

Faster-faster-faster!

Whirring wings whirring wings frantic.

Hurry hurry!

Sweet need sweet need *sweetneedsweetneedneed!*

Jannie bounced out of bed and dashed to the window. She pushed aside her frilly princess curtains. Morning sunshine dazzled in, early-summer morning sunshine, as light and yellow as the scoops of whipped butter they served at Becca's.

Her stomach pinged and poinged at the idea of crisp hot waffles with syrup oozing in maple-gold rivers to puddle on the plate, and powdered sugar. And those kind of strawberries or apples that were gooey like pie filling! And chocolate milk!

She looked out over their back fence at the golf course, which was still partly misty, especially down by the artificial lake. Dew glimmered on the bright green grass and in the treetops. A few golfers were there already, driving their little carts or towing their golf bags on wheeled frames. Most of them wore checkered pants with polo shirts and funny caps.

It made Jannie wonder if there was a special shop they went to, just for those clothes. Or maybe there were special shops just for old people. Like the old lady, Mr. Schromm's grandma or great-auntie or whoever she was, who'd just moved in with him next door.

Poor old lady. Jannie felt bad for her. She was *really* old, *old*-old, way older than the golfers. Like, ancient-old, all tiny, wrinkled, hunched frail and helpless in her wheelchair.

A nurse stayed with her while Mr. Schromm was at work. Though, as far as Jannie had been able to see, the nurse would basically just park the old lady by the bird-feeders and watch TV the rest of the day, pigging out on donuts and cookies.

She checked, but the old lady wasn't there yet. Their patio was empty, messy with stray leaves and windblown crumples of stuff that looked like tissue paper or discarded wrappers.

A golfer hit a ball that arched way high and white against the pearly blue sky. It plunked into the lake, sending circles of ripples across the smooth water. Sometimes, there were ducks paddling around. Sometimes, there were geese, which were mean, honked, chased people, and left long squiggles of slimy green-black poops.

More dew dripped from the fine mesh of net that hung between the golf course and the houses. Despite it, every week Jannie could count on finding at least a dozen golf balls. She collected them, and turned them back in at the clubhouse for a quarter apiece.

Breakfast, she decided, and then the great golf ball hunt. Maybe she could say hi to the old lady in the wheelchair. Who called her 'Jenny,' but that was okay. She seemed nice - the frump-a-grump nurse was another story - and it was neat to see the birds visiting the feeders.

Hummingbirds, mostly, in all kinds of rainbow-jewel colors. Their wings went so fast they blurred almost invisible, and they hung in the air like magic. With their long thin beaks, she imagined fairies could ride on them and have jousts or do fencing duels.

Giggling, she dashed around her room, holding her arms straight-out and not swoop-flapping them but vibrating them up and down way-super-fast. She swung her head around and jabbed her nose at things, as if it had a musketeer sword growing from the end.

Silly. But fun!

After a quick trip to the bathroom for bathroom-stuff, she got dressed in jeans, sneakers and a sparkly unicorn shirt, and did her ponytail all by herself. She went down the stairs two and three at a jumping time and skipped into the coffee-smelling kitchen.

"Can we have waffles?" she asked.

Her mother, filling a travel mug, said, "What, sweetie?"

"Waffles?"

"I think there's still half a box in the freezer."

"Mo-o-om," said Jannie, drawing it out and rolling her eyes. "I meant *real* waffles, like at Becca's!"

"I don't have time this morning. I'm already running late."

"You always say that."

With a laugh that might have sounded like it belonged to a crazy person, her mom said, "I'm always running late. Tell you what, though. This weekend, we'll make some at home. How about that?"

Jannie gave her a dubious look. "You always say *that,* too."

"I know. I know. I'm sorry. I'm just so busy." Mom smooched Jannie on the head. "I have to get going. Tell your brother to remember to bring in the recycling bins."

"He won't listen to me."

"I don't want to see them sitting out there when I get home," Mom went on, as if she wasn't listening either. "Another nasty note from the community association snootie-patooties is *just* what I need."

"I think that nurse next door is mean to the old lady," Jannie said, partly because she did think so, and partly to see if Mom was paying attention.

"That's nice, sweetie." Travel mug, purse, cell phone, stack of file-folders, car keys. "'Bye, and be a good girl!"

Jannie heard the engine, followed by the garage door rumbling open and shut. The house fell silent except for the burble of the coffee maker. She sighed, and dragged a stool from the counter across so she could clamber up to look in the freezer.

No toaster waffles. Lots of Stouffers-food, and the microwave junk Troy lived on - pizza rolls, burritos, pastry pockets. She stuck out her tongue and tried the fridge, but that was mostly leftover take-out containers, two-liter bottles of soda and about ninety bazillion canned energy drinks. A search through the cupboards finally rewarded her with a variety-pack of healthy cereal bars.

"Bleh," Jannie said.

She thought about knocking and seeing if Troy was awake yet and maybe wanted to drive them someplace, but decided against it. Probably he'd stayed up all night playing video games and drinking SugaRush Ultra-Blue, and would be mad about pesky sisters disturbing him in his basement lair.

Sighing again, she grabbed a couple of cereal bars - granola crunch and yogurt mixed berry - and did her own version of Mom's out-the-door checklist. Change, fanny pack, travel-size hand sanitizer, house key. No phone. Mom said she was too young for a phone.

Dad said maybe for her birthday. But Dad *also* said maybe a new bike, maybe he'd take her and Troy to Disneyland, maybe they could come spend Christmas with him and Brittnylynne, and yeah as if any of *that* was going to happen.

Outside was just like it had looked from her window. The whipped-buttery sun was warm, the shadowy shade was cool, dewdrops beaded the grass, and everything was picture-perfect, except for the trash cans and recycling bins waiting by the curb, and a couple more crumpled papery-looking wads on Mr. Schromm's lawn.

Mom said that theirs was one of the families who'd been 'grandfathered in' when the snootie-patooties made the new rules; all Jannie knew was that it meant there was hardly anybody around to play with. Not so bad during the school year. Summers and breaks sure could be boring, though.

A car turned the corner, but it was just the old lady's frump-a-grump of a nurse. She got out and gave Jannie a squinchy oh-great-*you*-again frown before grabbing her purse and her usual armload of bakery bags and clumping up the walk.

The sight of the bakery bags made Jannie's tummy ping and poing some more, despite the granola crunch cereal bar she'd eaten. Granola crunch *cardboard*, more like... and she just knew the nurse was stocked up on glazed donuts, chocolate snack-cakes, maybe those cookies with the frosting.

The nurse wasn't a total *fattie-fat* fattie, but she wasn't skinny either. She always wore stretchy pants with bright floral smock-tops. Today was no different. The pants were lime sherbet green, and the top looked like Hawaii lost a fight with a clown.

Jannie did a cheery smile-and-wave, which the nurse ignored. As soon as her back was turned, Jannie made a face instead, then skipped past Mr. Schromm's house to a little spur of path that cut across to strip of park following the edge of the golf course.

They called it a park, though in Jannie's mind, a park - a *real* park! - would have swings and slides, maybe places for soccer or baseball. Playground stuff. Fun stuff. Not a hardly-ever-used jogging trail winding along with only some benches and the occasional drinking fountain. There weren't even any picnic tables.

She searched the grass and poked through the bushes. Most of the golf balls were plain white. Some were neon-colored, orange and yellow. She also found a nickel, three bottle caps, a pretty rock, and a few things she didn't bother picking up, not even with hand sanitizer. Yuck. Cigarette butts and wads of A-B-C gum.

And a dead hummingbird under a bench, which was sad. Just a bunch of brittle feathers, purple-blue and red, with its long dark beak in the dust and its itty-bitty feet curled up stiff.

Poor hummingbird. She didn't pick it up either, partly because eew-dead-thing and partly with vague Mom-voice don't-touch-that-you'll-get-germs, but mostly because she didn't know what to do with it. Dropping it into a trashcan seemed mean, but what else was there? Bury it?

In the end, she settled for sort of kick-scooping a mound of gravel over it, then setting her pretty rock for a headstone. She wondered if it was one the old lady would recognize, if the old lady gave them names, even.

The hummingbird funeral brought an end to her great golf ball hunt for the day. By the time she got back to her street, the neighborhood had reached its maximum normal creepy-quiet levels.

Every day during the week was the same. The grown-ups left, and the houses sat there. Silent and empty... but alive somehow, with things on timers and remote control, and the tiny blinky red eyes of security systems. Like a ghost town. A robot-house ghost town of the future.

The only people she mostly saw coming and going were workers, cleaners, deliveries, and snooper-spy snootie-patooties eager to find something wrong so they could leave their nasty notes.

"Don't give them any more reason to come after me," Mom often said, if Jannie left toys outside or Troy's speakers were too loud. "They still wish I'd been the one to move out instead of your father. A divorced man, that's fine; but a single mother?"

Jannie knew better than to argue or ask, though it did make her wonder what the snootie-patooties would have thought about Dad and Brittnylynne, or Dad and Valerie, or Dad and Monica.

Down the block, someone's sprinklers came on, spitting water with a hishy-wishy noise. A Daily-Maid van and a UPS truck drove past. That was it. No barking dogs, no crying babies. No ice cream man jingling music - she *wished*; they *never* got the ice cream man driving by here. No sirens or explosions. Not even a radio turned way up.

Creepy, quiet, empty, and boring.

If only *something* would happen, something interesting and exciting. When she had to do her "how I spent my summer vacation" paper, it'd be nice to be able to write about more than collecting stray golf balls for quarters or listening to Troy cuss at noobs over the internet.

She went around the side of the garage, thinking to deposit her day's haul in the bucket where she kept them until she had enough to go to the clubhouse. Then maybe she'd see if Troy was awake after all. He didn't have to take her to Becca's, but he could at least drive her to the store for a candy bar.

Her gaze wandered across to Mr. Schromm's yard. Sure enough, the wheelchair was parked out on the patio. The old lady sat sort of slouched in it, with her head down and her bunched, shaky hands to her face. She looked like she might be crying, or trying real hard not to.

Jannie paused, nibbling on her bottom lip.

Did the old lady know somehow about the hummingbird funeral at the park? No, that was silly; there was no way she could know. But what if she really did recognize them all, even give them names? What if she was worried because that particular one hadn't shown up for breakfast? The bird-feeders - Mr. Schromm had put them in special a few days after the old lady came to live with him - were clear tubes with bright red horn-shaped fake-flower-looking-things sticking out of the sides. Every morning, the nurse refilled them from a pitcher. The humming-birds would go zipping from one fake-flower spigot to another, suspended on their blurred-invisible wings, fairy-rainbow-jewels of silver and turquoise, shimmery greens, purples, even gold.

Now that she really paid attention, Jannie saw there weren't very many flitting around the feeders at all. Hardly any, when on another day there'd be a dozen or more. Normally, they flew in smooth, graceful little dances, too; a birdie ballet. But, today, the few that were there moved in kind of jerky, jittery fits and starts.

Then, even as she watched with a confused frown, a bronzey-red hummingbird just fell out of the air, plop onto the patio, where it lay twitching feebly. The old lady covered her mouth to muffle a sob.

"Omigosh!" Jannie yelped. She dropped her golf balls, dashed to the low fence, and scrambled over it into Mr. Schromm's yard.

The hummingbird twitched again and stopped moving. It looked like a delicate, broken toy. Like a wad of colorful tissue paper someone had crumpled up and thrown away.

Like... the things she'd noticed earlier, and thought they were discarded windblown wrappers? Which she didn't see now, because probably the nurse had swept them up along with the stray leaves?

The thought of the nurse froze Jannie in her tracks for a second. With a huge guilty trespassing flinch, she stole a glance in the direction of the house. The blinds were partway open on the big picture window into the family room. She saw the TV set - on, tuned to the channel that did game-show reruns from fifty years ago - and the nurse kicked back napping in a comfy chair.

A relieved breath shuddered from Jannie's lungs. She resumed crossing the lawn, making more of an effort to be extra quiet. At the corner of the patio was a plastic yard-waste bin; when she peeked inside, she saw exactly what she'd been afraid of. Five or six brittle, feathery bundles in a drift of leaves and grass clippings. Hummingbirds, dead ones, just like she'd found in the woods, just like the one that fell ker-plop on the patio.

"Jenny?" The old lady's voice quavered.

"Shh!" She flung another flinching glance through the window. The nurse had a box resting crooked on her chest and a partly eaten glazed donut dangling in limp fingers.

"Jenny, dear, is that you? Jenny from next door?"

"Hi, uh... Mrs.... Mrs. Schromm?"

"Edith," said the old lady, wiping at her eyes.

"Ummmkay... Edith... I saw you, and the, um, the birds, jeez, what happened?"

This time, it was Edith who cast a furtive look at the window. "You won't believe me. Nobody believes me. My nephew doesn't believe me. He says it's dementia, paranoia. But I'm *not* senile! I *didn't* have a stroke!"

"Okay, okay, shhh!" Jannie hissed, bouncing from foot to foot as if she had to pee. Which, of course, now she did have to.

"It's that woman! That horrible woman, that lazy, lying, miserable *bitch*!"

Jannie's eyes almost popped. Hearing the b-word from her brother when he was gloating about pwning somebody in a video game was one thing. Hearing it from a nice little old lady in a wheelchair was another.

"Do you see what she did?" Edith went on. "Do you see what she's done?"

"Shhhh! She'll hear you! She'll wake up and we'll both be in trouble!"

"She's killing innocent hummingbirds!"

"Huh?" Jannie said, baffled. The nurse wasn't even out here... "Oh, hey, wait, you mean, like, when she refills the feeders? She *poisons* the birds?"

"Poison would be kinder!" Her wrinkled old eyes leaked more tears as she gazed, stricken, at the bronzey-red bird. "It's only supposed to be sugar-water, a simple syrup of sugar and water, boiled and let cool. It isn't expensive. It isn't complicated. But she makes it with *artificial sweetener*!"

"The... the diet stuff, the fake sugar? Um, well, so?"

"So? So, they starve! It has the right *taste* and they keep *drinking* it but not the *calories* and they *need* those for their quick little metabolisms! They *think* they're getting food but it's a trick, it's empty, and they *die*!"

"Okay, okay, shhh!" Jannie hissed again. "She must just not know..." "Oh, she *knows*, that crafty bitch! She does it on *purpose*! It's *murder*!"

"But why?"

"Because she's *evil*!"

That was enough as far as Jannie was concerned. "Can't you tell your nephew?"

"I have told him. He doesn't believe me. He believes *her*. I've tried to shoo them away, but the little darlings don't understand, and..." She flicked irritably at the armrest.

"Well we gotta do something!" said Jannie. She went over to the nearest feeder, poked her pinkie finger into one of the trumpet-shaped plastic spigots, examined the clear liquid on the end, sniffed it, and tasted it. Sweet. Not flavored like Kool-Aid, just way-whoa-*sweet*!

Another hummingbird buzzed past her head, so close she felt the whiffy-whirr of its fast-beating wings against her cheeks. The sound was a whispery flutter-hum that reminded her of riffling her thumb along a deck of cards. Its feathers were grey and blue-green, with a ruby-red throat-bib. She even saw the shiny black beads of its eyes.

"No, no, shoo!" cried Edith.

Jannie waved at the bird. "Psst, yeah, shoo! Go on, get out, stupid!"

"They won't," the old lady said. "They'll keep coming back, thinking it's food, until they die."

"What if we put in real sugar? Don't you have some in the kitchen?"

"And wake the bitch up?"

"Oh, yeah." Jannie waved at the hummingbird again. "I know! I'll get some from my house!"

Without waiting for a reply, she ran back across the yard, scrambled the fence, and dashed inside. Troy's door was still shut, but he must have been awake because she could hear electronic shooting and death groans from the basement, and the smell of recently-microwaved pastry pockets hung in the kitchen.

Sugar... sugar... the canister on the counter was empty except for a rock-solid crust at the bottom... she found a box of store-brand sweetener in the cupboard but that was the whole gosh-dang problem in the first place... Mom used that in her coffee because she said they already put too much sugar in those energy drinks...

Snapping her fingers, she whirled and yanked open the fridge. Not only was it packed full of black-and-yellow cans with jagged white lightning-bolt letters, but a bottle of Troy's SugaRush Ultra-Blue gleamed like a great big sapphire torpedo.

She dumped some cans into a plastic bag, tucked the two-liter under her arm, and bolted back out. Yard-fence-yard and to the patio, puffing and panting for breath. The old lady - Edith - was trying to ward off the hummingbird from the feeders, but it was really seriously determined to stick in its beak.

"Here, here, okay, hang on a second," Jannie gasped. She plunked down the bag of cans and struggled with the twist-cap.

The hummingbird zipped backward and forward and sideways at angles. It started to go all herky-jerky the way the bronzey-colored one had done right before dropping dead out of the air. Its wings went stutter-flutter. Jannie saw its shiny eyes again and thought they looked desperate.

The cap spun loose and the totally shaken up soda shot everywhere in a terrific, ginormous fizzy-foamy blue spray. A super-soaker blast of it nailed the hummingbird point-blank, knocking it into a spinny somersaulting cartwheel before pasting it to the patio. Jannie lost her grip on the plastic bottle, which hit the ground and skidded, rolling and squirting, in a circle.

"Glahgh!" Edith yelled, as she got a faceful of SugaRush Ultra-Blue. Her false teeth landed in her lap.

Jannie, also doused, ran to the spot where the drenched, feathery wad thrashed and splashed in a puddle. "Omigosh I'm sorry little birdie are you all right?"

The hummingbird's long, skinny tongue flicked from its beak. It flipped itself over. It wallowed and rolled. Droplets flew from its wings and tail as it shook off the flurrying way birds sometimes did at birdbaths. Its startled shiny-black eyes blinked a lot. Then its head darted. Its tongue flicked some more - flick flick flick! - lapping at the brilliant blue soda.

"Hey, cool! Look! The..." She broke off, tipping her head to the side. "That's weird."

"What's that, Jenny dear?" Edith asked, her words mushy and slobbery without her teeth. She wiped SugaRush from her face.

"The hummingbird," said Jannie, crouching.

"It isn't dead, is it?"

"Nuh-unh. But... it's... um... bigger."

Spraying more droplets in a sparkling blue mist, the hummingbird beat its wings as it righted itself. Its body, Jannie was sure, had been maybe as big as a fun-sized Snickers bar; now it was - and she was sure of this, too! - as big as a Twinkie.

And growing.

Growing even as she stared in jaw-drop astonishment.

Tiny feathers fell off as larger ones replaced them, to be in turn replaced by ones even larger. The black beak had been a sewing needle, then a golf-pencil, then a school-pencil.

"Um..." Jannie gulped and duck-walked backward a few steps. "Do you see that?"

"Oh, my goodness. It's the size of a bedroom slipper!"

And still growing. Growing, blundering around as it flapped clumsy wings that looked like soggy comic-book pages, jabbing its thin spike of a beak - which, Jannie realized, looked really sharp - and flicking its weird string of a tongue to drink up more spilled soda.

The size of an old lady's bedroom slipper, then a football, then the size of one of Troy's huge galumphy high-top sneakers he always left in the hall for people to trip over no matter how much Mom told him not to.

The puddle was almost gone, and the soda that had sprayed everywhere was drying to a sticky mess, but the bottle still had maybe a third of its contents that hadn't gurgled out. The hummingbird lurched for it, poking its beak into the cap-hole, lashing its tongue in the sloshing blue liquid. Its wings and tail fanned out. Where the feathers had been grey with shimmery blue-green before, they now had a sapphire sheen that almost seemed to glow in the sunlight.

"What in the *world* do they put in those sodas these days?" Edith pressed a hand to her chest.

"Chemicals and stuff, I guess?"

The bottle was pretty well empty. The hummingbird was bigger than Jannie's pillow, its shiny black eyes like golf balls. Like mean, mad, crazy golf balls. And that beak... that long sharp beak... had she actually thought how *funny* it would be for fairies to ride hummingbirds in jousts and musketeer-sword duels?

Not funny, no, not funny at *all*!

"We should maybe..." she said, rising from her duck-walk squat to grasp the handles on the back of Edith's wheelchair.

The hummingbird flapped its wings again and this time they made the kind of brisk whipcrack noises of kids snapping damp towels at each other in a pool-fight. Its body wouldn't have fit into a shopping cart. What had been itty-bitty bird-claws were practically dinosaur feet!

The feathers at its throat, which had been ruby-red but turned a deep rich pomegranate-purple, quivered. Then the hummingbird chirped, a screechy, squeaky shrill teakettle chirp that hurt Jannie's ears.

"I think it's still hungry," Edith said.

"It drank all the soda."

It screeched louder. It hopped, wings beating the air with wind and a whirring, humming vibration. But it couldn't quite take off, and came down stumbling. One of its dinosaur-feet tangled in the grocery bag and a claw punctured a black and yellow can.

"Uh-oh," muttered Jannie as the long-beaked head darted to inspect the leaking dribble of yellowish fluid. She tugged at the chair but it wouldn't budge; the brakes must have been on or something so that the old lady didn't roll away.

She finally figured out the brakes, but by then the hummingbird was bigger than a sofa and had treated the cans of energy drink like someone dying of thirst might treat Capri Suns. Punch and slurp, punch and slurp, its beak for the straw, and chug-chug-chug!

Jannie turned the wheelchair toward Mr. Schromm's house and got it moving. She'd only made it a couple of steps when all at once the patio door slid open.

"What in the hell is –" began the frump-a-grump nurse, stomping out. Her cotton-candy-pink kerchief was crooked, frizzy grey hair going wild. She still had the partly eaten donut in her hand, crumbs on her chin and flecks of glaze speckling the front of her bright floral smock-top.

The rest of what she'd been going to say, she didn't. Instead, she made a sound like a vacuum cleaner trying to suck up a penny. Her eyes went *way* wide and her mouth made a big shocked O.

With a piercing shriek worse than a million fingernails on a chalkboard, the hummingbird launched itself into the air. Its wings whirred so hard the wind almost knocked Jannie over. She ducked. It went past - *whoosh!* - in a buffeting rush of feathers and speed.

The nurse shouted the f-word and sprang butt-first through the door. A split-second later, the hummingbird was there, wedging itself at the door, flapping and fluttering, trying to squeeze in after her.

Those bright-colorful clothes, Jannie thought. And the sugar, all that sugar, glazed donuts and chocolate snack-cakes and cookies with the frosting!

She hauled the wheelchair in reverse as hard as she could. Edith was babbling something, but without her teeth, Jannie couldn't make any sense of it, and didn't really care.

A twisting heave, a crunch-rustle, bits of fluff filling the air, and the humming-bird crammed itself into the house. Furniture crashed over. The nurse screamed and screamed. The bird shrieked and shrieked. The half-drawn blinds leaped, rattled, clattered. Feathers bristled against the glass. Wings battered at the window, shaking it in its frame.

Jannie, running full-tilt backward and dragging the old lady with her, didn't even realize they'd gone onto the grass and most of the way across the yard until she bumped smack into the fence. The fence! What was she going to do about the fence?

There wasn't time to think of a plan. Feeling like she, too, was gonzo on sugary soda and energy drinks, she hauled Edith out of the chair, boosted her over the top with a yelp and a flailing of bony arms and legs, and followed in a vaulting tumble that might have made her gymnastics teacher happy for once. Then she hoisted Edith piggyback like with a toddler instead of an old lady. She staggered for the door; glad she hadn't bothered to lock it again.

Behind them, glass shattered and there was a splintering crackle of wood, and another screech that just about made Jannie's head explode. An immense whap-whap-whap, like flat thunderclaps, made everything shudder.

Troy emerged from the basement with a puzzled expression. "Hey, what's all the noise?" he called. "Sounds like a war zone." He saw Jannie, with Edith piggyback, and the puzzled expression switched to one of total confusion. "Sis?"

"It's a hummingbird!" she cried.

"A what?"

"A –" She tripped and bellyflopped, Edith landing on her, both of them going, "Oof!" Troy did come to help them up, glanced out the window above the sink, and gaped. *He* said the f-word, plus a few others, in a stunned, marveling tone.

"A hummingbird, I told you," Jannie said, panting. She risked a peek out the window herself.

It burst up from the wreckage of Mr. Schromm's house, shedding scraps of drywall and wallpaper, stirring a billowing cyclone of plaster dust. The furious whirring of its wings made a helicopter downdraft, sending ripples across the lawn, flattening chunks of fence on both sides. The next house over had a backyard pool, which whipped into a frenzy from the gales. A pool cleaner guy had just been bopping along doing his job with ear buds plugged in; he got one look at the massive shape rising out of the debris and dust-cloud, and keeled over on the spot.

"Jannie," said Troy, "that's a hummingbird."

"I *told* you, *duh!*"

A hummingbird as big as an airplane, body arched in a comma-curve... wings beating so fast they were half-invisible blue-sheened blurs... its long beak a black spear stabbing at the sky... the hum and the whirr and the deafening hurricane thunder... pieces of Mr. Schromm's house tossed around like playing cards...

"Whoa!" Troy seized Jannie and pulled her below the counter as a shiny gold thing smashed through the kitchen window in a hail of busted glass. The shiny gold thing broke off the sink faucet with a clang and a cold gushing shower, then bounced to the floor - a badly bent and dented golfing trophy.

"It's so loud!" Jannie hollered.

"What?"

"It's so *loud!*"

"*What?!*"

She gave up, risking another peek as a huge moving shadow blotted out the sun. More windows all along that side of the house cracked or shattered. The kitchen door banged back and forth. The table made a coin-flip and hit the wall so hard it sprang several years of framed school pictures from their nails. Gritty sandstorm gusts howled in through every gap.

Troy yelled, but she couldn't hear him or anything else through the destruction. He spun her around, pushed her toward the basement door - it was also banging back and forth, like it was in a haunted house movie - and went to pick up Edith. Jannie eyed the bangy-slammy door in alarm, and then saw the stool she'd perched on that morning while asking Mom about waffles.

Gosh that seemed like forever ago! And to think, she'd been grouchy and bored, wishing for something exciting to happen this summer!

The stool, though... Jannie grabbed it by the legs and shoved the seat-end at the basement doorway. The door whammed into it with a crunch, breaking one of the legs and snagging long enough to let her catch the edge and hold it open.

"Go, Troy, go!"

He went, carrying Edith, plunging down the stairs in a way that would probably kill them both. Jannie didn't even try to take the steps like a normal person, butt-whumping down. She got a brief glimpse of posters, a paused game on the big screen, laundry, clutter and mess.

A brief glimpse only, because there was a sudden pop and the power went out, hurling them into basement darkness.

Troy said the s-word. "I didn't save!" He drew his phone and used it to cast enough light for them to see by, and all three of them crowded into the closet-sized bathroom as the house shook and creaked and groaned overhead.

"My goodness," said Edith. "It's like a tornado."

Jannie's ears felt the way they did during take-off or landing when they flew to visit Dad. She closed the bathroom door - and locked it for no good reason; if the hummingbird came after them, it wouldn't try the knob!

"Are we gonna die?" she asked.

"If it caves in on us, probably," Troy said.

"I didn't mean to! I didn't know!"

"Wait, what? Didn't mean what? Didn't know what?"

"That your soda and Mom's energy drinks would do that!"

His eyebrows twisted in a way that said he didn't think he heard her right, but he didn't ask.

"Let's see what's going on out there," he said, waggling his phone. "I can still get online."

The community association might be snootie-patooties about their rules, but they'd had exterior security cameras installed all around the neighborhood that people could log in and look at, even from work. Edith and Jannie leaned close to peer over Troy's shoulders.

They watched in solemn silence, skipping from one view to the next, as the huge hummingbird laid waste to house after house after house. It bashed them apart with the gale-force winds of its wings. Muffled, and from a distance, they heard the destruction. They heard the shrill, piercing screeches and shrieks.

It drove its beak - which was now as long as a telephone pole! - into the wreckage, seeming to go for the brightest houses within the snootie-patootie acceptable paint range, impaling colorful bedspreads and furniture with floral-print upholstery. Epic splatters of blue-tinged whitish bird poop streaked lawns and driveways. And they'd thought the *geese* were bad!

Yard guys, pool guys, Daily-Maids, deliverymen, housekeepers and golf carts fled in panic. The garbage truck roared down the street so fast it jumped the curb, missed the turn, rolled two complete rotations with trash spewing every direction, and teetered to a smoking stop in somebody's just-trimmed hedges.

"Oh yeah," Jannie said to Troy. "Mom wanted me to remind you to bring in the recycling bins, but I don't guess it matters very much now."

Wings whirr wings blur zip zip zip and sip. Dart head. Beak and tongue. Sip sip. Pulse race flutter flutter. Up down forward back sample sip sip sip. Liquid sweet. Dart and zip. This one. That one. Wings whirr whirr whirr.

Craving hunger craving need. More more. Sweet. Sip and drink. Beak poke. Tongue flick.

Need need.

More-more-hurry-faster.

Zip. Whirr. Up-down. Thiswaythatway.

Faster-faster-faster!

Whirring wings whirring wings frantic.

Hurry hurry!

Sweet need sweet need sweetneedsweetneedneed!

Sadie and Tho'Thok

by

Konstantine Paradias

Sadie and Tho'Thok

by

Konstantine Paradias

THE LITTLE blue rock spins below, tossing and turning like a feverish child, with its Moon clutched in the tug of its gravity. The blue rock's surface is covered in obscene growths; green and browns and tiny screaming things that live and die in the blink of an eye, their populations waxing and waning on its surface.

Tho'Thok, too, was sick once; ravaged by such infestations that prodded and prowled its skin. It had begun as a minor infection that took hold in a small lesion on the surface, but grew out of proportion before Tho'Thok was even aware of it. Screaming like mad, the things stomped across the surface, drilled against Tho'Thok's skull and sent terrible vibrations into its brain. It got to a point where Tho'Thok was so weakened by their infestation that it could no longer break away from the tug of a mere sun. Tho'Thok stayed sick and powerless for countless revolutions, the sun's heat singing each side of Tho'Thok's sides, burning his skin to a matte black. When the infestation finally annihilated themselves in an orgy of nuclear fire, Tho'Thok was finally free again. Free to roam the vastness of space, to warn others like Tho'Thok, help them overcome the tyranny of those maddening growths. When Tho'Thok broadcast its signal by carefully bending the blue rock's tyrant sun rays, it received an answer almost immediately: *Save me*, the blue rock signaled, through a carefully mediated eclipse. Tho'Thok was more than happy to oblige.

J-762, tediously dubbed by worldwide media as 'Wormwood', entered the Solar System at July 2nd, crawling past Saturn at one-quarter light speed. Its size, scientists estimated, was so large that it could cause a significant shift in planetary orbits, effectively causing Earth's rotation to spin out of control and send it hurtling into space in just a few years' time.

"All life on Earth," the dour-faced scientists repeated on the TV channels, the radio stations, the message boards and the social media "is effectively doomed."

Plans were drafted; billions were sunk into the development of measures that would allow for the evacuation of the world's population. For the first time since the beginning of human history, mankind thought as one, fought as one, breathed as one for the sake of the survival of its species. It was a glorious thing, but early predictions showed that even non-stop work on the project at our current technological level would not allow us to be off-world on time.

So we wept and we beat our chests and we gnashed our teeth. The doomsayers nodded their heads and went 'I told you so'. There were riots in the streets, but those died out after a while. As a token effort, a crack team of astronaut-kings was sent out into space, their vessels stockpiled with enough nuclear weapons to reduce the surface of Mars to an irradiated, smoldering cinder. The entire effort was televised on every channel 24 hours a day. When the vessel made contact and burst with all the dignity of a mosquito flying into a bug zapper, everyone just shrugged and went on with their lives, slowly letting civilization fall apart. In the night above the sky, 'Wormwood' continued its slow, determined crawl.

Something stung Tho'thok's skin, as it carefully crawled around the red ball of gas that was fifth from the Sun. It made sure not to allow any of its sides or pseudopoda touch it. Gas balls were filthy things that littered the landscape, always grasping at everything with their grubby gravity fields.

Please hurry, the blue rock sighed, its message scrawled on its atmosphere through a calculated ventilation of its volcanic ducts.

Soon, Tho'Thok said, reassuring it by scribbling something on the fly by colliding two sizeable meteors against each other. It was all Tho'Thok could do, in that limited window of time.

Sadie was born on the night the world went crazy. She grew up watching the shows about how everyone needed astro-engineers. When she was 8, Sadie wanted nothing more than to work in the fields in the African Plains and make space-arks. She'd make sure that when she built them, she'd have a big bedroom for Mom and Dad and enough space for all the kittens and the doggies in the world but she'd install vents that would zap the roaches and the flies and the mosquitoes and all the creepy crawlies.

By the time Sadie was 12, everyone had given up. The ship that they'd stuffed to the brim with all the nuclear missiles had detonated after the astronauts drilled the hole at the top of its pyramid-shape, but it hadn't even made a dent. Dad took it really hard. He'd spent months just watching the astronaut shows, commenting on their livestreams and bidding on future chunks of 'Wormwood' on eBay. He'd wanted one big enough to make a house out of, which is why he sunk all the family's savings into it.

Sadie's Mom handled it better, of course. She would go out on dates while Dad was obsessing over the astronauts. She left two days before the detonation and didn't even ask Sadie if she wanted to come along. Sadie didn't mind that so much. After all, she was plenty busy taking care of Dad; making sure he wasn't lying on his back when he drank too much, or pull him into the bedroom when he'd pass out on the living room floor and make sure he'd eat his lunch so he wouldn't starve. It helped pass the time; after all, there wasn't any school anymore. Her friends drifted away and did stupid, grown-up stuff like hijacking cars and driving them into storefronts.

When the TV went out forever, Sadie kept herself occupied by drawing rough sketches of all the spaceships she wanted to make and posting them online on Facebook. Nobody liked them or commented, but it felt nice to get something done, all the same.

The little red rock shed its moons as Tho'Thok passed by. The twin rocks orbited Tho'Thok's top, whizzing past its field of vision, blocking his view. Tho'Thok twisted and turned in place, struggling to slingshot the moons, but all it ended up doing was causing the larger moon to slam into Tho'Thok's surface, while tearing the other moon into a fine power that blighted him with a ring. The little blue rock below made a sign by positioning itself in front of its moon, the universal sign for a playful giggle. Tho'Thok groaned, fighting against the stinging pain on its surface where the moon had punched a hole, leaving Tho'Thok's substratum exposed to the solar winds and radiation.

This blue rock was turning out to be a pain in the poles.

The bearded men in tattered suits came for Sadie on the night her Dad died. He had made a noise, that afternoon; a little coughing sound, then something like water, being sucked into a drainage pipe really fast. Sadie could have stopped it, if she hadn't spent the entire day trying to haggle their spare laptop for food. They were out of money and no one was printing them anymore and the supermarkets had stopped stocking up the shelves as soon as 'Wormwood's' horrible triangular shape cast its shadow over the face of the sun.

"Are you Sadie 'Twinklestar' McMahon?" the bearded man at the head asked.

"Please don't take the food. We've got a TV. I know it's useless but maybe you can sell it for parts..."

"We aren't here to rob you, Sadie. We're from NASA. Well, what's left of it."

"No way."

"Yes way." The men said and flashed their badges at Sadie. They had kept them good and polished and they twinkled like little suns. Sadie stared in disbelief. "We saw your spacecraft drawings on Facebook, Sadie. And we want to build one."

"Which... which one?" Sadie asked, already reeling.

"The one you had titled... er, 'Super Special Slither Streaker'"

"Are you serious?"

"The solar sail design needs work and we might have to seek an alternative to your suggested hyperspace drive as we do not have one that works on pizza, but yes. We're going to need your help."

"Are you going to go to another world?"

"No Sadie; we're saving this one."

Tho'Thok was half-blind and wholly in pain. The burning sensation behind its eyes had gotten worse, as he neared the planet. Perhaps some stray meteor slivers had made it into the rift on Tho'Thok's surface, or maybe the radiation had made it sick. Tho'Thok closed its eyes for a second, tried to reposition itself away from the red rock, approach the blue rock from another direction, but it ended up getting caught in the gas-ball's gravity field.

Tho'Thok struggled to free itself but the gas-ball gripped him tightly, wound it twice in its orbit and then sent it streaking across the Solar system, before Tho'Thok finally managed to catch itself in the gravitational tug of the Sun. It helped clear away the pesky ring, but it still had to fight with all its might, if only to keep itself from hurtling down into that horrible mass of burning gas.

What are you doing? The blue rock moaned by churning its oceans. *Save me already!*

Tho'Thok grit its mantles together, in a subtle display of anger. The little blue rock was bloody pushing it...

It took Sadie and the people from what was left of NASA four whole years to finish the 'Super Special Slither Streaker'. They built it in Baikonur, which the Russian President just gave away with a shrug.

"Do whatever you want. I'm going on vacation." He said and handed them the keys.

Sadie liked Baikonur, because it was huge and open and because everyone treated her like she was the boss and asked her for instructions. Most of the important stuff was kind of lost to her, but Sadie had to put her foot down about how the 'Super Special Slither Streaker' had to be painted gold and how the controls had to have candy-stripes painted on them, no matter what.

In the two-year mark, the great triangle shape went away for a while and the people cheered in the streets. The world wasn't gonna end after all! Sadie was kind of bummed about it, until 'Wormwood' suddenly reappeared, closer than ever before. Thankfully, the people from what was left of NASA had never stopped working. They even gave Sadie lessons in piloting a spacefaring vessel, for her birthday.

On the day of her sixteenth birthday, with the great pyramid shape obscuring the sun, Sadie blew her candles and was escorted outside, where the 'Streaker' waited, laid down on the field, primed and ready for lift-off. Sadie asked the men if she could pilot it. The men very politely told her no, after explaining to Sadie that their intent was to detonate the vessel's hyperdrives inside 'Wormwood' and create a black hole that would suck it in forever, destroying it. Sadie thought about dying for a moment, about Mom leaving and Dad dying and the world falling apart. She asked the men if she could come anyway.

The men said yes.

Tho'Thok was struggling against the Sun's relentless pull every step of the way, the part of its surface that faced the Sun scoured by the intense heat and naked radiation. Tho'Thok was half-blind and in immense pain. The rupture in its surface had done a number on it and Tho'Thok feared that perhaps it was infested with life again. It would make another run past the gas-ball, after it had saved the blue rock, to make sure that it cleared up the mess and avoid any mishaps.

Come on! Just a little bit more! The blue rock urged on and Tho'Thok beat his space-faring pseudopodia against the solar winds, felt the familiar almost-erotic tug of his gravity field and Earth's meeting together, the Moon caught in the throes of their meeting. Below, the blue rock shivered in naked anticipation. Tho'Thok grasped it, slowly began to pry it loose from its orbit around its sun.

The world shook and shuddered as the 'Streaker' took off into the Heavens. It moved as fast as Sadie had designed it too, whizzing past the Moon in six minutes flat, aiming at the huge shape in the night sky. Two astronauts were with her, inside the vessel. They tinkered with the hyperdrive the entire time, poking and prodding it with instruments.

"Sadie, we need to steer the vessel upward and land it somewhere inside 'Wormwood'." they squawked from the speakers. "Can you find a crater or a chasm, anything that we can fit the 'Streaker' into?"

"Will this do?" Sadie asked, as she whizzed around the giant black pyramid, staring out from the windows at the blasted lifeless surface of it, at the strange lakes filled with a liquid that flowed like molten silver. Up ahead, a giant crater adorned its tip, as wide as Australia. Sadie maneuvered it inside, past kilometers of rock and endless strata, all the way to its mantle. They stepped outside, Sadie and the men, carrying the engine on their backs to lay it on the mantle. Something squished and squelched under the soles of their feet. The rock was coated in some grimy green substance, like week-old soup molding at the back of the fridge. Below, the moon seemed to stretch, like it was made of silly putty.

"Engine is primed to blow, Sadie. Soon as Bob throws the switch, we're all going to run to the 'Streaker like Hell and gun it really-really fast, okay? Then maybe we can escape the event horizon."

"Okay" Sadie muttered. Except Bob never threw the switch. Something had crawled out of the sludge and caught him in its pincers, stuffed him in its mandible-mouth. Bob cut off communication, but Sadie still caught the sound of something a lot like teeth chewing tinfoil. The other astronaut reached for his emergency ignition button, but a puddle came alive and drowned him. Brown sludge with teeth slipped into his suit and stripped him down to the bone. Sadie thought whether being sucked into a black hole and decided it was better than this.

Her hand slammed the EMERGENCY IGNITION button.

Tho'Thok's gravity field had all but encompassed the little blue rock. Already, Tho'Thok could feel the blue rock's rotation slowing down, if only by a fraction of a meter per second. Just a little bit longer and he'd be able to halt its rotation, pull it into his own orbit and then...

Yes, yes yes! the little blur rock exclaimed by shattering its poles in ecstasy. Its moon wobbled in their shared orbit.

... maybe it was time for Tho'Thok to settle down with a nice little planet of his own.

Except there was this horrible sucking sensation and Tho'Thok watched helplessly as the Universe fell away from him, the totality of existence being reduced to a single point of infinite gravity that crushed him into such a fine powder that he was one exactly one atom thick and ten thousand kilometers long. When he screamed, Tho'Thok's voice was long and squeaky and it went on forever.

Damn, the blue rock grumbled, voicing its dissatisfactions on the Richter scale. On its surface, life cheered and whooped and made horrible stomping noise again, sent terrible drills into its core and sucked its lifeblood dry.

The little blue rock watched in horror, as the golden swarm zipped away from it, into the vastness of the dark beyond. The little blue rock crumbled into dust, its very last sight that of a girl's face, etched on the side of its Moon.

Sadie's face.

MegaGRONK!
by
Doug Blakeslee

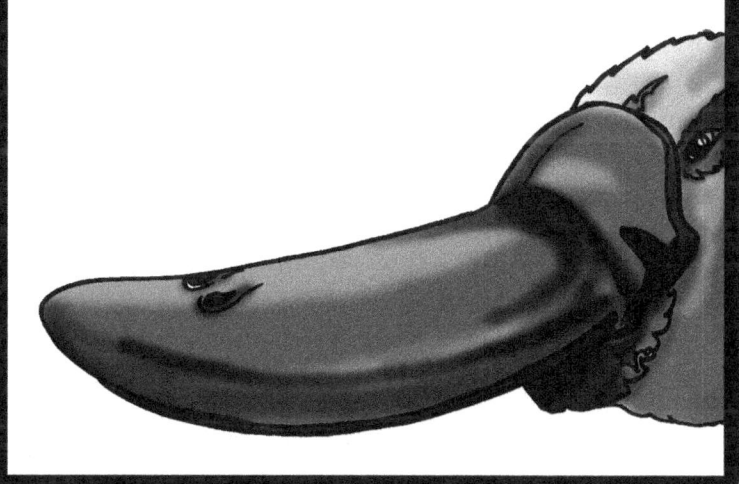

MegaGRONK!
by
Doug Blakeslee

HE SHIFTED in the muck, settling comfortably to digest his first meal since waking. The pack of scaly ones had descended upon him, seeking easy prey, and paid for their arrogance. Three died, crushed and swallowed against the massive plates of his bill. Four more succumbed to his spurs, thinking him defenseless from underneath and behind. The last scaly one died of shock and allowed the rest of the band to escape. This meal would sustain him for a few days, but instinct drove him onward to defend his territory and the strange rock that lay half buried in the river bottom. It gave him life while he slept and grew. His senses pinged to renewed activity above, on the surface and the shore. More of the scaly ones to hunt and fill his belly; both prey and a threat. He'd find their nest and devour their eggs to ensure his dominance.

GRONK!

The gulper gurgled and swished as it flopped onto the beach, rudimentary lungs gasping for breath. Frothy bubbles leaked from the gaping mouth, tinged red with blood. Dozens of small wounds peppered its hide, tearing away the scales to reveal a pale pinkish flesh underneath.

"Someone get the tartar sauce, the fish is done!" Private Linda Merchant cocked the pump-action and pulled it to her shoulder. The twelve-gauge roared, buckshot tearing into the mutant salmon's head.

"Quit showing off," barked Sergeant Chucks. "Tag it for recovery and continue the sweep."

"Yes, Sergeant." She pulled out a small pistol and fired a dart into the thing's back. A swampy smell of muck and decaying vegetation wafted from the corpse. Up the shore, the rest of her fire team moved up the beach on a final inspection sweep. She counted two dozen gulper corpses littering the beach. The eggheads called them Genetically Modified Aquatic Entities or GAMES. Troopers used gulpers for their obvious difficulties with breathing air.

"What's your count?" Tony Pike fell in beside her, cradling his M-15. "I got five with a probable."

She glanced at him and smirked. "Slacker. I nailed eight with two probables."

"Dammit. I thought I had you." He grumbled, kicking one of the bodies. "How the hell do you do it?"

"Blame my Great Uncle Steve. He taught me to shoot and hunt." She patted the Remington. "Slugs and buckshot, better than spray and pray."

"Damn woman, you won the pool again." He slipped her a wad of cash. "At least I got second."

"Thanks." She tucked the prize into a pocket and looked out over the waters of the Columbia River. "What the hell's driving them to shore? This makes the fourth incident in a month."

"Who cares? We get combat pay for this. Two more months of this and I'll be able to afford that DeLorean."

"Dream on." She frowned at the froth of bubbles that drifted on the currents. "This is weird."

"What the hell messed these fish up?" The rookie, Hunter-something, poked at the dead body with his boot.

"My cousin says they got a dose of radiation and chemicals back in the 50s. Either a chemical spill or a radioactive meteor. Been breeding and changing ever since."

"Radiation doesn't work that way," the rookie said.

"Tell that to the eggheads."

Before the rookie could respond, the Sergeant shouted, "Squad, fall in! The clean-up crew is here. Time to get your lazy asses back to the barracks."

Linda took a last look at the scene. *I wonder what Molly would say about their behavior.*

The Offspring sang about gangs and law as Fire Team Urchin disembarked from the APC. Three deuce and a half transports rumbled by, the white hazmat bags hidden under heavy canvas tarps. At the far end of the base, smoke rose as the gravediggers fired up the incinerators for another night of disposal.

"I wonder if they're serving fish at the mess?" Corporal Jackson made the same joke every time.

That brought a series of groans from the rest of squad as they marched across the tarmac.

"That joke still sucks," Linda said.

"Old ones are the best."

The Sergeant emerged from the front of the APC. "Okay, you screw-ups. Mess in thirty minutes. Get cleaned up and fall out for roll call in twenty-five."

A chorus of acknowledgments came from the team as they piled through the door, and stopped short.

"Officer in the room," shouted Tony, as everyone snapped to attention and saluted.

The tall, thin man saluted back. "As you were. I'm Captain Harr. Command has assigned me as your liaison for Task Force Flounder. You'll be paired with a newly formed armor team."

"Armor team, sir?" Even the Sarge looked confused.

"That is correct. Operations is pairing infantry and armor squads to create mobile task forces in the event of an emergency. Here are your operational orders." He laid a packet of paperwork on the table. "Starting at 0800 tomorrow, you'll be reporting to motor pool seventeen. Any questions?"

"We're armor jockeys now, sir?" This came from Hunter-something.

"No. You'll be acting in a support role for the armor units that are being deployed."

"Support?" The Sarge's voice held that tone. The one that even the densest of recruits recognized as anger.

Linda watched the officer, wondering if he recognized it. He ignored or remained oblivious to it. "That's correct. The pilots will need training in dealing with future GAME intrusions. You'll be trained and reclassified as a heavy weapons team."

"We're no longer going to be deployed for field operations?"

"Private Merchant; am I correct?"

Linda nodded.

"With your personal achievement and that of your squad, command has decided that your talents are bested suited to support our new operational focus."

"Aren't tanks overkill in dealing with the gulpers?"

"Everything will be explained in the morning. I've kept you long enough from your duties." He walked to the door and nodded. "Continue as you are and I'll see you all at 0800."

The screen door banged shut after him, leaving the squad in silence.

He swam lazily along the bottom, digging into the silt for hidden morsels that hid there. His bill sensed the faint electrical signal that pulsed through the muck. Smalls bits of food, barely enough to take the edge off his hunger. Smaller creatures flanked him, snapping up the stray pieces that escaped his notice. They danced at the edge of his presence, keeping a safe distance away, instinctively sensing they would be added to the menu without hesitation. At his burbling rumble, they fled towards the shore and perceived safety of the shallows. Alone. Hungry.

Vibrations tickled his senses. A steady thrum of noise and signal. Enticing, despite the unfamiliar source. It crawled across the surface, a slow and tempting target. More than that; full of scaly ones. Enough to fill his stomach; to suppress the hunger that gnawed at his belly and occupied his thoughts. He pushed off and paddled towards his dinner.

GRONK!

Linda glanced around the motor pool, focusing on the three large objects off to the side covered by green camouflage tarps. The squad sat on the folding chairs, peering at the three clean-cut officers standing at attention across the way. All had second Lieutenant stripes on their shoulders and the smell of freshly minted commissions oozing from them.

Tony leaned over and whispered in her ear. "That must be the armor crew."

"What gave it away? The fresh faces or their lack of experience?"

He chuckled. "I wonder if they'll listen to us. Like Major Blowpork."

"Windham. To be fair, he listened to us before transferring out."

"Yeah, after a gulper nearly ate his nuts."

"Thanks for reminding me of that image."

"Attention!" barked the Sarge. As a unit, the soldiers rose up and saluted.

"At ease." Captain Harr marched across the floor. In his wake trailed three men, two in tech jumpsuits and one in a business suit.

"Holy crap, those guys are from Bishop Industries," Linda whispered to Tony.

"How do you know that?"

"My uncle ran into them back in the day. He said they were a bunch of bush-whacking sidewinders."

"Sidewinders?"

"He's from Texas."

"Thank you for coming. Let's get to business." Harr gestured behind him. "These are Lieutenants Wheeler, Cleo, and Georges. They've been assigned as pilots for the new Combat Reactive Armored Battlers."

The cloth coverings dropped away. Linda stared at the revealed machines. Six spindly legs, an oval body, and two large claw arms. A large windscreen across the front with four lights slung underneath, along with strange red-lensed camera. On top, nestled in the middle, sat a turret with two barrels, flanked by ammo bins. Someone had painted the things a bright red. Call signs were painted on the side in black. Antigua. Yukon. Sumatra.

"What the hell are those?" Tony's voice carried over the dead silence. The officers shot him a look of annoyance.

"Glad you asked, Private Pike." Harr walked over and patted the closest one. "The CRABs, as the techs call them, are personal combat machines, designed to engage GAMES on land and in the water. No longer do we have to wait for an incursion, but we can track down colonies and eliminate them before they threaten the population."

"Excuse me, sir, but how are those things better than foot soldiers?" The Sarge stood up.

"I'll let Mr. Leon Bishop answer that. He's the chief engineer on the project."

The suit stepped away from the techs, looking at the assembled troops over a set of too small glasses. "We can reduce combat casualties by eighty percent according to the projections. The Combat Reactive Armored Battlers are state of the art machines. Fully armed and armored. Our projections show they'll be able to withstand the strongest blow a GAME could generate. They're fully amphibious with an operational life of three hours underwater."

"There goes my DeLorean," Tony said under his breath.

Linda rose to her feet. "Sir, how do those vehicles handle urban environments, such as clearing a building or protecting civilians?"

"Those scenarios are considered to be obsolete. We'll be able to prevent the GAMES from reaching population centers."

The suit gave her a look, raising an eyebrow. "Miss... ?"

"Private Linda Merchant."

"Private, we understand that there may be doubts about the unit's combat prowess, but we've tested them extensively and feel they'll more than adequately handle any situation that arrives in the field. If not, then you and your fellow soldiers will be there to assist."

A corporal walked swiftly across the warehouse floor, stopping next to the captain, and whispering in his ear. He nodded, and then stood up. "Sorry for the interruption, but there's been an incident with the GAMES. Sergeant, please have your men fall in and prepare for a clean-up operation."

Linda followed the rest of her squad out, glancing back at the red painted vehicles. *We might, just might, be replaced.*

The barge rested in the shallow mud, leaning heavily to the left. Steel sides and deck crumbled and pierced, scorch marks marring the surface in places. Cargo containers, a bishop stenciled on the grey-metal sides, lay strewn about like toys. A few bobbed on the surface of the Columbia, stuck on the bottom but forced upright by trapped pockets of air. The tug lay on its side, the conning tower bent nearly ninety degrees. Fuel leaked out, creating a glistening, rainbow-colored slick. Four white sheets covered the remains of the crew.

Linda whistled at the sight of the wreckage. "Did one of the containers explode during the attack?" Behind her, the rest of the squad unloaded their gear with the Sarge barking orders.

80

"Looks like the gulpers did a number on this ship. Never seen them this destructive," Tony said.

"They didn't," a voice said from behind them.

"Molly!"

"Linda." She nodded, taking off the cap, letting her pony-tailed hair fall down her neck. "There's no way they could manage that much destruction. Something larger attacked the ship."

"Miss Wilson, a pleasure to see you." Leon Bishop wiped his hands on a cloth. "I see that the government's brought you in on a private matter."

"The National Science Board is concerned about an incursion by an unknown creature or that the GAMES have developed sophisticated methods of attack."

"There's no proof that this is nothing more than an accident. Clearly, the barge sustained structural failure of some sort or the cargo experienced a thermal event."

Molly scowled at him. "An explosion would've sent the barge to the bottom of the river."

"I'll leave the conclusions to the maritime officials, not some scientist with her newly minted degree."

"Explain all the dead GAMES then."

"We don't need to hear your theories on a giant creature living in the river again. It's been proven that none of your mother's creations have survived the last two decades." He glanced back up the hill at the limo. "Now, if you'll excuse me, I have some important matters to attend."

Tony leaned over. "Who's the blond?"

"Tony, this is Molly Wilson, my cousin. Her dad's the one that taught me how to shoot. She's an expert in biology."

"Pleased to meet you," he grinned. "Single?"

"Yes and we're not really cousins." Molly turned to Linda. "My master's in genetic science, not biology. Why are you here?"

"Clean up detail."

"That would explain why Bishop was sliming about."

"You two have history?"

"He's put off that I refused a job offer and a visit to his bedroom." Molly pulled out a notepad and pen, gesturing at the river. "There's something out there."

"Oh come on, you still think there's one of those Gronks still alive?"

"Ornithorhynchus anatinus mutans. And yes, there's one that our dads didn't find. It's survived, I know it."

"What the hell is a Gronk?" Tony looked back and forth between the two.

"I'll tell you later, the Sarge's here." Linda looked as the burly man stomped down the hill, leading the rest of the squad in tow. She looked at Molly. "I'll talk

81

with you later on."

"Here's my card. Give me a call if you find anything interesting."

"I will." She tucked the card into a pocket. *Geez, she's not changed a bit since high school, but she has a point. What the hell did destroy that barge?*

Satiated, he settled along the bottom the river, paddling lazily with the current. The hard thing hadn't matched his strength. They'd fought, but to no avail and he'd eaten his full in a matter of minutes. Strange scaly ones, young and fresh. Not like the unclean ones from before. Tasty. Filling. He'd ignored the non-scaly creatures, sensing they weren't a threat at first. Until they used fire. Then he'd crushed them with a single blow, burning the webbing on his foot in the process. It tingled in the cool water, healing quickly like the wounds he'd received from the scaly ones.

For now, he'd rest and sleep. The muck enveloped him, sloughing off his oiled fur. Until hunger woke him again. Until he needed to follow the trail to the nest of the new scaly ones. Up the smaller, dirty waterway.

"Bored," Tony said, staring at the slowly turning ceiling fan. "Entertain me!"

Linda looked away from the hunting magazine. "I hear that Captain Harr needs someone to shine his boots. Or you could go take a turn guarding those toys."

"I'm a month from mustering out, why do I need to suck up to the brass?"

"Maybe you can get a cushy job with his buddy over at Bishop Industries. You might get CRABs."

"Hur, hur. I'm a funny ball-buster."

"You're jealous that Molly shot you down."

"Man, no way she could resist my charms."

"Better men than you have tried to get in her pants."

"There's no one better than me," Tony said.

"Dream on."

The alarm bell echoed loudly in the barracks, sending the soldiers scrambling for their gear. Sergeant Chucks stormed into the room. "We've got a situation. We're acting as back-up on this one. Don't engage unless threatened or directly ordered."

Linda tossed on her flak jacket and snagged the shotgun out of the weapons locker. "Gulpers?"

"Intel's found a small nest of them. Armor's going in to clear it out. We'll provide containment."

"Sentry duty. Whee." Tony pulled the vest strap tight and slung his M-15 over his shoulder.

The trip lasted less than half an hour, taking them to the far end of Hayden Island; a landscape of scrub grass, stunted pines, and gravel beaches. On the shore of the Willamette, a long flatbed and semi-tractor blocked the access road. Captain Harr and Leon Bishop conversed in low tones as the last of the armored battlers scuttled down the ramp. The trio gleamed in the sun as the guns tracked back and forth at the rippling water. Around them, a dozen techs setup an array of radio equipment and electronic gear.

"Sergeant. Deploy your men along the perimeter. Make sure they're far enough back so as not to interfere with the operation." Harr laid out a map with red line drawn on it. "That should be close enough to help if necessary."

"If necessary. I doubt they'll be of much use." Mr. Bishop sniffed, looking at the assembled troops.

Sarge scowled. "Listen up, grunts! Get in position; I want a nice spread along the area of operation. Don't take chances and keep your weapons free, but don't engage unless they get into the danger zone."

"Yes, Sergeant!" Linda and the rest yelled, as the battlers headed towards the far end of the beach. They reached the line just as the sounds of gunfire echoed across the landscape. The radio burst alive with chatter.

"This is Yukon, I've got my sights on a pocket of GAMES coming from the left."

"Acknowledged. Sumatra, circle to the water and cut off retreat."

"Roger that, Antigua. Weapons lock on lead element. Estimate three dozen targets."

Tony leaned over. "That's not a small nest."

"Intel. Go figure." Linda checked the magazine again. "Sounds like they're taking them apart."

The scent of the scaly ones drew him forward. An instinctual urge to feed and defend his territory. A stirring that he'd not felt in years. Not since leaving the nest and hunting down his brothers. There were other signals. Strong ones like from the metal floating box. Sensations rippled and tickled his bill, strong and persistent. Not food like the scaly ones, but an irritant. Like the eels that occasionally found purchase on his feet or tail. An itch to be scratched. With a push of his webbed feet, he rose from the river bottom.

Yukon cut in. "Telemetry incoming from sentry buoy."

"Roger that, Yukon. Receiving now," replied an unknown voice. "We've got a large contact moving on your position from seven o'clock. Please confirm."

"Negative visual here." The other two replied with the same. "Command, the GAMES are contained in the AO, please advise on new contact."

"This is Sumatra. I've got a large wave coming in."

"Can you identify the contact?"

"Target's breaching the surface now. Holy shit! Command, we've got an Omega class contact!" Sumatra's pilot screamed into his radio.

"Acquiring target! Firing solution recalculating!" That was Yukon.

"Repositioning. Command, this thing is larger than background would indicate. Please advise." Antigua's voice barely raised above a normal tone.

The sound of automatic gunfire filled the air.

GRONK!

A hump of oiled fur rose above the stand of pines. A ball of fire erupted as the massive, flat tail descended, shuddering the ground.

"Sumatra is down. Repeat, unit down," yelled the pilot of Antigua. "Requesting reinforcement!"

"Holy, shit, Molly was right." Linda flicked on her radio. "Sarge we've got a situation."

"Captain Harr, permission to deploy to AO?"

"Permission granted." Panic laced the command.

"Fire team advance, keep inside the tree line. Jackson. Huntermin. Hump that TOW. Everyone else lay down cover fire," said Sergeant Chucks.

"Let's go, Tony." Linda sprinted through the scrub grass. She skidded to a stop as the grove gave way to the beach. One of the CRABs sat motionless; a crushed and flattened tangle of metal. Sparks spit from the wreck along with smoke. Nearby, an orange-suited figure lay sprawled face down. The other battlers fired into the massive bulk that filled the beach. Black, oiled fur. Webbed feet. Duck's bill. Beaver tail.

"Dad's gonna shit a brick on this one," Linda said.

"What the hell? How's that possible? That's a giant..." Tony stood there with his mouth open. As did the rest of the squad.

"I'm going to church on Sunday," Private Davis said, with a couple of agreements.

Summers fished out a small flask and tossed it aside.

"That's a Gronk," Linda said. At the far end of the trees, she saw the TOW crew pause, then start scrambling to setup their weapon. She looked at her shotgun and gave a laugh.

As if on cue, the beast raised its bill and uttered a thundering GRONK! The trees swayed and the ground vibrated as the sound impacted into the fire team.

"Okay, I see why." Tony shook his head. "There goes my hearing."

"Negative effect on weapon fire!" Yukon cut in over the chatter. "Please advise!"

"All units pull back!"

"What about Sumatra?" Linda toggled her radio. "Should we attempt a rescue?"

"Negative!"

She looked at Tony. "Radio reception stinks here."

"Yeah, couldn't hear a damn word over the gunfire." He slid down the hill after her. "Sarge's going to kill us."

"Right after he buys us a round." The rock and dirt crunched under foot as they sprinted. To their left, the Gronk lumbered after the retreating CRABs, shaking the ground with each step. In its wake, it tore up large divots and crushed undergrowth. "He's really interested in those toy suits."

"Better them than us."

Linda knelt beside the prone man, checking his pulse. "Alive and breathing. Looks like a knock to the head."

"Fire in the hole!"

Linda covered the wounded man as the TOW launched with a whoosh and trail of white smoke, Fire erupted on the Gronk's left flank as the missile impacted, leaving a dark smudge on the heavy fur coat. There was a pause as the beast lumbered around, dark eyes following the smoke back to the source.

GRONK!

"Negative effect on impact!" Linda recognized the voice as Jackson. He and the new guy, Hunter-something, scrambled away, dropping the gear like it had grown fangs.

"Evacuate AO! Repeat, evacuate AO!" Harr again, screaming like someone had given him a nut shot.

"Help me." Linda lifted the pilot up. Tony took the other shoulder and they stumbled towards the tree line.

"We got bigger problems. Gulpers incoming."

A dozen of the mutant salmon floundered along the shore. Linda sagged under the shifting weight of the pilot. "Tony?"

"I'll cover you. Get him out of here." He unslung the M-15 and flipped off the safety.

"Don't be stupid." The ground shuddered, as Gronk lumbered towards them. "We can make it."

"Go! I'll be right behind you." He pulled the rifle to his shoulder and fired, dropping the lead gulper. "Run!"

"Dammit, Tony! I'll set you up with Molly."

"Deal!" Another gulper went down. "And Chinese from Wu's?"

"Yes, lets go!" Linda hauled the pilot towards the tree line, trying to ignore the sound of gunfire, gurgling, and a heavy tread.

GRONK!

"The army issued a statement that the sightings of GAMES along the shores of Willamette are greatly exaggerated. Captain Harr, head of Task Force Flounder, said that a few strayed into the area and were contained before they threatened anyone. Reports of a giant creature were dismissed as the overactive imaginations of witnesses."

"Bullshit. That was a Gronk or my daddy's a big fat liar," Linda mumbled into her beer.

"Uncle Dale tells a lot of tales, but he's not one to lie." Molly slid onto the barstool next to her, ignoring the stares from the rough and tumble crowd. "Drinking this early in the morning?"

"I'm off-duty." She stared at the pitcher and empty glass, wondering where the hell all the beer had gone. "You were right, one of those things survived."

"The black one. I saw the footage. The same radiation and chemicals that changed the GAMES must have affected him as well."

"That video's top secret stuff. He's a goddamn mountain of fur. Shrugged off a direct missile hit without injury."

"I'm sorry to hear about Tony," Molly said. "He was kinda cute."

"A cute idiot. Only a month left and he had to go be a hero." She waved at the bartender. "I disobeyed orders and he paid for it."

"You saved the pilot."

"Yeah." Linda stared at her. "How do you know that?"

"Your Sergeant told me and said you'd be here."

"Good for him. He chewed me out and then handed me over to the Captain. Now I'm looking at a court martial for disobeying orders." The bartender placed a full glass of beer in front of her. "That asshole Bishop blamed me for the loss of his toy."

"You and your team were set up." Molly grimaced.

"What do you mean?"

"Bishop's breeding GAMES. One of the survivors of the barge told investigators that they loaded a container of GAMES and then dropped off eggs on Hayden Island. They were supposed to dump the live ones further down the river."

"Why?"

"To sell those CRABs to the military. Create a few incidents and then offer a solution. Get rich or in his case, richer."

"Bastard."

"How would you like to settle that score?"

"Hell, yes. What do you need me to do?"

"I need more proof. All I've got is hearsay and an irregular cargo manifest. It's not a smoking gun. Leon's got to have a lab somewhere, I need to get proof for my bosses."

"Need me to rough him up?"

"No, he has an office at Swan Island. I'm sure that the evidence is there."

"Count me in." Linda chugged the beer. "Let's get some stuff at my place."

The train chugged through the switchyard, click-clacking along the tracks as it pushed cars towards the far end. It vibrated the windows and shook the floor as it passed. Linda winced and closed her eyes, trying to wish away the pounding in her head. On top of the smelly ashtray, the office lacked any sort of class.

Molly tucked the bobby pin back into her pocket. "This has got to be the place."

"I thought this was a quiet town," Linda said, "and I didn't think they taught lock picking in college."

"Mom taught me. She learned it from Dad and told me always to carry a couple in case of emergency."

"All he taught me was how to shoot."

"Hold this." Molly thrust the flashlight into her hands, and then opened a cabinet. "Shine the light so I can see."

"Hurry up. Those guards will be back soon."

"I am."

Linda watched Molly rifle through files, muttering under her breath. In the light of sobering up, she began to have doubts that this was a good idea. If they got caught, it'd be a trip to Leavenworth, not just a dishonorable discharge.

"Got it. Here are his private notes on a Project Carapace."

"Can we leave now?"

The lights flickered on. Leon Bishop, smiling, pointed a pistol at them. "Not so fast."

Molly stood up, clutching the folder. "You're breeding GAMES!"

"Yes. Release a few to stir up trouble and the military's tripping over itself to buy my battlers." He gestured with the gun. "Please put down the file, I can't let you leave here with that."

"We'll talk. You can't cover this up."

"No one will believe you. A disgraced soldier and a radical activist caught breaking into my office to assault me. The guards are calling the police right now. By the time you tell your story, the lab will be cleared out of the building. Just empty storerooms."

"What does he mean?" Linda looked at Molly who stood there blinking.

"The lab's here?" Her voice raised a few octaves.

"Right under the nose of the military. We just loaded up a boxcar with the GAMES and delivered them to the destination. Cheap and easy, no one asks any questions if they're paid enough."

"You don't understand. It's looking for the main nest and will track it back here."

Leon frowned. "It? What 'it'?"

GRONK!

The call blasted across the yard, rattling the window even more than a passing train.

"This day's just getting worse," Linda muttered.

He rested his bill on the ground, sending out electro-static pulses, and feeling the returns. The nest of the scaly ones was close. Past all the boxes of metal that floated and the small life that swarmed the bank, not the scaly ones. His tail slapped the ground, sending a ripple across the packed dirt and metal rails. The narrow, moving boxes fell over as the nest structures shook and swayed. None of the scaly ones fled as normal. This was their spawning ground. He'd feed well this evening.

GRONK!

Leon screamed and fired. Behind them the window shattered as the round impacted ineffectively against the oncoming beast. "Die, monster!"

Linda flicked the ceramic ashtray across the room. It smacked him in the mouth with a crack, spray of blood, and a cloud of ash and butts. The pistol clattered to the ground, sliding under the desk. She pulled the sidearm from the under her shirt, as he ducked out the door, pulling it closed behind him. "Why is that thing here?"

"It's following the GAMES to their nest. It thinks this is a spawning site."

"He's not wrong." She gestured towards the lumbering monster. "Get that file and let's get the hell out of here."

Molly nodded and snagged another file from the drawer. "Insurance."

"Whatever!" She snagged her cousin's arm, ran to the door, and yelped as a loud zap delivered a shock. "Damn! What the hell?"

"It's Gronk. They use an electro-static sense to find prey. This one must be able to generate a charge."

From outside came shouts and screams as train cars were crushed under its massive tail.

"Wonderful." Linda kicked open the door. "Which way?"

"Left."

The building shook as the Gronk lumbered closer, webbed feet tearing up the railroad track and spraying gravel in the air. Men shouted and ran, tearing off into the night. A few idiots stood and took pictures of the monster. Fires crackled to life and oil tankers caught alight, sending clouds of black smoke into the night air.

Sparks danced around the edge of the bill; small bolts of lightning grounding out to nearby metal objects. A sharp tang filled the air. Shots rang, ineffective gestures of defiance, panic, and bravado. They did nothing to stop the beast's progress. It crashed into the laboratory, digging into the floor and bringing up limp, scaled forms to devour.

Blue and red lights flashed as police cars and fire trucks arrived. The responders stared at the scene. One car peeled away in reverse, bouncing over the tracks before landing in a ditch. Shouts and gunfire. A spray of water washed over the oiled fur from a tanker truck, ignored by the feasting Gronk.

"You did this!" Leon's voice screamed from a CRAB's loudspeaker, as it scuttled out from the warehouse. "It followed you here!"

"He's gone nuts," Molly said.

"Stay behind me." Linda pushed her back and looked up at the darkened windscreen. "It's over. You've lost."

The twin guns tracked around, the barrels spinning up. "I never lose!"

GRONK! The edge of its tail caught the battler, sending it tumbling and rolling across the yard coming to rest in a smoking wreck.

"It's leaving," Molly said.

The Gronk flopped and waddled towards the water, retracing its steps through the ruins of the train yard. A giant wave washed over the edge of the pier as its bulk slipped into the river, dousing a few of the smaller fires. Ships rocked in their berths as the Gronk swam down the Willamette, headed back towards the Columbia.

"The paperwork's going to be a bitch to fill out," Linda said.

Linda knocked on the hospital door. "You decent?"

"No, but come in anyway."

She slipped into the recovery room, balancing the vase of flowers, cartons of Chinese take-out, and a couple of bottles of beer.

"You're late." Tony lay in the bed, propped up with pillows, with his leg suspended in a giant cast. "You got the good stuff?"

"Chicken chow mein, complete with extra soy sauce." She plunked the array of cartons on the plastic tray. "I got the kung pao pork."

"Oh thank god. Hospital food's worse than the usual mess hall crap." He snagged a set of chopsticks and dug in.

"Be glad the MP owes me a favor."

"Speaking of which, how did the review go?" he asked, slurping a mass of noodles.

"Bishop Industries is now in the hands of outside investors who want nothing to do with the military. Bishop and Captain Harr were working together to create incidents and profit from military contracts."

"They're court martialing his ass?"

"Nope. He's retiring for personal reasons. The brass decided to disband the squad and give everyone medical discharges, provided we sign papers to keep our mouths shut."

"And if we talk?"

"A stint in Leavenworth for spilling government secrets." She dug into the spicy food.

"What are you going to do now? You were all set on military for life."

"Got a new job." She waved a slip of paper at him. "Brass offered the squad reenlistment into a newly formed branch of the armed service. Monster Armed Response Specialists."

Tony's eyebrows furrowed. "Who thought of that?"

"Some desk jockey with way too much time on his hands." Linda put an envelope down on next to the carton of rice. "Here's your offer."

"Go back in? I nearly got killed out there."

"You were playing hero."

"No."

"They'll double the reenlistment bonus and you get boosted to sergeant with full back pay for previous time served."

"Hell, no."

"We're going to be attached to the National Science Board." She paused and watch him shake his head. "Molly's our attache with them. She said you were kinda cute."

"That's a low blow."

"Here's the pen."

"I hate you."

He swam into the big water and dove deep. The threat to his territory eradicated. No more would the scaly ones breed. He pushed his bill against the strange rock, absorbing the waves of energy as it filled him with the need to sleep. It thrummed as he slipped underneath, curling up in the large hollow. Hidden from view and predators, a place of rest and sanctuary. He curled up into a ball and faded into slumber. Only once did he stir to give a faint but distinctive call.

GRONK!

The Wicked Big Monstah Ovah Bawstin

by

David Bernard

The Wicked Big Monstah Ovah Bawstin
by
David Bernard

AIR TRAFFIC controllers at Boston's Logan Airport started filing reports of something large and fast showing up on radar. The Federal Government leapt into action, passing the buck from one jurisdiction to another with spectacular speed. TSA to FAA to USAF to - you name an agency, the odds are they were told to investigate, right before they passed it on to someone else. Finally, the Massachusetts governor cornered the FBI Regional Director at a cocktail party and since no one refused the governor face to face, it immediately became an FBI matter.

Since the regional director wanted to deal with a UFO outbreak as much as he wanted to have a root canal, he dumped it on me. Special Agent Travis Tredman, at your service, fresh from the academy and too new to turn down any fieldwork.

I went over to Logan and interviewed the controllers who filed the reports. They all basically said the same thing - something as big as a bus had just appeared on the radar, traveled at speeds nearing supersonic and then dropped off the radar. I noted the dates on the report and wondered what I was going to next. The FAA had reviewed the radar reports and decided they were "inconclusive." I had no idea what to do next - the FBI Academy hadn't offered a course in unidentified radar blips, and there are no X-Files (believe me, I looked).

I decided I should approach it like a crime and just follow the fact trail, assuming I could find one. I took the date of the first reported incident and ran it past every record-keeping department I could think of. Weather service had no unusual weather patterns. Military had nothing to say, as usual. Boston Police Department had a couple of oddball reports but none of them involved supersonic UFOs.

Out of clever ideas, I looked at the Boston Police reports. It seemed a couple more light panels had come down in the Tip O'Neill Tunnel after midnight, which by itself was odd because they had already fixed the problem (again). A maintenance worker claimed he felt a tremor in the tunnel, which he blamed for the light panels falling, but the USGS showed no unusual seismic activity. The other report was even odder - the police had been dispatched to an access road behind the Boston Garden at 1:15 AM to investigate reports of a sinkhole opening up near the Bill Buckner Bridge. The Department of Public Works dispatched a structural engineer to make sure the bridge was safe and then dumped gravel into the sinkhole to fill it.

I was getting nowhere fast. So, just to make it look like I was trying, I drove down to the river to look for the sinkhole. Maybe it was really a crater from a meteorite crash. Maybe it was a secret underground dirigible launch site. In other words, I had no clue at all. I parked the car and walked toward the bridge. There was a huge circle of gravel, about 20 feet in diameter. Sinkhole? The damn thing was wider than a subway tunnel! I decided to visit the DPW.

The receptionist was not impressed by my arrival. Sensing that I was going to annoy her until she actually did something resembling work, she pointed to a burly man with a bright red beard standing in the corridor.

I walked up to him. "Hi, I'm Travis Tredman with the FBI. Can I talk to you about that sinkhole on the river?"

"I'm Liam O'Malley, a track inspectah. The sinkhole was caused by an old watah main breakin' and washin' out a section of ground next to an old abandoned subway tunnel. We fixed the watah main and filled the hole with gravel. I inspected the tunnel and saw no signs of damage. We don't expect any futhah trouble."

I stood there jotting down notes and realizing that I was starting to translate a Southie accent into English without thinking about it. I found that somewhat unsettling.

O'Malley looked at his watch. "Listen Agent Tredman, I'm headin' down to inspect the tunnel one last time. Why don't you tag along?"

I had nothing better to do, so I climbed into his battered truck and we drove out to North Station. Instead of walking down to the shore, we started into the Green Line station.

He glanced at me. "You look confused. The tunnel next to the collapse isn't on a track in use. We need to do a little walkin' through Bawstin's past." He unlocked a door and I caught a whiff of stale air. He grabbed a hard hat and a flashlight and tossed them to me.

He grinned. "Not a lot of folks get to visit the old tracks. And just to make it fun, powah's been shut off for decades." He turned on his light and slammed the door shut. The flashlight really didn't really light up a lot of the tunnel. I followed O'Malley to a ladder leading down even further. As we descended, it got cool and damp.

At the bottom, I paused. "O'Malley, should I hear water dripping?"

O'Malley snorted. "Relax. That's just ground watah. If the watah main was still leaking, you'd be up to your shawts in watah."

We walked along a dust-covered set of rails, O'Malley scanning the sides as we went.

"This heah was supposed to be a route from the rivah to the mahkets back in 1907 to alleviate congestion in Bawstin Hahbah. The plan was to have the ships sail fahtha up rivah and unload cahgo directly on the rail line."

I looked at the walls as well as the flashlight allowed. "Let me guess. The company failed?"

"Absolutely. Almost as soon as it stahted. They ovah estimated the congestion in the hahbah and ships didn't want to sail up the rivah when they had to sail past available slips in the hahbah propah. And the damn fools made the trolley tracks the wrong scale. You couldn't move goods any fahtha than Haymahket Station because the main subway track was a widah scale. So you had to tranfah the goods to another cah anyway. So why botha?"

We had been walking for a while. "O'Malley, can I ask you an engineering question?"

He turned to me. "Okay. What's the question?"

"Why is it getting light in this tunnel if you sealed the sinkhole?"

He frowned and shut off the flashlight. The tunnel was definitely getting lighter. "Damn," he said. "I musta left the lights on."

I looked at him. "You have lights down here? Why are we walking in the dark?"

He was still frowning. "Not that kind of lights. You see that metal stripe down the middle of the tunnel?"

I looked at the ceiling where a copper stripe ran the length of the tunnel.

O'Malley followed it with the light so I could see it was continuous. "That's the old powah line for the trolleys. We still use the same basic technology above ground. Now, the cahs have poles that contact to an ovah-head line. But in this tunnel, they just put the powah on the ceiling. It's so well built that we can still kick the powah on in a pinch. So we juiced up the transformahs enough to connect pohtable lights for inspections and maintenance."

I looked at the age of the tunnel. "So you're using a century old electrical transformer for a flashlight?"

He grinned a little sheepishly. "The T ain't got the funding to do propah maintenance on abandoned tunnels. I just make do with what I have."

We approached a wider stretch of tunnel. Sure enough, there were several construction work lamps jury-rigged to an ancient transformer. O'Malley headed over to shut off the lights. Just as he got there, I noticed something reflecting in the light.

"Hang on a second," I yelled and walked over to the wall. I found myself staring at something hard and shiny and as large as a SUV.

"What the hell is that?" O'Malley suddenly said from behind me.

"I was hoping you knew." And I meant it. Whatever it was, it almost looked organic. It seemed almost translucent with a yellowish tint. I poked it with the flashlight. It felt solid. More importantly, it didn't poke back. I snapped a piece off an edge and tucked it in my pocket.

I turned and looked at O'Malley. "I don't know what it is, but I'm going to find out. And I wouldn't mind getting the hell out here either."

O'Malley nodded. "Lemme kill the transformah and we can get going."

I was never so grateful to be back in the sun, or at least as much of it as you could see in front of the Garden. My cell phone sudden sprang back to life and I received a text alert. I was to report to Boston Police headquarters immediately.

BPD was waiting. They ushered me in to the commissioner's office. He was sitting there, looking perplexed. "You're the Fed looking into the UFOs?"

"Yes sir. Special Agent Tredman."

He picked up a remote control for a TV on the wall. "There was another UFO report. And then this." He turned on the set.

"This is WBZ reporting live from the Esplanade. Witnesses are claiming a giant insect grabbed a jogger and flew away. We have just learned that the creature was actually picked up on radar before disappearing. There is no word on the identity or the fate of the jogger."

He shut off the TV. "This is on all the stations. Your UFO is now stealing people. I assume it's feeding, but I officially have no comment. What have you got?"

I couldn't tell him I had a sinkhole. I stuck my hand in my pocket and remembered the sample from the tunnel. "I have a couple of ideas, but I need to talk to someone in your labs."

He stood up and looked out the window at the growing collection of news vans in front of the building. "You talk to whoever you need to and get back to me. I'll be here, preventing a panic."

I left his office and headed down to the lab. A man in a lab coat met me at the door. "I'm Nick Detaranto, head of the forensic lab. I'm under orders to assist you. What can we do?"

I handed him the fragment from the tunnel. "I found a very large object where it shouldn't be. Can you identify it?"

He looked at it. "This is chitin."

I looked at him blankly. "And exactly what is that?"

He kept turning it. "Chitin is a nitrogen-containing polysaccharide"

I took the fragment back. "In English?"

He looked at me. "Chitin is the hard shell that makes up the carapace, an insect's exoskeleton. How big did you say the original was?"

I was beginning to feel a little nauseated. "Very big. Can you tell me any more?"

He paused. "I could look at it through an electron microscope, but something that big in a mutant specimen. You need Eva."

I had a giant Bostonian-eating insect on my first investigation. I felt so lucky that I could have thrown up right there and then. "And may I ask who Eva is?"

Dr. Detaranto apparently noticed the clenched teeth. I don't think the hysteria was evident in my voice yet. "Professor Eva Caperon at Harvard. She's an entomologist specializing in mutative genetics."

"Thank you, Doctor. Could you update the commissioner? I need to get to Harvard."

"Mr. Tredman?" I stopped and looked back. "An insect drops its carapace for one of two reasons. Either it's dead and the soft parts have already decomposed, or it's molted because it's outgrown its exoskeleton."

I drove over the Longfellow Bridge into Cambridge. Traffic was so bad I had plenty of time to look up Dr. Caperon on my smart phone. She was definitely an egghead. She had won last year's Nobel Prize for achievements in comparative behavioral physiology and communication between insects, whatever that meant.

The rent-a-guard at the parking lot was very impressed by my credentials. Perhaps it was a good omen. At this point I'd take any good omens. I entered the building and quickly found the entomology lab.

I opened the door to the lab. A coed in a white lab coat was hunched over a microscope. I knocked on the wall. "You can leave it over on the desk," she said without looking up. "And so help me, if you put mung bean sprouts on my salad again instead of alfalfa, there will trouble."

I cleared my throat. "I didn't touch your alfalfa."

Suddenly, she turned around. "You're not the kid from the deli." She looked over at the desk, just in case. I like a woman who has her priorities in order.

"No Ma'am. I'm the kid from the FBI, Special Agent Travis Tredman. Dr. Detaranto at the police lab suggested I see Dr. Eva Caperon about a piece of chitin I found. Is she available?"

She looked at me suspiciously. "I'm Eva Caperon. And why does the FBI have chitin?"

I had honestly thought she was a grad student - she seemed too young to have a Nobel Prize and be heading up a Harvard department. If first impressions count, I was not off to a good start. I pulled out the fragment from the tunnel and handed it to her. She stared at it in disbelief. "Please tell me this is some sort of prank."

I shook my head. "Sorry Professor. Turn on the TV - something big with wings just picked up a jogger and flew away."

She turned and walked away. I assumed I needed to follow her. We walked into a room at the back of the lab that looked like Victor Frankenstein's wet dream. The doctor went to a table and started scraping across the chitin with a scalpel.

She looked up at me and then went back to scraping the chitin. "Well Agent Tredman, go ahead and ask."

I looked at her blankly. "Ask what?"

She took the scrapings and put them on a glass slide and placed it on some sort of platform. "Whenever I get brought into a criminal investigation, I get one of two questions tossed at me in the first 3 minutes. The first question is usually something like 'Aren't you a little young to be a Harvard professor?'"

"Well, it did cross my mind when I Googled you on the way over," I admitted. "I'm almost afraid to ask what the other question is."

She threw a switch and all sorts of lights started flashing. "The second question is usually 'how did an entomologist end up with such a great ass?' Boston cops are a classy lot. Let's take a look at this under the electron microscope while the mass spectrometer is looking at it."

She turned back to the worktable. "And before you ask, the answer is yoga." She took the chitin and shaved a paper-thin section and placed it in another electronic gizmo that I assumed was the electron microscope. A pattern came up on a computer screen.

She stared at it and frowned. "This is impossible. It's a yellow jacket. The molecular cohesive ratio is too big. How big was the original carapace?"

I pulled up a photo I shot in the tunnel. "Big enough to cover your car."

She stared at the photo. "I don't drive. It's ineffective in an urban setting. And this is against the laws of science. Something that big can't generate the lift needed to fly."

I checked the news feed on my phone. The monster had just slammed into the Charles, grabbing someone off a boat and caused a wave that capsized the rest of the sculls. That probably saved their lives by dumping them in the water. "Dr. Caperon, I don't know about the laws of science, but you might want to take it up later with the bug crowd. Things are getting worse out there, not to mention closer."

She was unperturbed. It must be nice to be able to focus that narrowly at the matter at hand. She went over to the big blinking light machine. "Agent Tredman, you're in luck. We have an hour to kill before spectrometry is complete. Since the deli never showed up, I'm going to let you take me to lunch." She took off her lab coat and headed out the door. She turned and smiled. "Are you coming?"

I looked around in total confusion and decided what the hell; the day couldn't get any odder. I did notice as I caught up with her that although the Boston cops may have been rude pigs, but they were not incorrect.

Apparently dive-bombing giant wasps tended to thin out the lunch crowd in Cambridge. Dr. Caperon picked at a salad while I poked at a burger. The television above the register was reporting a window washer had been picked up off the side of the Hancock Tower by what the media was calling "the biggest wasp in Boston this side of the Cabots and Saltonstalls." Which would have been a brilliant line if anyone still remembered who the Cabots and Saltonstalls were. Obscure Boston history aside, it was evident there was a full-blown panic taking place. The Mayor's assurances that the FBI was handling it did nothing to lessen the panic, although the sudden number of calls I was getting from higher-ups at the agency was making me a little panicky too.

Finally, she looked up. "This may actually be worse than you think."

I looked at her. "Is that possible?"

She put her fork down. "The pattern I saw on the electron microscope is that of a yellow jacket, a common wasp, *Vespula Vulgaris*. Here's the problem - adult wasps are not carnivorous."

I let that sink in. "If the wasp isn't eating those people..."

She interrupted me. "I said *adult* wasps aren't carnivorous. The larvae are. They'll eat anything the adults bring them. The larvae then secrete a sweet, sugary liquid that the adults eat."

I looked at her. "Larvae? Like in baby wasps? As in 'wasps' plural?" She nodded quietly.

I grabbed the tab and threw some money on it. "I think it's time to get back to your lab. This is getting worse."

Back at the lab, Eva went over her data while I had a conference call with the Mayor, the Boston bureau chief, a senator and a group of minor politicians looking to feel important. The senator wanted to send in a bomber, but the Mayor thought firing missiles downtown was a bad idea.

Finally, Eva came over to the table. I slid the phone over to her.

"Gentlemen, I'll be brief because we're on a shorter timetable than you can imagine. We're looking at a female wasp that has been mutated by more chemicals than I can analyze. My best guess is that the wasp was contaminated underground in Back Bay."

The Mayor asked "Back Bay? What does that have to do with it?"

Eva rolled her eyes at me, which meant I was supposed to know why Back Bay was important. She was incorrect, but she continued. "The history of Boston, Mr. Mayor, starts with the Back Bay being swampland 300 years ago. It was filled in over the decades by the residents using it to dump all their trash - including industrial waste chemicals. If you dig deep enough under the topsoil and filler, the Back Bay is a toxic chemical stew that's been simmering since 1630. This wasp somehow encountered the waste and mutated."

My bureau chief spoke up. "Agent Tredman tells me that the wasp may be feeding baby giant wasp mutants?"

She looked at her notes again. "Yes and no. Adult wasps are not carnivorous. They feed off nectar produced by the larvae. Assuming the life cycle time line is vaguely similar to that of a non-mutated wasp, it must be preparing for asexual reproduction."

The room fell silent, an impressive feat with that many politicians on the phone. I looked at her. "Asexual reproduction? This thing doesn't need two to tango? So the people it's been grabbing..."

Eva sighed. "Probably dead and being stockpiled for the larvae once partheno-genesis commences. There is good news. In this case, parthenogenesis is being triggered by the wasp due to a bacteria infestation. Even if we can't kill the wasp quickly, we can at least spray it with an antibiotic that will kill the bacteria and prevent the eggs from undergoing parthenogenesis upon hatching, which prevents a breeding colony." She noticed the room was still silent. She cleared her throat. "Of course, killing the wasp before it lays eggs would be a good thing too."

The meeting continued. It was decided that the mayor would ask the governor to mobilize the National Guard to look for the nest. I was to stick close to Dr. Caperon - apparently there was a local shortage of entomologists specializing in mutative genetics. I looked over at her and she just winked. I have giant insects eating civilians, Senators ready to launch stinger missiles in an urban setting and now I'm getting mixed signals from an entomologist with a great ass. I was beginning to think a career in retail shoe sales was looking better and better. The call ended and Eva started looking at her printouts. She had said something that triggered a thought.

"Eva? How would a wasp get underground to the contaminants?" I had a bad feeling that no matter what she said, it was not going to make me a happy FBI agent.

She looked at me. "Wasps usually build their nests on any structure than can support it. But..." Her eyes grew wide as she thought it through. "But they will use an abandoned hole or tunnel to start a nest."

I was already calling O'Malley at DPW. "Liam, this is Travis. I need to get back down in that tunnel as soon as possible. The water main didn't break and cause that hole. The pipe broke when the hole was being made. Meet me at North Station."

I checked local traffic and slipped the phone in my pocket. I'd check my gun, but it seemed pointless against a giant insect.

Eva ran into the back room and brought back a bucket. "I always keep a supply of insecticide, in a convenient, powdered concentrate form. I use it during expeditions to collect my samples undamaged."

I was hoping she had a flamethrower too, but insecticide couldn't hurt.

I pulled up a traffic app on my phone. "The roads are completely jammed with panicked Bostonians trying to leave town. We may have better luck taking the subway. That is, assuming you don't mind being underground right now."

She smiled. "It's probably safer than trying to cross the Longfellow Bridge on foot."

The Red Line was empty going into the city and Park Street Station was a ghost town. North Station, on the other hand, was bordering on a riot as people were rushing to catch any train heading anywhere that wasn't here. I checked the news feed again. Apparently the Senator had jumped the gun and gotten the Air Force to scramble a jet. It gave chase and discovered the wasp was too maneuverable to shoot down and didn't have enough body heat for the heat-seeking missiles to lock on. The jet did manage to blow up the WLVI transmitter tower in Needham and a taxi in Dorchester, which was sufficient damage for the Mayor to get the Air Force called off.

O'Malley worked his way through the crowd. "This had best be a pissah good idea. This city's going nuts!"

I introduced Eva and we again descended into the murky past of Boston. I quickly explained to O'Malley why we were heading into the tunnel. "Wait a second," he said. "If you think the wasp is down heah, why not just seal the tunnel off? I'm too young and pretty to be used as monstah chow!"

Even Eva seemed to be getting nervous as she clutched her bucket of poison. "We're not sure it's down here and it can probably rip through anything you use to block it in."

We came up on the transformer where O'Malley had left the work lights. "Turn on the lights and let Eva get a good look at the carapace. Maybe it'll give her a clever idea."

O'Malley muttered under his breath as he warmed up the transformer. "Only clevah idea I want to heah is that we need to get out of heah wicked fast."

The lights snapped on and Eva started looking at the carapace. It occurred to me that the patchwork from the "sinkhole" repair was still intact. So how was the wasp getting in and out? I shouted toward the transformer. "O'Malley, where did you say this tunnel ended?"

He looked up from the transformer. "I told you. It stahts down at the rivah. You can still see it from the watah. Big tunnel opening with metal bahs blocking access."

Eva looked up. "Metal bars? Wrought iron might slow down the wasp enough to make it look for another tunnel, assuming it's been maintained."

O'Malley looked her. "Maintained? Doc, I hate to break it to you, but this heah is an abandoned tunnel. The only one who might have looked at those bahs in the last 50 yeahs would be a homeless guy looking for a way in for a dry place to sleep. We wouldn't know if the bahs have rusted through, unless someone filed a complaint."

She looked at him. "Then how do we know the wasp hasn't ripped the bars open and is using it for an entrance?"

The question had no sooner echoed down the tunnel than a noise came echoing back. A skittering, clicking noise with a low humming. I looked at Eva. She looked at O'Malley and he looked down the tunnel.

"Don't botha telling me." He looked at Eva. "Lemme guess. Giant wasp noise?" Eva just nodded.

I pulled out my pistol and felt puny. Then I had an idea. "Eva, give me your bucket of poison and get behind the carapace. Even if this doesn't work, the wasp will be coming at me. You and O'Malley can get out through the river end."

I took the bucket and placed it in the middle of the tracks, lining it up with the copper on the ceiling. A better idea suddenly came to me that made my survival chances go up to at least 10

He looked at the equipment. "I've nevah tried. I suppose like I can powah it to full strength without it blowin' itself to kingdom come. But we don't have a trolley."

I checked my clip. "But we have a giant wasp that could make contact with the power and electrocute itself."

O'Malley went to work, apparently more optimistic than I was. I stood in the middle of the track, trying to look fearless while concentrating on not soiling myself. Soon the clack got louder and there it was, it's carapace gleaming in the light, every facet of its compound eyes looking directly at me and not one of them particularly happy to see me. It slowly advanced. The damn thing was filling the entire tunnel, which helped me since it couldn't move much faster. It approached the bucket and when it was just about on top of it, I fired into the bucket.

The bucket exploded into a cloud of insecticide, which did absolutely nothing. It continued forward. From behind the carapace, Eva suddenly shouted. "Um, about that powder... Wasps breathe through spiracles in their thorax. Dumping it in its face will just make it angry."

I looked at her and then at the annoyed giant insect coming toward me. She picked a hell of a time to give me a biology lesson. "*Now* you tell me this? Have them write that on my head stone, will you?"

I kept backing up slowly. I was hoping to at least get the wasp beyond the siding, which would give Eva and Liam a chance to make a run for it. The antennae were flailing around and getting dangerously close. I was slowly backing out of the lit area and I'd be willing to bet Eva forgot to tell me the damn thing could see in the dark better than I could.

I stepped into the shadows. "Now would be a really good time to turn the power on, Liam."

"I'm tryin'. You want to try coaxin' an antique transfomah to play nice, feel free to come up heah and try."

He sounded a little nervous. He should come down here and see those jaws slowly progressing toward me. That'll show him what nervous really is.

I decided to go old school and emptied my clip at the monster's head. It did as much good as the insecticide. One of the antennae suddenly caught me across the ribs. It was like getting hit with a steel rod and I went flying into the wall headfirst. I couldn't catch my breath but I knew I couldn't stay put. I tried to crawl down the tunnel, just to stay away from the jaws.

"Tredman, the tunnel narrows as you go fahthah in. If you go fah enough, it might get stuck."

O'Malley was still working on the transformer, and I couldn't see Eva behind the wasp. I struggled to my feet and watched as it got closer. I coughed up a little blood and felt my knees start to buckle. I wasn't going to be able to keep moving much longer.

Suddenly the tunnel lit up like a spotlight. I heard the clacking stop and a crackling sound. Then the wasp exploded. Wasp parts slammed into me and the last thing I remembered was the triumphant hooting of O'Malley.

I came to, pinned down with something across my chest. I could feel blood rolling down my forehead, but I seemed to be in one piece, more or less.

"Travis? Can you hear me?" It was Eva Caperon's voice.

I managed to get an eye open and Eva was straddled across my chest holding a rag to my head. The rag looked suspiciously like the sleeve of my custom fit and very expensive shirt. I wondered if that counted as an operating expense. I tried to smile and coughed instead.

She looked at me. "Are you okay?"

I had some sort of head wound, so I knew I was a bloody mess. "Seriously," I croaked, "How did an entomologist end up with such a great ass?"

She blushed. "I told you - yoga." She leaned in close. "And if you survive, there are some other benefits to yoga I'd like to discuss."

I tried to laugh. It hurt. That meant broken ribs, a personal favorite of mine from the training academy. Let's just say I did not ace the hand-to-hand combat exam.

"Stop squirming, I'm trying to stop the bleeding." She got off me and helped me into a sitting position.

"Don't bother," I said. "It's a head wound. Unless you see bone or brains, it's superficial but messy." O'Malley strolled up. "If it's all the same to you two, I'd like to get the hell out of heah and try to explain to the supervisahs how I blew up a hundred yeah-old transformah." He looked at me. "And maybe drop you off at a hospital?"

I thought that sounded marvelous. Then I passed out again.

They had me in Mass. General for three weeks. The mayor wanted to give me a medal, which is against FBI policy. O'Malley didn't want his name in the papers, so while the Globe made "an unknown FBI field operative" into the hero, the Herald lauded the praises of "the Bug Babe who Saved Boston," which I'm sure Eva appreciated almost as much as Harvard appreciated the Herald photographers skulking after her on campus.

After I was released, I met up with O'Malley at a diner near the DPW. He looked no worse for the wear while I still looked exactly like someone who went face first through the explosion of a giant wasp. He sipped his coffee with a little smile on his face.

"So, I heard from your bug lady doctah." He said. "She got permission to have the remains sent down to the college for study."

I remembered how big the charred husk was. "How are you going to get that thing out of the tunnel and move it to Cambridge?"

Liam smiled again. "Already done - nothin' to it. We took a couple of fohk lifts and hoisted it onto a flatbed rail cah. Then we wheeled it over to Haymahket Station and brought out through a maintenance access and then trucked down to the college."

Suddenly I realized he was smiling in anticipation. I asked the question he was waiting for, wincing as I did. "Really? And then what did you do with it?"

Triumphantly, he grinned. "We did exactly what you think we did - we pahked the cahcass in Hahvahd Yahd."

The Knot

by

Edward Martin III

The Knot
by
Edward Martin III

S HE QUIETLY watched him.

She was expected to take notes, but she always spent a little time first, just watching. It often revealed more than any pile of notes.

His hands shook as he tied the knots. The rope was a green, hempish kind of rope, with lots of chaos in the weave. She imagined how rough it would feel running through her fingers. His hands were old, sporting wrinkles and dark brown patches. She watched as the knot grew in complexity. His shaking fingers slid rope in and out of loops, twisting and tugging.

After an intense twenty minutes, he seemed done. He held the ball of string in the air, staring at it.

Nothing happened, but Elizabeth found herself leaning inward, also looking at the knot.

He stopped staring and set it on the floor. His face was filled with disappointment. After a long sigh, he started untying the knot, unraveling his sculpture.

Once he had nothing but loose rope in his hand, he stared off into the distance a moment, and then started tying the rope into a knot again.

"He'll do that all day," said a voice behind her.

She jumped.

The intern was a young man and he smiled at her. "Sorry," he said. "I didn't mean to scare you."

"You didn't," she said, "I was just..." she pointed back at the old man. "That's what he does?"

"That's all he does. All day. Every day." He offered a hand. "I'm Jefferson. Carver. But everyone calls me 'Bug'."

She shook it. "Elizabeth," she said. "Elizabeth McClaren. I don't have a nickname. Sorry."

This time, he jumped. "Wait, you're Doctor McClaren?"

When she nodded, he asked, "Why didn't you let us know you were here? We've been waiting for you."

106

She shrugged and smiled. "I don't like making a big fuss."

"It's not a fuss, Doctor McClaren, it's just that we had an orientation planned and everything." He stepped away. "Is now a good time?"

She glanced back at the man in the white room, alone with his piece of string. "I suppose," she said.

They left.

He finished another knot and stared at the new one. When nothing happened, he wept, then started untying it.

"Hello, Douglas," said Doctor McClaren.

He spared her a glance, and then went back to work.

She watched a moment, and then asked, "Can you tell me what you're trying to do?"

He shook his head, and continued knotting the rope.

"It's okay," she said. "I just want to know. I'm not here for any other reason than to understand."

He glanced up again, a little longer, focused on her, and then bent back to his work. "Not right now," he muttered.

When she was sure he was done, she tapped on the door and it opened.

"Not bad," whispered Bug, as he relocked the door. "Doctor Finch worked with him for six months before he even spoke to her, and you're getting a verbal response after three weeks."

Elizabeth watched Douglas through the observation window. His old fingers unwound the latest knot as he shook his head in frustration.

"There's something about him," she said. "I can't put my finger on it, but there's something just past what we can see."

Bug nodded. "Everybody's got a pet project," he said. "Douglas isn't too bad. Pretty quiet. At first, we were worried about the rope thing, so we only gave him little pieces, but we figured out he wasn't being trouble, so the docs have pretty much let him have what he asked for, rope-wise." He watched the old man through the glass. "He's still dangerous, I guess, but he's content with his rope."

"No," said Doctor McClaren, shaking her head. "He's a lot of things, but he's not content."

"I can't remember," muttered Douglas. "Sometimes I come close, but then it's gone and, so far, it never works anyway."

He held up his finished knot, turned it in his hands, staring, and then sighed. "I keep trying," he said. "I have to get it right eventually."

"What happens if you get it right?" asked Doctor McClaren.

"You'll see," he replied, and bent his head to concentrate.

"You're not tired of him, yet?" asked Bug.

"No. Not yet," said Doctor McClaren. "I think it's a sort of game. I think he's waiting to see if I'm still willing to play."

"A game?"

She nodded, watching the old man weave rope through the glass.

"I think he wants me to know - I think he even wants me to help, but I have to unwrap the layers of meaning, first. I get the feeling that the things he says and does are several layers of abstraction from what he thinks he's really doing in there."

"Living a secret life?"

"In his head, yes. Maybe not secret so much as veiled. Maybe he can't quite peel it open alone, and he wants help."

"Doctor Finch tried for quite a while before you."

"I know, but I think she approached it wrong. Or maybe he wasn't so close to giving up."

Bug cocked his head. "Giving up?" he asked.

Elizabeth crossed her arms. "I think Douglas is getting desperate," she said. "The way he moves seems jerkier and more frightened than when I came here."

Bug stared at the old man's hands.

"You figured all this out in three months?" he asked.

"I figured in out in six weeks," she said. "The rest has been filling in the details."

"Well, don't forget one detail," said Bug.

"Which is that?"

"He's a murderer."

She watched him for ten minutes before speaking.

"Douglas."

He glanced up at her, then back to his rope. That was his way of greeting her.

"Do you know why you're here?" she asked.

"It's a pause," he said. "It's between breaths. I'm here because no one's sure if I'm mad or not. If I am, then one thing. If I'm not, then another."

She thought about it. "Pretty much," she said.

"It's important to be mad for a little while," he said, "until being not mad isn't a problem."

"Do you think you're mad?" she asked.

"The question means a different thing to you than it does to me."

"Why?"

"Because when you ask it, you know what the answers will mean. When I answer it, I'll know what the answers mean. But your meaning and my meaning are different."

"How are they different?"

"You'll think my answer means I'm a murderer, Doctor McClaren."

"What will your answer mean to you?" she asked.

"My answer will mean I've shown you I'm not a murderer," he replied.

"I'm not here on a legal basis," she said. "I'm just a doctor interested in you."

"That's why I talk with you and not that other gal. The one that was here before you. With the horse face."

Elizabeth stifled a grin.

"I've seen pictures of her," she said. "She's not that bad." "Try being locked up with her," he replied. "She was here because the State wanted her here. The State wanted to know if I was mad or not, so they put her here; assigned me to her."

"What do you suppose she thought?" asked Elizabeth.

"I'm still here, so I expect she decided I was mad."

She nodded.

"Are you?"

He smiled a little, but kept working the rope.

"When I do this right, you'll see. When you see what I see, you'll know the question has no meaning."

"Do you think you'll ever find it, Douglas?" she asked.

"I need to."

"To prove your innocence?"

"We've all done terrible things," he said, "and I'm not an innocent, but at least to prove I'm not a murderer."

"I've read the police report," she said.

He hesitated, uncertain, and then continued.

"Then you already know what you need to know, I guess," he said. "I'm sure I appear quite mad."

"I'm not so sure I can make that conclusion," she said. "There are some... irregularities. Some things I wanted to ask you about."

His only reply was the scratchy hiss of rope sliding through his dry fingers.

"How did you know they were sick?" she asked.

He stopped and stared hard at her. "How were they sick?"

"They were anemic," she said. "Not even their doctors knew."

He sighed, and renewed his knotting.

"They weren't," he muttered.

"I talked to the M.E.," she said. "He remembers it like it was yesterday. It was the one thing that didn't make any sense. Six completely unrelated children, severely anemic. No one else on the playground that day, and no medical history suggesting it, but you knew. How did you know?"

"They weren't anemic," he repeated. He put his knot down and his voice rose. "I'm not being stubborn - I'm being factual. Nobody knew they were anemic because they weren't anemic. They..."

He stopped. His face turned pale. He looked down at his knot.

"I... I have to start this again. I've lost track of where I was."

"Douglas," she started to say.

"I have to get this right, Doctor. Could you please leave me alone."

He began to unweave the cord, but his fingers were shaking more than usual.

It was late. Past eleven. She wasn't wearing her suit - just jeans, a turtleneck, and a jacket. A purse.

She didn't close the door behind her as she entered the cell.

Douglas woke up when she flicked on the lights.

"What are... Doctor McClaren?" he asked, blinking back the stars.

"Not right now," she said. "Just Elizabeth. We've been talking for nearly six months, Douglas, I think we can be on a first-name basis."

He sat up. "How can I help you... Elizabeth?"

"No more games, Douglas. No more layers or tricks or riddles. I've learned more. I've talked to people. People you've never heard of. Some of them even know what you're trying to do with your rope."

His eyes flickered to the edge of the bed. The length of rope was never far.

"I want to know," she said. "No more games - I want you to tell me everything. I want to hear it from you. I want to know what you saw, Douglas. I want to know everything."

He waited a long time before speaking.

"I used to make animals," he said, "out of rope. When you're retired, you drift away and I didn't want to drift away, so I went to the park and made animals. Gave them away to anyone. It was fun, and once in a while, someone else who knew about it would come and teach me a new animal. The kids loved 'em and the moms knew I was harmless."

"I've seen some," she said. "People showed them to me. You realize that a lot of them still can't believe what you did."

"They don't know what I did."

"They know what it looked like," she said. "And unless you explain, that's going to be what they come to believe."

"Why do you think I do this?" he asked, and waved the rope at her.

She waited until he continued.

"I wasn't paying attention one day, just tying, and it got bigger. It wasn't an animal, but there was something to it, something compelling, and I kept going. I was almost out of rope, but I had to keep going."

He shook his head, disbelieving his own words.

"Time and space are weird," he said. "We think of travel and we think of boxes and cylinders and things like that, but I think there's other ways to travel, other ways to connect places, and I think I found one. I think I found it in the knot."

Elizabeth nodded. "What happened?"

"As soon as I finished it, I knew something was different. I knew something had happened to me. The world tilted, but not really tilting, if that makes sense. I could see things differently. I could smell and hear things differently. It even felt different. The air was electric, the sky was brown and yellow, and the land was a plain of smoking craters and ancient death.

"But I wasn't gone from here. I could still feel the bench beneath me, still hear the birds, still hear the laughter of the children in the park. I could even see them, ghostly and faded.

"In my hands, the knot felt like a living thing, throbbing and pulsing, and I was in two places at once. One was my world - our world - and the other was this horrible place, that stank of sulphur and hurt my eyes to see and my soul to consider."

"I know what you did," she said. "I talked to a man who told me. You built what he called a treph. The word means a sort of path or route. It's pretty rare."

"A 'treph'? You mean someone knows about this?" His breathing rate increased. "Maybe they can talk to the police!"

"Someone was willing to speculate," she said. "A treph is more than just an object, it's a part of the person, too. I couldn't build the same one you did - only you can, and usually, a person can build only one, and it only goes to one place. What did you see, Douglas? It's important."

"I told you what I saw," he said.

"You told me what the area looked like. You didn't tell me what you saw. You didn't tell me why you did what you did."

He glared at her.

"I think you can rest assured that I'll believe you," she said. "You've already told me more than you've told anyone, and I'm still here. And I've told you something you didn't know. But I need to know what happened next. I need to know what you saw."

He took a deep breath and fingered the string in his lap.

"I don't know what it was," he said, "but it was huge. It was like a football field. No, more like two or three. Huge."

He closed his eyes and she saw the pain in his face as he remembered.

"I thought at first it was just smoke, you know? A big cloud of black smoke. But I guess I also knew it wasn't. It was moving. It was galloping. It had legs and a body, but it was all made of smoke. And it was coming toward me. I knew that. It wasn't just out running; it was coming toward me. Toward us. It shook the Earth. Well, maybe it was Earth. I don't think it was, but it shook the ground, anyway. And it shook me. It shook my soul. Every footstep I could feel in the ground, but I could also feel in my heart, like each step was another beat lost. It was... was so dark.

"I should have stopped, should have torn the rope apart, but I was mesmerized. I kept watching it as it came closer. It moved like air, but moved like an animal, too. Then, it arrived. It came here and stood high above us, high above the park and the plain in front of me. I could hear something - I'm not sure I can call it 'breathing' but it was air moving through, it was a sound of life. Maybe it was some sort of vocalization, but it was deeper than that, and all around us.

I saw tendrils of smoke come from its sides and drop down, down to the plain, and strike the ground. I saw those tendrils spinning and pulsing. I saw it drawing something from the ground, and I saw it pushing something back down through.

I looked up to its body and then I saw its eyes. Its eyes were so deep, so dark, like the sky without stars, like space forever, like hellish nothing. Its eyes were forever and empty. I stared into them and knew we were lost.

And then I heard a scream. Not a scream, but more like a squeal. I looked back down to the ground, to the blasted plain at my feet, and I also saw the playground in front of me, and I saw where the tendrils had landed. I saw what it was doing. I saw that each tendril had touched the plain where, on my end of the Universe, there was a child. I saw children sitting and playing games, I saw children standing, puzzled, and some just caught mid-step, pausing.

I saw the tendrils pulling light out of the children, pulling them out of their own shells. I saw them darkening as something else came in from the tendril, something cloudy, something not of this world, and barely of this Universe.

I realized then what the plain was, what this hell was I had tied us to. It used to be a place a lot like Earth, filled with life and growth and joy, and then this thing had come to it and had eaten it. Had eaten everything. This one thing had destroyed an entire world, and now it was here, and reaching through to ours.

Now I saw why it had waited. I had thought that it was trapped on that planet, and I was right, but it wasn't quite trapped - it had a path, and it was waiting, and now it was doing what all things do after they eat.

"It was reproducing."

He looked up at her.

"I'm not a murderer," he said. "Those children were already dead the moment it touched them - they were husks and it was hollowing them out, feeding on them one last time to fuel its... reproduction. It was making them into another one of its kind."

"I know," she said.

"Does it have a name, too?" he asked.

"No, Douglas. It has no name, but you described it right. You described it how I was told it looked. It's the closest thing to death this Universe ever experiences. It's the final and permanent end of everything. You were right to stop it. You succeeded. You're not a murderer, you're a savior."

She stood up, reached into her purse, and drew a pistol, aiming it at him. His pistol. The one he used on that day.

"And you're its only way to get back to Earth."

She fired twice.

She took the rope from his hands, and pulled a cigarette lighter from her purse. She lit the rope and watched it burn. The last of the flames burned her fingers, but she didn't care. It had to be all gone.

Douglas struggled for breath, his hand twitched as he tried to reach up.

Then she sat down next to him, and looked one last time into his shocked face.

"I'm sorry, Douglas. I'm so, so sorry," she said.

She held him close until he slipped away, and she kept holding him until the others arrived.

Hellgrammite!

by

Martha Bacon

Hellgrammite!

by

Martha Bacon

D EPUTY RAY paused, momentarily distracted by Vanessa's Hello Kitty bobble head. It appeared to be the only object on her shattered desk that had escaped unscathed. Its fat, white head danced merrily, responding to each distant vibration, rocking ever more enthusiastically as crumbling mortar and ceiling tile confetti rained down sporadically from a gaping hole in the station roof.

The old joint has seen better days, he ruminated as he weaved to the back of the building, kicking the bobble head into a pile of wreckage that had once been an efficiently organized filing desk.

As he rooted through a meager collection of confiscated weapons in the lock room, Deputy Ray felt unwelcome waves of nausea roiling beneath his vest. He slipped a Glock and two full clips into his jacket pocket and thought of his truck, once the most coveted beast in town, now little more than a flapjack of leather and chrome. He slid a pair of twelve-gauges into a duffle bag, stuffing handfuls of shells all around them like Styrofoam peanuts, and recalled Vanessa's last expression; a mixture of confusion, disbelief and abject terror.

Not how he wanted to remember her.

Lastly he slung Old Man Murphy's bazooka over his shoulder, confiscated for the fifth and final time. As the antique tank-buster dug into the sore spot between his shoulder blades, Deputy Ray considered the monster outside. The big, black thing that bucked and stamped and snapped and crushed as it tore his beloved town a new asshole.

He stepped through a freshly made hole in the side of the station into the cruiser lot. None of the vehicles remained intact. To the North, just beyond the high school, the night sky glowed, tinged by a hundred fires. To the south, fresh tongues of flame licked the heavens; beacons denoting a smattering of desperate last stands. The screams of men and women mingled with bursts of gunfire, and the muffled *whoomps* of small explosions punctuated a cacophonous symphony of destruction.

116

There was too much going on for Deputy Ray to process, too many good people missing, so he focused on the one thought that continued to propel his shaking legs forward; to find it and kill it.

To blast that motherfucker back to hell.

Six hours earlier

"It's Maggie. She says Bert's missing."

Ray sighed, long and low, and tossed his book onto the side table before draining the remains of his third beer and levering himself out of his La-Z Boy. His sister, Janet, held the phone out to him with a telling smile, and he grimaced as he took it.

"Yeah, Maggie, this is Ray. No, you won't get him. Sheriff Roberts is in St. Louis right now, I'm running the store until next Wednesday." He tried to catch Janet's eye, hoping to coerce her into bringing him a fresh brew, but she had already disappeared into the kitchen faster than a rattler down a rabbit hole.

"Now, Maggie, slow down. I don't want to spend another night trawling every bar in Warsaw looking for your old man. He's probably curled up under a tree right now, cradling one of Earl Johnson's quart jugs..."

Ray held the phone away from his ear and Janet laughed out loud from the kitchen at the volume of Maggie Boone's ranting.

"Alright, alright," he barked as the hysterical woman on the other end took a break to breathe, "I'll be right out. Give me ten minutes."

He hung up and made straight for the rack next to the front door where his hat, gun and keys hung; the sooner he found Bert, the sooner he could be back in his chair.

"I'll be back in twenty."

He was already out the door before his sister could reply.

It was a good forty minutes before Ray finished his search of the local bars and 'shine shacks, and Albert Boone was still AWOL. One possible lead from Nancy in the *Pig Pen* was his last resort. She'd seen Bert and his pals loading up the back of Bert's wagon with tackle boxes and rods, and several cases of beer.

Deputy Ray now had his foot to the floor, knowing full well that drunken fishing trips usually ended badly, either in fisticuffs or a near drowning. He approached a tight left bend on the I-83 but didn't slow, carrying onto Lone Star Road before hanging a hard right onto the dirt track that would take him down to Bert's favorite spot, a tendril of still water that snaked off the Truman reservoir, home to the biggest smallmouth bass in Missouri. Abel's Finger it was called, a pool blessed with perfect conditions for bug breeding, which brought the bigger larvae flooding in and subsequently, the bass. As he neared the crest of the last hill before the descent to the pool, several flashes to the Northeast caught his eye, but when no thunderous rumbles followed, he filed it away as something to look into after he had chewed Bert out for not calling his missus.

A pair of small lanterns glowed wanly on the shore of Abel's Finger, but Bert and his cronies were nowhere in sight. Deputy Ray cursed and climbed out of his truck, wondering where Bert's wagon was parked, and *what the hell was that thing glistening in the moonlight?*

He received both answers when he reached the water's edge.

The rear fender of Bert's station wagon peeked out of the dark waters and, even in the murk, Ray could see that the frame of the vehicle was twisted, corkscrewed, as it disappeared beneath the surface. Several feet further along the pebbly shoreline, Ray ground to a halt. The familiar tang of fresh blood assaulted his senses and he could finally make out the mystery shape, retching as he did so. It was a man's chest and stomach; looping entrails and jellied organs splayed out across the rocks, the tip of a shattered spine poking out the top. Opened beer cans bobbed in the pool, their dull *clinks* reminding him of distant warning buoys. A scrap of denim lay next to the partial corpse and Ray could make out a few embroidered letters; ... *a c k*. Mack Haggard, the finest mechanic in Warsaw and Bert's drinking buddy.

A sound, further back, toward the tree line. It was the gurgling rasp of a death rattle, a noise Deputy Ray was all too familiar with. He sprinted toward the sound, trying to gain some purchase on the loose stones, and finally reached the poor lad emitting the sounds. It was Charlie Marks, Dan's boy. A good kid, undoubtedly there for the fishing and not the drinking. Ray knelt and pressed his fingers to the boy's neck and Charlie's eyes fluttered open.

"Dad?"

Ray cradled the boy's head and pressed his thigh against a gaping wound in Charlie's side, "It's Deputy Ray, son. Hold on for me, won't you?"

"It, it killed Bert. Killed Mack... tore them up..."

"Who did this, Charlie?" Ray drew his gun and scanned the trees, his rage building. No man deserved to be ripped apart like this.

Charlie Marks coughed a scarlet globule into the deputy's face and his eyes grew wide, "Not... man. Bug. It was... huge."

"What are you talking about, Charlie? What do you mean, *a bug*?"

The dying boy reached up and took hold of Ray's shirt, his bloody fingers slipping on the polyester, catching the gold star on Ray's breast and tearing it free as he gasped, "Hellgrammite..."

Charlie Marks shuddered and died. A few last vestiges of steam wisped out of the gash in his side and disappeared into the warm night air. Ray stood up and took several deep breaths. Thoughts tumbled. The boy made no sense; what did he mean by *Hellgrammite*? Back by the dismal lanterns, Ray had seen a couple of plastic boxes and a pile of overturned rocks. The men had been digging up bait, that was for sure, and hellgrammites would land them the most bass. On the two occasions that Ray had actually fished, he had been shown how to hook and cast the evil-looking larvae. On average, each hellgrammite had been four inches long, its dark, chitinous armor segmented like a stretched pill bug, a multitude of black spikes for legs and a pair of over-sized pincers at the business end that could cause the worst pain imaginable when locked onto naïve flesh, and Ray would know. He rubbed the small scar on the skin web between his thumb and forefinger as he contemplated the boy's dying words.

How could hellgrammites do this to grown men? And where the hell was Bert?

Deputy Ray's initial shock ebbed away, smothered as years of experience kicked in. He reached for his radio and cursed himself when he realized he had left it at home. This had meant to be a simple drunk retrieval...

As he made his way back to the truck, he pulled out his cell phone and called the station. Vanessa should still be there, filing the day's reports in her overly professional manner, and she would be able to relay his message to the boys in Buffalo. He would need more tech out here; this was out of his league.

The phone rang, and rang. He tried again but there was still no answer.

"Damn it, Nessa!" he spat as he crunched the gears and reversed back up the track, spinning the truck and roaring back up toward Lone Star Road. As he bounced onto the paved road, his headlights picked out several deep indentations in the grassy field to his left, like someone had gone mad with a jackhammer. The indentations were evenly spaced and ran like stuttering train rails, straight and true, in the direction of the township of Warsaw.

Normally, Warsaw would have been a swift ten-minute drive from the reservoir, but Deputy Ray hadn't taken into account the possibility of running into a monstrous hellgrammite two minutes into his trip as it straddled the 83 like a footbridge. He certainly didn't anticipate crashing into one of its mighty forelimbs or rolling out of his beloved truck seconds before two more armored legs pummeled the vehicle flat, or then watching, bloodied and dazed, as the creature continued on its fixed route toward the soft glow of the distant town. The giant beast, as long as three buses and twice as tall, had disappeared over the next hill before Ray regained enough sense to draw his gun.

Three hours later, Deputy Ray reached the outskirts of Warsaw, and the town was already ablaze. He should have been there in half the time, but a sharp pain in his upper back had reduced his journey to a miserable collection of small, agonizing steps. He could see where the giant insect had entered the town, straight through Albin's wood mill; a once proud structure that was now little more than a pile of toothpicks. The creature had then ploughed through Hope's Lane, the gentle suburb now dotted with plumes of water and flame; former homeowners wailing or laying crushed in the street. Beyond that a strip mall sat in ruins. Shattered mannequins shared a glass-strewn resting place with the torn bodies of former shoppers. Thick, black smoke billowed up from the gas station at the rear of the mall and broken streetlights flickered spastically, illuminating the path of destruction like an abysmal runway strip.

Gunshots sounded and people screamed. A lilac Beetle careened past Ray. Its roof had been sheared off and a woman's headless body still sat bolt upright, held in by the seatbelt as the car bounced across four lanes and parked nose-down in a ditch.

"Godammit!" Ray yelled, feeling a new wash of adrenalin basting his tired flesh, willing his legs forward into the beleaguered town and toward the police station.

He was just blocks away from his workplace, his center of refuge, when he found Vanessa. She was sitting on the curb, her auburn hair frazzled, singed at the ends; her pencil skirt shredded, revealing long lacerations down her legs, her beautiful legs. Ray ran as fast as his injuries would allow and squatted beside her, wanting to hug the woman he had fallen for over the past four years, wanting to reassure her that *everything would be OK*, but when she stared at him with unseeing eyes and started to scream and scream, he knew he had lost her. He kissed the top of her head and continued on his trek to the station, wishing he had never found her, vowing to destroy the beast that had done this to the woman whom he had never told he loved.

Despite increasing his speed, spurred on by his percolating rage, Ray's half-skipping, half-shuffling gait meant it still took him a good ten minutes to reach the station and arm himself. Ahead of him, the monster rampaged, unseen but definitely heard; Warsaw's former rustic charm now a soundscape of tire squeals, human screams and thunderous violence.

Ray thought back to the couple of occasions he had used hellgrammites as bait. He recalled how they arched their backs when threatened, like a scorpion's tail, exposing their segmented underbellies. He remembered the pain that coursed through him when the little bastard he had been trying to hook had latched onto the skin next to his thumb, sinking its tiny pincers into the soft meat of his palm, refusing to relinquish its grasp until Ray had separated its head from its body using a flat rock as a chopping board. There was a weak point, just behind the head. Mack had taught him how to drive a bass hook into the gap between the insect's head and thorax, twisting the barb completely through which made the live bait thrash and curl wildly, resulting in an irresistible lure. He just needed a big enough hook.

By the time Deputy Ray caught up with the colossal hellgrammite, a raging battle was in full effect. The beast appeared to be cornered on the grounds of the library at the intersection of Commercial and Jackson. Its abdomen disappeared into the old, brick building and its swollen midsection was stuck between the two, massive steel installations that had been erected a decade ago in lieu of stately columns, much to the detriment of the townsfolk. The beast's front end was far from pinned though, and it thrashed wildly from side to side as over a dozen men and women fired hunting rifles and shotguns from the opposite corner, a good distance from the vicious mandibles. The creature stamped its forelimbs into the grassy lawn, more annoyed than pained, trying to gain a solid foothold, and Ray could see that the buckshot and bullets were having no effect on it. The exoskeleton was peppered and flaking in places, but hardly breached, and Ray could spy no discernible cracks to exploit. Even the creature's eyes seemed unharmed; any holes made those black pits would be indistinguishable anyway.

A hunting rifle cracked loudly next to his right ear, and he twisted to his left as a high-pitched whine filled his head. From the corner of his eye, Ray could see a small group of men, heavily armed good old boys, advancing on the thrashing beast; unloading their rifles with staggering speed. One of them, clad head to toe in garish camouflage, was whooping wildly, delighted that all his Christmases had come at once. His joy was short-lived however when he squatted a little too close to the beast's head and fumbled with the sliding bolt on his Remington. The enraged hellgrammite strained against its steel restraints and broke free as one of the sculptures toppled in a shower of earth and sod. In less than a second it had scooped the hunter in one of its giant mandibles and tossed him into the air, slicing him neatly in half upon his return.

The rest of the crowd quickly lost their collective appetite for this particular hunt, and scattered wildly, running in all directions as the enormous beast dragged its abdomen out of the ruined library and curved its back, raining bricks down into the street.

Ray watched all of this from his hastily acquired shelter, a partially flattened fire truck, and pulled one of the shotguns from the duffle bag. He quickly fed a handful of shells into the chamber like chocolate drops into a fat dog, and cocked it, all the while never taking his eyes off the creature.

The hellgrammite appeared to be in no hurry. It half-heartedly scuttled this way and that, responding to gunfire and sudden movement, but apparently in no mood to give chase. Ray hoped that perhaps the previous barrage had indeed weakened it. He shuffled around to the crushed cab of the truck and peered through an empty window frame. He had flanked the bug, and had a clear shot of its exposed underbelly, but the chitinous loops that slid against each other as the abdomen curled into the night sky looked as tough as the armor that covered the rest of its hide. It would be pointless to attack. He knew his shots would be little more than a distraction, and then he would be snipped apart along with Warsaw's other lost souls. Ray felt utterly useless. The pain in his upper back, forgotten in the preceding moments, now compounded his despair.

Sudden gunfire snapped him out of his daze as efficiently as a slap to the face and Ray craned to see where it was coming from. Four figures had returned to the fray. He could see two of the good old boys, a third shooter clad head to toe in body armor and, bringing up the rear, Nancy from the Pig Pen, unleashing a hail of bullets from her assault rifle. The hellgrammite stamped furiously and turned to face this new annoyance. As it aligned itself along Jackson Street, the burred tip of its abdomen scraped across Ray's hiding place, shearing off red metal panels and scattering equipment. The bug's tail lifted once more in a threat display and the entire truck shuddered as it momentarily lifted a few inches off the ground. Ray saw that something was looped around the rear barbs of the beast; a hose, shredded but still strong, and a thick cable attached to a three pronged grappling hook that threw up sparks as it was dragged across the asphalt by the giant larvae.

Ray flung himself back as the fire truck jolted forward, pulled by the entangled beast straining against its restraints as it tried to reach the small band. The grappling hook dangled a few feet away from him and he lunged for it, thankful that there was enough slack in the cable for him to drag it back and latch two of the steel prongs around the base of the nearest cast iron street lamp. The hellgrammite jerked back as the cable went taut and its spear-point limbs scrabbled upon the road as it fought against its anchor. The old street lamp held its own, and Ray knew that he had to act quickly.

As the beast thrashed back and forth, torn between freeing itself and murdering the creatures before it, Ray stepped out from behind the truck wreckage and cupped his hands to his mouth, yelling to the quartet across the way, "Keep it busy! Piss it off!"

"It's already plenty pissed off, Ray!" yelled Nancy as she slapped in another clip and unloaded it into the monster's head.

Her compatriots did likewise, and the hellgrammite responded by trying to arch its back once more, straining against the hose and cable holding its tail against the pavement. The iron trunk of the street lamp groaned, and Ray heard a popping sound from within. Ignoring the stabs between his shoulder blades he leaped forward, landing both feet on the flat tip of the monster's tail, and then proceeded to run toward the thorax, stepping from segment to segment as if climbing an escalator in an earthquake. He was barely halfway along the abdomen when a terrible snapping sound announced the creature was free. A length of cable whistled past the back of his head and he fell to his knees as the hellgrammite lurched forward, barreling across the road into a row of parked cars. Nancy and the other men scattered, but the two hunters closest to the action were clipped by a tumbling Volvo and pinned beneath it as the monster advanced.

Deputy Ray tried to right himself, but the bucking monster made it impossible to stand. Then he felt his world rise sharply, and suddenly he was flying through the air as the tail curled up, flicking him toward the monster's head. The shotgun fell from his grip and clattered to the ground as Ray landed face down on the broad back of the creature's thorax. He desperately reached out with his left hand as he began to slide off the blood-slicked shell and managed to snag a thick bristle protruding from a gap where the thorax met the head. The gap was wider here and Ray could see gray, sinewy flesh beneath the plates. Drawing on the last of his strength, he hauled himself up until he could lay spread-eagled on the monster's back. Then he began to shrug off Old Man Murphy's bazooka.

On the ground Nancy and the armor-clad hunter had returned to the fight, emptying their weapons into the creature's head in an attempt to keep the scythe-like mandibles away from the pinned men. Their efforts slowed the beast but did not stop it as it pushed on, determined to dismember its quarry. Several townsfolk emerged from the shadows, working as one to roll the car off the men as others grabbed hold of the hunters and started to drag them toward the nearest doorway. The hellgrammite stamped furiously and lunged forward with terrifying speed, snatching up the armored man as he reloaded. Nancy raged as she poured lead into what she hoped was the weak spot where the mandibles joined the head, but her efforts went unrewarded and she threw her empty rifle down in frustration as the night echoed with the sound of polycarbonate body armor splitting open like a pecan.

Then, a voice from up high. "Get back!"

Nancy peered into the gloom behind the monster's head as she staggered back to join the other people who were rapidly melting into the surrounding buildings. The image before her would have been laughable, if it hadn't been accompanied by the noisy dismemberment of her former shooting partner.

His graying hair backlit by distant flames, Deputy Ray crouched upon the monster's neck, his hands wrapped around the firing mechanism of the 70-yr-old tank-buster. The front of the bazooka disappeared into the gap between the thorax and head. Ray checked to see that the sidewalk was clear, then he squeezed the trigger.

"What are you waiting for?" Nancy shouted from a darkened doorway, "Shoot it already!"

"I'm trying!"

Ray twisted the bazooka and looked at the firing mechanism. As far as he could tell, everything was in the right place. The trigger guard was fully open; *why wasn't it working?*

"Flip the safety!" Nancy had returned to the sidewalk and was glaring up at him.

"There isn't one!" shouted Ray, splaying himself across the beast's back as it lurched forward once again. It was determined to crash through the wrecked cars before it and grab the small, fleshy thing screaming in its general direction.

"Try again, dammit!"

Ray twisted the ancient weapon around and studied it. There were no levers, no other switches to flip. Then he saw the trigger guard wasn't fully opened, and it needed to be for the magneto sparker to launch the rocket. He fumbled at the guard, all the time gripping the beast's thorax with his knees, trying to survive the hellish rodeo. His thumb and fingers bled as he tried to force the rusted cover fully open, but it wouldn't move. Then, in a moment of clarity as the hellgrammite inched closer to the building sheltering Nancy and the others, Ray pulled out the Glock and pistol-whipped the trigger mechanism. The guard finally locked into place and he rammed the end of the bazooka back into the fleshy gap behind the monster's head and pulled the trigger.

It had taken Nancy and three more townsfolk ten minutes to dig themselves out of the doorway through a sticky pile of gray meat and black shell fragments. By that time, Ray had already clambered down off the smoking carcass that straddled Commercial and Jackson and had limped off in the direction of the police station. Nancy watched the battered man disappear into the smoky gloom; a battered man that wouldn't be paying for another drink for as long as he lived.

Vanessa was still rocking on the curb when Ray reached her and he crouched next to her, hugging her tight, wishing he had the balls to tell her how he felt. Killing a giant force of nature was a cakewalk next to spilling his heart. Vanessa lifted her head slowly and he gazed into her eyes. Some of the light had returned.

"Is it dead?"

"Sure is, Nessa."

She smiled and held him close. Every tiny pang of pain in his body melted away and a glorious warmth caressed his bones. He inhaled deeply, smelling her perfume that punched through the smoke and oil fumes. He cleared his throat. Now was as good a time as any.

"Deputy Ray! Deputy Ray!"

Ray turned wearily and felt his chest tighten as a man rushed toward him, his face bloodied and twisted in terror.

"Deputy Ray," the man gibbered, panting as he collapsed in the road next to him, "it's the reservoir! It's boiling! There's things in there! Giant things! Hundreds of giant things!"

Ray sighed. He stood and stretched, wincing as his entire body screamed at him. Then he reached down and took Vanessa's hand, pulling her upright before kissing her on the mouth.

Long and soft and deep.

Xan-Ti-Maca: The Pit of Hell

by

R. Allen Leider

Xan-Ti-Maca: The Pit of Hell
by
R. Allen Leider

D OWN THEY PLUMMETED, millions per minute - perfect, clear droplets plunging from the balmy summer heavens into the depths of the Yucatan rain forest. They bounced off giant palm leaves and splattered their souls on the soft jungle floor where the thirsty flora and fauna awaited their morning baptism. In the distance, thunder could be heard, both from the clouds and from the 5,000 horse power turbines of the great Sikorsky AirLab helicopter plowing its way through the clouds and rain. Aboard, Dr. Scott Lambert of the University of Mexico and Lt. Hector DeJesus of the Mexican National Police peered outward, searching for signs of their objective.

"The city of Gualtecata was discovered by long range telescopic satellite some five years ago," Lambert explained to the preoccupied policeman. "Those onboard cameras are powerful enough to read a license plate from hundreds of miles out in space. They were looking for geological signs of possible oil deposits when the city was discovered under deep layers of jungle growth."

"Really?" mused DeJesus in an absent monotone as he shuffled his paperwork.

"It took Dr. Montez from the university and his assistants over a year of planning and painstaking labor to excavate just the main square of the city," Lambert continued. "The satellite data shows that at least two thirds of the site is still buried under the jungle." Lambert took a long pull from his canteen, then added with a sad note, "But, there's no telling when the funds for the completion of the project will come through."

"You don't say," replied DeJesus, his tone implying thorough disinterest. The officer was thumbing through his folder of notes on the disappearance of the five man team that had preceded Lambert's own expedition just three months earlier. The missing scientists included the man DeJesus considered the actual discoverer of Gualtecata, the famed Dr. Alejandro Morales.

From the chopper, the team could see the mysterious great pit-style lake Morales had described in his transmissions. Half a mile from the ancient city a 600 foot deep crater, two hundred feet of it filled with transparent, green bubbling ground water, stood as it had for the last 4,000 years. The location of Gualtecata and the ancient legend of the mysterious god, Xan-Ti-Maca, were recorded in Mayan hieroglyphs on artifacts the original university team had returned with ten years earlier. They had promptly been stored, then forgotten, in the basement of the museum.

"It was only three years ago that modern technology advances in gamma ray scanning were able to clearly detect the markings on the tablet and record the location of this place," Lambert clarified. "We were then able to decipher the ancient glyphs once we had the original X-ray plates enhanced with sophisticated computer software."

"That's very good," DeJesus mumbled while he continued to sort through his unruly stack of papers.

"The real break for us was when Isidore Crenshaw left the University thirty million in his will for the express purpose of archeological advancement regarding Mayan culture."

"Huuuummm," drawled the lieutenant, his voice almost betraying interest in his companion's prattle at last. "That's quite a lot of money, Senor Lambert."

"It's really been stretched, too," the doctor continued, still not paying any real attention to the policeman's general lack of enthusiasm, "our share of it paid for the initial excavation, and both the first mission to uncover the mysteries of the lost city as well as the mythical treasure of Xan-Ti-Maca. They say this expedition was mounted to complete Dr. Morales' last project. But frankly, I'm pretty certain the treasure is all the university is interested in."

The policeman sat up straight, rubbing his back against the brace bar in his seat. Adjusting his glasses, he addressed the doctor with focus.

"Yes, the mythological lost treasure of the Mayans. Let's review that first mission's connection to that, shall we," DeJesus started. "Three months ago Dr. Montez and his team came down here to excavate the main square of Gualtecata and to recover that treasure you said - yes?"

"Yes, the hieroglyphs we found on the underside of the original tablet told of a great treasure that was thrown into the lake in the pit to placate some deity or other that supposedly lived at the bottom. We figure that there's about 100 million dollars in gold, silver and jewels down there. And that's just the bulk, market share monetary value. The treasure's value in terms of antiquity worth, that's indescribable, priceless. The carvings and hieroglyphs on the artifacts and jewelry will fill in so much that we don't know, so many of the unexplained mysteries of the Mayan civilization... I don't know how to explain it."

Lambert took another drag on his water bottle, then splashed a bit in his hand to use to cool his eyes and forehead. Beaming with enthusiasm, he added, "It's even possible that many of the pieces will have DNA in their cracks and crevices.

With today's tools, I mean, we stand to learn so much about the people themselves, oh my God, I mean... oh my God!"

"A fortune in science versus a fortune in pesos?" DeJesus replied, his eyes wide open.

"Oh, honking yes. Priceless pieces for sure," Lambert replied. "Hundreds, thousands of them. But, that doesn't matter. I mean, even if we only recover a dozen pieces, it will take years to fully evaluate their contributions to furthering our understanding of the Mayans. This is the one ancient civilization that hangs just beyond our reach. To finally know what happened to them, to unlock their secrets..."

"Hmmm. The first team, they all disappeared while investigating this treasure in the lake. Two scientists and their three assistants? That's a lot of people to disappear without a trace... all at one time."

"I know," replied Dr. Reid MacNamara, who had come to the front of the helicopter as it circled the landing pad. "That's what makes it all seem so mysterious. And dangerous. The locals disavow any knowledge of the disappearances. They have a shaman, named Marcuso, sort of a local politico religious leader who says the men just left the camp one day and never returned. Even their equipment was gone overnight! He says it was because of the legend."

"I want to talk to this man Marcuso first," said a grimly determined DeJesus, biting the tip off a large Cuban cigar. "And what legend are we talking about?"

"Approximately 4,000 years ago," Lambert explained, "when the Mayan culture was at its peak, a brilliant light was seen high in the sky, according to the information we got from our relic. Tumeca, the high priest at the time, described the vision as a message from an approaching deity. He told the people that this deity was a god named Xan-Ti-Maca coming to judge them. They amassed a great treasure of jewels and gold and silver and placed it on top of the temple for Xan-Ti-Maca to see as he passed overhead. But the god did not 'drive by' as Tumeca had told them it would."

DeJesus lit his cigar as the doctor continued.

"The meteor plummeted through the atmosphere, a ball of white fire that terrified the people. The molten mass of space rock burned its way through the dense foliage and impacted a half mile from Gualtecata. It carved out a huge crater in the Earth's crust which immediately began to be filled by the green spring water from an underground aquifer. Tumeca told the people that Xan-Ti-Maca now dwelled in the lake and they must take the treasure, a little at a time, and throw it down into the depths to placate the angry god."

"The Mayans were a very superstitious lot," MacNamara interjected.

"They may still be," DeJesus answered, stuffing his paperwork into the folder and thumping it on the window sill, "and someone may be exploiting that weakness to get at that treasure. Your scientist friends did not disappear because someone wanted to advance archeology."

No one said anything to contradict the lieutenant as the great Sikorsky AirLab finally began its descent near the site of Gualtecata.

DeJesus left camp for the village before noon, determined to interrogate Marcuso. He was convinced the interview would shed a great deal of light on the mysterious disappearances of the first University team. At the same time, back at the pit, MacNamara sent the team's twin robotic cameras, Floyd and Lloyd, down to the bottom of the lake. Hiding from the 100+ degree equatorial sun within the main work tent, the scientists and a few of their native helpers watched the TV monitors intently. Each flickered slowly into life, then lit up to reveal an underwater field of gold and silver jewel-encrusted adornments which seemed to completely cover the lake bed. The decision was quickly made to loosen the treasure piece by piece with the robotic arms on the camera platforms.

At the same time that those in camp stared with sweat-filled eyes at the dazzling sight on their monitors, white streams of steam lifting from the jungle leaves were the sight which greeted Lt. DeJesus as he arrived at the nearby village. Marcuso's five room house was far more solid than the simple one and two room adobe huts in which the native workers and local farmers lived. Marcuso had other conveniences as well, such as a chemical toilet and a large private water tank. Such extravagences saved him the commonality of the communal wells and group outhouses. He also owned a small diesel generator which chugged away 24 hours a day churning out electricity for the very private residence.

Lt. DeJesus was ushered into a comfortable living room by two of Marcuso's guards. An electric fan whooshed above them, whipping the thick, humid air into a nearly bearable atmosphere. Marcuso entered the room dressed in semi-formal, Mayan-themed leisure attire. He wore large sunglasses that obscured almost a third of his face and a thick mustache that hid his mouth. Behind the sunglasses, Marcuso's piercing eyes explored his visitor carefully, searching for a window into his soul so he might anticipate his adversary's questions.

"You wanted to speak to me, Lieutenant?" Marcuso asked in a low voice.

"Yes. I was interested in what you might know about the disappearance of the five scientists from the University who came to explore Gualtecata and the great pit three months ago," DeJesus replied. "I understand some of your people worked on that expedition. They didn't die. That tells me they should know something that could shed some light on the disappearances."

"I don't believe the scientists disappeared," Marcuso replied in a cold monotone voice. "I think they finished their work and returned to the University."

"My notes indicate that they arrived, set up camp, then communicated via satellite with the University for six hours before communications went down. No one has seen or heard from them since."

"I can check with the local men and see if any of them were asked to work the project," said Marcuso. "I am sure they would take the work if it were offered. The people here are very poor and the University pays well for workers."

"I can ask them myself," DeJesus said. "Thanks just the same."

"Whatever pleases you," Marcuso replied coolly.

"Do you know what would please me?" the policeman snapped, looking about the room, his eyes inspecting every object. "To know just exactly what is it you do here."

"I give guidance to the natives," Marcuso replied as he began his carefully rehearsed answer. "I came here as an agent for a wealthy benefactor who wanted to develop the area as a tourist attraction after the discovery of Gualtecata. That deal is taking forever to materialize, but while I waited I became attached to the people. As I have a formal education, I decided to stay here to help with the upgrading of the village, the local schools, things like medical aid. Once the tourist thing happens they'll have the money they need for a hospital and other improvements."

"I see," DeJesus said as he nodded, then walked calmly and deliberately out the door. "You're just a humanitarian."

Marcuso watched as the unwelcome guest spoke to some of the villagers. He continued to observe the lieutenant until an hour had passed and the officer returned to his Hummer and drove off in a cloud of thick, brown dust.

"That man could be trouble," Marcuso said to Bokut, his six foot six body-guard.

"Why, boss? He's just another snooper, like the others," replied the larger man, "and he can disappear just like them if he causes trouble."

"The others weren't National Police," Marcuso spit back. "That damned Montez recognized me. That condemned them all. It had to. There's too much at stake."

"You should have known that sooner or later someone from the university would come back here, someone who could finger you, or someone who would follow up when those others disappeared," said the giant. Marcuso paced the floor a bit, then sat down at his desk.

"I've worked too hard on this to have anything go wrong. I dug on my knees with my bare hands when they found this place. Afterwards, I put in 24 hour days at the University sifting through rubble, identifying the bits and pieces. Then, Dr. Alejandro Montez, the great authority, takes all the credit and I am passed over for tenure. Miserable bastards, telling me to teach classes to teenage morons while Montez got millions to come back here for the treasure."

Marcuso exploded then, his open palms slamming repeatedly against his desk as he screamed, "NO!! I should've been a full professor years ago. Montez and the others were plagiarizers, nobodies. I did all the work! This is my city! My treasure!"

He stood then, slapping his chest with his fist as he shouted; "Mine! Mine!"

"I hope you're right," Bokut said as he turned to leave the room. "I didn't really enjoy killing all those people, especially that young couple. But, business is business and I expect my reward."

"You'll get your share."

"That's all I ask."

Bokut smiled, then left the room, letting the door slam behind him. Marcuso stared out the window, watching nothing in particular, simply sinking deeply into a series of random, nervous musings.

At the Gualtecata camp site, MacNamara was in his tent with Lambert briefing Willie Rivas, the native foreman, on the plans for recovering the treasure. As he did, an excited Dr. Melton, accompanied by divers Bryan and Louie, entered the tent. They all three were covered with sweat and an odious bug repellant almost as repulsive to humans as it was to the swarms of local mosquitoes.

"Scott," interrupted Melton, "We have some interesting readings here you should see."

"Oh?"

"We sent the platforms down this morning to check out some fifty square feet of lake bed where we figure to start our recovery of the artifacts. Just now we checked our data over once more and we got these readings from the instrument packages."

"So...?" replied Lambert, releasing a small, white puff of smoke from his pipe as he took the printouts from his colleague and began to study them.

"So, they don't jive with the earlier data–in the least. The lake was 200 feet deep when we first checked, right? Now, it's shrunk to close to 175 feet deep? How's that possible? In just a few hours... how? Where in hell did all that water go?"

"Hmmmm," mused Lambert, "Have you sent any divers down there yet?"

"No, we wanted to check with you first before we went down," Brian replied.

"Okay, you checked. Now do it."

Melton and the divers left. Lambert and Willie went back to their discussion on how best to recover the treasure, but before even two minutes had passed, Jesus Reyes, a junior geologist, burst into the tent gasping for breath.

"Senor, we find it. We find the words of Tumeca on the wall of the pit!"

The men rushed out of the tent and gathered at the northern wall of the pit where a small platform had been rigged for a TV camera to shoot footage for the Discovery Channel. Some of the natives had gone over the edge down rope ladders to install supports under the platform. That was where they uncovered the new carvings under a rich carpet of thorny, green moss.

"These Mayan hieroglyphics are from the period of the High Priest Tumeca," said Melton with excitement. "See, look here–here's where they detail how, after the meteor crashed, some of the inhabitants of Gualtecata disappeared. Tumeca said they had been devoured both..." the doctor began a direct translation, "...'flesh and bone, by the angry god, called Xan-Ti-Maca, who came down to Earth, in a fiery ball to live within our lake.' The inscription went on to say that Tumeca had claimed to have seen Xan-Ti-Maca in the lake and that the only way to appease the god was to adorn a virgin with treasure and toss her into the lake on the night of the full moon."

"My god," exclaimed Lambert. "Then the whole freakin' lake is a boneyard!"

"It looks that way," replied MacNamara. "The writings say that on the event of every full moon, that means for hundreds of years, a chosen virgin was laden with jewels, gold and silver and then ceremoniously sacrificed to the unseen god Xan-Ti-Maca at the bottom of the pit."

"And it didn't stop," added Melton, "until the Conquistadors came and wiped everyone in the region out with the measles."

While those gathered pondered the implications of what they had just discovered, others were raising and securing the cameras. At the same time, Bryan and Louie suited up and made ready to dive as soon as the cloud of mud settled. They were just about ready to go when Lt. DeJesus' Hummer roared up the embankment. He was not smiling.

"Did you speak to Marcuso?" Lambert asked the officer.

"Yes and no," DeJesus replied. "Marcuso was very elusive, but I have a feeling he knows more about what happened than he's letting on. He pretends to be a peasant who made good, but he doesn't talk like one, he's too refined, too worldly. Also, a call back to Mexico City told me there are no records of him anywhere in the country. It's as if he came into being when the excavations began."

"Sir," a student assistant interrupted. "We just finished the new reading."

"And...?"

"I don't know what to say, Dr. Lambert. This time the reading says there's only 158 feet of water, but still no drainage fissures were detected."

The assembly looked at each other. Finally, Lambert exhaled hard, wiped at the sweat stinging his eyes and said "Send in the divers."

The two men waiting in the small launch out in the middle of the lake understood the hand signal given them. In seconds their smooth, hard bodies shattered the placid surface of the deep, green lake. Thirty minutes passed.

Nothing.

"Well," mused MacNamara. "This is a bit troubling."

"Troubling," snapped Melton. "They should be back by now. Twenty minute intervals, that's what we said. Twenty minutes."

"So," asked DeJesus. "Where are they?"

"I don't know," responded Lambert, "but I'm going to find out. Myles, send down Floyd and Lloyd down again. Find out what the Hell is going on down there!"

Dr. Melton and Willie turned on their camera equipment. Floyd and Lloyd slipped off the platforms and plunged into what they now recorded as only 143 feet of water.

"What's wrong?" DeJesus inquired, still not understanding the gravity of the situation.

"My divers haven't come up," said Lambert. "They're the best in the business, worked the Titanic recovery crew. This is nothing compared to that. It's a lake–still water–clear for the most part. I don't understand."

"Any snakes or other predators in there?" asked MacNamara.

"No life of any sort," Melton answered, "and that's bothered me for days, too. This is a dead lake, but it should be teaming with life, fish, turtles, algae, et cetera. But it's not. There aren't even plants beneath the waterline. All we see on the monitor is the lake bed and the treasure, some trinkets embedded in the mud."

"Oh, is that so?" DeJesus mused.

The search continued for two hours further but yielded nothing. There were no signs of Bryan or Louie or even their equipment. The blazing yellow sun turned bright orange, then blood red and slowly retired behind the ancient mountains. With the light lost, the search was abandoned for the day. Shadows crawled over the ruins of Gualtecata and blended into the same thick mysterious darkness that had enveloped the region nightly since time began.

In the village, massive bonfires dotted the intersections of the local streets and spit their embers high into the air. The fires lit torches and these beacons, in the hands of the locals, formed a line of dancing flames that followed the narrow road from the village to the edge of the pit of Xan-Ti-Maca. The distant chanting jolted the slumber of the visitors from the University. The scientists stumbled from their tents, their emotions ranging from frightened to angry. In the village square beyond, Marcuso strutted like a peacock dressed in the robes of an ancient Mayan high priest. Before him marched his muscular henchmen, Bokut and Naga, looking far more like members of the Hell's Angels than Mayan soldiers.

"Xan-Ti-Maca has been offended by the outsiders," Marcuso told the gathering throng of nervous, frenzied natives. "Our ancient god Xan-Ti-Maca demands sacrifice, new flesh and treasure must be offered up or he will come forth from the lake and destroy all of us. Your wives and children will be devoured and your homes blown to the four corners of the Earth. We must placate our god, drive the outsiders away. We need gold and silver, jewels, and a new virgin sacrifice."

Marcuso turned suddenly, shouting, "Her!"

The self-proclaimed chief pointed at a teenaged native girl named Chanika who had rejected his romantic advances since he had first arrived in the village. Chanika turned to run for her hut. She sprinted less than ten yards when Naga grabbed her roughly and, as the crowd cheered, Marcuso forced her to drink from a jewel encrusted gold cup containing cheap red wine and a powerful narcotic. The girl struggled with Naga as he forced his huge, thumbs into her mouth and wrenched her jaw opened. Quickly Bokut poured the potion down her throat. She choked on the bitter brew, but the two men held her mouth shut tight and forced her to swallow every drop of it. Slowly Chanika's pupils dilated and she became limp in the arms of her captors.

The drugged girl was stripped naked in front of the crowd, her tan, nubile body glistening with sweat in the torchlight. Marcuso's henchmen dressed Chanika in traditional Mayan sacrificial garb, then adorned her with half of the gold and silver jewelry they had taken from the villagers.

The full moon shone over the mountains, the blue-white light of the lunar goddess slowly turning ruddy. Behind it, constellations spread out like a million haunting eyes waiting for the sacrifice. The gathered masses gasped collectively and looked skyward as a large shooting star lit up the heavens from East to West. Marcuso took advantage of the event to announce that it was a friend of Xan-Ti-Maca's, who would come down and eat their children and curse their souls for eternity if they did not continue their sacrificial traditions. The woozy Chanika was dragged to the edge of the pit and the drums beat fiercely as the bonfire crackled and the flames reached upwards for the death moon above.

Over a hundred Mayan descendants gyrated in a frenzy around the bonfire as Chanika looked alternately at Marcuso, the thugs securely holding her arms and then into the India-inky depths. The two henchmen held her wrists so tightly she could barely feel her hands. Marcuso glared with anger at the girl who had refused him. This would not only teach her a lesson, but serve as well as a lesson for the next girl he fancied.

Then, out of nowhere the music was pierced by a shotgun blast. A frightened silence followed, then a second thundering blast rang out from MacNamara's weapon. Lt. DeJesus stood at the other side of the pit taking aim at Marcuso with the laser sight of his M-16. Marcuso noted the red dot on his chest and bolted immediately. His men followed suit, abandoning their captive. While the crowd scattered in screaming disarray, Willie ran around to the west side of the pit to Chanika, scooping her up before she toppled into the pit. The native foreman wrapped a blanket around the shivering, disoriented girl and brushed her long black hair off her sweaty face. While DeJesus stood guard with his M-16, Willie brought Chanika a mug of hot, black coffee. Above this scene, the clouds blew across the pitch black western skies and wrapped themselves around the death moon obscuring it from view. The villagers cowered as if they had never seen such a terrible portent.

From his vantage point, DeJesus could tell what the locals were thinking. Try as he might, he found he could not disagree with them.

Sunrise came too early for everyone, and with it thick, Nimbus rain clouds that moved like an invading swarm over the peaks of the ancient mountains. The humidity rapidly climbed to 100

"In thirty minutes," Marcuso told his sidekicks as they began their descent back down the cliff, "the side of this mountain will come down and crush the camp below, and that will be the end of the university and its intrusion into our affairs."

In the archaeologists' campsite below, Melton sent the camera assemblies and instrument packages down to search once more for the lost Bryan and Louie, but nothing had changed.

"It's as if the lake is alive," Willie offered quietly. "And has swallowed them whole."

"I don't understand this," Melton muttered. "There're no underwater caves or any places for them to get stuck or for their bodies to be obscured. I have a dozen printouts here and they all show the same thing, that the lake bed is one huge, smooth, muddy surface. You can see the treasure embedded in it, but no bodies or any of their equipment."

Lambert looked at Dr. Melton and Lt. DeJesus. His expression queazy, he whispered, "Like they say in the movies, I have a very bad feeling about this."

Melton acknowledged his colleague with a nod.

"Is that your scientific opinion?" DeJesus asked.

"It's my gut feeling," Lambert replied, wiping the sweat cascading from his brow. "I don't like things that can't be explained. I don't like the native situation either. That shaman Marcuso, he reminds me of someone I met at the university back when this city was discovered."

"Really?"

"I'm pretty sure it might be him, forget his name, one of the minor players, but he was too interested in treasure..."

Lambert's recollections were shattered as every tree in the forest shook. Animals panicked, running mindlessly for shelter. The mountains rumbled and the sky filled with birds. Then, the grumbling of the Earth was counter-pointed by Willie's shrill voice.

"Senhors, run ... run for your lives!! Rock slide!!"

The scientists looked above the pit and saw an avalanche of rubble descending upon them, behind which was an immense boulder, some thirteen tons in weight. The monstrous rock impacted the side of the mountain in irregular spins and twists but veered away from the campsite at the last moment and headed downwards, not for the tents, but for the center of the lake. The boulder crashed through the water's surface, a plume of white-green water rising from the lake to splatter everything and everyone around.

Silence.

Slowly, the leaves in the jungles rustled once more. One by one natives from the village poked their heads from the leafy, green maze that was the forest. Marcuso walked proudly out of the thicket and waved his priest's staff.

"The intruders have offended Xan-Ti-Maca!" he announced.

Little did he know how right he was, for suddenly, all the water in the lake rose in Biblical quantities to spill outward in huge waves over the ruins of Gualtecata. Most everything in the camp was swept away into the jungle gullies. The scientists did not lament their belongings, however. Indeed, paltry details such as possessions and food were banished from their thoughts, erased completely as Lambert and his crew looked up in astonishment.

"Wha..." MacNamara's gagging syllable was all any of them could utter, as that which no living human had seen for thousands of years rose from the center of the lake - Xan-Ti-Maca!

Big it was, as large as a skyscraper, with nails the size of churches. Its outer skin, which had been mistaken for the lake bed, was rough and wrinkled like a rhino's, coated with mud and encrusted with jewels, gold and silver ornaments. The thing was a gargantuan humanoid, with clearly delineated appendages, but it was nothing like anything ever previously recorded by man. Its head was a mass of fins and tentacles, all of it just so much hair adorning a skull filled with a mad face, eyes the size of eighteen wheelers, a maw the size of a baseball diamond.

As the scientists stared, their minds trying to make sense of the horror before them, they noted that the forms of many types of fish and amphibians seemed to move beneath the skin of the monster, life forms it had assimilated throughout the ages. And then, they began to note other shapes, human shapes, appendages which could only be human, some still in their diving gear.

The minds of the scholars struggled to get past the surface of what they were seeing, searching for an answer. Could it be some organism whose DNA or dormant spore had come down inside the original meteor thousands of years ago? Might not the vegetation of the lake and the living creatures provided it with an abundant supply of nutrition which the monthly human feasts of flesh and blood then supplemented?

Other ideas came to them as well, wilder, more fantastical. Still, none of them moved until finally the creature lurched upward out of the pit.

"Run!"

"To the helicopter!"

The university men and their workers turned and ran, slamming one into another, sliding and falling in the mud caused by the creature's first appearance. As they made to stand, the horror reached out, scooping up scores of villagers. Lightning lit the hideous scene, even as Marcuso and his underlings tried to head off Lambert, DeJesus, Chanika and the rest of the team as they headed for the helicopter.

"See what you have done!" Marcuso shouted at the intruders, waving a machete over his head menacingly. Bokut raised his blowgun and pointed it at Chanika, but a shot sounded, sending a hollow point bullet through the back of his skull. MacNamara lowered his M-16 as Bokut's body jerked around and stumbled.

"Enough," cried Lambert. "We've got to get out of here."

MacNamara nodded, his hands shaking violently. He had never before killed a man. Had never watched a human head explode, felt the blood and bone of it splatter against his chest and face. But then, the back of his mind screamed, he had never seen any of the things he had seen that morning. With a shudder, he wheeled about and followed the others down into the village.

Marcuso shouted for the natives to stop the team, then motioned for Naga to follow him back to his villa. Once inside he called for Carlos, foreman of the fuel depot, to join them as he unlocked a cabinet hidden behind clothing in the back of his hall closet. Naga's eyes widened as Marcuso pulled out three explosive backpacks and a pair of rocket launchers.

"What's all this?" Carlos asked.

"Insurance." Marcuso replied. "I never intended those rich gringos to control anything around here. We dug out Gualtecata with our hands and now rich Americans wanted to make it a tourist attraction with us cleaning the bathrooms and waiting the tables. With that thing out there, we can make it all **ours**!"

"But..."

"Silence!" Marcuso snarled, tossing Carlos two of the back packs. "Set those on the fuel tanks. If that creature gets loose we're ruined. But if we kill it we can blame all the deaths on it, rebuild the area ourselves! It can all be ours, hotels, casinos, everything! Maybe we might even capture that hell-thing, keep it as an attraction."

Marcuso and Naga took the rocket launchers and the third back pack and headed for the fuel depot with Carlos. Once there, the foreman attached the bombs to the biggest of the diesel fuel storage tanks and enabled the remote detonators he held. Marcuso and Naga took up positions on the sides of the fuel depot, armed their rocket launchers and waited for their 4,000 year old, extra-terrestrial prey.

On the other side of the village, the university team had reached their transportation. Behind them Xan-Ti-Maca gorged itself on native flesh and blood. The screams of the villagers echoed throughout the rain forest as the chopper's engines sputtered. The rotation started as a slow whine, then the rotors began to spin faster and faster, their sound growing louder, more fluid. Chanika was frightened as she had never been on, let alone seen, a helicopter before, but Lambert put his arms around her and hugged her gently.

"It's all right," Lambert assured her. "We're almost gone. We'll get you away from Marcuso."

"Now, I remember that guy," MacNamara said grabbing DeJesus by the shoulder. "He's Dr. Marcus... Dr. Alejandro Marcus."

"He's a nut case," said Lambert. "He was just a minor player at the excavations. He was psychotic, acted as if he discovered the place and resented the other university staffers who got the credit."

"I can't check that now," DeJesus said. "but, it fits."

"He left the university, disappeared completely shortly after the awards were given out," MacNamara added. "He must have came back to retrieve the treasure for himself."

DeJesus nodded. It was no mystery to him now as to what had become of the first team, or how their bodies had disappeared without a trace.

"Hang on!"

The helicopter jerked sharply, slowly rising in a series of spasms through the rain-laden air to a height of about 500 feet. Beneath the hovering chopper Xan-Ti-Maca swelled, seeming to sense the morsels in the tin box above it. As the helicopter moved south, the beast followed.

"Just a half mile to the fuel depot," reported MacNamara. "We take a quick dip, refuel, and we're gone."

"That t-t-thing," stammered Willie. "It's moving after us!"

"There's 50,000 gallons of diesel fuel, kerosene and gasoline on those docks," shouted Lambert. "Maybe we can slow it down some while we get what we need."

As the chopper approached the depot at low altitude, the scientists watched helplessly as Xan-Ti-Maca slithered through the village, gathering up dozens of the fleeing natives. Juices ran from its maw as it fell atop five men pulling a wagon stuffed with possessions. Their muffled screams were never heard by human ears. A careful observer would have seen them slowly dissolve. First, the monster's digestive juices caused their skin to burn red, then turn purple and black, peeling from the raw flesh which liquefied in the acidic jelly that rippled beneath its scaly hide.

No one in the helicopter cared to witness such horror, however. The only person watching for anything was Marcuso. When he spotted the chopper - saw Chanika and Lambert - the blood boiled in his veins. Raising his rocket launcher he aimed it at the hovering AirLab, his rival and the girl who had scorned him. He took careful aim and slowly squeezed the trigger.

"Jesus Christ," Lambert yelled. "Climb! That bastard has a missile launcher."

Marcuso laughed with anger, but then, just as he was about to complete his attack, a cold, wet blob of slime fell on him from above. His attention shattered, he looked upward just in time to see the monstrous hand of Xan-Ti-Maca closing over him. The false priest swung his weapon up, but all too slow as the massive paw close over him. His brief screams resounded through the jungle, only to be cut off as he disappeared into the behemoth from the pit he had exploited for so long.

Above, as the giant AirLab circled the village, Dr. Melton lit the short fuse on a six stick dynamite package rigged to a spare cartridge belt. He held onto the grip bar on the opened doorway of the left side of the chopper and swung the belt around like a sling. His target below was the millennia old creature terrorizing the village.

Suddenly, however, Lambert's eyes widened and he became cogent of the reality of their situation.

"Don't!" His scream froze his colleague's hand. "This thing, it's no mere animal. It must be of xenomorphic origin, born from a single cell or spore on that eons old meteor from the far reaches of outer space."

"If that's right," MacNamara threw in, "blasting it to bits would splatter millions of its reproductive cells across the landscape. It might spawn millions of such creatures."

"We could doom the entire planet."

Melton stared out the door of the helicopter helplessly for a moment, then threw the deadly package on the floor of the chopper. Melton quickly doused the sparkling fuse with the remaining water in his canteen. His actions turned out to be futile, however, as Carlos detonated his explosives on the ground. The resultant fireball was visible for a hundred miles. The chopper shifted violently from side to side as it dodged debris and shrapnel, the latter being mostly metal shards from the framework of the fuel tanks. One piece caught Naga in the chest, killing him instantly, his death spasm causing him to fire his rocket. The missile caught Xan-Ti-Maca squarely in the maw. The beast lurched upwards, hundreds of thousands of flaming globules of skin, and jewels and precious metal fragments flashing outward from its burning body as the helicopter rose away sharply.

"Oh, my Lord," exclaimed Lambert. He was staring still as Gualtecata faded into the distance and the fireball's column of thick, black smoke slowly dissipated into the air.

The cool morning rains came early the next day as they had always come. The large, tropical droplets pummeled the palms, joined forces and formed streams that ran into gullies in the sandy soil, through the rough-hewn streets of the ruined village and over the paved avenues of ancient Gualtecata. Torrents poured down the black granite rocks of the mountain slopes. The fresh streams poured into the great green lake at the bottom of the pit, filling it, renewing the lake and washing away the minutest remains of Xan-Ti-Maca, bits and pieces of DNA laden alien jelly into the great river that flowed toward the ocean twenty miles away.

At the bottom of LaPlaya Bay, a small yellow fish swam about in steady circles, gulping morning mouthfuls of sea water rich in plankton and microscopic bits of vegetation. Under him a slightly larger form moved silently across the ocean floor.

In the blink of an eye the fish disappeared.

Above the bay the rain continued to fall upon the smooth surface of the ocean. Within moments, a red fish with black stripes disappeared. Then, another.

Before long it would rain again, in the jungles near Yucatan and in Mexico City and on the verdant lawns of the great University where Dr. Lambert would debrief his associates and where Lt. DeJesus would file his report.

And where, before they would finish, the staggering shadows of a hundred thousand ancient evils would soon fall.

Bring Back
the Hound

by

Amy Braun

Bring Back the Hound
by
Amy Braun

"HEY, Charon," my companion grinned. "Who let the dog..."
"If you finish that sentence, I am going to kill you."

Hermes rolled his eyes at me. I showed him my back and continued walking as yet another screaming human ran past me.

"I'm just trying to lighten the mood, here."

I tightened my fists at my side, forcing myself to breathe deeply and calmly. *It is the assignment that is exasperating me. Not Hermes. He is merely being himself. His young, foolish, irritating self.*

"This is not a circumstance to be joking about, Hermes."

"Yeah," he replied, glancing down at the corpse on his left. "But being serious all the time takes all the fun out of the job."

I turned on him so suddenly that he bumped into my chest. Hermes was one of the oldest gods in existence, but he still acted and looked like an eighteen-year-old boy. His light brown hair was perfectly curled around his head, his was skin completely free of blemishes, and his eyes were a sparkling, sky blue. He was dressed in jeans and a plain white T-shirt, but he was wearing his sandals with the gold wings on the side. Aside from the shoes, he looked remarkably human.

"This is not supposed to be *fun*," I seethed."The Hound of the Underworld is loose. Do you not understand the ramifications of that?"

Hermes rolled his eyes again. I suppressed the desire to hit him. In the body I was currently using, I would have been able to. It was more youthful than my true form, which was a hunch-backed old man. The body that Hades provided me was young and strong. It had olive skin, thick black hair, and violet eyes. It was wearing a long black shirt, black pants, and black combat boots. I was able to bring my trusted black skull tipped staff with me to earth. A weapon I had modified specifically for this mission.

I do not know what Hades did with the soul once I took the body, but it did not matter. We were on a very important errand, and I was forcibly reminding Hermes of that.

144

"I have two eyes, Charon," his lips twitched into a blinding white smile."I can see the dead people."

I shook my head and made myself keep walking. Hermes spent most of his time with mortals, and often spoke with their popular vernacular. As the ferryman for the dead, I was accustomed to hearing these manners of speech from the dead humans I took into the Underworld. Every time I did, I thought about throwing the soul off my boat into the River Styx.

But I needed Hermes to help me retrieve Hades's hellhound. He moved with speed and efficiency, skills that would be invaluable in retrieving the prized Hound of Hades. Hopefully the two of us would be able to lure the hellhound back to the Underworld without further loss of life.

Which, seeing the current trail of Cerberus's destruction, did not seem like an easy task.

We were walking through the ruins of Greece's capital city. White stone buildings were caved in and smashed to reveal their decimated insides. Rubble and blood covered the two narrow roads and the concrete median splitting them. Cars and trees were burning and tossed around the street. Thick, choking smoke curled up toward the dark night. The smell of death and blood was heavy and familiar to me. Screams filled the air as terrified humans charged down the street, trying to escape the city. The shredded corpses on the ground said nothing. Their souls had long since departed their bodies.

Luring Cerberus might not be simple, but tracking it would be.

In the distance, we could hear a low, echoing roar and the steady crack of gunfire. The humans were not prepared to deal with something like Cerberus, and they were defending themselves the only way they knew how. Regular bullets could not harm the Hound of the Underworld, and would only serve to make it angrier. But with that anger would come more bloodshed, and military action would be called for. If that situation arose, there would not be much we could do.

"We must move quickly," I told Hermes as I started jogging."We cannot let the humans further engage the Hound."

Hermes was the quickest of all the gods, and had no problem keeping pace with me."Since when did you start caring for the mortals, Charon?"

I narrowed my eyes, though my temper was rising."I do not," I admitted."I do have concern for the wrath of Hades should we not return his beloved Hound to him."

For once, Hermes didn't have an argument to offer. When Cerberus had accidentally broken free of its cage, eaten the minions feeding it, and made its way onto earth, Hades was devastated. More than that, he was embarrassed. He wasted no time in ordering us to retrieve the creature. It was too late to conceal the incident from the other gods, but Hades was not concerned with the displeasure of the Olympians. He would accept a just punishment once Cerberus was returned to the Underworld.

If it was not... well, neither Hermes nor I would be around to witness the trial.

As we ran further down the street, it became harder to avoid the screaming humans fleeing the path of the monster. They ran blindly, barreling over one another in an attempt to save their own lives. Most did not care if they trampled an unlucky person who had tripped and fallen.

The majority of the humans were shrieking with no care for words, but others were more articulate.

"Demon! It's a demon!"

"Where's my family? I have to find my family!"

"Help, someone, help!"

"Oh god, oh god, oh god!"

Hermes and I were the only ones who ran toward the madness. We were forced to shove many of the humans aside. It was tempting to use my staff and toss them away, but the amount of power I had on earth was limited. Even Hermes was running on both feet instead of flying in an effort to reserve as much energy as possible.

The greatest clamour was coming from the road on the left about sixty feet away from us. The apartments obscured my view so I could not see what was happening, but it indicated that we were close to Cerberus.

Humans were shouting orders and curses over the clustered chatter of their guns. Both noises stopped when Cerberus roared.

It was an enormous sound, like a clap of thunder during an earthquake. It echoed through the broken streets of Athens, made the cracked roads shiver, and shattered glass in the distance.

I had only heard Cerberus roar twice before this time. It was a sound I prayed I would never hear again. I am a servant of Death, and there is little that terrifies me.

Cerberus is one of those things.

I stopped running the moment I heard Cerberus's howl. Hermes stopped beside me, staring at the corner with wide, horrified eyes.

"All right," he admitted. "I'm taking this seriously now."

I did not waste time with a withering retort. I began a dead run and finally turned the corner to the street where the gunfire had been. Hermes lingered a little ways behind me. I stopped again when I laid eyes upon the beast.

Whenever I ferry a dead soul to the Underworld after receive them from Hermes, I pass by Cerberus's cage. No matter how often I see it, the sheer size and ferocity of the beast astounds me.

It was a thirty foot tall monstrosity that looked as if it had once been set on fire. Its body was charred black and cracked in some places to reveal raw, bloody flesh beneath it. The ridge of its spine stood out like small mountains. All four legs were thick and bulging with muscle and the paws were edged with four black claws that resembled those of a tiger. Its tail was about twelve feet long and covered in burned scales. On the edges of the tail were sharp, bony spikes as wide long and wide as my arm. A heavy shackle with three broken, dangling chains circled its necks.

Cerberus's back was to us, but I knew all too well what its three faces looked like. They were shaped in a similar fashion, with a pointed snout, pointed ears, three bloodshot eyes on each head, and pointed yellow fangs as thick as my leg.

There were subtle differences that could only be seen if one dares to look closely, or has to pass by the monster's cage every hour of every day for the last ten thousand years. The head on the right was missing its outer ear, nothing but an unprotected hole remaining on its head. The muzzle of the left head had a piece bitten off near the nose, exposing even more of the terrifying fangs. The centre head had a scar on its neck from a bite, and three claw slashes on its muzzle.

Cerberus was so volatile it could not get along with its other heads.

The beast could hardly fit in the narrow alley, its bulky body smashing into the brick buildings on either side of it, rubble and dust tumbling down each time. Flames billowed out of apartment windows. Snapped power-lines hung against the buildings like limp vines. Cars were either burning or crunched pieces of metal around Cerberus's feet. Bodies of unfortunate mortals were crushed to pulpy red smears close to the cars.

I was able to see a band of humans bravely standing their ground before the beast's terrible maws . From their fatigues and weaponry, it was clear that they were military personnel. The bullets hit Cerberus, but barely made it flinch. Even with its exterior burns, the Hound's flesh was tough to penetrate with a weapon. There were no tanks or larger machines of war, but they could not be far away. The harm they caused Cerberus would be far more severe.

The Hound was not aware of this. It dipped its head low to the ground, as if preparing to pounce. It drew in a huge breath like it was about to roar again. Instead, it opened all three of its mouths and belched an enormous blaze of fire. The flames were so bright that they painted the broken walls in orange and red. The screaming of the militants died quickly. Cerberus continued the fire even after they were ashes.

"Gods," Hermes breathed beside me. "Well, there's something you don't see every day."

I would have finally given into impulse and struck him if he had not sounded so terrified.

"We must draw it out of the alley," I said, never moving my eyes from the creature's back. "The previous street held two lanes for traffic past the median. That should provide us with enough space."

"To do what?" Hermes protested, looking at me with a shocked expression. "Did you bring a juicy bone for Yeller's deranged cousin there?"

This time I looked at Hermes and smiled. Even though I was in a new body, my smile was the same cold, malicious one that could strike fear into even the dead.

"I was thinking more along the lines of fetch." The smile faded from my lips. "You know what must be done?"

Hermes nodded. Before he sent us on this quest, Hades had provided us with his runes, which would subdue Cerberus long enough to return it to the Underworld. The rune was embedded into our skin, so all we had to do was touch the shackle on each head, and the spell would temper Cerberus.

The vexatious part of this plan was going to be getting close to the Hound, and not being eaten or set on fire by it.

"Take to the skies," I ordered Hermes. "I shall distract Cerberus to buy you time."

Hermes gaped at me, "Charon, that's insane! Did you take crazy pills this morning or something?"

I gripped my staff in both hands.

The glow from the fire began to fade as Cerberus relaxed its body. A deep growl built in its chest. It raised its head and began sniffing for its next prey.

"We do not have time to argue!" I shouted at my partner.

As the guardian of the Gates to the Underworld, Cerberus has excellent hearing. The moment I shouted, it began to twist its body around. The three red eyes on the left head found me, and narrowed angrily. Its lips trembled as it began to snarl. The other two heads were barking ferociously. They smelled something, but could not see it yet. Cerberus began turning, its tail snapping across the apartments and shops, sending debris flying in various directions. Its body was beginning to angle toward us, massive black shoulders moving through the caved in parts of the buildings it previously created.

Soon all three heads were facing us, the three chains under their jowels dangling over the road. I swung the black staff in my hands in a wide arc. A heavy black mist seeped out of the hollow eyes and mouth of the skull on the tip of my staff. Before departing, I placed some magic from the River Styx into my staff. Since the River is poisonous, I was able to release a thick black smog that would sting the eyes and open cuts on Cerberus. The poisonous cloud would not kill it, yet Hermes would have the chance to fly away unseen.

Cerberus stomped toward us, leaving deep impressions and cracks in the road.

For such a large creature, it was alarmingly quick. But then the left head stepped into the black smoke, and it stopped. The poisonous fog went into the left head's eyes, the crevices of its skin, and was inhaled through its nostrils and mouth. The result was instantaneous.

The left head thrashed even further left, straining its thick neck and smashing the back of the apartment behind it. The other two heads began snapping and snarling, pulling to the right and trying to get the left head to do the same. The left head barked savagely, snapping at the centre head. The centre head snapped back, nearly sinking its teeth into the muzzle of the left head.

I glanced at my accomplice. He frowned deeply, then sighed.

"Stupid is as stupid does," Hermes muttered.

He looked at Cerberus again, a serious look crossing his face. He bent his knees and then darted down the other end of the street. The shoes made him move so fast he was a blur to my violet eyes. He disappeared and I wondered how the shoes were going to help him crawl up onto Cerberus.

I quickly forgot about Hermes's plan, because the effects of the poison had worn off, and now Cerberus was seeking vengeance.

I turned on my heel and ran down the now vacated street. I ran as fast as I could, wishing I had a pair of Hermes's infamous shoes. It might have kept Cerberus away from me for a little while longer.

There was no need to turn and see if it was following me. I could hear the heavy pounding of its feet on the concrete, fracturing it with every step. The ground shook beneath me. The chains dragged heavily on the cement. Its shadow was stretching before me. I pushed myself harder, but Cerberus bellowed at me. The force of its breath crashed into my back like a gale wind.

I began to smell burning sulfur, and knew that Cerberus was about to unleash his wrath. I did not think about the damage my human body would endure. I simply looked at the median on my right with two unaffected trees, and hurled myself across it.

My smaller size made me just a little quicker in reaction than Cerberus, allowing me to escape the immediate blast of its fire. The rest of my action was less than ideal. I landed face first on the grass; dropping so hard the air was forced from my lungs. I did not bounce or roll, I simply landed flat on my chest and obtained a substantial bruise on my torso.

While I struggled to breathe again, the air behind me began to heat. I ignored the pain and forced myself to roll off the median onto the next street. Just as I landed on the concrete, the grass and trees burst into flames. I continued tumbling along until I was lying on my back next to a flattened, bloody corpse. I looked over my shoulder at the wall of flame. I gripped my staff and started to get to my feet, just as Cerberus stuck its heads through the fire. Instinct kicked in and I swept the front of the staff at the Hound's right head.

The smoke blanketed the right head, causing it to rear up and howl so loud I could feel the tremor in my chest. The centre and left heads continued to surge forward, trying to drag the right half of its body over to devour me. Just as I was about to begin running again, I noticed a small figure moving on Cerberus's back.

Sometime during my running, Hermes had zipped onto Cerberus. He was clinging to the ridges of the beast's bony spine, pulling himself along with the speed of a hummingbird. He managed to maintain his footing, and was suddenly upon the Hound's shoulders, nearly at the shackle by the left head.

Hermes placed his hand on the shackle, imprinting Hades's rune onto it. A thick black smoke circled the left head, fastening in place. The left head suddenly dropped, nearly pitching Hermes off. It was as if the left head just had a rock released over it. The chain under its chin slammed into the ground, making me jump back on instinct. The centre and right heads twisted to the left, craning their necks until they saw the tiny Hermes standing on their shoulders.

The small god did not panic as I expected. He sped for the centre head, reaching out to touch the shackle. Cerberus's spiked tail launched over its back, aiming to strike Hermes down. If it were not for his magic shoes, he would have been crushed.

Two things suddenly happened. Hermes touched the shackle of the centre head, placing the rune onto it and ordering it to submission. At the same time, the remaining two heads heaved to the right with too much force for Hermes. The god was whipped off of Cerberus's shoulders, spiraling through the air until I lost sight of him in the smoke and darkness.

Fear gripped my heart for a moment. I was hesitant to call Hermes a friend, but he was a familiar face. He provided decent conversation when he brought me souls to ferry across. He was the only being I saw who had been alive for as long as I had. He was in his immortal body, but I was not sure of the damage he might sustain from such a fall.

Cerberus's angry roar deflected my thoughts. I saw movement from the corner of my eye and backed away. The right paw lifted heavily and crashed down into the space I had been standing in. I jumped as the concrete shook, the heavy chain swinging back and forth mere feet from me. The other two heads were hanging uselessly now that the black smoke circled their necks, but the rest of Cerberus's body was moving perfectly well.

It completed its turn, its huge head filling my vision. Cerberus contorted its body until the tail was curled around to its right paw, cutting off my escape. I flicked up my staff, but Cerberus anticipated the move and titled its head back. The chain nearly crashed into my chest, but I stepped away in time. I hesitated as I looked at the dropping centre head, then took my chances.

I ran for the centre head, pressing myself against its neck. The centre head did not so much as flinch. Darkness consumed my sight and made me look over.

Cerberus's jaws were opened, and I was staring at my own death, the irony of which was not lost on me.

The cavern of Cerberus's mouth seemed to stretch endlessly, a dismal black circled with jagged fangs and carpeted by a blood red tongue. The smell was so putrid it burned my nostrils and flipped my stomach.

I did not have time to draw my staff across Cerberus's mouth. I had only time to react. I dropped into as low a crouch as I could, letting the right head of Cerberus sink its fangs into the neck of the centre head.

The sharp growl that erupted from Cerberus's throat was thunder to my ears. My gambit had almost failed. I was still pressed against Cerberus and felt his scratchy, torturously hot skin on my back and chest.

But I was in range of the final shackle.

There was barely any room to move, the air was humid and congested, and the scent of scorched flesh was making my eyes water. But I threw out my hand and touched the searing metal shackle.

Scalding pain filled my hand at first, and then I could feel Hades's icy cold magic spiral out from my heart. It shot up to my shoulder and down my arm like a rush of frozen water, yanking itself through my palm and filling the shackle.

Black smoke twined around my hand and circled the metal binding around Cerberus's throat. The Hound twitched suddenly, the movement throwing my hand away and pressing my back against the beast's harsh chest.

The spell was completed, however. The final head of Cerberus lolled to the side, hanging to its chest. There was pressure at my back, and it did not take me long to understand that Cerberus was tilting forward.

I jumped and raced through the tiny crevice of between the centre and left head. I stumbled out just as the right head *thunked* onto the ground. I twisted around, holding my staff in front of me in case the rune had not been effective.

Cerberus's heads were lying on the road, every shackle now covered in wispy black smoke. All eighteen eyes were staring blankly ahead, but the heads did not move. I put the blunt edge of my staff onto the road and slumped against it.

After this, I would be able to use my staff to draw Cerberus into a portal and back to the Underworld. For now, all I wished to do was rest my weary body. It amazed me that humans could endure a battering like that and survive.

There was a rustling on my right and I turned quickly.

Hermes had blood plastered on the side of his head and in his curly hair. His arm was scraped and bruised, part of his jeans torn from thigh to knee. His shirt was covered in dust and blood that did not appear to be his own.

His smile went from ear to ear.

"Out of sight, Charon!"

I amazed even myself by laughing. He annoyed me to no end, was abhorrently chipper, and was keen on reciting the most amusing phrase he could think of, but I was relieved to see that Hermes was alive.

He walked over to my side and looked at the submissive Hound. He whistled long and low.

"That's a sight I never thought I'd see."

"We do not know how far behind the human army is. We must begin transporting Cerberus back to its master."

"Roger."

Hermes took a step forward to assist with creating the portal, then looked over his shoulder at me. His grin was playful and eager.

"At least we don't have to worry about the Hound getting loose again. After all this, who'd let the dog out? Who, who?"

Avanc

by

D.J. Tyrer

Avanc

by

DJ Tyrer

THE MEDIA was referring to it as a 'perfect storm of a PR disaster'. Sir Lionel DeMauncy, Bart, Junior Minister for Energy Production was vowing that heads would roll as he wiped egg from his expensive suit. Not that he could quite understand what had gone wrong. Surely the people of the town with its ridiculous, unpronounceable name would be grateful to know their silly little town would solve England's looming energy crisis?

"Minister, do you seriously believe that fracking should be carried out in the vicinity of a nuclear power station?"

"Well, I..."

"Minister, do you recognize that you were not the best person to visit a Welsh former pit town, being a posh Tory who can't even pronounce Llandwrafanc?"

"Well, I..."

"And, Mr. Minister, was it advisable to make the sheep joke after being asked why these developments haven't led to local jobs?"

"Well, I..."

The questions kept on coming and he didn't receive a chance to answer, which was probably for the best given his performance so far.

Another egg came flying his way and he quickly ducked into his waiting limo. "Get me out of here!" he ordered his driver.

He couldn't wait to return to the sanity of London where nobody complained about what the government did to obscure, provincial towns.

Llynafanc had been a beauty spot before the great grey bulk of the nuclear power station was built and was still quite beautiful when you looked in other the directions. The lake and surrounding woods were upstream from the town of Llandwrafanc, but the slag heaps that surrounded the pit had never impinged upon it. Now, those heaps were gone, replaced by slag spreads filling streets and gardens thanks to the vibrations engendered by fracking.

It didn't matter that a powerboat and, at the far end of the lake, a pair of jet-skis were roaring across the water, removing the idyllic silence, for the din of the protests outside the power station had already ruined the calm. There were the usual opponents of fracking and nuclear power, and a whole slew more worried concerned about fracking nearby a reactor. Welsh nationalists and British nationalists were standing side-by-side to complain that the plant staff had been imported from China rather than being sourced locally. Then, there were the local conservationists worried that the power station threatened the newly-reintroduced family of beavers in the lake.

The noise didn't bother Bill Easton because he was listening to eighties pop on his iPod. He was sitting on an inflatable chair on a jetty, half-asleep, with a fishing rod clutched in his hands. Not that there was a hook on the line; he didn't see the point with catch-and-release. Instead, sitting like that was a ritual dating back to when he'd join his dad down at the canal on a Sunday morning, an escape. His wife and son were out on the powerboat, giving him a bit of a break.

Noticing the sun was starting to drop towards the west, he glanced at his watch. Time was getting on. He shielded his eyes and looked out across the lake; he couldn't see the boat. The jet-skis were being loaded onto a trailer along the shore. He popped the earphones out of his ears. There was no sound of the boat engine, although he could hear airhorns from the direction of the power plant.

"Odd," he murmured, fishing in his pocket for his phone. Natalie and Steve both had their phones with them. He tried both of them, but they went straight to voicemail.

Bill was starting to worry now. Where could they be?

He gave them another five minutes, tried their phones again, then called the police.

A short while later, a police land rover drove up and an officer climbed out. Quickly, Bill reiterated his worry.

"Are you sure they haven't gone back to your chalet?" the officer asked. They were renting a holiday chalet in the woods nearby.

"The boat isn't here and they aren't answering their phones."

"Well, let's got take a look, eh? Climb in."

They drove the half-mile up the track to a cluster of chalets, but the one they were staying in was locked and empty. The policeman knocked at the couple of chalets that had people in, but nobody had seen them.

"Okay," the officer said, "it seems they may still be out on the lake. I'm going to call the chopper in to take a look."

He made the call and then they drove back down to the jetty. There was something white out on the lake.

"Hey, what's that?" exclaimed Bill. "I think… Yes, it's the boat - it's overturned!"

"Oh, dear," said the policeman.

"Well, aren't you going to do something?"

"Like what? It's right out in the water."

"Swim out to it! Save them!"

"No fear! Health 'n' safety, you know. I'll call in for specialist help."

"But, that'll take too long!"

"Sorry, nothing else I can do..."

"Dammit!" Bill jumped into the water and began to swim out to the capsized boat, but there was no sign of his wife or son.

Taking a deep breath, he dived down underneath the boat, but they weren't there, not that he could see much in the murky waters. He groped about, to no avail. Surfacing, Bill swam back to the shore and climbed out, then collapsed.

"I have made a note of your reckless behaviour," the policeman told him.

Bill wished he had the strength to get up and punch the officious twit, but he wasn't the fittest of men and the swim had left him exhausted.

Laying back on the narrow band of pebbles that passed for a beach, Bill watched as a police helicopter flew overhead and made a few cursory sweeps of the lake before heading back south. Eventually, a search team arrived with an inflatable boat. They brought the upturned boat in and the Landrover's winch was used to drag it out of the water.

Pointing to an enormous chunk missing from the side of the boat, a policeman told Bill, "The boat obviously struck an obstacle, capsized and your wife and son drowned. Sorry."

Bill didn't think the man sounded sorry. He sounded bored. He couldn't believe what he was hearing.

"You don't know they're dead! You haven't even looked for them!"

"The chopper took a look and there was no sign of them. The lake is treacherous, bodies can get caught on underwater entanglements or sucked into hidden cavities below the banks. Sometimes they wash up, sometimes they never do."

"Then, you need to search, drag the lake, dammit! Do something!"

"Oh, dear, sir, we don't have the budget for that... No, the best you can hope is that they'll surface eventually. Right, well, we'll be off, then."

"That's it?"

"Sorry, sir. We just don't have the budget for anything else, I'm afraid."

Somehow, Bill had eventually managed to get some sleep. He'd stayed by the lake, staring out over the water hoping to see some sign of Natalie or Steve, but there was nothing. Exhausted, he'd stretched out on the jetty, using the chair, half-deflated, as a pillow. As he slept, he dreamt of his wife and son in the water somewhere, the ominous da-dum, da-dum of the *Jaws* theme playing as something stalked their dangling legs beneath the murky waters.

Bill woke with a start.

"You okay?"

He looked around in confusion and saw a figure looming over him. After a moment, he recognized it as one of the men who'd been out on the jet-skis.

"No, I'm not okay," he said, voice thick with exhaustion and loss.

"Oh."

"It's my wife and son..." He explained what had happened. "The police haven't done anything, haven't searched."

"That sucks... Hey! Can you ride a jet-ski?"

Bill yawned. "Sure. I rode one on holiday in Corfu once." That had been back before the downturn had made a staycation the best he could afford.

"Then, I think I can help you... My mate's got a gippy stomach, so I've got a jet-ski going begging, here... We could take a look around..."

"Really? You'd help me?"

"Sure, why not? Oh, by the way, my name's Doug."

"Bill." They shook hands.

"Right, well, help me unload them and we can get going. You hungry?"

Bill hadn't considered it, but realized now he was. "Uh-huh."

"No problem, I've got some energy bars in the car. Not much, and they taste awful, but they'll keep you going. Here you go."

"Thanks." He quickly ate them, not caring how they tasted, then helped get the jet-skis down and into the water.

They began to sweep the lake back and forth.

"You see that?" Bill called to Doug. "Bubbles."

"Yeah. I think that's from the fracking."

Bill wasn't entirely convinced. "Hey! Look!"

"What? I can't see anything."

"I thought... nothing."

"What?"

"It's nothing," Bill told him. "For a moment, well, I thought I saw something swimming below the surface."

"A fish."

"Something large."

"A big fish? A shoal of fish, perhaps."

"Yeah, probably. Or, maybe a log..."

A moment later, there was a loud crashing sound from the shore as if something huge were smashing through the trees.

"Jesus!" Doug exclaimed. "What was that?"

"I dunno. It was over on the far bank. Let's look."

They sped over and found an area where a number of trees had indeed come down, as if something enormous had passed by and shrugged them aside.

"Look," said Bill, "some of the trees look like they were... bitten by something. Something huge." He shuddered. "I think there's something in the lake, and I think it got my wife and son..."

"You might just be right..." Doug nodded, surveying the scene.

"Come on, let's get to the authorities."

That evening Bill was in a pub in town drowning his sorrows. Doug was with him, commiserating. The authorities had not only been uninterested in what he tried to tell them, but they'd treated it as a joke.

"Oh, dear me," the officer he'd spoken to had laughed, "you imagine you've seen the Avanc. I'm sorry about your family, but, oh, my!"

When he met up with Bill afterward, Doug had taken out his smartphone and searched for 'Avanc'.

"The Avanc, the Welsh usually spell it with an 'f', is a sort of water monster or ogre that lives in rivers and lakes. The lake here is named after it, as is the town, Llandwrafanc means 'Church by the Avanc water', meaning the lake, obviously. There's a legend that the Avanc here used to steal cattle and attack swimmers. They suppose it was the way they explained the undertow or whatever; it was notorious even then." Doug paused, chuckled. "Well, that's appropriate."

"What is?" Bill wasn't in the mood for levity.

"Avanc can also mean 'beaver', and the lake is where they've reintroduced beaver."

"How very convenient," Bill said, sarcastically, taking another gulp of beer. He was determined to get very, very drunk.

Bill had a pounding hangover the next morning, but refused to give up the search for his family. As long as there was a small chance they were still alive, he'd keep searching, and, if something had killed them, then he was determined he'd have his revenge. To that end, he'd rented another powerboat and fashioned a makeshift harpoon from a length of scaffold pole he'd 'liberated' from a building site. He really wished Britain had liberal gun control laws or he knew criminals who could get him a gun. He was half-convinced there was some sort of monster in the lake.

Doug was with him, a large, possibly illegal, hunting knife strapped to his side, and was steering the boat while Bill scanned the lake, harpoon in hand.

"Hey," exclaimed Doug, after they'd been skipping waves for a while, "I thought I saw something over there." He pointed.

Bill raised the harpoon, searching for it.

That was when the water exploded, the boat shot into the air and everything went black.

"Mr Easton, you've been unconscious for several days. Your boat overturned. I'm afraid your friend was killed, decapitated by the propeller blades. You are very lucky to be alive. Welcome to Cardiff, by the way."

Bill stared dumbly at the doctor as he left Bill's room. They'd made up their minds, created a narrative. He stood no chance of convincing the authorities about what had really happened, he was certain.

With one arm in a cast, his neck in a brace and veins full of morphine, Bill sought solace from the old TV hanging forlornly at the end of his bed.

"After the devastation that struck the town of Llandwrafanc, the village of Dinas T has been obliterated from the map."

The screen showed the remains of a dozen houses smashed as if they were matchwood and puddled with water.

"The authorities say that the damage was caused by a freak flood due to global warming, fully justifying their fracking of the region and the construction of a controversial nuclear power station, and not, as some of their detractors maintain, as a result of a localized tremor caused by fracking."

The image changed to show Sir Lionel DeMauncy, Bart, Junior Minister for Energy Production, at a press conference in London, saying, "It is all perfectly safe, let me reassure you. Indeed, these floods only serve to illustrate why we need more fracking and more nuclear power stations and less whinging from the Welsh. I am certain there is no danger."

Bill tried to laugh, then groaned from the pain. "Easy to say when you're nowhere near."

A map showed the relative positions of Llandwrafanc, Dinas T and Cardiff. Despite being rather drug addled, Bill realized that the cause of the devastation was coming downstream towards the Welsh capital. Flashes of memory showed an enormous black shape erupting from the water, great chisel-like teeth snapping, a frenzied thrashing. There *was* a monster, an Avanc, and it was headed this way.

It took him two more days before he was able to discharge himself. He was still in a bit of a mess and dosed up with painkillers, but he could walk and just about think. Another village, a hamlet called Croesdu, had been destroyed, confirming his suspicions about it coming downstream.

As his mind had cleared a little, the flashes of what he'd seen when the boat was overturned began to coalesce into an image he couldn't quite believe.

"A beaver?" He was certain that was what he'd seen, a gigantic beaver, yet he couldn't quite believe it. It seemed preposterous, and, yet... he'd seen it...

He began to wonder. There were beavers in the lake; he knew that for a fact. There was the power station on the shore of the lake and in every movie with giant, mutant animals, radiation was always was always to blame. But, that was the movies, did such things happen in real life? He'd heard nothing of giant beasts near Chernobyl going on the rampage but, then again, it wasn't as if these attacks were being accurately reported on the news. For all he knew, there could be dozens of monsters rampaging across the Ukraine without anyone realizing. Then, there was the franking, the protesters claimed it could cause the pipes or reactor to crack, releasing radiation. It all made sense, if a gigantic killer beaver could be said to make sense...

The authorities wouldn't believe him, he knew, and going to the media would probably result in public ridicule, if they even listened at all. He was the only person who knew what was happening, which meant he was the only person who could stop it...

"What did I do in a past life to deserve this?" he muttered as he jerry-rigged a set of scaffolding poles, purchased this time, into harpoons. At the very least, he would get his revenge.

Based on what little he knew of the mega-beaver's passage, he knew it would shortly be passing through a bend in the river that created a promontory called Y Pen Goch after its heavy red soil. Which was where he now was, sitting in a rusty folding chair, waiting.

"Finally," he said, standing when he spotted a dark shape and a wake approaching down the river towards him. He hefted a homemade harpoon, ready. He'd practiced with his weapon, luckily needing only the one arm to throw it as the other was still in a cast, until he was good at hitting the same spot with decent force again and again. "You're mine..."

The sleek dark shape grew closer. It was huge. Enormous. It looked bigger than a house. Even if fear and lack of comparison were causing him to overestimate its size, it was still bigger than a car. As it grew closer, he guessed his first estimate was probably right and began to doubt he could pull this off.

It was in range. At least it was a big target.

He hefted a harpoon and threw it; it glanced off the creature's spine, leaving a thin red line. It did, however, get its attention and the beast began to swim towards the promontory, towards him.

Bill threw a second harpoon, but missed. A third embedded itself in its shoulder and a moment later it burst out of the water, churning up the blood-red soil as it charged him.

It was almost on him. He held the harpoon as if it were a pike receiving a cavalry charge. It drove onto it, blood bursting out of its chest, and he thought he saw the light die in its eyes, but the momentum carried it on, burying the shaft ever deeper into its body.

Bill's last thoughts as it ploughed into him with all the force of an express train were a hope that he really had killed it, a sudden wondering whether any of the other beavers had grown to prodigious size and the question of what the authorities would make of the giant beaver when they found its corpse. A joke began to form in his mind, but he was dead before he could realize it, smeared deep into the bloody soil, with his family again at last.

Blood Run

by

Kerry G.S. Lipp

Blood Run
by
Kerry G.S. Lipp

"L OOKS LIKE they finally found us," Rose said, squinting through her binoculars. "We knew it'd happen sooner or later."

She offered the field glasses to Thomas who took a look for himself. The warm wind whipped across the top of the tower.

"Inevitable," he sighed as he watched dust rising off in the distance. Dust kicked up by giant feet. "Fuck."

"We're almost out of ammo, too," Rose said.

"That doesn't matter much. We tried to fight them with guns and rockets back in Pittsburgh. And we ended up here. We killed a couple, crippled a few more, but we couldn't stop them. They overran the city, ripped it to pieces. Ripped us to pieces," Thomas said, shaking his head, remembering that painful day, "We knew they wrecked the country, but we still didn't believe it," Thomas added, "We just didn't know how giraffes could be so dangerous."

"Well, they're mutated for one. They're three times the size of a normal giraffe."

"Yeah," Thomas said, "but we thought, so what? What's a fucking giraffe, even a huge one going to do? They usually aren't aggressive, they just eat leaves and shit and walk around. That's what we thought, until they ran amok and trampled the Pitt."

"I've heard what they can do but I never would've believed it."

"Believe it. They're lethal and with the vegetation mostly gone, they've developed a taste for meat. Human meat mostly, with the other animals so scarce."

"I can't believe they eat people," Rose said.

"That's not even the bad part," Thomas said. "They use their heads like wrecking balls, skulls like iron, and with their new size came enhanced bone structure and they can knock holes in the biggest buildings, shatter foundations and support pillars like snapping twigs. And their kicks? Jesus, I watched one kick an APC 200 yards. It shattered as it struck a building. Killed everyone inside, brought half the building down too. Nastiest fucking creatures I've ever seen."

"And firepower did nothing?"

"Not a damn thing."

"So what are we going to do?"

"The opposite of what we did last time."

Rose turned to look at Thomas - she didn't understand.

"We're already dead," Thomas said, "but I've got an idea. If we're lucky we might only lose half the settlement. We'll see. Let's get everyone together, we don't have much time."

Rose looked at the ominous dust rising on the horizon, looked back at Thomas, and started ringing the air raid siren.

People all around the settlement came running. Some carried children, others screamed, panicked, babbled incessantly that they couldn't believe this was happening. Some came carrying rifles, ready to go to war. Only a handful of them appeared to have seen the dust off in the distance and knew about the approaching threat.

Once they gathered, Thomas laid out his plan.

Like a war general commanding troops, he gave his orders with the air raid sirens howling in the background. Some tried to argue. Thomas shut them up. He'd faced off against the giraffes more than once and tried different things each time. He was one of few that had even engaged them in combat. This idea was all he had left. He didn't know if it would work, but he knew it'd work better than shooting the monsters with guns. If they tried that again, the creatures would storm the city in seconds. Eat them, trample them, and raze it all.

"We're going," he said and pointed to a group of settlers who came forward, Rose among them. "The rest of you know what to do. We're risking our lives, and we're all dead anyways, so make sure you do your part. We're going on a blood run so that we can take out the tower."

"The tower?" A young guy, Rory, who was leading the plan at the settlement, asked.

"That's what a group of giraffes is called. A fucking tower."

It might've sounded corny if their lives weren't on the line, in the crosshairs of hungry, stampeding giraffes.

Despite the cold fear induced at the blood-curdling siren and the oncoming storm, people sprang to action.

"Alright then," Thomas said to his crew. "Let's do this. This is our last chance to hold our defense. We've got nowhere to run but the ocean."

"This is our turf," Rory said, "and we ain't giving it up to no pussy bitch giraffes."

"Don't underestimate them," Thomas said.

"We won't, but we ain't never fought them this way before either."

Thomas nodded. "Let's go," he said to the chosen few around him.

They went.

"Do you really think this is going to work?" Rose asked.

"Actually," Thomas said, eyes on the road, "I do. If it doesn't, we're pretty much dead anyway. They'll overrun the city sooner or later, we're just making it happen on our terms instead of the theirs."

Rose nodded. "So what? We're just going to lure them back to the city?"

"Exactly," Thomas said. "It's an ancient war tactic called the blood run. You send a man or a small group out looking lost or hurt straight at the enemy. The enemy spots them, hunts them and the blood runners hightail it back to camp. Lead the enemy into an ambush."

"But we already know the giraffes are heading our way," Rose said.

"We do, but we need them to head our way at full speed, in a rage. Only way this is going to work."

"How long do we have?"

"From up in our high rise it looked like the tower was a ways out, but don't let that fool you. Giraffes are fast as shit, god knows how fast these mega-giraffes are."

"Fast as shit?" Rose asked and Thomas could hear the smile in her voice.

"Yep, the long necks can hit 35 or 40 miles an hour if they really want to. These bigger ones, probably faster."

"And how fast does this hummer go?"

"Max?" Thomas asked.

"Yes."

"Probably 60 or so."

"Christ," Rose said.

Thomas grinned, laughed like a lunatic, and gave the horn three blasts.

The two hummers on either side of him gave three answering honks, the gunners riding out the top flashed thumbs up followed by middle fingers in the direction of the tower.

Dust from the giraffes' hooves hung in the distant air like a foggy sandstorm. Thomas eased the accelerator as the caravan crested a hill and there, on top of the hill, they saw the enemy. Had to be at least fifty of them.

They looked innocent enough, trotting through the wasteland of what was the United States not that long ago. Giant heads atop more giant necks, their black tongues lolling out of some of their mouths like unrolled rugs. Their muscular legs supported their sturdy frame as their powerful hooves carried them across the plains. Their spotted hide covered their bodies in intricate patterns that would give you pause, captivate you, and make you stare like art. A few years ago you would've, happily stared in awe at the majestic, almost mystical creatures munching leaves from high trees. But now, stopping to enjoy the patchwork of their fur or their unique anatomy would get your head kicked right off your shoulders. And then eaten.

"Jesus," Rose gasped, "Look at those things. They've gotta be fifty feet tall."

"Can you hear them?" Thomas asked.

Rose looked at him.

"I'm serious. Roll down your window."

Rose did. At first only hear the distant air raid sirens. Then she heard the giraffes. First just the beat of their feet on the dry ground, but as she kept listening, she heard the... what were they? Honks? That wasn't quite right. The sound was high and shrill and almost mocking. Terrifying. She shuddered and raised the window.

"Yeah," Thomas said, "those noises only get scarier as we get closer. Imagine being holed up in a building with those fuckers beating down on you. And the sound they exhale as they ram their heads into buildings like artillery shells? Shit, that'll haunt my dreams forever."

"How did you survive?" Rose asked.

"Luck," Thomas said. "Glad we've got a little strategy on our side this time."

There was a long silence in the hummer barreled down the hill into enemy territory.

"You ready?" Thomas asked.

"Does it matter?" Rose said.

"Nope," and Thomas gunned the gas to the bottom as he blared the horn.

The other two hummers in the convoy kept pace and blasted their own horns. From the sunroof of both, two men emerged with assault rifles and started taking pot shots at the giraffes. Good ol' spray and pray.

The tower shrieked at all the noise and finally registered the hummers in their field of vision. They'd been looking much further into the distance. Several redirected themselves and picked up their trot as they dashed at the hummers.

Thomas slammed the brakes and jerked the wheel, the tires throwing stones and dirt. He reversed and had the big vehicle facing the opposite direction, back toward the settlement, within a couple seconds.

He lead-footed the gas pedal and the hummer's engine roared as it charged back up the incline.

"Well," he said, "we're half done. Too bad that was the easy part."

Rose didn't speak. Instead she white-knuckled the center console and the armrest on the inside of the door.

Thomas stared straight head, then glanced left and right and realized the other members of the convoy weren't there.

"Oh fuck," Rose screamed and spun backwards in her seat.

Thomas couldn't afford to stop or turn around or even look back, but he glanced into the rearview mirror and watched the horror unfold.

"Why the fuck did they wait?" he screamed and pounded the steering wheel. "Those mother fuckers. Goddammit."

Rose did not know if he spoke about the giraffes or the other hummers.

She faced out the back window and watched the carnage as the stampeding giraffes caught up to the other hummers and made short work of the large metal vehicles. Rose had heard all the stories of the chaos and violence the giraffes were capable of, but she'd never witnessed it. What she watched was a million times worse than the stories she'd heard.

The hummers had pretty much stopped, either fear from the driver or a vehicle malfunction, but the brave gunners didn't retreat. One giraffe, about as fast as a flash of lightning, shot his head down and chomped off the top half of the gunner, chewed a couple times and swallowed. Rose saw the bugling torso as it slid down the giraffe's massive throat. The gunner's lower half slid back into the hummer. The giraffe licked its lips and then it swung its head.

The comparison to a wrecking ball wasn't quite accurate. The giraffe's head hit much harder than that. The giant beast whipped its neck and smashed its head into the hummer. Glass blew out and the vehicle catapulted fifty feet in the air and god knows how far it actually flew before it landed on its top crushing the two others inside.

The other hummer had the same shitty luck. A different giraffe put its front feet straight through the windshield stomping bloody holes into the crew riding inside. With a minor stroke of luck, the giraffe tangled its feet up in the shattered windshield and lost its balance trying to free itself. It went down like a sack of hammers.

Thomas struggled to keep control of the car as the giant giraffe's downfall shook the ground like an earthquake.

The other members of the tower didn't pause to help their fallen member. They trampled over him, crushing him under their massive hooves as they chased the hummer that carried Rose and Thomas as they lead the blood run.

The road rocked beneath them as they topped the hill and now the city settlement was in sight.

They better be ready, Thomas thought, gripping the steering wheel hard enough to hurt. The shaking ground made the wheel jerk in his grasp, but he held steady.

"Faster, faster," Rose demanded still staring out the back window. "They're closing in."

"Pedal is all the way down. I press any hard and my foot is gonna go through the fucking undercarriage."

The thundering stampede hurtled after the hummer and their shrill squawks were enough to freeze blood.

With the front wheels of the hummer finally on the other side of the hill, Thomas commanded Rose to face front and buckle up. She turned and strapped herself in. Thomas didn't ease his foot of the gas at all as the hummer throttled itself at breakneck speed down the hill.

He chanced a glance in the rearview mirror and saw the first of the herd topping the hill. True, the hummer would move faster down the hill, but so would the tower.

Maybe they would trip.

They didn't trip.

Rose couldn't face forward anymore. She stayed strapped in but craned her neck. "Fuck Thomas, they're all over us! What are we going to do?"

"Win," he said, "We're almost there. Let's hope they did their job."

The giraffes were running almost even with them now. They could've trampled the hummer but they didn't. Probably remembered what happened to the one a few minutes ago. Instead, Rose screamed as she saw one start to swing its neck. *Like we're the golf ball and its head is the driver*, she thought.

"Almost there," Thomas said.

"Go Go Go," Rose yelled.

Thomas guided the wheel perfectly between two massive buildings on the outskirts of the settlement. The giraffes broke off. Some followed dead on, others went on different paths as the countryside turned to city streets.

The hummer jetted straight through to the middle of town and the giraffes followed, but they followed in two pieces. Headfirst.

Thomas parked the hummer inside the safe zone and told Rose to get out and run. To get to cover. They both dove out their doors just as the giraffe's head came crashing down on the hummer. Glass burst out like a bomb went off inside and the giraffe's neck stump, at least 6 or 7 feet of it oozed blood out both ends. It's eyes closed and it let out a squishy cry as its tongue flopped out of its mouth.

"Holy shit," Rose said. "What the hell was that?"

Thomas started to answer but another crash rocked the ground. Then another. Giraffe heads pelted the earth like a meteor shower.

"Get to cover," he yelled and together he and Rose ducked into a nearby office building.

They made it to the basement where Rory waited with a giant grin on his face.

"It worked?" he asked.

"It's working," Thomas said. "Hopefully it continues to work."

"I can't believe it. Razor wire, you smart son of a bitch," Rory beamed and offered his hand.

Thomas looked down, but then shook it.

"What?" Rory asked.

"The others didn't make it," Thomas said.

It was Rory's turn to look down.

"Any chance they'll make it back?" Rory asked.

Thomas shook his head.

"We watched them die," Rose said, and wiped away a tear.

With the adrenaline gone, reality burrowed itself back in and the commune mourned the loss of six good men and women.

"We must honor their sacrifice," Thomas said.

Rory and Rose agreed. They sat huddled together with some others. Thomas and Rose told them what happened. After half an hour or so, things above grew eerily quiet.

"It sounds like it's over. Let's head topside and see what we can see," Thomas said.

"Yeah," Rory said.

"Look, I know they're dead and it could've just as easily been me and Rose, but we all agreed to go on the blood run. We knew the risks, now we've got more work to do. They made the ultimate sacrifice and we must honor that."

The three of them ordered everyone else to stay inside the basement of the office building. They emerged to find a lot of dead giraffes. Most of their heads were cut clean off. A few of them were stuck, half cut off and dying slowly, being strangled by razor wire. Blood poured from the severed stumps and deep lacerations, open mouths. The blood ran in the streets, dripped from the wire and washed itself down the sides of several buildings.

On the other side of the wire several decapitated giraffes lay sprawled in obscene directions. Some plopped over with dead legs dangling. Others lay propped on three legs like an awkward, bloody tripod. Only a few giraffes remained outside the city fortifications. They were angry, and somehow Thomas could sense their sadness as they wandered around trying to figure out what happened and mourning the loss of 90 percent of their tower. They could see far and wide, but couldn't register the thin wire that brought their tower crashing down.

Considering the massacre he saw and the confused giraffes wandering around, Thomas almost sympathized. Almost. But then he remembered what happened in Pittsburgh and knew that the giraffes felt nothing as they wrecked his town and took from him everything he loved.

170

One giraffe let out a sad bellow as it studied its headless comrade.

"Fuck you," Thomas yelled and gave it the finger.

Rose laughed.

"So what do we do now?" Rose asked. "How are we going to get rid of the other ones?"

"Hopefully they'll just eventually run away," Thomas said.

"Yeah, I don't want to fight them," Rory said.

"But are we safe for now?"

"You've got razor wire lined all around the city right?" Thomas asked Rory.

"Sure do," Rory said, "Even got plenty to spare if we need to put up more. Some of it looks bent by the...um...impact. We can go check it all in a bit."

"So we're protected?" Rose didn't look convinced.

"Chill Rose, giraffes can't limbo," Thomas said and the three of them burst out laughing.

Rose relaxed.

"So what do we do now?" Rory asked.

"We go get everybody, we let them know it's safe and we bring them out here. Then we start cutting them up."

Rose and Rory gasped.

"What?" Thomas said. "Have you seen what's out in this wasteland? It's full of cannibals and raiders and wild animals. We've got a great fort here, but our food won't last forever. If we work hard for a day or so we can have enough meat to last us damn near forever."

"That's a good point," Rose said.

"Mmmmm giraffe burgers," Rory said, "looks like we're grilling out tonight!"

Thomas smiled, "Then let's get busy."

Over the next couple hours the settlers at the encampment came together to harvest the giraffes. Much like the Native Americans, they didn't waste any part of the majestic animals. They saved the fur to fashion clothes and blankets. The meat to eat. The bones for a purpose that would be determined later. Some of the children played catch with giraffe eyeballs. If they lost one, there were plenty more in a big barrel.

When they were down to only four giraffe heads left to harvest Thomas stopped them.

"Don't touch those," he commanded and the people stopped. They listened to Thomas, respected him. He was the closest thing they had to a leader, a king, a general.

"Why not?" Rory asked.

"We're going to use those to protect us from all other threats," Thomas said.

"How can those..." Rory started.

Rose swallowed hard. She knew.

"That's awful," she said.

"I know," Thomas said, "but we're living in a new world. It's the Wild West all over again. We put those heads on spikes around the town and we can show animals and people alike that we took down the threat. It will protect us. Either get people to leave us alone or respect and fear us during whatever interactions we may have."

"I know you're right," Rose said, "but it still makes me sick."

"Me too," Thomas nodded.

Rory didn't speak, he just looked around at the abandoned city now inhabited by their flock, their herd, their *tower*. The survivors in this mad new world. He looked at all the blood and the people harvesting the giraffe carcasses that lined the streets. A few surviving giraffes bellowed off in the distance.

"Our protection came with a price," Thomas said, "And we can't forget that. It cost of several of our own and three of our best vehicles."

"And our innocence," Rose said, watching the children play dodgeball with giraffe eyes.

"A price that will pay dividends in the end. We must guarantee that," Thomas said.

No one said anything for a few moments. Then Rory clapped his hands together and said, "I'll bring the crane around," then disappeared.

A few minutes later, Rory approached with the giant piece of machinery. The hollowed out settlement had plenty of vehicles and technology left intact, but those resources wouldn't last forever.

It took a long time, but they hoisted the giraffe heads and placed them at the four corners of the settlement. Even on the side by the sea, just in case anyone approached that way.

Thomas and Rose recruited a few others to help guide the large, heavy necks down on the impaling spikes and in no time, dead mutant giraffes heads flew like flags, long black tongues flapping in the breeze.

They returned to the town square where people celebrated and the smell of cooking meat made all of their mouths water. They'd eaten nothing but canned goods and boxed meals for months now.

The carcasses had been skinned and thinned of meat, a feast cooked and the rest of the meat treated or stored. The day's work was done. Several days' work, actually. Everyone was tired, everyone was hungry, and everyone was triumphant.

Rory wiped sweat from his brow and asked, "So chief, what now?"

"Now we eat, and we relax," Thomas said, and looked to the four corners of the city sporting giraffe heads. Some blood still dripped from the severed necks.

"And we watch the blood run."

The Devil's Avatar

by

Michael Thomas-Knight

The Devil's Avatar

by

Michael Thomas-Knight

CORBIN CAME upon the small cinder-block building as his Jeep Cherokee crested the hilltop. The structure looked odd in this rural area, nestled among the trees and craggy mountain rock formations jutting from the roadside. If Roger had summoned him to the lab to mend their partnership, he was smoking too much of his own homemade hashish. Corbin was done with Roger, with all his secrets and his backstabbing.

Roger's intern had called Corbin, telling him to pick up his belongings.

"You can come pick up your stuff," Jarrell had said.

Even through the phone Corbin could feel Jarrell holding back, wanting to tell him something, but not releasing his secret. Corbin knew there was more to this visit than an electron microscope and some books on ancient texts. He held great suspicions about Roger's motives, but wanted his items back. Most of all he didn't want Roger using his things and gaining any benefit from items he owned. However, he did concede a faint tinge of curiosity surrounding his visit.

He parked and exited the vehicle. From this vantage point he could see the whole town of Windham in the valley. He knocked on the door and Jarrell let him into a small reception area. Old chairs with torn upholstery and white wear spots crowded the small room. Beyond a wooden desk was another door leading to the lab. Why an archaeology major needed a lab in the mountains, escaped Corbin's comprehension. Jarrell buzzed with excitement as he poured himself fresh coffee from a brand new coffeemaker.

"You want a cup?" Jarrell asked.

"No, I'm good," Corbin said.

"I'm so glad you came. I think you're going to be amazed," Jarrell said.

"Don't get your hopes up, Jay. I told you, me and Roger don't work together anymore."

Jarrell sat on the edge of the desk and took a sip of coffee. "Yeah, I wanted to ask you about that...if I'm not being too nosey."

"No, I'm not the one with secrets. I'd be glad to tell you. Roger kept hitting on Gwen. I had told him several times to stop, that Gwen was not interested, but he wouldn't relent. Then last month, he ran into Gwen at Rusty Pete's. He was drunk and he tried to force himself on her."

Jarrell gazed at Corbin, not understanding.

"He attacked her," Corbin said.

Roger entered the room catching the last part of the conversation.

"I did not attack her. Besides, what Corbin fails to mention is how he stole Gwen from me in the first place."

"I did not steal Gwen, Roger, and you know that."

Corbin turned to Jarrell, wanting to explain further. "We both met her at the same party and she made up her own mind about who she wanted to date." He nodded in Roger's direction. "Someone's just a sore loser," he said.

Roger mumbled under his breath, gritting his teeth.

"What's that?" Corbin asked. It was clear the two men were getting agitated with each other.

"Not a loser," Roger said, clearing his throat. "Just not a winner...yet."

The men paused, with nothing more to say to each other.

Corbin spoke first. "I'm only here to collect my belongings."

"Fine, then get your stuff and get out."

Roger opened the door and Corbin stormed into the back room. He stopped short when he saw what was in there.

A machine from a time before machines, made of stone, copper, and brass, obscured the south wall of the lab. It was an alchemist's imagination set loose upon the physical world. Three petrified sarcophagi were lined with copper planting. Copper wire led to coils along both sides of each box, each coil progressively larger and set upon progressively larger gear mechanisms. Affixed to the foot of the middle sarcophagus was a brass plate impressed with an ancient German writing.

The parts had been excavated from a site in northern France some years ago. On loan from the University of Iowa and the Michigan Museum of Old World Cultures, these thought to be unrelated artifacts were assembled into one monstrous contraption, a mysterious relic of the Bronze Age. Corbin could not fathom what the device was or its application.

"What is this, Roger? Did you transcribe the inscription?"

Roger stepped up, admiring his own work. "Loosely translated, The Devil's Avatar," he said.

"The top half looks like a transmitter of some sort, but I don't understand. Copper wires for conductivity, but there's no energy source," Corbin said.

Roger laughed. "Come now, Corbin, the source is obvious in its design. You just fail to comprehend it."

"Wait, the excavation was dated, 1200 AD. There were no conductive energy sources at that time."

"So we were led to believe. Keep looking, it's painfully obvious."

Corbin absorbed the sight of the artifact. His eyes were wide as he struggled to understand. It was revealing its secret slowly, but Corbin was having trouble unhinging his own preconceptions. He walked to it and touched the middle sarcophagus. The gruesome idea sparked in his head.

"It's the sarcophagus, isn't it? It transfers energy from a dying person?"

Roger smiled and pulled on his goatee. He liked seeing Corbin squirm to comprehend things, especially things that came so easy to him. "You are half right, Coby, but what would a dead man need energy for? This machine transfers energy from a living person."

Corbin looked at him, astonished.

Roger continued, "Each coil stack magnifies the energy to the tenth power. That's an enormous amount of energy, but where does it go? It runs in series to the top of the machine and then what? Is it transmitted into the air?"

Corbin's excitement waned. He saw a flaw in this impossible contraption. It was impossible. That should've been Corbin's first suspicion, twentieth century science and knowledge imposed upon relics of yesteryear. Corbin began to feel foolish; he realized he was being duped. Now he wondered if Roger was purposely trying to deceive him or if he was delusional. Corbin admitted it took quite an imagination to assemble these random artifacts into something so impressive, but random and unrelated they were. The proof was high on the mechanism, a stone and brass plate that acted like a car distributor cap. Clear markings inscribed its surface and they were Egyptian, not Germanic. The excitement drained from Corbin like the stale air from a badly sealed balloon.

Roger began a story, perhaps a tale that would conclude with a pitch for research dollars. Roger was a swindler, a shyster, a carnival charlatan, looking to bait his next mark.

Corbin made a gentle turn from the machine and walked to a bench. He opened a plastic case with foam cushion cut-outs and began to dismantle his microscope.

"This machine and the science behind it was pre-Black Plague. Unfortunately, when the plagues ravaged the land killing seventy-five percent of the population on earth, all the knowledge of these older sciences was lost," Roger explained.

Corbin continued packing, placing lenses into the corresponding slots in the foam-guarded case. Roger barely noticed, continuing with his oration. Jarrell listened intently; obviously this was the first time hearing Roger's theory.

"Do you know the biggest cultural difference between pre-plague and post-plague culture?" Roger asked.

Corbin snapped the locks on the microscope case and pulled a second case out from under the bench. Without looking at Roger he offered a half-hearted answer. "I don't know, the advancements in war strategies?"

"Wrong," Roger said. "The biggest shift was in the kind of legends and stories told. After this great loss of knowledge, there were no more legends of giants or dragons. No one witnessed any more trolls or ogres. There were no longer tales of griffins or three-headed dogs. The monsters were gone."

"And this is important why?" Corbin asked.

"Because, my dear Coby, this machine is the missing link."

Corbin was not impressed and closed up a second case packed with carbon dating supplies, slides, chemicals and test-tubes, used in determining the age of relics. He pulled the case angrily from the bench top and turned to his ex-partner. "Roger, you're a clown!" he said.

Jarrell turned to Corbin, his mouth agape, and his brows rose. Unlike Corbin, he believed every word of Roger's theory and wasn't prepared for Corbin to question Roger's authority.

Roger pursed his lips and raised one eyebrow in dramatic fashion. "A clown, eh?"

"You expect me to believe this ranting, asinine, fairy-tale of yours; a hodge-podge of unfounded assumptions. If you're going to make up a tall tale, keep it closer to historical facts. I don't believe it or your fantasy, Frankenstein contraption," Corbin said.

"I guess I have no choice but to show you its powers."

"Do whatever the hell you want, but just count me out. I don't have time for this charade."

Corbin left the lab with his microscope case. Outside, the bright sun caused him to squint. He opened the back door of his jeep and set the case flat on the carpeted floor. When he returned to the lab room, Roger was naked and climbing into the main sarcophagus.

Corbin ignored him and went to a bench with drawers, emptying them of books and spiral notebooks. He grabbed a bag and packed the materials in it. He stepped up to a desktop computer, removed wires from an external hard drive, and placed the drive in a cardboard box.

As he packed other items in the box, Jarrell slid up beside him and spoke in a low tone. "Corbin, we should stop Roger from trying this machine on himself. We don't know what it does."

Corbin blew air through his lips, disgusted at Jarrell's naïveté.

"Jarrell, the machine is a farce. Roger made it up in his mind and slapped it together with wires and screws. It does nothing. The components aren't even from the same time periods."

"Really?" Jarrell asked.

"Yeah, the cup thing at the top is Third Dynasty Egyptian, the stone gears are seventh century Chinese and the turbine mechanisms are probably from the 1800s."

Roger interrupted. "Don't listen to his weak opinions, Jarrell. I'll make a believer out of him and Gwendolyn, too."

Corbin turned to Roger sitting naked in the coffin-box. "Rog? Go fuck yourself!"

Roger lay back, disappearing from view. Corbin folded the flaps on the cardboard box, lifted it, and grabbed the bag with the other hand.

"I'll be right back for the rest of my things. If you want a ride into town then, let me know," Corbin said to Jarrell.

As Corbin was on the way out, Roger chanted some gibberish. Corbin shook his head in disbelief.

Outside the skies had turned overcast and dark clouds swirled above the mountainside. Corbin rearranged items in the back of his jeep to fit snug so they wouldn't bounce around driving down the mountain road. He heard the crackling of leaves off to his right side and backed his head out of the Jeep. He looked through trees lining the dirt driveway. He expected to see a deer or some other animal in the clearing, but it looked quiet. The air was still, no breeze, but he saw the tall reeds sway in several places. He followed the movement, his eyes jumping from one place to another. The unnatural movement sent a chill down his back and the hair on his arms stood at attention. Someone grabbed his shoulder from behind and he jumped. He spun around with his fists raised for protection.

"Sorry, didn't mean to scare you," Jarrell said.

"Jeez, you really got me good." Corbin held his hands to his chest, feeling his own heartbeat.

"I think you should come inside, something is happening."

Corbin glanced back at the clearing, saw nothing unusual, and then headed to the lab. Jarrell followed close behind him.

At the front door Corbin stopped. He turned to Jarrell. "Jarrell, you look like a smart kid. I want to give you some advice. Don't hitch your wagon to Roger. I used to think he was a genius, but it's all a bluff. He lives in a fantasy world and if you fall into his trap, it will ruin your chances for a real career. Do you understand what I'm saying?"

"Yeah, I think so."

"And I'm not doing this to hurt Roger. I'm doing this to save you from the mistakes I have made. Roger thinks he's going to make some great discovery that will make him rich and famous one day. He bends truths to fit his goal and he's getting increasingly further from reality. He'll do anything to get people to support his fantasy."

"I understand what you're saying, Corbin, but something is *really* happening in there."

"I'll get to the bottom of this," Corbin said, and entered the lab.

Blue lightening engulfed the mechanism. Corbin stopped short, taken aback at the loose energy in the room. The machine produced a loud whine that increased in tone and volume. He inched his way to the coffin-box to look at Roger. He cupped his hands around his mouth and yelled to him.

"Roger, how do you turn this off?"

Roger's eyes rolled up into his head, showing only whites. Corbin attempted to reach into the box and a violent jolt knocked him clear across the room. Jarrell ran to his side and helped him up.

"Damn, that's one powerful electromagnetic field."

"So the machine is working?" Jarrell asked.

"No. This must be plugged in somewhere, set up to feed the illusion. We have to shut it down before Roger kills himself," Corbin said. "Look around the back of the machine for a wall outlet."

Both men looked for an energy source but found none. The machine's whine increased its pitch, deafening the two men. Corbin had to yell just to be heard.

"Where are the circuit breakers?"

"Front wall," Jarrell yelled, pointing to the metal box.

Corbin flicked every switch to the *off* position. The lights winked out, the computer screen saver went off, and the telephone on the wall lost its LED, but the machine continued. Corbin stared in disbelief, letting the information sink in.

"Now what?" Jarrell asked.

Corbin ran to the work bench, grabbed a small axe and swung it down upon the machine. The axe blade snapped back, deflected by the swirling electric, and flew from his hands. Jarrell ducked and the axe went whizzing passed his head. It crashed into the cinder block wall and stuck there. The earth rumbled, shaking the walls of the lab. Loose items tumbled to the floor and the glass in the south wall windows cracked in their frames. Jarrell heard the snapping of tree branches outside. He ran to the window and peered through the broken glass. Trees were crashing to the ground and the earth was pushing upward.

"Corbin," Jarrell shouted, "Something strange is happening outside!"

Both men ran through the front door and out to the driveway. Trees were down along the path. They moved to higher ground behind the lab. Standing upon a rock formation enabled them to see the meadow clearly. Something had surfaced, pushing its way through the high grasses.

A solid object rose as dirt fell from its folds and boulders the size of car engines were tossed in the air and sent rolling down the mountainside. Corbin couldn't make out the nature of the object. Colors; white, red, blue, and green, blurred in the rising motion. An appendage rose and hinged forward, planting a firm footing on the hardened earth in front of the birthing area. Corbin could see what it was clearly, though it took a moment to register that a giant blue shoe had risen from the ground. The appendage straightened and another leg was pulled from the meadow dirt, this one wearing a pink shoe with blue stars. With both feet free, it continued forward, heading down the mountainside. It was a football field away before the men realized a giant clown had climbed out of the hole in the meadow. The clown crashed through a line of trees getting a good view of town. It paused for a moment and called out.

"Gwendolyn!"

The voice, although two octaves lower, was Roger's voice.

Corbin ran into the lab, followed closely by Jarrell. The machine had settled into a steady hum making the lab much less chaotic. He pulled at his shirt, popping all the buttons and sending them flying in all directions. Jarrell grabbed him by the shoulder, attempting to stop him.

"Corbin, what are you doing?"

"I'm going after him. I have to stop him."

"How do you intend to do that?"

"That monstrosity is obviously an extension of Roger, somehow brought to life by this machine. We can't stop the machine so I'll have to fight Roger on his own terms." Corbin unbuttoned his cuffs and removed his shirt.

"Okay, but let's come up with a plan that will work."

"He's going after Gwen. I don't have a minute."

"So what are you going to go after Roger as? What will be your avatar?"

"What are you saying?"

"I'm saying Roger chose a clown because you called him a clown. You have to choose a form, a physical manifestation."

"Why can't I just go as myself?"

"I don't think it works that way. It says Devil's Avatar. I think you have to choose."

"You might be right."

Corbin undressed slowly, thinking things through. He unbuckled his pants.

Jarrell added some additional thoughts. "He's halfway down the mountain already and by the time you form an avatar, he'll already be in town. You might want to be something with wings so you can fly above and find them."

"I don't think a bird will be able to fight Roger."

"Not a bird. This was used in ancient times, I was thinking more like a dragon."

"How will Gwen know it's me if I'm a dragon?"

Corbin removed his shoes, socks and pants while forming a plan. "How big do you think that clown was?" he asked.

"I'd say fifty feet."

"You know that big statue on Route 66? How big do you think that is?"

"About forty feet," Jarrell said, but realizing what Corbin was getting at he added, "But it has an axe!"

"Do you think it'll work?"

"It's worth a shot. If the machine allows you, you would take over the statue at about the same time that Roger reaches town. You'll be right there to stop him."

"See if there are any excavation explosives in the road cases and rig the lab to blow. When we get back, we'll destroy this machine so no one ever uses it again."

Corbin jotted Gwen's number down on a piece of paper and handed it to Jarrell. "Call Gwen and warn her about what's coming." He removed his jockeys and climbed into the first sarcophagus. "What did Roger chant when he was in the box?"

"It was pig-Latin. He was just stating his intentions to the machine, or perhaps to himself."

"Could it be that simple? Wish me luck." Corbin laid flat in the box.

"I intend to take over the Paul Bunyan Statue on the east side of town and make it come to life under my control. Then I plan to save Gwen and stop Roger from hurting innocent people." Corbin closed his eyes.

Within seconds, the turbines alongside Corbin's sarcophagus began to buzz and spark with energy.

Officer Frank Helen was stuck in the 'rookie of the month' club, a training match-up that partnered newbies with experienced men in the department. Frank was a tough cookie and everyone called him Helen, just to get under his skin. It didn't bother him at all, not nearly as much as having to hold hands with a rookie through thirty days of patrol car duty. The young punk he was hitched with this month was the worst to date. Billy-Bob Drayton was the kid's name. Everyone called him Bilbo for short, and Helen couldn't believe the dimwitted kid ever made it into the force. They were pulling away from Marge's Coffee House with fresh java when they got the call.

"Forty-nine from dispatch." "Go, dispatch."

"Helen, we got a call from old-man Hanley. He said some clown let loose his goats and cows and chased them into Route 40."

"Probably some prankster kids, we'll check it out, Sue."

"Roger that. How's that rookie working out?"

As if to answer the question, the FM radio blasted 'on' at high volume, filling the car with dance beats and electronic sounds. Helen jumped in his seat, surprised by the loud outburst and he smacked the rookie's hands away from the radio knobs. He shut off the music.

"Damn it, Bilbo, I told you not to play that hip-hop crap in the squad car while we're on duty."

"Hip-hop? Hip-hop is music they use in cereal commercials and advertisements for Wal-Mart. I listen to Dub-step."

"Whatever the hell it is, leave the God damn radio alone or you'll be double steppin' your ass back to the station by foot." Helen realized he was still holding the radio mic pinned, and finished up with Sue at dispatch. "Yeah, Sue, we're coming up on the west edge of town now."

"Roger," Sue said, trying to hold back a giggle.

Helen made a left onto West Windsor Drive, where the buildings thinned out leading up to Route 40. The first thing he witnessed was a brown and white goat running full steam up the road at them. Helen swerved to miss the wild-eyed goat, only to see two bovine and a white-tail deer not far behind.

"What in jumpin' Jehovah is going on?" Helen said.

Helen pulled the car to the side and let the animals pass. Bilbo turned his head with each passing animal, giving a "Whoa!" for each one. Helen kept his eyes ahead, where Route 40 crossed Windsor, and where the tree line on its far side signaled the upward slope of Munser Mountain. He witnessed some unnatural movement along the treetops. One lone car moved along Route 40. Call it a cop's intuition or Murphy's Law, but Helen knew something bad was about to happen. He opened the car door and stood up to get a better sense about his feelings. He could see it clearly, treetops moving and shaking in a direct line to intersect with Route 40, and the small blue car racing toward the meeting point.

A large bull moose broke the tree line and crossed over the 40 to gallop up Windsor, but Helen looked beyond it, to the inevitable cataclysm that was about to occur. Like watching a child spill milk and not being able to stop it, Helen could do nothing as the next few moments unfolded. A giant figure crashed through the trees sending branches sailing in all directions. The blue car jammed on the brakes and pitched sideways as a large shoe cut off passage down Route 40. The giant... whatever... it was still inconceivable to Helen at that moment, lifted its other big shoe and stamped down on the vehicle causing it to explode; a fireball blooming into the sky. The giant thing moved away from the fire.

Helen turned away and rubbed his eyes before looking back at the surreal sight. A giant clown with a powder-blue costume, white ruffles, and a big painted smile that revealed sharp yellowing teeth, stomped up West Windsor toward the police cruiser. The moose darted off the road. Then Helen witnessed the damn rookie running toward the giant clown from the right side of the road, gun drawn and screaming commands at the top of his boyish voice. He shot three rounds that echoed off the mountainside.

"Bilbo, NO!" Helen screamed.

It was too late. The clown's white-gloved hand reached down and seized Bilbo. The rookie screamed in pain as his ribcage was crushed. Bilbo took one last shot as the clown studied his captive and hit the clown in the left eye. It exploded like a blood-filled balloon. The clown screeched in pain, then bit Bilbo in half. Bloody entrails strung from the clown's mouth to Bilbo's lower torso in the clown's meaty white hand. He threw the bottom half away, then spit Bilbo's half-chewed chest and head onto the road.

Helen grabbed his shotgun from the car, checked to see it was loaded, and then pulled the radio mic to its full length as he stood behind his open car door for protection.

"Sue, this is Helen. I need back up support with shotguns, barricades, tear-gas... Bilbo is dead, this is a Code-9 emergency situation..." Helen's voice was frantic, unlike his usual cool, gruff demeanor.

"Roger that. How many back-up units did you need?" Sue asked.

"All of them," Helen yelled.

Helen took two shots at the giant looming over him and then a giant pink shoe flattened him and the patrol car.

Sue heard something about a Code-9 emergency, and an officer down. She heard gunshots and then she heard Helen scream. She had never heard a man scream like that, a scream of sheer terror, and she would've never suspected she would hear it from Helen. She called every available man and squad car to respond. Outside the window, she could see two plumes of black smoke on the horizon.

On the east side of town, at the exit ramp off Route 66, Dogwood Road was the main artery into Windham. A visitor center and rest stop greeted motorists with racks of town attraction flyers, from go-cart racing to mountain hiking, to restaurants, to the logging industry plant on the Melville River. However, the main attraction of the town stood on that very piece of property. A forty-foot tall, fiberglass and steel statue of Paul Bunyan watched over the highway entrance. Blue jeans, red plaid flannel shirt, brown knit cap. Black hair and blue eyes. In its right hand it gripped an axe handle. The axe ran parallel to the ground and rested in the left hand of the statue. When the axe moved, it startled a couple who were taking a picture with the famous landmark.

"What was that?" the woman asked her boyfriend.

"It was nothing, Cindy," the man said. He snapped a photo.

Cindy looked straight up from between the statue's legs, seeing Paul's smiling face gazing down at her. Birds flew from the statue, where they had been perched. The screech of metal joints shattered the quiet afternoon. Cindy ran to her boyfriend, who had switched the camera to video mode and commenced shooting. People ran out of the restrooms, called by the loud grind of metal joints. Paul dropped to one knee upon the rectangular foundation he had been mounted upon and watched the young couple back away from him. His head turned in unison as they moved to a safe distance. Paul stood and stepped off the foundation. The small crowd gasped. Cars skidded to a halt on Route 66 as drivers saw the giant take a practice swing of his axe, then turn and march off toward the center of town.

Gwendolyn had just finished getting her nails done at the new salon on Main Street. She stepped out of the shop with her girlfriend, Allison, into a big commotion. Police cars raced down the street, sirens blazing and lights flashing. People were running, many with worried expressions on their faces. A fire truck screamed down the street at high speed and the women followed with their eyes. Twin plumes of smoke rose into the sky on the western horizon. Store and shop owners came out of their establishments and turned their attention to the west. It was quite a ruckus for a town in which nothing ever happened. Allison suggested they stop at her apartment, and see if there was any information about the excitement on the local news.

Allison's apartment was above Jo-Mar's TV and Appliance Repair, just off of Main Street. As soon as they entered the apartment they heard an explosion and ran to the window. A new fireball rose into the sky, considerably closer to downtown than the other smoke trails. Allison turned on the TV and *Breaking News* was reporting the disturbances. However, the news was on the east side of town, at the visitor's center, where the giant Paul Bunyan statue was clearly missing from the view.

"Gwen, you gotta' see this," Allison said, but Gwen's attention could not be pried from the window.

Gunshots rang out in rapid succession and both women jumped at the sound. Gwen backed away from the window and turned her attention to the television, which now showed scenes of a clown, a giant clown, tossing a police cruiser into the glass storefront of an IGA Grocery Market. The women heard the breaking glass, not through the television, but through the opened window. Allison ran to close the window while Gwen pulled out her cell phone to call Corbin. She had two missed calls from a number she didn't recognize. As she held the phone, it began to vibrate. Another call from the unknown number was coming in.

"Hello?" Gwen said.

There was a frantic voice on the line. "Gwen, thank God. You don't know me but I work with Roger and Corbin. I have no time to explain, but you have to get out of town immediately."

"Wait, who is this. What do you mean, get out of town?"

The voice on the line yelled, "The CLOWN is coming for YOU!"

"Clown? Is this some kind of joke?"

Behind Gwen's back, Allison backed away from the closed window as a giant eye filled the frame. Before she had a chance to warn Gwen, a giant white hand crashed through the wall and ripped Allison from the apartment. Gwen turned just in time to see her friend disappear from view and she joined her in unison screaming in a high-pitched wail. Gwen heard a 'crunch' and Allison's scream stopped instantly. Blood rained down in front of the gaping hole in the apartment wall.

The clown's bloody, one-eyed face peered into the apartment at Gwen, then the big hand reached for her. After a brief and futile struggle, she was pulled from the apartment and whisked up into the air, high above the rooftops. It was chaos outside as bullets ripped through the air, sirens blared, and a cop with a megaphone barked out orders to the clown, which were ignored.

"Gwendolyn," the clown's deep voice said.

Gwen was on the verge of passing out because of the dizzying height and fast movement in the hand of the clown, but she recognized the voice. It was impossible, but it was Roger's voice.

Several stories below, an officer kneeled with a short rocket launcher resting on his right shoulder and fired a shot. A rocket flew past Gwen's head and almost caught the clown in the face as he ducked. The clown roared and turned to the left, smashing waist-high through the building and emerging in the next block. There were no police on this block and the clown had a moment of peace here. He opened his palm, the one holding Gwen, and with his forefinger, stroked Gwen's body from under her chin, down to her crotch. It was sexual in nature, dirty and intrusive. Gwen struggled to keep her top up as it was pulled by the clown's probing, fondling finger.

The ground shook like an earthquake, distracting the clown and setting off car alarms in a three block radius. From down the street, a deep low voice called, "Roger!"

The clown looked to the intersection and Paul Bunyan stood there with his trusty axe.

Roger-clown set Gwendolyn down upon a rooftop. "Now don't go anywhere, my dear," he said. "If you run, I will find you and you don't want me to get mad. You won't like me when I'm mad."

Roger-clown turned to Paul Bunyan. He screamed into the air, a war cry, and charged the giant at the end of the street. Paul Bunyan charged too and the giants collided in the middle of the block. Paul held the axe horizontally, fists wrapped around opposite ends of the handle. Roger-clown grabbed the handle with both hands and the two pushed and pulled, each trying to dominate the other. A plastic flower on the clown's costume squirted water into Paul Bunyan's face but it had no effect on the giant's fiberglass eyes. Paul twisted the axe handle straight up and the clown tumbled left into a three-story, store front. Bricks, glass and cement rained onto the street. The clown stood and grabbed a utility pole, ripping it from the ground. Wires snapped and sparked as they whipped through the air. The clown swung the pole and struck Paul in the left shoulder. Paul recovered and swung his axe. It connected with the clown's leg, gouging a tear in the cloth and skin. The clown backed up several steps to look at his wound. Pink goop oozed out of the gash and the clown moaned in pain.

The clown picked up a box truck parked at the curb and threw it at Paul. The giant raised his arm to cover his face and the truck smashed into his elbow, breaking into dozens of pieces. The clown charged and grabbed Paul by the legs. He tackled Paul and they both fell into Main Street amid a barrage of bullets and rockets fired from a police barricade set up down the street.

Jarrell lowered the binoculars from his face. He had been watching the melee from the rock formation behind the lab, but something in the lab had changed, grabbing his attention. The blue electric light seen through the door and windows had changed. It seemed less intense. He jumped down from the rock and entered the lab. At first Jarrell didn't notice a difference. The machine was humming and an electric wall swirled about its surface, protecting it from tampering. When he stepped closer the change became evident. The electro-magnetic field no longer covered the sarcophagus where Roger lay. It occurred to Jarrell that he could end this now, just by waking Roger and forcing him out of the box. Even the turbines alongside Roger's box were quiet. Jarrell walked up to get a closer look and saw that Roger was dead. His skin was shriveled and his eyes were black and lifeless. He looked like a mummy. All the life was drained from his body, presumably sent to his avatar. Jarrell backed away from the withered husk. He ran to the window and looked through the binoculars. The two giants continued to fight. All of Roger's life energy had been turned into that giant clown. Jarrell thought about Corbin. Was it possible to reverse this process before it was too late? How was he going to tell Corbin there was no way back? Climbing into this machine was a one-way trip.

The clock tower at the center of town fell with a dull clank of the tower bell. When the iron bell broke loose from brick, cement and wood beams, Roger-clown scooped it up in his right hand and swung it full force at Paul Bunyan's head. The bell rang much louder this time and Paul's feet lifted off the ground. He landed atop the Masonic Temple building and crashed through to the basement. The marble columns fell on top of Paul along with a stone edifice of Masonic symbols. The stones completely immobilized Paul Bunyan. Roger-clown stared with his one good eye upon the unmoving Paul. He pulled a bouquet of paper flowers from his sleeve and placed it upon Paul's chest. He let out a shrill laugh then turned and ran back to the street where he had left Gwendolyn on the roof.

Gwen was not on the roof at this point. She was several blocks away running the best she could in her bare feet. She had kicked off her heels after twisting her ankle racing down the stairs from the roof of Bakers Street Cafe. She was out of breath and making moans and grunts with each exhale. From somewhere behind her she heard, *thud-thud-thud*, and the ground shook.

A booming voice called, "Gwendolyn."

She glanced back to see the one-eyed clown peering around the corner at her. She ran faster, ignoring the rough sidewalk on her feet. The loud *thuds* of footfalls resumed and she was scooped up by the white hand of the clown.

A small unit of the police force, armed with tactical gear and weapons, turned the corner of Lancet Street to see the giant boots of Paul Bunyan sticking out of the rubble. A rookie rounded the corner late and immediately opened fire on the boots, triggering every other cop into a firing frenzy.

The squad commander yelled "Hold your fire!" several times before the officers settled down, but not before the rookie shot off a grenade rocket.

The officers had stopped shooting and watched the solitary rocket scream into the air then come down on top of Paul Bunyan. They couldn't see it land upon the stone block engraved with symbols. The grenade exploded, pulverizing the stone facade to bits, and Paul sprang to a sitting position. The officers stood their ground for a few moments. Paul Bunyan stood, brushing cement dust from his chest. The officers opened fire as they retreated.

Paul located Roger-clown's head above the line of buildings north of the town square. He ran up Lancet and turned onto Carson Blvd. Roger-clown glanced behind him, alerted by Paul's heavy footfalls, saw him, and began to run. His big feet knocked over cars, tossed garbage cans and shattered windows on the street. Trees at the curb were snapped and uprooted along his path.

Having longer legs, the clown was able to extend the distance between him and Paul. He was nearing the north edge of town where most of the utility buildings and infrastructures were located. He ran to the giant water tower and began to climb. Paul crashed through the Milton Furniture Factory, sending debris into the air, as he tried to cut corners and catch up to his nemesis. Roger-clown stood atop the water tower tank, his oversized feet dangling off the sides. He held Gwen out in front of him and the other hand palm up to the sky. He cleared his throat and sang *That's Amore*, Dean Martin style.

"When a big pizza pie, hits you straight in the eye, that's amore!"

Paul reached the water tower and looked up. He had to get that psycho down from there, and decided on a risky plan. He wielded his axe and swung into one of four legs holding up the water tank. It made a nice dent and a visible vibration rose to the top of the tower. The clown yelped like a dog and steadied himself. When the vibrations stopped, he resumed singing. Paul swung again and the leg tore and buckled. The staircase going up the center of the tower broke from its mount and tilted, leaning against the far legs.

"I'm giving you one chance to climb down from there and do the right thing," Paul Bunyan yelled.

"Go to hell, Corbin!" Roger-clown said.

"Okay. You asked for it."

Paul Bunyan took a final swing and his axe sliced through the steel leg. The other legs buckled and the tower tilted. Roger-clown dropped Gwen, and Paul Bunyan caught her. He ran her to high ground and safety as the tower tumbled behind them. The tank busted and the north side of town was deluged by five hundred thousand gallons of water. Roger-clown wallowed in pain and in water.

Paul Bunyan had only seconds to complete his plan. He ran to the high-tension wires that fed the town with power. He ripped the thick black wire from the tower and a shower of sparks exploded in the air. He towed the line until he was standing next to Roger-clown. He knew it was suicide but it was his only chance to save Gwen. He threw the wire down into the flooded street. Electric fractals traced the bodies of both giants as all of the energy that ran the town now unloaded into the water. Roger-clown shook and trembled then fell still. He split opened and pink ooze bubbled out of his torso. Paul Bunyan stiffened into the lifeless statue he had started as, and fell forward. In the lab on the side of Munser Mountain, the machine overloaded as the polarity reversed. The machine blew out a burst of energy then died. It slowly crumbled as the burnt out copper and stone turned to ash. Jarrell ran to Corbin. He looked as if he had aged twenty-five years, but he was breathing. Jarrell helped him out of the box and walked him outside for air. He sat Corbin in the passenger side of his jeep. Corbin struggled to speak.

"Is the lab rigged?" he asked.

"Yes, it is," Jarrell answered.

"Then blow it," Corbin said.

Jarrell set the timer for five minutes. The jeep cut across the meadow grasses meeting the road away from the fallen trees.

As they headed down the mountain, the lab exploded behind them.

Four days later, Gwendolyn visited Corbin at the hospital; her arms full of muffins and balloons. She had been beside herself with excitement ever since receiving the message that Corbin was feeling well and should be discharged soon.

"Ugh, balloons," Corbin said when she first entered the room. Gwendolyn tied them to a cabinet.

"What, no good? They're colorful. They're meant to cheer you up," she said.

"It's just that... they remind me of clowns."

Gwen winced at the thought. They made light talk until they were sure no one else was in the vicinity.

Corbin propped himself and reached for a muffin. "What have the police been saying? I saw some things on the news but not much."

"They are really trying to down-play the whole event. They're not even investigating. They're just trying to get past it as quickly as possible. I'm the only one that knew it was you and Roger. And Jarrell, but he's good; he wont say anything."

"When I see some of the news footage on TV, it's so weird. It's unbelievable. It seems like a long forgotten dream."

"More like a nightmare," Gwen murmured, "of which I've been having quite a few."

"When I get out of here and we move in together, I'll protect you from those nightmares."

"Move in together? When did this epiphany occur?" Gwen smiled. She had been wanting to take their relationship further but always sensed resistance from Corbin.

"Just now, when I saw how beautiful you looked," Corbin said.

Gwen's smile grew even deeper and her face glowed with warmth. "You know, you don't even have a job. How are you gonna' keep up your half?" she teased.

"I'll get a job. I've been thinking about making changes in my life and now's a good time to start. I'm going to look in a different field of work, though."

"Really?"

"Really. No more Alchemy Science."

"What would you even think of doing, outside the science field?"

He smiled and reached for a second muffin, "I was thinking something more aligned with nature, maybe becoming a lumberjack."

They both laughed. Gwen leaned over the bed and they kissed.

"So, how 'bout it? Will you come and live with me?" Corbin asked between mouthfuls.

"Of course," she replied, stroking his recently grayed hair, "I love you in plaid."

Where Gods Roam Freely

by

D.G. Sutter

Where Gods Roam Freely

by

D.G. Sutter

THE RANGE ROVER bounced over the dirt-laden road, its four-wheel drive employed. It dipped and steered over hills of clay, between gum trees, through naturally sprawling expanses of pure nature. So far, Australia had been everything and more than Jamie had dreamt about since age five. From the clear waters off the coast of Perth, to the mountains just north of the capital, the western coast of the continent was breathtaking.

From the start his mind was set on traveling to Sydney to see the opera house, but somewhere along the trip his wife, Rachel, had convinced him that the site was cliche, and they were better off engulfed in the rarities. He finally agreed with her, seeing as most depictions of Australia included the famous structure; they could easily view it from a postcard. It was the intrinsic beauty of the rugged outback that could not be eternalized in a glossy eight-by-ten photograph.

Jamie leaned forward in the backseat, against the restriction of the blistering seatbelt. "Is it much further?" he asked the guide, Reed.

"Can't be more than a few kilometers now." Reed replied, elongating his vowels in a hearty Aussie dialect.

"It's pretty barren out here," Rachel said.

"Kimberly region is less populous than other parts of Australia. Don't want to get all factual on ya, dear, but it's about eight square miles per person."

Rachel mimicked Jamie, leaning forward with a smile. "No, that's good. What would be the point of going to another country if you walk away without learning anything?" She raised her voice then, as if she had deemed the volume previously insignificant. "That's why we hired you!"

In the rear view mirror Jamie noticed a smile crack across Reed's face of bushy gold. "I hope that's not all you lot walk away with."

His toned biceps tensed as he yanked the wheel to the left, curving the vehicle around a fat boab tree with spindly branches and pale bark. After the turn a couple of kangaroos bounced across the road. As a worried passenger usually does with the threat of an imposing accident, Rachel voiced her concern, which typically came out as a series of frightened, unhelpful noises.

"Woah, woah, woah!" In synchronicity she grabbed what Jamie liked to refer to as the "Oh, shit!" handle, which most would actually hang their dry cleaning on.

Jamie was surprised when Reed's foot did not ease off the accelerator, and the car actually seemed to speed faster.

"Just hold on," Reed said. "If I can teach ya' anything worth knowing, it's to keep a watchful eye when you're driving in the bush. Otherwise, you'll hit a cow or a 'roo. 'Specially at night."

For the remainder of the drive Jamie could tell that Rachel was on edge. Every bump, turn, and pothole was met by a firm grip of the nylon padding of the seats. It wasn't until the utility vehicle came to a complete stop outside of a one-floor ranch washed in dirt that relief showed on his wife's face. Even then a trace of tension was undeniable in her shallow breaths.

Reed jumped out of the Range Rover first and opened the door for Rachel. He gave her a gentlemanly pat on the shoulder.

"Calm down, missy. I wouldn't let nothin' happen to you and your hubby." He indicated to Jamie with a dirt covered thumb.

Then he started toward the building, pulling air over his shoulder to tell them they should follow.

"I wish you would drive home," Rachel said.

"It wasn't that bad, it's rough terrain."

She turned to him, lowering her head in disbelief. "You've got to be kidding. He drives like a fucking madman."

Jamie grabbed her hand. "Be nice. You know he's better than we could have asked for."

Her head bounced, considering, back and forth, and her thick lips twisted to one side. "Yeah, I guess you're right."

They followed him into the ranch. Reed stood holding the screen door open for them. As Jamie passed, Reed winked a powder blue eye at him, guiding him through the door with a friendly hand on the back. The room was a dimly lit, square bar. Around the outside of the bar, were tables with inverted chairs on top of them.

"This doesn't look like an inn," said Rachel.

"Cause it ain't," Reed replied. His boots clunked across the sand covered floorboards, until he reached the bar counter, where he pulled on a dangling metal string. A slightly brighter light illuminated a patch, which had previously been a void.

A much larger section spread out beyond the bar, reminiscent of a dance floor. Sitting at the counter with their backs to the open space were two men; one very thin in a rattlesnake vest and one very bald, who shielded his eyes from the projection of fresh phosphorous. Baldy lowered his thick club of an arm, but continued to squint as he took a swig from his half-filled glass of amber.

"That's Rick," Reed pointed at the bald man with the snake tattoo on his forearm, "Skinny bastard is Teddy."

Teddy's smile was missing a left incisor, but it was a warm smile. He raised his glass above his head of short, curly brown hair. "Unwind a little?"

Reed pulled off his khaki jacket and hung it over the back of one of the bar stools. Underneath he wore a tight white tee that showcased two firm pecks and eight rows of abs. Jamie would have been mad at Rachel's stare had he not been watching with equal measure of awe and jealousy.

"I believe our guests need to get settled and put some grub in their stomachs first."

Jamie and Rachel both concurred. Jamie said, "How about after dinner?"

Teddy poured the liquor from the bottle into his empty glass. "I ain't goin' anywhere."

They had settled in, unpacked their clothing for the night, and then eaten dinner. Reed presented a meal of damper, a soda wheat bread, and cattle stew. The meat was the freshest Jamie had ever eaten. Even Rachel enjoyed the small feast, despite her not being a fan of soup.

Afterwards, they drank until they were quite buzzed. Reed turned the on the jukebox in the corner of the dance floor area. Springsteen sang overhead.

"Good American music," he said. "Bar's open for business."

Jamie thought he was having a laugh, but no more than half an hour later, a crowd started to pile into the building. Reed hadn't told them it was an operating business, and it worried Jamie a bit to know they'd be sleeping not twenty feet away, in an extension of the dive bar. It looked like a rough crowd; men in leather, and muscular monstrosities, guys with tats and facial piercings. From outside he could hear the sound of engines rumbling closer.

Rachel scootched closer to him and her stool screeched over the wooden floor. "I don't like this very much," she whispered into his ear.

Jamie smiled. "It's all right, just relax. Have another drink, you rarely do."

She listened, sipping her vodka and cranberry. He tipped his draft back and stole half of it into his stomach. Reed was chatting up a storm with the gentlemen, and at the same time, collecting money from them. He would sift through the bills, and then would pull out a small pad of paper and jot into it. As he waded through the crowd - collecting from every spectator - Reed acknowledged Jamie's stare with a wink and a nod.

Jamie leaned his shoulder up against Rachel's upper arm. "What the hell is this, a gambling ring?"

"Looks that way, don't it?"

"Yeah, but what the fuck do Aussie's bet on?"

Rick and Teddy were manning the bar, keeping Rachel's cup full and Jamie's beer coming. He wasn't sure if he should tip, or if their service and free drinks were simply hospitality, but either way he felt compelled to do so. After Reed had collected his till, he made his way over to Jamie and Rachel.

"Havin' a right time?"

"Sure are," Jamie said.

Rachel gave him an exaggerated smile. "Yes, thank you so much for letting us stay here so cheap! And for the free drinks." She held her glass up in salute.

"No worries, lass. It's what I do."

He held his hand up and Rick caught the gesture. Without a word, the bar hand slid a bottleneck down the counter, where Reed's thick hand received it. It seemed very ritual to Jamie.

The crowd on the dance floor started to clear away, toward the walls, and Jamie could sense the main event was about to begin. "What's this all about?" he asked, indicating the change with his index finger.

"Special treat. You came during the right time of year."

Adjacent to the opposite side of the bar, a door opened. Teddy came prancing out, dressed in a pair of shiny, red trunks with white stripes down either leg. His hands were bound in white wrapping and he threw quick punches into the air. The crowd of ruffians started whooping and whistling through their teeth, much to the dismay of Rachel, who looked almost ready to cover her ears from the noise.

"How many rounds?" Jamie asked, grabbing blindly for his beer.

Reed's smile darkened and he gnawed at his wad of chew, making his cheek puff out. "To the death."

Jamie jerked back, knocking his beer all over Rachel's lap. She jumped out of her stool instantly, her jeans looking as if she had pissed herself.

"You gotta' be fucking kidding, right?"

Reed chuckled. "You'll understand in a minute. Teddy's undefeated."

Rachel grabbed Jamie's hand. "I'm going to change. I'll be back." She gave him a kiss on the cheek.

"I'm so sorry."

"It's okay," she said and exited the bar, all eyes alight with horniness, watching her go.

Once the door closed behind her, Jamie relaxed, knowing that none of the sketchy guys had followed.

There was a garage door at the far end of the dance floor that started to rise with a hearty rumble by the hands of one of the leather-clad guys. It commanded the attention of the masses.

A man in a safari hat and khaki clothing came through the opening dragging a chain. The chain became taut and he was forced to yank on it for more guidance. A very reluctant animal was pulled into the building with drooping ears and shuffling feet. The kangaroo tried to bounce back through the door, but safari man was too strong. Once he and the animal had cleared the entrance, leather-clad closed the garage door with a resounding slam.

"Come one, come all," Reed muttered to Jamie under his breath. He left the bar stool and made his way to the crowd, which had become a circle, enclosing the kangaroo and the guy in the safari garb.

Teddy weaved through the people, emerging into the circle like a weasel, his thin arms cutting the air like whips. When the animal was released, it cowered into the corner of the dance floor by means of tiny sideways hops. Teddy started towards the marsupial with his hands squared aggressively.

The 'roo bounced to its left, past a sudden jab. Teddy threw another punch and scraped the furry, brown face. Finally, he connected with a sucker shot to the stomach, as the kangaroo rubbed its nose with its short limbs. A yelp escaped from the wild creature's body.

It looked around, frightened, for an escape route. Jamie felt sorry for the creature, but knew there was nothing he could do about it. The elongated feet of the kangaroo flew out, slamming into Teddy's chest. The man slid across the wooden floor, groaning. Holding his chest with one hand, he staggered into a fighter's stance, his small eyes reflecting pure anguish.

The 'roo had caught on to Teddy's aggression and came bouncing towards him. It landed a few short punches, but Teddy used a human maneuver, kicking its legs out. The thing didn't fall completely, just onto its side.

Some of the spectators booed while others cheered, the usual reactions at any "sporting" event. Reed was particularly happy with Teddy's success, jumping up and down, and throwing his own punches into the air. Then, to Jamie's disgust, Teddy straddled the neck of the creature, and commenced to pound its head into the wooden floor. Jamie had to turn away, but he could hear the weak moans of the poor animal as it drew its final breaths, reminiscent of a child sobbing through a bedroom door.

Reed made the rounds, collecting and paying out. As he did so, Rick dragged a metal locker onto the dance floor, or boxing ring, and with an effortless lift, tossed the corpse into the box. He returned to the bar, with the meat locker in tow. Not only did Reed not wash his hands, he licked them clean.

After that he wiped them on the bar apron he wore, caught Jamie watching, and smiled. "Can I getcha something'?"

Jamie had to prevent his face from showing disgust. "No, thank you." He was glad Rachel had not seen the match. She certainly wouldn't have approved or appreciated it.

When she did reappear, she was dressed down in a hooded sweater and 'roomy' sweatpants. He noticed, as she moved through the crowds, that the eyes no longer lingered, but actually turned away. She smiled genuinely and took the seat next to him.

"You look ready for bed," he said.

"I looked *over* the bed many times before deciding to come back."

Jamie gripped her knee and rubbed it. "I'm glad you did."

She placed hers on top of his resting hand. "So, did I miss all of the fun? I heard quite the ruckus."

His tongue was itching to tell her, but how to word it. "It was fucked up... they had Teddy box a kangaroo."

Her face didn't disguise her appall. "You're kidding me."

"No. He killed it."

Rachel's eyes watered when he said it and Jamie realized that despite his own disgust, he was describing the act with excitement.

"I don't want to be here anymore."

"We can't just leave now, he brought us all the way out here."

"Ask him, please."

"I thought you wanted to see the aborigines tomorrow?"

She weighed the thought for a moment, her head teetering. "Fine. But right after that, we're heading back to Perth. I don't care if I have to pay extra. It's just plain wrong, Jamie."

"The Northern Territory is some of the wildest terrain in the world," Reed said when they stepped free of the Rover, "some of it even uncharted."

He led Jamie and Rachel up a steady slope, and near the peak, laid down into commando crawl. Looking over his shoulder, he pointed to the ground. "Gotta' get down here, don't want them to see you."

Over the crest of the hill, Jamie could see a flat expanse of uninterrupted wild. There were Bloodwood trees and small bushes, the occasional red Holly tree. Here and there were grassy stretches of Spinifex, and far off, the barren Great Sandy Desert could be seen. In the gully was a village where comparatively small people walked and played. They glistened in the sun like black pearls.

Reed continued, "What you're seeing is amazing. The government thought they caught the last in the 1980's, but this is an un-contacted aboriginal tribe."

"What's that mean?" asked Rachel.

"They're completely separated from society. They're hunter-gatherers living off the land, with barely an inkling of what goes on in the world, if any."

"Are they dangerous if we get too close?" Jamie murmured.

Reed chuckled. "Last week they caught a sight o' me. Let's just say I narrowly escaped a spearing."

Jamie edged higher up the slope and squinted to get a better view. A few of them sat around half-naked in a circle, while a group of younger ones chased each other. He couldn't imagine living such a carefree existence. No worry about getting to work on time, no worry about bills, he had to admit the concept *was* oddly enticing.

"How did you find them if the government couldn't" Rachel asked.

"It's not that they couldn't, they kinda' just stopped searching after awhile. I stumbled across them on one of me kangaroo hunts. I'm always out in the bush looking for more."

He clicked his tongue then, as if to seal the fates of the creatures. Out the corner of his eye, Jamie could see Rachel's eyelids close a few millimeters. She had voiced her disgust long into the night, reprimanding him for not researching their guide extensively. They came to a mutual agreement to stay just one more night, but she wouldn't be hanging in the bar. Jamie hadn't expected Rachel to bring her discontent into conversation with Reed.

"Is it legal to *murder* kangaroos?"

Reed peered over his shoulder, his ruffian face sour. "Lass, it's not murder. They're beasts. Government issues a nationwide culling of three million annually. Damned things outnumber us three-to-one."

"For some reason I don't think death by beating was on their agenda."

He waved her off. "Oh, pardon me. Like you Americans are any better with your slaughterhouses and deer hunting seasons."

Jamie's hand tensed. He was getting angry as it became personal, but he knew he had to be the diffuser. Swallowing his malice, he spoke, however, not without intended sarcasm. "Why don't you just show us something interesting?"

"Okay. Follow me, stay low."

He rose into a crouch and treaded carefully in that stance until he was a little further down the trail, then stood. Jamie and Rachel followed suit. They made their way back toward their vehicle and then took a sharp right, which led through an out of place patch of trees.

Once through the trees a clearing was laid out, circumvented by a circle of sitting stones. In the middle was a totem carved into the form of a kangaroo.

"Totems like this can represent either a person or a tribe. They're physical embodiments of the land, deity, a certain food, or even a believed past life. They come here to pray for food or rain, perform religious rituals. It's not clear cut."

Reed walked around the circle and sat down on one of the rocks. He dug through his pockets and pulled out a wad of tobacco. He spit a dark brown dollop through the trees and put the fresh batch into his cheek.

Jamie and Rachel walked to the totem to examine it closer. The carving was intricate, done by the hand of a person, rather than just another machine. Jamie pulled the totem towards them with one hand.

"Ooga-booga-booga!"

Rachel's laugh was cut short by the harsh protest of Reed. "Hey! You can't go messin' with that!"

Jamie carefully eased the statue into place and let go of it. "Sorry."

"Their religious sites are law-protected," he said. Then he spit a trail of black from his mouth into the dirt.

What a hypocrite, Jamie thought. Along the left side was a stone wall with a hole in it.

Reed caught Jamie eyeballing the gap and said, "It's a cave. Some beautiful paintings in there."

Rachel tugged Jamie's hand. "Let's look at them."

Painted on the walls of the cave were humans and animals in earthly reds and pigmented yellows and oranges. The human bodies were skinny with large heads, and oddly no mouths. They looked to Jamie like bulbous aliens. Reed's voice made him jump.

"*Wandjina* - they bring the wet seasons. Piss em' off and they bring floods and lightning. Obviously done in clay. The aborigines believed the Gods lived during a time called "The Dreaming", in which the landscape was created by their travels. With each movement they made, something was left behind; a teardrop… a lake, a footstep… a canyon. You get the idea."

Outside, lightning cracked and Rachel jumped. She grabbed onto Jamie's arm with a gasp. "Is it supposed to rain?" she asked.

Reed scratched his head. "Eh, rarely does around here. But ya' did come during The Wet. *Wandjina…*" The cave echoed with the sound of pattering rain. He cackled. "It obviously comes down sometimes, and when it does, it's a doozy. Better get back."

The cave seemed darker than when they had entered it.

"Roads'll flood and ya can't get home. Or worse, a cyclone."

"Cyclone?" Rachel worried.

"Aw don't worry," Reed said with a snicker.

The Range Rover splashed through the mud as Reed pressed on the accelerator. Rachel was tense in her seat, and Jamie couldn't blame her. Reed was driving too fast for comfort in the weather.

Lightning streaked fluorescent blue and yellow across the purple sky, shearing through it like live ripples of the ocean. The thunder followed, but more frequently than it should - like the footprints of a huge man. Water from the excess rain on the ground splashed up due to the tires cutting through trenches and gullies.

Reed was humming, unaffected by the fierce storm.

"How can you be so calm in this?" Jamie yelled over the pouring rain, which fell so hard it blurred his vision and hearing.

"I'm not calm, I'm composed," Reed said between notes.

Jamie wasn't sure, but he thought they were and the same. "You're singing."

"It's a songline. Local tribe of aborigines taught me. Each sound refers to a landmark... to guide you in a certain direction."

"So basically we're lost?" Jamie asked raising his voice again, this time from anger.

"Yes and no."

Jamie tapped his fingers on the arm rest. Lightning flared, brightening the windows of the car like bursting television screens.

"I think we're almost there. Right around this bend, should be... " Reed said.

The car swiveled around the corner and lost traction. Reed spun the wheel quickly to regain positioning. As the SUV nearly tipped, Rachel audibly cringed.

"Careful!"

Reed's arms locked the wheel and the car straightened. He didn't slow, despite the puddle ahead. Jamie had a bad feeling about it, and he was right. The Rover slammed to a stop, dipping front first into the puddle.

Jamie and Rachel were snapped forward and Reed was knocked back by his airbag. Reed wrestled the airbag, finally deflating it. "Dammit, dammit," he said.

"You okay?" Jamie asked Rachel.

She rolled her neck and nodded. "Yeah... fucking idiot."

She slammed the back of Reed's headrest. "You should have slowed down."

Reed eyeballed her in the rearview mirror. "Nothing I can do now."

He threw the car into reverse, but the only result was the useless spinning of tires heard over splattering mud and the strange continual thunder.

"Dammit," Reed said again. "Wanna help me push, Jamie?"

"Not really, but I don't really have a choice."

They hopped out of the car, and Reed vaulted right into the puddle. Jamie took a deep breath and followed suit. They pushed for a moment, but then Jamie realized that someone should probably power the tires. He banged on the hood. "Honey! Get in the driver's seat!"

Rachel's head lifted, nodded slightly, and then she clambered through the space between the two front seats. The tires spun endlessly through the mud, as

Reed shoved with his shoulder and Jamie with his hands. The car rocked a little, but then fell back into the puddle.

The sky cracked and Jamie wanted to jump out of the water, knowing how dangerous it was to be in there. "On three," Jamie said. "One, two, tha-ree... "

They both grunted and heaved their shoulders into the bumper. The rear tires spit mud onto their faces and clothes, but finally the Range Rover escaped; fish-tailing out into the middle of the track.

Reed climbed out quicker than Jamie and offered his hand. Jamie took it, grateful to get back in the vehicle.

As he climbed into the car he noticed a large shadow, dark against the misty sky. Once buckled in he cleared the rain from his face and turned to look out the rear window.

Rachel had returned to the back and asked, "What is it?"

Maybe a mile back, in the direction that they had come from, a giant shadow moved over the landscape. There was no telling just how big it was and it was gaining ground fast.

It was Jamie's turn to bang on Reed's headrest. "I think there's a cyclone coming! What do we do?"

"Get back home, and get into my shelter is what."

Reed juiced the engine and swerved around the puddle and up a steep incline. The tires didn't protest, but clung to the hill. Around the bend, as promised by Reed, the ranch came into view not more than a mile down the trail. He stepped on it.

The road straightened and the Range Rover tore towards the building. Jamie looked behind them. The shadow took the turn. It seemed to be *following* them, and with it came the thunder, rhythmically shaking the Earth.

As the speedometer reached sixty, Jamie started to worry. The bush pushed past his vision as a series of pastel brush strokes. Going that speed it took less than a minute before they were sliding into park. They left their belongings in the car for the time and rushed into the dim building.

The screen slapped shut behind them. The foundation shook with thunderous reverberations.

"This is too scary, Jamie," Rachel whispered.

"I know," he said squeezing her hand.

At the bar sat Teddy and Rick, unbothered once again, and in the dark. Reed flicked the light on, which flickered then steadied.

"What gives?" asked Teddy.

"There's a cyclone comin'. We gotta' get the shelter ready."

"What're you mad, Reed? There ain't been a cyclone warnin'. We had the radio plugged in."

Sure enough a small FM radio quietly serenaded Bob Seger's "Against the Wind". Reed stomped over to one of the windows and drew the blinds. He bent over and peered through the slats.

"What in the hell?" He staggered back, away from the window, revealing a view of sandy brown fur. It filled the window, blocking the outside view. The fur *moved* and Jamie's stomach wrenched. A giant quake rocked the bar, nearly toppling everyone inside.

Rachel moved closer to him, and Jamie felt the urge to be near the middle of the room.

Reed circled the bar and grabbed the twelve-gauge off the wall. He cocked it and rested the barrel on his shoulder with his finger on the trigger. There was another boom, this time farther away. Jamie feared the shotgun was going to fire aimlessly as Reed tried to regain his balance.

Reed drew the blinds on another window, to the right of the front door. There was nothing but the slow drip of an abated rain. It had only lasted an hour.

Then the ceiling over the dance floor caved in with a crash, catching Ricky and Teddy off-guard. They shielded their heads, but debris spewed over them. Splinters of wood spit across the bar, the jukebox smashed with a two-by-four studded with rusted nails.

Two enormous feet stood in the center of the dance floor, covered in mud-matted brown fur. A floppy tail fell onto the garage door, guiding it onto the ground outside. The feet hesitated for a moment, but when Teddy swiveled in his stool, they came off the ground and kicked him like a pebble through the ceiling.

In the middle of the bar lay a pool of blood, directly underneath the puncture in the roof which allowed Jamie a view of a massive kangaroo head against a navy blue sky. Pieces of skin stuck to the edges of the jagged peek hole. The 'roo's head bent lower to the hole, so close that Jamie could see its whiskers twitch as it sniffed.

Rachel screamed when the shotgun exploded. The kangaroo whined and hopped into the air, the ground shaking as it left. Rick fell off his stool after being sprayed with shotgun buckshot in the shoulder. Behind him, the building collapsed unto the dancing area.

"Shit!" Reed yelled. He rushed to his pal and knelt by his side. "I'm sorry. Oh shit, Rick, I'm sorry!"

Rick lay on the ground bleeding through his chest. Jamie wanted to hold Rachel, but knew that she had the best capabilities to take care of Rick, being a nurse and all.

"Give me your shirt," she said to Reed.

Reed ripped his shirt off revealing his chiseled physique and Jamie hated him more than ever.

She compressed the shirt onto Rick's chest. He grimaced in pain and grabbed at the fabric.

"Stop it," she said. "You need to stop the bleeding."

He complied and she asked Reed where the nearest hospital was.

"A good twenty miles east."

"Then let's go."

Reed grabbed Rick's shoulders and Rachel and Jamie each took a leg. As the thunder echoed all around them and pieces of wood sprinkled to the floor, they hauled Rick carefully through the front door and planted him on the backseat of the SUV. Rachel offered to sit with him and hold the compress. The Rover pulled a quick one-eighty and they were off.

As they drove, Jamie thought about Teddy and how they hadn't even looked for him. It made him remember why Rick was shot in the first place, and also made him check the rear-view mirror. The creature the size of the Statue of Liberty bounced into the middle of the bar, crushing it like a deflated balloon. It didn't stop there, instead it continued down the dirt road.

"Pick it up," he yelled "it's coming!"

"Aw, shit," Reed said making the speedometer needle flick to the right. The bounces shortened the distance between them, and Jamie gripped the door handle.

"C'mon, c'mon, c'mon."

The next hop shook the car and Jamie could have sworn they went airborne. He put his hand on the dashboard. "It's gaining on us!"

"I know, mate!"

From the back Rachel started to sob and Jamie couldn't take it anymore. "Turn off the road! We're better off on our feet."

"No we ain't."

"It can see us clearly in this thing."

"We're too slow on our feet," Reed said.

Jamie grabbed for the wheel, but Reed yanked it away. "What're ya tryin' to do, crash us?"

"Turn off the road dammit!"

This time when Jamie grabbed for the wheel, Reed yanked it a bit too far and the Range Rover tipped. The car flipped end-over-end down a rocky slope. It was a short crash, but bounced them about like beans in a bag. Rachel screamed in agony.

The car came to a window shattering, metal crunching stop. Jamie opened his eyes, aware of a stabbing pain in his neck. He put his hand there and came away with a slight amount of blood where a piece of glass had sliced him. The car was upside-down and he hung in space.

"Rach... "

"I'm okay."

For a second his heart had stopped beating, then it quickened. He craned his neck and saw Rick lying on the roof of the car, as pale as a ghost. His eyes were closed and Jamie couldn't see his chest moving. Rachel hung above Rick, holding onto her seatbelt so that she wouldn't fall.

Jamie realized that only his torso was in the air and his legs were actually on the roof of the car. He kicked the glass away and spun towards his passenger window. Before he could fully spin, he caught a glimpse of Reed staring at him, with blood dripping down his temple.

"Go get help, mate... I can't move."

Jamie nodded and kicked the rest of the glass out of his window frame. He crawled through the square, embedding glass into his palms. "Aw, fuck!" he screamed, scrambling to his feet.

He looked around and saw that they were surrounded by trees. Among them moved a giant shape. Jamie hurried to open the crushed door and help Rachel out while behind him branches crunched and snapped.

Rachel gripped his arm with both of her hands, and kicked against the back seats in order to push herself out of the door. When she sidled against Jamie, she stopped dead. Her vision line was over Jamie's head and he knew what was there.

She cowered against the decrepit vehicle and Jamie remained still. He could feel the hot breath on the back of his neck, and he could picture the huge head right behind him, its pointy nose nearly poking his head. Jamie took a deep inhale of the freshly moist air, closed his eyes, and slowly walked forward.

After a few small steps around the car he opened his eyes. The ground shook, and Jamie turned abruptly. Branches snapped and a tree fell over. Jamie looked up to see the kangaroo in the air. Then, it started to drop, its feet aimed right at the car.

Jamie grabbed Rachel's hand and pulled her away toward the hill. There was a smashing sound and pieces of metal sliced through the thicket. The thumping of giant feet continued as the couple staggered up the hill. Rachel was slower than Jamie, but he dragged her along.

When they reached the edge of the road, they nearly fell backwards down the hill as the monster dropped into their path. It bent over and clawed with its two short arms and Jamie flung himself in front of Rachel.

He was surprised when no pain came. Instead, he was gripped in a giant paw and lifted seventy feet in the air. He looked down at Rachel reaching up and crying, as if it would do something to help his situation.

His surprise continued when the marsupial used its free paw to spread the pouch away from its stomach, and then dumped him inside.

It was warm in the pouch, blissfully so. For an all too brief moment, Jamie felt comfortable, protected. It wasn't until the kangaroo launched into the air and Jamie rolled onto a floor littered with sharp sticks and then into a furry, snuffling mass, that he felt the first pangs of fear; a fear that evolved into abject terror when he realized he had landed amongst a pile of bones.

Picked clean human bones.

On the Strangest Sea

by

Pete Mesling

On the Strangest Sea

by

Pete Mesling

H IS ARMS HUNG heavy as he pulled the small door shut behind him. Climbing the steep, narrow planks from the lower cabins to the deck of the *Lonesome Buccaneer*, he noticed it in his legs, too. His whole body, in fact, behaved as if weights hung from his black leather vest, sailor's blouse and pantaloons. Abel Sykes was too weary to revel in his recent accomplishment, but he was determined to try. He dragged himself to the gunwale and stared beyond the bowsprit, out across the unbreakable sea before him, hoping to find a revelation in the repetition of blues and grays that stretched in every direction. Perhaps a new calling.

Something came upon him eventually, but it wasn't the quiet reassurance he'd been hoping for; the unshakable affirmation he sought. After an hour or more of witnessing the sea in one of her quiet lulls, he realized that something special was on its way. It was a knack that some old sea dogs picked up after too much time away from land. A sense that maybe the sea wasn't so unbreakable after all, that there was a universe of constant change beneath the surface, no matter how calm it appeared from above, and maybe some particle of that flux was thinking of breaking free, or laboring at it even now.

Never had a calmer sea borne him across its glassy top, and he could have put it no stronger than that, it being his twenty-eighth year on one whaling vessel or another. Not a cloud in the sky, either. Conditions were maybe a little too perfect. His job on the *Buccaneer* had been to flense the hides off the enormous sea mammals and harvest the blubber. Toughest job on a whaling sloop, too, if you asked him, although the waste disposal men and the hash slingers probably felt the same way about their work. He'd certainly never known a captain who didn't harbor the opinion.

The point here is that Sykes knew the manner of an ocean about to be breached by a sperm whale. He'd seen the hesitant lunge preceding the arrival of a monstrous cetacean many times. And he'd observed the upwelling of cool waters from beneath warm. This wasn't like either of those phenomena. This was a swell so sweeping and vast he could have sworn he heard the drifting timbers of the

Buccaneer and her two flanking whaleboats groan in response, though she was a clear two-and-a-half knots from whatever was pushing all that water skyward.

And then it broke. A rolling arc of gray flesh, as long as an armada of frigates moored prow to stern, and considerably thicker. And that was just what he could see of it, for no head or tail had made an appearance yet, unless he'd missed the emergence of the former. He let a deep shudder pass through him before calling to the deckhands to alert them to the fact that they were headed straight for the most immense creature of the sea that Abel Sykes had ever set eyes on. It was a momentary lapse. Of course there was no one to hear his hollering. He was alone.

He did what he could to batten down and tie back sails, but it was beyond the endurance and speed of any one man. Periodically he allowed himself a glimpse of the ponderous movement of the thing that still refused to reveal either end of itself. The *Lonesome Buccaneer* was without a helmsman, and she pitched violently in the worsening tumult. Abel had planned to die on her deck this very day, or by jumping off of it, but now curiosity had him by the throat. The creature, it was clear, continued to glide from where it had emerged to where it was returning, rolling gently as it did so. It was no whale. That was certain. But just how large could the thing possibly be? Where was the end of it? Abel was transfixed.

He imagined the hand of Captain Fulsome gripping his shoulder. "If you have any ideas about what that might be, Sykes, I'd love to hear them," the captain might have said in his guttural yet clipped voice. It always had the uncanny ability to cut through the roar of any storm, that voice. Designed not only to be heard but obeyed.

"No sir," Abel said out loud, seeing little difference between the real and the imagined as he watched the impossibility of the sea creature on the move. "I ran out of ideas at least fifty yards ago. He just keeps coming. I've never seen anything like it."

And that's when the suspense ended, and the terror began. For when the great gray monster finally did come to an end, it was no tail fin that could be seen following the rest of its bulk into the depths. It was simply a tip, as if belonging to a tentacle.

Sykes stared into the nonexistent eyes of his make-believe companion, seeking comfort, or at least reassurance. Then came a long stillness, and any seamen Abel knew would have testified to the fact that there's a certain kind of lull on the open sea that's far worse than the most tempestuous squall of lashing rain and ripping wind. All that could be done now was to wait for unbending Fate to rush in and break apart all that silence and dread.

Was the thing grinning, down in its unknowable depths, aware that the longer it held any onlookers in thrall of what was to come, the greater would be the shock of its full emergence from the sea? Abel sensed this was so.

The first hint of the actual magnitude of the beast came not from the horizon where Abel's eyes were trained but from directly below. As if Neptune had the sloop on a chain and now gave it a sudden tug, down dropped the *Lonesome Buccaneer*. It was a considerable drop, too, but more considerable still was that the ship never plunged beneath the surface. The water in her immediate vicinity had fallen along with the vessel.

There was barely time to register this odd phenomenon before the horizon claimed his attention once more. As if the very world were giving birth to a new moon, a bell of ferocious water rose up from the depths. Immense waterfalls dripped from the thing that rose and pulsed in the aroused sea. Its dimensions were dizzying, because if something could be this enormous, what did that say about the actual size of things as Abel had been perceiving them since infancy? Was all judgment relative, or so easily shattered?

The time for marveling over such things was soon over, though, for what goes down must come up, and up shot the *Buccaneer* as the water reacted again to the expulsion of the beast, rippling in gigantic waves, any one of which would have been the most impressive sight of Abel's life twenty minutes ago. Not anymore. Now all was insignificant in the face of the sea-dwelling wonder.

Timbers cracked, then snapped. A deafening report echoed from below deck, and the *Buccaneer* lurched to port. She was coming apart at the seams. And suddenly Abel was flying toward the creature, launched into the spume-filled air by a twisting wrench of undercurrent that doomed the *Lonesome Buccaneer* to a dark, wet grave. Fate was closing in as he tumbled through the air.

He had no choice but to breathe deeply of the ocean's salt. It loomed so large now, the thing from the deep, that it brooked absolutely no comparison to anything from Abel's world. Little waterfalls, only fifty feet in length by this time, still dribbled from its lowest regions, but it appeared to be mostly free of the water, and its shape was as clear as such an amorphous thing was likely to get. Abel had been right about the tentacle. Dozens more of them flicked in and out of the water all around the creature, a skirt of snakes that must have held the wriggling mass afloat.

Soon he stopped tumbling and remained flat, stomach down, arms out in front of him, but his descent put him on a course toward the most tumultuous water encircling the beast. That's when he saw its horrible mouth. He felt the presence of the Angel of Death then, but its touch wasn't cold or hard. Rather it applied a friendly pressure to his shoulder and seemed to whisper, "Is it such a bad way to go, Abel Sykes, being swallowed into a beast as impressive as this?"

But he was kidding himself. There was plenty of unpleasantness ahead if he kept a course for this behemoth's maw. For he could now see that its throat was studded with teeth designed to puncture and tear. Near its dead-gray lips the teeth were far too large to be thought of as sharp or pointed, but they quickly diminished in size the deeper inside Abel's gaze wandered. Whatever the thing was, it was clear to him that it had but one sole purpose in life: to ingest as much living meat as it could before it died. The ravenous, lolling eyes, too accustomed to the sunless fathoms of the ocean's deepest pits, confirmed this. So did the hungry agitation of the flexing rows of teeth.

But the leviathan had seen enough of the bright topside world, and down it plunged like a sinking continent. Abel was so close now he could smell the thing's breath, which was a rotten wind to be caught up in. Thankfully it twisted away from him as it dove, so he didn't have to stomach the offending air for long. But he was sucked into the quickening maelstrom of its wake. Even before he reached the water level a vacuum was at work on him, and now he, too, was in a mighty plunge for the ocean's bottom.

To the extent that Abel could hold a coherent thought together in the spiraling torrent that dragged him down, he assumed he was destined to drown at last. Yet the rushing tunnel ensconcing him showed no signs of narrowing, at least not enough to prevent something as tiny as a man from passing through. A more immediate danger than drowning, though, was the dizziness beginning to claim him as he tumbled away, glancing off the curved wall of the tunnel and ricocheting back across, over and over. Ever downward.

But whatever the real dangers to his person, Abel's mind soon focused on a single inescapable reality; it was getting dark. He'd never adored the warmth and brilliance of the sun more than now, when the prospect of its permanent withdrawal closed around his neck like a garrote. Still he crashed around and down, losing more light with each revolution of his body.

He was completely blind by the time the rushing water deposited him roughly on some kind of rock shelf. It took him several moments to realize he was no longer in the water but in some kind of grotto. How was it possible, he wondered? How could there be an air pocket in the very ocean? Then he realized it was probably temporary, the result of the raging eddies left behind by the descending monster. Which meant it was only a matter of time before water refilled the cavern, drowning him after all and washing him out of existence. He could still hear the din of water being siphoned away, but it wasn't close, yet. Once he found the strength to lift his weary body from the stone floor, he got up on his knees and began feeling around with his cold, shivering hands, desperate to gauge the dimensions of his new habitat.

On his left he quickly encountered an edge and violently recoiled from the fathomless abyss he imagined extended forever from it, but in so doing, he backed into a wall, giving his head a good knock in the process. *Dear God*, he thought, *how confined am I?* He soon had his answer. The ledge he occupied seemed to be roughly crescent shaped, extending no more than four feet ahead and eight across. Venturing to stand on wobbly legs, Abel reached as far up the wall as he could. He found no edge, not even a handhold. Abel Sykes had found his watery grave, and now he longed to return to the whaling life.

But that was impossible. There was no whaling life to return to, for one thing, even if he were to risk a fatal case of the bends by finding his way to water, or waiting for it to find him, and letting himself shoot to the surface. His vessel sunk, her crew gone, he had no hope of existence beyond this underwater shelf.

Perhaps for the first time in his life he contemplated the connectedness of things. He was no student of metaphysics, but how could he not wonder if his ultimate fate was tied up in his own actions prior to the colossus's breach? Murder hadn't been on his mind when he fell asleep the previous night, nor when he awoke in the morning. Suicide was another matter. That had been in the works for some time, as tends to be the case with those whose crimes are so numerous and dire that most of them defy the reach of memory. But he'd never understood the blackguards and miscreants who felt the need to take as many innocent lives as possible with them when they destroyed themselves. Why couldn't they just slice open their own throats and be done with it?

Well, Abel Sykes would now die the perfect hypocrite. He'd slaughtered an entire whaling crew with every intention of making himself the last victim, and now that death was an imminent certainty, he wanted life more than he could remember ever wanting anything before. To step once more onto dry land and take in the spiced air of autumn. To observe again the fashionable elite as they thronged the city streets at night, and maybe lighten their purses by a coin or two. To swell with the hope of future voyages and the profits they might bring. All of it was gone from him. In a sense, he was already dead. The rest was formality.

Again the feeling came over him that it hadn't needed to be this way, that the creature might not have come if Abel hadn't so recently left the good captain's quarters after separating his head from his neck with an axe. Hadn't laid the bloody implement against the doorframe before exiting the scene with such moral certitude. Hadn't prided himself on the mass murder so newly concluded. And maybe under those alternate circumstances that could never be, Abel Sykes would have found a reason to go on.

At least his situation could get no worse. Surely he'd arrived at the nadir of his existence. Death would come as a kind of release, a blessing even. He almost smiled in the dark.

But then the clicking began, as did the echoing trickle of water nearby. Something was climbing out of the pit, skittering up the rock face to the edge of Abel's roost. Faster now, and louder. *Tchck! Tchck!! Tchck!!!* Whatever it was, there was more than one. It wasn't the sound of their ascent that he was hearing, however. As they poured onto the ledge and over his body, dozens, at least, of the wretched stinging and gnashing things, he recognized the clicking noise as some sort of communication among their ranks. This was their call to feast, and Abel's only comfort now was that he was spared the sight of whatever tore him open and gorged on his red wet insides in the dark. For he was spared no measure of agony or regret as he loosed a litany of final screams.

Ibrahim and the Karkadann

by

David Longshore

Ibrahim and the Karkadann

by

David Longshore

IBRAHIM SAT CROSS-LEGGED on his woven mat and closely watched Saleem as the over-fed traitor sauntered across the work yard and into the entrance of the prison camp's main building. As usual, an unbearably smug Saleem was smiling, and his white teeth, cleaned every six months by the camp dentist, gleamed in the hot tropical light as brightly as the beach sands that ringed the isolated outpost.

In a brutal instant, Saleem's perfect teeth were shattered to a pulp, their slivered, meaty remains suddenly flushed from his mouth by a torrent of blood. In the following second, his head exploded like a ripe melon from the camp garden, spraying shards of white bone across the work yard's dusty, sun-baked soil. Now headless, Saleem's plump body, once pampered and protected by the oppressors, plunged forward to the ground, lifeless and finally damned.

With a chuckle, Ibrahim watched as a crimson stain spilled from what was left of Saleem's fat neck.

"Are you thinking what I'm thinking?" one of his friends, Abbas, quietly asked in Arabic. Both men knew the work yard, like all of the prison's sinister spaces, was filled with electronic listening devices, and so barely spoke above a whisper.

His revenge fantasy against Saleem now spent, Ibrahim turned to the old clerk and simply nodded. The elder laughed, a rattling chest yawn that the camp doctors only paid passing attention to.

"The exploding head scheme again, I gather."

Ibrahim again nodded, and they laughed together, much louder this time. Abbas knew all of Ibrahim's inner worst wishes for Saleem, and the younger man in turn knew all of his. Like every other prisoner at the camp, Ibrahim had spent many secluded hours contemplating Saleem's demise.

At best, Ibrahim would have liked to torture Saleem before killing him... and at worst, he would have wanted to torture him some more, keep him alive just long enough to recover a bit before setting the scalding knives to his flesh again.

"It will be soon," Ibrahim said, watching as Saleem pulled open the door and disappeared inside the main building. No doubt the man who had promised everything to Abbas but delivered nothing was going to meet with the warden, ostensibly to get more privileges for them all, but more likely to deliver his daily spy report and receive his instructions.

"You seem so certain, Ibrahim. Too sure for the perfection of success."

"The whole thing," Ibrahim continued, his eyes scanning the prison camp's familiar grim outline... the imposing main building... the long cell wings... the soaring guard towers with their permanent machine gun installations, search lights, and blinking laser surveillance beams. "The whole thing will be destroyed."

"It will only be destroyed when our oppressors want it so," the old man added, punctuating his cynicism with another bout of coughing. Ibrahim wondered if they would ever let Abbas return home to die in peace and dignity.

"I did not always know how monsters were made," Ibrahim said. "But now I do."

"It must be an expensive quest... as priceless as a human soul."

For a few moments, Ibrahim sat silently, watching the play of the sunlight on the prison's clay tiled roofs. He shook his head in disagreement. "I... you... have already paid for this blessing. We have spent a decade here, held without charge or trial. We have been subjected to the most cruel abuses of body and soul, and an entire decade of our lives has been forever denied us."

"Once again, your sense of certainty frightens me, Ibrahim. And no matter the reasons for it, what you seek is powerful, yes, but terribly so."

"It must be so if we are to be successful."

Abbas looked up at his young, but brash, friend, and said nothing. The Caribbean sun was at its height, and the radiating heat reminded him of his own arid homeland. The land was dry, but his home was simply warm, and if he were to die here, it would at least be less disagreeable to his desert soul than if he were in icy climes.

Ibrahim looked back at his friend, and a silent message passed between their eyes. Ibrahim knew it was hard for the old clerk to believe in anything these days, and so he would simply have to suffer, faithless, until the final reckoning became apparent. It troubled Ibrahim that Abbas so doubted because when the creature of vengeance did finally rise upon them, it was important the alleged terrorist know what to do in order to survive and escape.

"I am listening, Ibrahim." Abbas truly did not believe a scintilla in Ibrahim's revenge fantasies, and was well aware this was simply another version on a familiar theme, just on a grander scale. But he indulged the younger man because he reminded him of his own son, and because they had been taken together, ten years earlier, by another rampaging monster, one long and camouflaged and mechanized with steel treads.

"It will come from the bay, so that will be the first place it strikes."

Abbas laughed. "And I, who can hardly breathe and am nearing my 66th birthday, am supposed to run between its legs?"

"Once it breaks through the outer wall and enters the first yard, you should be able to escape. I will help you."

"There's no other way?" The sun had already begun moving across the work yard, and Abbas reasoned that even if they were nonsense, Ibrahim's fantasies did at least help pass the time.

"I will help you," Ibrahim replied. "I will help anyone who wants to escape this hell."

A bemused look crossed Abbas' face, and his heart sank when he realized Ibrahim had noticed it.

"There is no other way out of here," the younger man persisted. "They aren't going to put us on trial, and they aren't going to release us. We'll be here forever!"

Abbas began another round of coughing, and his face momentarily grew ashen. Ibrahim realized his words had troubled his friend, intruded on whatever mental paradise he had constructed to deal with his own life's horror, and had hurt him with the truth.

He reached out and patted Abbas on the back, hoping his touch would magically remove the phlegm from the old man's lungs. When he had recovered enough to speak with a hoarse wheeze, Abbas said that whatever came out of the bay, whatever oppressed the oppressors, as long as it killed Saleem, he would die a contented man.

But no sooner had they finished laughing at the justice of it all, than an enormous boom echoed across the bay and swept across the work yard. It caused the few palm trees to rustle, and sand whirls to form in the otherwise stark concrete corners. One of the windows in the guard tower nearest the water's edge cracked, sending its occupants scurrying to their posts in surprise and awe.

In an instant, Ibrahim was on his feet. Using his hand to shade his eyes, he looked toward the bay, trying to see what had caused the bang. His heart pounded on the wall of his chest, its beating a form of sonar that he hoped was signaling to whatever it was that had come to liberate them all.

Because of the high concrete walls, he was unable to see much. Immediately following the reverberating boom, a gargantuan geyser of water shot up from the surface of the bay. Tall enough to be clearly seen from the prison work yard, the watery pillar seemingly parted the clouds like a giant spear before dropping down again in a tremendous smack.

Immediately thereafter, Ibrahim and Abbas heard a loud snorting noise.

218

"The Karkadann," Ibrahim exclaimed, falling to his knees and placing his hands out before him.

"Is that what it's called?" Abbas said, his eyes widening at the sight that had just emerged before him. Up over the prison wall, but still some distance away, rose the tip of an oversize horn, like that belonging to a rhinoceros. Dark gray and approximately 50 to 60 feet across, it kept growing larger and longer until it stood like an enormous mountain on the horizon.

Ibrahim may have been right after all, Abbas thought as his sandaled foot went out and kicked the younger man in the rump. Scrambling to his feet in anger at being so rudely disturbed in his grateful ablutions, Ibrahim's anger at the old man was immediately dissipated as he, too, caught sight of the giant rhinoceros horn piercing the bright Caribbean sky.

Others in the work yard had seen it as well, as had the prison camp's guards and military garrison. While many stood rooted in place, their mouths hanging open in surprise, others were shouting or scampering for cover. The snorting noises had grown louder, and the horn - which by now was attached to a block-like head so large it cast a shadow across miles of the tropical landscape - had clearly begun to advance toward the prison complex.

"The Karkadann," Ibrahim repeated, the wonder in his eyes so great that Abbas feared he had become mesmerized and would miss his long-awaited opportunity for escape. When it seemed Ibrahim was again going to fall to his knees, Abbas suddenly reached out and grabbed his arm to stop him.

"Your genie has granted your wish," he told the younger man. "It's time to pray on your feet."

Ibrahim nodded in understanding. "We should stand to one side of the work yard," he added. "That way when the Karkadann attacks the prison, we will be able to get past it to freedom."

"Just a few minutes ago," Abbas said, his eyes grown large from watching the advance of the gigantic rhinoceros, "I truly doubted your belief. But now... yes, I am willing to take the chance."

Trailed by a wheezing Abbas, Ibrahim moved away from the table and chairs and toward the work yard's far wall. Fashioned from concrete, reinforced steel, and topped with razor wire, it was set perpendicular to the wall facing the monster's approach. He reasoned that he and Abbas could slowly move down it, gauging the Karkadann's movements as they went. Then, when the creature had penetrated well into the prison, they could make their break for it through the shattered wreckage of what had, only an hour before, been their impenetrable hell on earth.

With each passing second, the Karkadann's monstrous silhouette grew ever larger, finally reaching the point where it cast much of the prison expanse into virtual darkness. This worried Abbas, but Ibrahim assured him it was to their advantage.

It was at that moment that all the prison's lights snapped on, mockingly flooding the work yard with starkly revealing white light.

Holding the old man's hand as he turned away from the glaring lights, Ibrahim had just begun to lead him down the wall, toward the corner where other prisoners were already cowering, when he heard the first staccato blasts of machine gun fire. The guards in the towers, horrified by the spectacle of the enormous rhinoceros bearing down on them, had opened fire indiscriminately.

As it was, those few bullets that did reach their target had no effect upon its armored mass. Even the rhinoceros' vast, heavily-lidded eyes were impervious to machine gun fire, no matter how concentrated and relentless. It was, Ibrahim thought, like the oppressors themselves, one monster battling another.

While Ibrahim and Abbas waited with the others for something to happen, the prison's loudspeaker system squawked in Arabic that all prisoners were to immediately return to their cells. Guards with automatic weapons were already beginning to fan across the work yard, jabbing their guns in the air while at the same time keeping a frightened eye on the terrifying specter now bearing down on the camp.

Ibrahim and Abbas huddled in the corner with approximately half a dozen other prisoners, hoping that they would not be confined in their cells while a natural phenomenon of unprecedented size and appearance tore its way out of the bay toward them. Ibrahim, in fact, was determined not to go inside any part of the accommodation wing; they would have to shoot him.

Abbas, his gray beard beaded with perspiration, nodded his agreement. "One way or another," he said, "now that your monster is here, we are to be liberated or finally executed."

Ibrahim heard another fusillade of gunfire erupt from the bayside guard towers, and reveled in the thought of the fear and surprise currently being experienced by the guards and soldiers and prison administrators as they confronted the shocking result of his most terrible curse. Under any other circumstances it was a curse that would have come at an equally shocking price, but as he had told Abbas, they had already paid for it in advance.

It was, Ibrahim thought as he heard the shuffle of even larger guns being frantically pointed toward the bay, also the sort of curse that would not work unless he who leveled it was in the right... that it was the just thing to do to those who had deserved such punishment.

Ibrahim watched as the guards continued their sweep of the work yard, corralling several of the other prisoners toward the two doors leading directly into the accommodation wings. As he feared, it was not long before two of the guards turned and spotted the tight cluster of human beings cowering in the work yard's far corner.

Shouting at Ibrahim, Abbas, and the others, the guards pointed their guns toward them and menacingly advanced across the work yard. It was at that moment, when Ibrahim was about to give up all hope of achieving his mission that the camp's lights suddenly went out. From what he knew of the prison's layout, the power station was situated near the bay, and the Karkadann's four giant legs must have destroyed it.

Everyone in the complex could now clearly hear and feel the rhinoceros beast's advance upon the complex. The air was filled with echoing snorting noises, as well as a strange howl that at times seemed more like a cry of triumph and invincibility. The ground now continually shook, rhythmically, and in four-time cadence with the Karkadann's lumbering stride. A large tsunami had accompanied its landfall, one that washed away the docks and warehouses that lined the bay front. Two large cranes crumpled beneath its gray heft, while the creature's giant feet left footprints the size of several swimming pools in the beach sand.

Between the bay and the prison were several residential suburbs that housed the prison's staff as well as personnel from a nearby Army base. Laid out on palm-fringed streets, many of the houses were of two and three stories, and rendered in a tropical architectural style. As Ibrahim shuffled along the wall, trying to avoid the gaze of the still-advancing guards, he thought of all the carnage the Karkadann would wreak on the oppressor's possessions.

Just as his life had been destroyed... just as all his family's possessions had been taken by the monster who had abducted him from his bedroom so long ago... the oppressors were now to be treated in kind. Under any other circumstances, the beast's appearance would have struck the utmost fear and horror in his heart... but not now. After ten years of air-conditioned imprisonment, Ibrahim yearned to breathe real air, the arid but fresh air of a free homeland.

While he held Abbas' hand, and listened to the booming, blasting, shattering sounds of the Karkadann's march toward the prison, Ibrahim thought of his mother and father, and of the brother who had been killed in an air strike on his home village nearly five years ago. Once a month, Ibrahim was allowed to call his parents and speak to them for fifteen minutes.

His feet remained shackled to the prison floor each time, and he knew his call was being recorded. In trying to maintain some semblance of privacy, Ibrahim spoke guardedly and in code - something that only increased the oppressors' paranoia.

This had now been going on for a decade, and it had changed, twisted and gnarled, his once cheerful personality. He wanted them to take away his telephone privileges, every one of his privileges, if need be, until his wormy suffering, like a chrysalis, morphed into a free-soaring martyrdom.

The more he suffered now, the greater the size of his vengeance later.

During his last call home he discovered his father had recently suffered a heart attack. His mother told him he was alive, but bound to his bed, probably to the last. As Ibrahim held Abbas' trembling hand, he thought of his father, lying frail and afraid thousands of miles away, and tried to commune with him through the old man beside him. The tremendous beast, sent by the universe at Ibrahim's command, would soon make it possible, one way or the other, for he to be reunited with his family, and this gave Ibrahim new found hope... even as the guards neared his position, their bayoneted guns drawn in fear and determination.

Accompanied by a cascade of wreckage, the gigantic rhinoceros finally reached the prison's outer wall. Standing as tall as a 15-story building, the creature was so huge it was difficult for even Ibrahim to comprehend its full scope. Even though it was tall enough to simply step over the wall and into the first of the camp's ringing courtyards, the Karkadann took the time to symbolically smash its bony tusk against the reinforced concrete wall like a medieval battering ram. In an instant, the edifice collapsed in a shower of concrete dust and sparks.

At the same time, the razor wire atop the wall pulled apart and whipped back, slicing into several of the soldiers and guards who had tried to defend the wall. The guards in the towers leveled their machine guns on the creature, again to no avail. The rhinoceros was simply too large and too well armored for anything less deadly than a nuclear weapon. They knew from their radios that the Army was nevertheless moving in heavy artillery, and that a nearby aircraft carrier had dispatched several fighters with missiles to attack the monster. But with sinking morale and mounting fear all around them, they knew it was now just a matter of time.

At last, Ibrahim thought with glee, I have found something the oppressors lack.

And even if the fighter jets and heavy cannon arrived before the Karkadann completely demolished the prison complex, what next? Could the oppressors be so certain that any weapon would be effective against a creature so large and so powerful? Even to the dumbest of their military strategists, would it not be apparent that the 300-foot-long rhinoceros was only a partial manifestation of something bigger?

It was, Ibrahim pondered, just like the mechanized creature that had so many years before snatched Ibrahim from his bed, and Abbas from his desk, in that it was just a part of something much bigger, something much mightier, and therefore that much more invincible.

Accompanied by a series of crashes that made the ground tremble, the Karkadann thundered into the first courtyard. Almost immediately, it turned its colossal head left and right, and destroyed the guard towers on either end of the breached wall. To the sound of shattering glass and exploding ammunition, the two structures toppled over, their red-tile roofs and terrified occupants scattered across the prison landscape like confetti.

Barely audible over the sounds of destruction, the screams of the oppressors as they confronted - mainly for the last time - the fulfillment of Ibrahim's curse, brought strength and pleasure to his mind and soul. It wasn't just that so many of them, his enemies, were now dead or dying, but that they had gone in a shower of terror and a hail of pain that gave him such joy. It was important to Ibrahim that the oppressors not only die, but perish with the knowledge of why it was so necessary for them to do so.

After crushing the two guard towers, the Karkadann advanced upon the prison's main administrative building. Lying directly in front of its massive tusk, the building was six stories tall. Stuccoed in white and embellished with a red tile roof, the building was the primary hub for all activity in the prison. It housed the offices of the warden and his staff, as well as the offices of all the military personnel assigned to the camp. It also contained the prison infirmary, and the security center.

Just as the two guards were about to round up the prisoners, a stream of men and women gushed from the administrative building and into the work yard. One or two of them were screaming, but the majority of them were silent as they ran, occasionally looking over their shoulders to the see the lurking mass of the Karkadann looming behind them. In the darkness created by the monster's approaching shadow, Ibrahim tried to see if Saleem and the warden were among them, but the Karkadann's dim shroud make it difficult to know for certain just what was going on.

The two guards, more alarmed by the gaining creature than they were by the prospect of Ibrahim and Abbas disobeying instructions, then faltered. Pointing their weapons at the Karkadann, they paused in mid-motion for several seconds before deciding that it was a futile gesture. Turning, they joined the exodus of prison staff making their way across the work yard and through a small, unlocked door, into the adjoining courtyard.

Ibrahim gripped Abbas' hand, and realized the Karkadann had turned them into prisoners of their own jail. Under different circumstances, he might have expressed his happiness at their predicament by loudly chanting insults at them, but at the moment his mind and energies were focused solely on escaping from the shattered prison.

Turning to Abbas, Ibrahim whispered that it would not be much longer now. Through the darkness, he could see that the old man was terrified to his wit's end, and could feel his overwhelming anxiety in the grip of his hand.

Ibrahim considered pointing out that next to ten years of unjust incarceration, the Karkadann was a minor annoyance, but instead kept silent. It would do neither of them any good to alarm Abbas further.

For his part, Abbas clung to Ibrahim and drew some strength and courage from his hatred, palpable and cogent in the midst of unsympathetic catastrophe. The Karkadann did not terrify him as greatly as the idea that a revenge-crazed young man had successfully conjured up such a force, and deployed it for his own purposes. While no one liked the *oppressors*, as Ibrahim relentlessly called them, Ibrahim's thirst for liberty and his quest for vengeance were only tolerable when he was playing the role of fantasist.

Now that it seemed Ibrahim's plan might just work, Abbas was confronted by a much bigger and more horrifying dilemma than the rampaging rhinoceros. The creature was, after all, just the first of many such destructive manifestations. It was the "of many" that most troubled the older and wiser man and he pondered what his options really were.

Out of the corner of his eye, Ibrahim watched in shock and awe as the Karkadann bore down on the administration building. Butting its horn against the 100-foot tall tower, the creature smashed several windows and large sheets of stucco sailed to the ground. Desks and file cabinets next tumbled into space as floors were undermined, and great cascades of paper and other detritus floated through the dusty air. The building's tile roof sagged, then disintegrated. A moment later it collapsed beneath the full weight of the Karkadann's attack.

Huddled in the corner where two courtyards met, Ibrahim and Abbas listened to the carnage as the Karkadann demolished the administration building. They prayed that in the next few minutes they would not be crushed beneath the footfall of a mystical Arabic rhinoceros born into the reality by one of them, and nurtured by the other. It was a day of ironies, Abbas thought, and so everyone was more vulnerable to the turn of the bolt under such circumstances. Anything was now possible, he mused, peering through the dust clouds at Ibrahim's profile, set dark and angry against a roiling white background of violence and despair.

Sticking his head around the corner, Ibrahim searched for the gargantuan rhinoceros. Unable to see much of the creature through the murky atmosphere, he tracked its progress by the length of its gray shadows. It began to dawn on him that he may have made a miscalculation, and rendered the creature too big for his plans. As it plowed through the broken ramparts of the administration building, the Karkadann steadily grew even more massive in stature and sheer size. Ibrahim feared that once it entered the work yard, it would overwhelm it, and that their present shelter was nothing of the sort.

Gripping Abbas' hand even more tightly, Ibrahim whispered in his ear that they needed to go in the next few minutes.

"Like I said," Abbas replied. "You want me to run between its legs after all."

"They're as tall as trees!"

Abbas shook his head and coughed. The heavy dust aggravated his lungs and he tried to breathe through his shirtsleeve. The kernel of a plan popped into his head.

"If I do, will you come with me?"

"Until the end," Ibrahim said. "Any minute now." Even though the dusty air was warm and humid, he shivered at the realization of how imminent and even certain his freedom now was... it was as close as the Karkadann as it at last took its first steps into the work yard.

Plowing forward like a crashing meteorite, the Karkadann roared into the work yard. Another two guard towers were knocked to pieces, their terrified guardians, unable to desert their posts, sent screaming into the void with bone-crunching finality.

All around Ibrahim and Abbas, chaos reigned as the oppressors were called to justice. Chunks of concrete tumbled to the ground as the prison walls began to fold in on themselves. With a sickening twang, the coiled razor wire atop the wall nearest Ibrahim and Abbas snapped and contracted, its slicing blades narrowly missing Ibrahim's face as it writhed through the air like an enraged metal python.

Next, the corner gave way, and a few of their companions were buried beneath the concrete rubble. Ibrahim and Abbas had no time to stop and help dig them out - the Karkadann was now moving through the work yard, and the time had come for them to make their escape beneath the cover of the havoc it was wreaking on their behalf.

As the monster's enormous bulk passed overhead like a giant thunderstorm, Ibrahim wasted no further time in mounting his escape. Releasing Abbas' hand, he left the corner, weaving his way across the mounds of debris littering what was left of the work yard, until he was a quarter of the way beneath the Karkadann.

Hurriedly following Ibrahim's lead, Abbas moved beneath the beast, but more toward its rear legs. Ever since his capture by the mechanized monster a decade earlier, Abbas had told himself of his confinement that the best way to get through was to go through, which he now did. He kept an eye, as best he could, on Ibrahim's progress. He wasn't relying on the younger man for direction, so much as for timing.

While earlier cowering in the corner, Abbas had come to realize that at some point he would have to kill Ibrahim. It was his ultimate duty to himself, to his country, and to his faith that he should in some way put an end to Ibrahim and his terrible magic of hate and vengeance. He reckoned he was a dying man, and even if amid all the chaos he should be arrested for the crime, or in some other way called to account for his actions, he would not have long to suffer any new torments.

Among those refreshed tortures was the prospect of a world dominated by Ibrahim and his mythical posse of avengers. Only the universe knew of what might be next, what means of terror would come down the road as a liberated Ibrahim rendered his judgment on a shocked and paralyzed globe. Abbas had no idea how he would undertake this bloody necessity, and many times he doubted he possessed the physical strength to accomplish it.

It was then, as Abbas watched with a mixture of horror and hope, that the Karkadann lifted its left hind leg. Soaring into the air like an entire acre of land ripped from the earth, the creature's foot moved forward, and directly over the spot where Ibrahim was picking his way through the smoking, dust-and-blood coated wreckage. Abbas saw the entire thing unfold, but deliberately said nothing before the beast's foot came down again, thudding into the earth just behind Ibrahim's location.

Abbas hardly had time to rue the failure of the Karkadann to kill its evil creator before he felt a curious pressure, almost like a strong breeze, descending from above his head. Unbeknownst to him, while he was watching and hoping for Ibrahim's destruction, the giant rhinoceros' right hind leg was moving forward, and directly over the debris pile where Abbas was standing.

The old clerk looked up, his eyes wide, his mouth agape, and watched the dark spot as it rapidly descended toward him, growing larger and darker and relentlessly closer with each passing second. The creature's foot was so expansive that even if he had tried to run, Abbas would not have been able to move fast enough to escape its reach. His last few moments of life were spent watching Ibrahim as he scurried away from him like a spooked dog, looking over his shoulder, and no doubt aware of what was about to happen to his old but doomed companion.

Ibrahim did not have time to mourn Abbas. While he would have liked to save him, brought him home to his family to die with the dignity he deserved as a man, he had warned him to remain close, and not to stray. And yet, it was Abbas who went in the wrong direction, and went there too slowly, thereby sealing his fate. There is only so much a man can do to lead people to righteousness, Ibrahim thought as he scrambled through the dusty air and heaps of wreckage toward the light beyond the beast's shadow.

Hours later, after Ibrahim had emerged into clear, open air and passed through the prison's trampled outer fence, the Karkadann turned and retreated back into the bay. As Ibrahim clambered up the side of the hills that surrounded the devastated bay and tried to avoid being spotted by the helicopters that swarmed the area, he paused to look back at what he had wrought.

Clouds of smoke poured from shattered neighborhoods, and there was absolutely nothing left of the prison camp except an indecipherable heap of smoking wreckage, punctuated by the stumps of two or three of the destroyed guard towers. Military assets were already being moved into the area, but it would be many months before anything could be rebuilt and by that time, praise be to the universe, Ibrahim would have safely returned home.

Turning his attention toward the bay, he watched as the scaly mound that was the Karkadann's back slowly submerged beneath the azure waters, leaving another shore-pounding tsunami in its wake. A swarm of fighter jets zoomed over the creature's trail, uselessly firing missiles into a vast and enveloping sea. He couldn't help but smile broadly, convinced that he had won a great victory against the oppressors.

Then, turning his back to the carnage, Ibrahim continued to ascend, all the while formulating his plans for the Karkadann's return.

About the Authors

Neil Baker

Neil Baker (editor) is a former fish-fryer, dinosaur builder and school teacher. After a spell as an award-winning filmmaker and traditional animator, he returned to his first love, writing, and within a year had sold stories that appeared in *Ugly Babies, Cellar Door II, World War Cthulhu, Atomic Age Cthulhu* and *Occult Detective Monster Hunter: A Grimoire of Eldritch Inquests*. He now runs April Moon Books and his first publication, The Dark Rites of Cthulhu, enjoyed a great critical reception. Neil is based on the outskirts of Toronto and he is married with two small children. You can reach him via the contacts page at www.AprilMoonBooks.com.

CJ Henderson

CJ Henderson's second published novel was a mythos novel and it seems he never looked back. Creator of supernatural investigators Teddy London and Piers Knight, reviver of Inspector Legrasse and Carl Kolchak, he has had scores more books published as well as hundreds and hundreds of short stories, including one book he was particularly proud of, Baby's First Mythos, created with his daughter, Erica. Sadly, CJ Henderson lost his fight against cancer in early July, 2014. He is survived by his loving family and legions of fans.

Aaron Smith

Aaron Smith is the author of more than 30 published stories in genres including horror, mystery, science fiction, fantasy, and espionage. His books include the spy thriller Nobody Dies for Free and the zombie horror novel Chicago Fell First. His Sherlock Holmes stories have appeared in 4 volumes of Airship 27 Productions' Sherlock Holmes: Consulting Detective anthology series. More information about Smith's work can be found on his blog at www.godsandgalaxies.blogspot.com

Patrick Loveland

Patrick Loveland is a self-taught screenwriter and author from San Diego, California. He studied Experimental Filmmaking in San Francisco and worked as a projectionist before moving back to his hometown in the early 2000s to use only one of those skill-sets; guess which one. At his longtime place of current employment, he has achieved near expert status in moving chairs and tables and helping people use dvd players, although the latter is debatable. Patrick lives with his wife, stepson, and young daughter.

Christine Morgan works the overnight shift in a psychiatric facility, which plays havoc with her sleep schedule but allows her a lot of writing time. A lifelong reader, she also reviews, beta-reads, occasionally edits and dabbles in self-publishing. Her other interests include gaming, history, superheroes, crafts, cheesy disaster movies and training to be a crazy cat lady. She can be found online at www.christine-morgan.org

Konstantine Paradias is a jeweler by profession and a writer by choice. His short stories have been published in Third FlatIron's Master Minds anthology, World War Cthulhuand the BATTLE ROYALE Slambook by Haikasoru. His short story, "How You Ruined Everything" has been included in Tangent Online's 2013 recommended SF reading list and his short story "The Grim" has been nominated for a Pushcart Prize.

Doug lives in the Pacific Northwest and spends his time writing, cooking, gaming, and following the local WHL hockey team. His interest in books and reading started early thanks to his parents, though his serious attempts at writing only started a few years ago. From time to time he blogs about writing and other related topics at The Simms Project at http://thesimmsproject.blogspot.com/. His current project is an urban fantasy novel featuring a group of changelings fighting a war in Arcadia. He can be reached on Facebook or simms.doug@gmail.com.

David Bernard is the pen name of Dave Goudsward, a native New Englander who now lives (albeit under protest) in South Florida, a paradoxical place where, when temperatures drops below 60û, locals break out parkas to wear over their shorts and sandals. His latest books are Horror Guide to Massachusetts (Post Mortem Press) and H. P. Lovecraft in the Merrimack Valley (Hippocampus Press).

The principal creative force behind Hellbender Media, Edward is an award-winning writer and filmmaker. His latest movies include adaptations of H. P. Lovecraft's stories "The Statement of Randolph Carter," and "The Dream-Quest of Unknown Kadath," the only complete adaptation of TolkienÕs "The Lord of the Rings," and "Flesh of my Flesh," a live-action horror/thriller. He's currently in preproduction for a horror/sci-fi feature based on his latest novel "Through the Night". Find him online at HellbenderMedia.com

Martha Bacon moves around a lot, for very good reasons. She has dabbled in extreme body art and enjoys working with people a quarter of her age. She has been writing since before you were born, but you really shouldn't read any of it. She is happily unmarried, twice, and has enjoyed the company of several pets long after their demise.

Film reviewer/screenwriter R. Allen Leider began his career in 1970 at CBS TV Network News as copy boy for The Walter Cronkite News. In 1973, he became a Featured Interviewer and Associate Editor for The Monster Times, then moved on to be Associate Editor and FeaturesWriter for Show Magazine. He created the original story and screenplay for the independent horror film *The Oracle* in 1985. After the film was released, he became Art Director and Film Reviewer for New Jersey Living Magazine and hosted his own radio show 'Cinemascene' on WWFM, Mercer County, New Jersey for five years. Presently, he writes and edits the online entertainment and business magazine The Black Cat Review at www.blackcatmedia.com and is working on the Wicca Girl trilogy novel/movie project, featuring Druscilla Marie d'Lambert, her blood sister Cheralyn Rose Moskowitz, Countess Jocelyn Von Hagen and Satan. Rick's Wicca Girl and Hellfire Lounge books are published by Bold Venture Press. He lives in Manhattan, NYC with wife Barbara, a professional photographer, and numerous feline Egyptian gods.

Amy Braun is a Canadian urban fantasy author who started writing when she was in middle school, and then never stopped. Her published work includes the short story Call From The Grave as part of Mocha Memoir Publishing Toil, Trouble, and Temptation series, and the novella Needfire, as well as the upcoming Charlatan Charade in Lost in the Witching Hour anthology from Breaking Fate Publishing, and Secret Suicide in Lincoln Crisler's dark ritual anthology. When Amy isn't writing, she's reading, watching movies, taking photos, and trying to overcome ice cream addiction and choco-holism. You can find Amy on the web by following her blog, literarybraun.blogspot.ca, following her on Twitter, @amybraunauthor, and liking her Facebook Page.

DJ Tyrer is the person behind Atlantean Publishing and has been widely published in anthologies and magazines in the UK, USA and elsewhere, most recently in Steampunk Cthulhu (Chaosium), Tales of the Dark Arts (Hazardous Press), Cosmic Horror (Dark Hall Press) and Serial Killers Quattuor (JWK Fiction), as well as having a novella available on the Kindle, The Yellow House (Dynatox Ministries). DJ Tyrer's website is at djtyrer.blogspot.co.uk The Atlantean Publishing website is at atlanteanpublishing.blogspot.co.uk

Kerry teaches English at a community college by evening and writes horrible things by night. He hates the sun. His parents started reading his stories and now he's out of the will. Kerry's work appears in several anthologies including DOA2 from Blood Bound Books and Attack of the B-Movie Monsters from Grinning Skull Press. His story *Smoke* pioneered The Wicked Library podcast's explicit content warning. KGSL blogs at HorrorTree.com and will launch his own website newworldhorror.com sometime before he dies.

Michael Thomas-Knight is the author of numerous horror short stories, bending the scope of reality one word at a time. Michael's style ranges from classic ghost stories with violent conclusions to atmospheric Eldritch tales steeped in mysticism, cynicism, and irony. His stories have been published in publications, Dark Eclipse, Infernal Ink, SNM Horror Magazine, Fiction Terrifica, and Microhorror.com. His work has also appeared in numerous anthologies, Terror Train, From Beyond the Grave, Shadow Masters, Cellar Door II, O Little Town of Deathlehem and others. You can find Michael at his blog, Parlor of Horror, which deals with all things horror: movies, books, and articles for the horror enthusiast. http://parlorofhorror.wordpress.com - Amazon author page: https://www.amazon.com/author/michaelthomasknight - Facebook: https://www.facebook.com/michael.thomasknight.9

D.G. Sutter is a writer and editor. His work has appeared in several anthologies in the underground of small presses. ÒWhere Gods Roam FreelyÓ originally appeared in his collection Oddly Chilling, out now from Chupa Cabra House. Look for his debut novel, La Maquina Oscura, due out this year from Westphalia Press.

Pete Mesling

Pete Mesling's silhouette can, on rare occasions, be glimpsed prowling the watery byways of Seattle, Washington. When not writing frightening fiction, Mr. Mesling is probably dreaming up not-so-frightening acoustic guitar music, broadcasting his ever-eclectic Bare Knuckle Podcast (where you can hear him read his tales of terror from time to time, incidentally), or dreaming up new ways to scare the bejesus out of his fiancÕe. He also revels in bike rides with his daughter, whose nickname is taken from a character in a Boris Karloff film. Check out his author page on Amazon!

David Longshore

Born in Ipswich, Massachusetts, in the heart of H.P. Lovecraft country, David Longshore holds degrees from Amherst College and the Naval Postgraduate School. A veteran of the U.S. Navy, he is the author of the Encyclopedia of Hurricanes, Typhoons, and Cyclones, as well as other non-fiction works. Previous examples of his horror and dark fiction have appeared in The Horror Zine, SNM Horror, and numerous other anthologies.

Future Releases from April Moon Books

2015

Black Star, Black Sun by **Rich Hawkins**
A novella of cosmic dread in the English countryside.

Flesh Like Smoke edited by **Brian M. Sammons**
Shapeshifters galore from today's best authors!

**Short Sharp Shocks Vol. 3:
Ill-considered Expeditions**
Pith helmets at the ready for some unfriendly welcomes!

**Short Sharp Shocks Vol. 4:
Spawn of the Ripper**
Our homage to Hammer, bosoms and blood!

**Short Sharp Shocks Vol. 5:
The Stars at my Door**
Optimistic Sci-Fi to cleanse the palate.

www.AprilMoonBooks.com